Southern
Lights

DANIELLE STEEL

Southern
Lights

A Novel

DOUBLEDAY LARGE PRINT HOME LIBRARY EDITION

Delacorte Press
New York

Published in the United States by Delacorte Press, an imprint of The Random House Publishing Group, a division of Random House, Inc., New York.

DELACORTE PRESS is a registered trademark of Random House, Inc., and the colophon is a trademark of Random House, Inc.

ISBN: 978-1-60751-322-3

Printed in the United States of America on acid-free paper

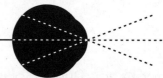

This Large Print Book carries the
Seal of Approval of N.A.V.H.

To my very wonderful children, Beatrix, Trevor, Todd, Nick, Sam, Victoria, Vanessa, Maxx, and Zara—who are the light of my life. May your lives always be full of joy and blessings, and happy times!

With all my love,
Mommy/d.s.

Southern
Lights

Chapter 1

The man sitting in the threadbare chair with the stuffing pouring out of it appeared to be dozing, his chin drifting slowly toward his chest. He was tall and powerfully built with a tattoo of a snake peering out of his shirt on the back of his neck as his head shifted down. His long arms seemed lifeless on the arms of his chair in the small dark room. There was an evil cooking odor coming from the hallway and the television was on. A narrow unmade bed stood in the corner of the room, covering most of the filthy, stained shag carpet. The drawers of a chest were pulled open and the few clothes he had brought with him were on the floor. He was wearing a T-shirt, heavy boots, and jeans, and the mud encrusted on his soles had dried and was flaking into the carpet. As peacefully as he had been sleeping, suddenly he was wide awake. He jerked his head up with a snort, and his ice-blue eyes flew open, as the hair stood up on his arms. He had an uncanny sense of hearing. He closed his eyes again as he listened, and then stood up and grabbed his jacket with a single stride across the narrow room. With his head erect, the snake tattoo disappeared back into his shirt.

Luke Quentin slipped quietly over the windowsill and made his way down the fire escape after closing the window behind him. It was freezing cold. January in New York. He had been in town for two weeks. Before that, he had been in Alabama, Mississippi, Pennsylvania, Ohio, Iowa, Illinois, Kentucky. He had visited a friend in Texas. He had been traveling for months. He got work where he could find it. He didn't need much to live on. He moved with the stealth of a panther, and was walking down the street on the Lower East Side, before the men he had heard coming reached his room. He didn't know who they were, but he was smarter than to take a chance. They were cops more than likely. He had been in prison twice, for credit card fraud and robbery, and he was well aware that ex-cons never got a fair shake, from anyone. His friends from prison called him Q.

He stopped to buy a paper and a sandwich, shivered in the cold, and went for a walk. In another world, he would have been considered handsome. He had huge powerful shoulders, and a chiseled face. He was thirty-four years old and, with both sentences, had done a total of ten years. He had served his full time and hadn't been released on parole. Now he was free as the wind. He had been back on the streets for two years, and hadn't gotten into trouble so far. Despite his size, he could disappear in any crowd. He had sandy nondescript blond hair, pale blue eyes, and from time to time he grew a beard.

Quentin walked north, and west when he got to Forty-second Street.

He slipped into a movie house just off Times Square, sat in the dark, and fell asleep. It was midnight when he got out, and he hopped on a bus and went back downtown. He assumed that by now, whoever had come to visit earlier would be long gone. He wondered if someone at the hotel had tipped the cops off that he was a con. The tattoos on his hands were a dead giveaway to those who knew. He just hadn't wanted to be around when they walked in, and hoped they'd lose interest when they found nothing in the room. It was twelve-thirty when he got back to the dreary hotel.

He always took the stairs. Elevators were a trap—he liked to be free to move around. The desk clerk nodded at him, and Luke headed upstairs. He was on the landing just below his floor when he heard a sound. It wasn't a footstep or a door, it was a click. Just that. He knew it instantly, it was a gun being cocked, and moving like the speed of sound, he headed back down the stairs on silent feet, and slowed briefly only when he got to the desk. Something was off, very off. He realized they were behind him then, halfway down the stairs. There were three of them, and Luke wasn't going to wait and find out who they were. It occurred to him to try and talk his way out of it, but every instinct told him to run. So he did, he ran like hell. He was already down the street by the time they made it out the door at a dead run. But Luke was faster than nearly any man alive. He had run track in the joint for exercise. People said that Q was faster than the wind. And he was now.

He was over a fence, behind a building, and grabbed the roof of a garage and swung over another fence. He was in the thick of the neighborhood, and he knew by then he couldn't go back to the hotel. Something was very, very wrong. And he had no idea why. He had a snub-nosed gun shoved in his jeans, and he didn't want to be caught packing arms, so he dumped it in a trash can, and ran behind a building into an alley. He just kept running and figured he had lost them, until he hit another fence, and suddenly a hand came up behind him and grabbed his neck in a viselike grip. He had never felt anything so tight, and he was glad as hell he'd dumped the gun. Now all he had to do was get rid of the cop. His elbow shot into the ribs of the owner of the grip, but all he did was tighten his hold on Luke's neck, and squeeze, hard. Luke was dizzy almost instantly and despite his impressive size fell to the ground. The cop knew just where to grab. He landed a resounding kick into Luke's back, who let out a stifled groan between clenched teeth.

"You sonofabitch," Luke said, grabbing for the other man's legs, and suddenly the cop was down, and they were rolling on the ground. The cop had him pinned in a matter of seconds, he was younger than Luke, in better shape, and he had been waiting for the pleasure of Q's company for months. He had followed him all across the States, and had already been in his room twice that week and once the week before. Charlie McAvoy knew Luke Quentin better than he knew his own brother. He had gotten special permission from an interstate task force to track him for almost a year, and he knew that if it killed him, he was going to get him, and now that he had, he wasn't going to lose him. Charlie got on his knees and slammed Luke's face into the ground. Luke's nose was bleeding profusely when he looked up, just as the two other detectives came up behind Charlie. All three of them were plainsclothesmen, but everything about them screamed cops.

"Easy boys, play nice," Jack Jones, the senior detective, said as he handed Charlie the cuffs. "Let's not kill him before we get him to the station." There was murder in Charlie's eyes. Jack Jones knew Charlie had wanted to make him, and why. Charlie had told him in confidence one night when he got drunk. Jack had promised him not to say anything to anyone when he saw him the next morning. But he could see what was happening to Charlie now, he was shaking with rage. Jack didn't like personal vendettas getting into business. If Luke had moved a hair to break free and run from them, Charlie would have shot him. He wouldn't have winged him or shot him in the leg, he would have killed him on the spot.

The third man on the team radioed for a patrol car. Their own car was several blocks away, and they didn't want to move Luke that far. They weren't going to take that chance.

Luke's nose was bleeding copiously onto his shirt, and none of them offered him anything to stop it. He would get no mercy from them. Jack read him his Miranda rights, and Luke looked arrogant despite the ferocious nosebleed. He had icy eyes, and a stare that took them all in and gave nothing away. Jack thought he was the coldest sonofabitch he had ever met.

"I could sue you bastards for this. I think my nose is broken," he threatened, and Charlie gave him a scathing glance as the other two men pushed him toward the car. They shoved him into the car, and told the cops driving they would meet them at the station.

The three men were quiet on the way back to their car, and Charlie glanced at Jack as he turned on the ignition and then slumped against the seat, looking pale.

"How does it feel?" Jack asked him as they drove downtown. "You got him."

"Yeah," Charlie said quietly. "Now we gotta prove it and make it stick."

By the time they got downtown and into the station, Luke was looking cocky. There was blood all over his face and shirt, but even cuffed, he was strutting his stuff.

"So what are you guys doing? Looking for someone to pin a mugging on, or stealing an old lady's purse?" Luke laughed in Charlie's face.

"Book him," Charlie said to Jack, and walked away. He knew he'd get credit for the collar. He'd been following him for way too long. It was just sheer luck Quentin wound up back in New York. Providence. Fate. Charlie was happy to have nailed him in the city where he worked. He had better connections here, and liked the DA they worked with. He was a tough old guy from Chicago, and more willing to prosecute than most. Joe McCarthy, the DA, didn't care how full the jails were, he wasn't willing to let suspects go. And if they proved everything Charlie hoped they would about Luke Quentin, it was going to be the trial of the year. He wondered who McCarthy was going to assign the case to. He hoped to hell it was someone good.

"So what's the beef you trumped up for me?" Luke asked, laughing in Jack's face, as a rookie shackled him and started to lead him away. "Shoplifting? Jaywalking?"

"Not exactly, Quentin," Jack said coolly. "Rape, and murder one, actually. Four counts of each so far. Maybe you'd like to tell us something about it?" Jack asked, raising an eyebrow, as Luke laughed again and shook his head.

"Assholes. You know it won't stick. What's the matter? You got a bunch of murders you can't solve, so you figured you'd do some one-stop shopping and pin them all on me?" Luke looked totally undisturbed, and almost amused, but his eyes were like steel, and an evil shade of blue.

Jack wasn't fooled by the bravado. Luke was slick. They had evidence that he had committed two murders, and they were almost sure of two others. And if Jack's guess was right, Luke Quentin had killed over a dozen women in two years, maybe more. They were waiting for a more conclusive DNA report on the dirt from his shoes that Charlie had gotten out of the shag carpet in Quentin's hotel room. If the dirt was a match, as Charlie hoped it would be, Quentin had just been on the streets for the last time in his life.

"What a crock of shit," Luke mumbled as he shuffled away. "You know you won't make it stick. You're just fishing. I have an alibi for every night. I hardly left my hotel room in the last two weeks. I've been sick." Yeah, Jack thought to himself, very sick. They all were, guys like him, sociopaths who didn't bat an eye after they killed their victims, dumped them somewhere, and then went out to lunch. Luke Quentin was handsome and looked as though he could be charming. He was the perfect type to spot some innocent young girl, and lure her to a secluded spot where he could rape her and then kill her. Jack had seen guys like him before, although if the stories were true about this one, he was one of the worst. Or the worst they'd had in a long time anyway. Jack knew there would be a lot of press on this, and every last detail had to be handled right, or Quentin would get a mistrial on some finicky detail. Charlie knew it too, which was why he had let Jack handle the booking, and after Luke was taken away to be searched and get his mug shot done, Jack called the DA himself.

"We got him," Jack said proudly. "All our hunches paid off, and luck was on our side. That and Charlie McAvoy, who ran his ass off and caught him. If I'd had to run down all those alleys and hit all those fences, he'd have been halfway to Brooklyn before I got over the first one." Jack was in good shape, but he was forty-nine years old, and he and the DA teased each other about their weight. They were the same age. The DA congratulated him for his good work, and told him he'd see him in the morning. He wanted to meet with the arresting officers to decide how they were going to handle the press.

By the time Jack left the station half an hour later, Luke was already in a cell. They had decided to put him in a cell alone. He was being scheduled for arraignment the following afternoon, and Jack knew the press would be all over them by then. Arresting the man who may have killed a dozen women or more in seven states was going to be big news. And if nothing else, it was going to make the NYPD look extremely good at what they did. Now it was up to the DA's office, the prosecutor, and the investigators they used to do the rest.

He drove home with Charlie that night, after they made the arrest. It had been a long day watching the hotel all afternoon. They had seen Luke when he left, and Charlie had wanted to grab him then, but Jack told him to wait. Since he didn't suspect they were on to him, they knew he'd be back. And there were too many people around then, Jack didn't want anyone in the hotel to get hurt. It had worked out just right for them in the end. And not so well for Luke.

Luke Quentin was sitting in his cell then, staring at the wall. He could hear all the familiar sounds of jail. In an odd way it was like coming home. And he knew that if he lost, this time he was home for good. His face gave away nothing, as he stared down at his shoes, and then he lay on his bunk and closed his eyes. He looked totally at peace.

Chapter 2

"Hurry! Hurry, hurry!" Alexa Hamilton said to her daughter as she shoved a box of cereal and a carton of milk at her. "I'm sorry for the lousy breakfast, but I'm late for work." She had to force herself to sit down and glance at the paper, and not stand there and tap her foot. Her seventeen-year-old daughter Savannah Beaumont had miles of pale blond hair. She wore it straight down her back, and she had a figure that had made men whistle at her in the street since she was fourteen. She was the hub of her mother's life. Alexa looked up from the paper with a smile. "You're wearing lipstick. Someone cute at school?" It was Savannah's senior year in a good private New York school. Savannah was working on her applications to Stanford, Brown, Princeton, and Harvard. Her mother hated the thought of her going away to school. But she had fantastic grades and was as smart as she was beautiful. So was Alexa, but she had a different look. Alexa had a long lean body and a model's looks, except she was healthier and prettier. She pulled her hair back tightly in a bun, and never wore makeup to work. She had no need or desire to distract anyone with her looks. She was an assistant DA and was thirty-nine, turning forty later that year. She had gone to the DA's office straight out of law school, and had worked there for seven years.

"I'm eating as fast as I can." Savannah grinned and reassured her.

"Don't make yourself sick. New York's criminal population can wait." She had gotten a text message from her boss the night before that he wanted to meet with her that morning, hence the rush, but she could always tell him the subway had been slow. "How did the essay for

Princeton go last night? I was going to come in and help, but I fell asleep. You can show it to me tonight."

"I can't." Savannah smiled broadly at her, she was a gorgeous girl. She played varsity volleyball at school. "I have a date," she announced as she scooped up the last of the cereal, and her mother raised an eyebrow.

"Something new? Or should I say someone new?"

"Just a friend. We're going out with a bunch of people. There's a game in Riverdale we all want to see. It's no big deal. I can finish the application this weekend."

"You have exactly two weeks to finish all of them," Alexa said sternly. She and Savannah had been alone for almost eleven years, since Savannah was six. "You'd better not screw around, there's no give on those dates."

"Then maybe I'll just have to take a year off from school before college," Savannah teased her. They had a good time together, and a loving relationship. Savannah wasn't embarrassed to tell her friends that her mom was her best friend, and they thought her mother was cool too. Alexa had taken several of them to the office with her for Career Day every year. But Savannah had no desire to go to law school. She wanted to be either a journalist or a psychologist, but hadn't decided yet. She didn't have to declare her major for the first two years of college.

"If you take a year off, maybe I'll do it with you. I've had a run of crappy cases for the last month. The holidays bring out the worst in everyone. I think I've had every Park Avenue housewife shoplifter in town to prosecute since Thanksgiving," she complained as they left the apartment together, and got in the elevator. Savannah knew that in October her mother had prosecuted an important rape case, and put the defendant away for good. He had thrown acid in the woman's face. But since then, work had been slow.

"Why don't we take a trip when I graduate in June? By the way, Daddy's taking me to Vermont for ski week," Savannah said breezily as the elevator headed down. She avoided her mother's eyes when she said it. She hated the look on her face whenever she mentioned her father to her. It was still a mixture of hurt and anger, even after all these years—nearly eleven. It was the only time her mother looked bitter, although she never said anything overtly rotten about him to her daughter.

Savannah didn't remember much about the divorce, but she knew it had been a bad time for her mother. Her father was from Charleston, South Carolina, and they had lived there until the divorce, and then she and her mother moved back to New York. Savannah hadn't been to Charleston since, and didn't really remember it anymore. Her father came to see her in New York two or three times a year, and when he had time, he took her on trips, although his schedule changed a lot. She loved seeing him, and tried not to feel like a traitor to her mother when she did. Her parents communicated by e-mail, and hadn't spoken or seen each other since the divorce. It was a little *Charlie's Angels* for Savannah's taste, but that was just the way it was, and she knew it wasn't going to change. It meant her father wouldn't come to her high school graduation. Savannah was hoping to work on both of them in the four years before she graduated from college. She really wanted both of them there. But her mother was great, in spite of the animosity between her parents.

"You know he'll probably cancel at the last minute, don't you?" Alexa said, looking irritated. She hated it when Tom disappointed their daughter, and he so often did. Savannah always forgave him, but Alexa didn't. She loathed everything he did and was.

"Mom," Savannah scolded her, almost sounding like the mother and not the daughter. "You know I don't like it when you do that. He can't help it, he's busy." Doing what? Alexa wanted to ask, but didn't. Going to lunch at his club, or playing golf? Visiting his mother between her United Daughters of the Confederacy meetings? Alexa pressed her lips tightly together, as the elevator stopped in the lobby and they got out.

"I'm sorry," Alexa said with a sigh and kissed her. It wasn't so bad now, at seventeen, but Alexa had been furious when Savannah was little and he didn't show up and her big blue eyes filled with tears and she tried so hard to be brave. It broke Alexa's heart to see it, but Savannah could handle it better now. And Savannah excused her father for nearly everything he did. "If his plans change, we can always go to Miami for the weekend, or skiing. We'll figure something out."

"We won't have to. He promised he'd be there," Savannah said firmly. Alexa nodded, they kissed each other good-bye quickly, and then Savannah ran for her bus, and Alexa walked through the freezing morning to the subway station. It was bitter cold outside and there was snow in the air. Savannah didn't feel the cold as much as she did, and after a stop-and-start ride on the subway, Alexa was frozen to the bone when she got to work.

She saw Jack, the detective, and one of his young assistants heading for Joe McCarthy's office, just as she strode toward it herself.

"Early meeting?" Jack asked easily.

He had worked with her often over the past seven years, and he liked her a lot. He would have liked to ask her for a date, but she seemed too young to him. She knew her stuff, and was a no-nonsense kind of person, and he knew the DA thought the world of her. Jack had worked with her on the big rape case three months before. They had gotten a conviction. Alexa always did.

"Yeah, Joe sent me a text last night. He's probably just catching up on all the two-bit cases I've had lately. I've had every shoplifter in New York," Alexa said with a grin.

"Nice," he laughed, and introduced her to Charlie, who said hello, but nothing after that. He looked distracted, as though he was thinking about something else. "Good holidays?" Jack asked as they reached the DA's office, and he told Charlie to wait outside.

"Quiet. My daughter and I stayed home, and I took a week off. College applications. This is her last year at home." She said it sadly, and he smiled. She talked about her daughter frequently. He was divorced, but had no kids, and an ex-wife he would have been happy to forget. She had married his partner twenty years before, after cheating on him for two years. Jack never wanted to get married again. He always suspected that Alexa felt the same way. She wasn't a bitter person, but she was all business, and he didn't know a single soul in the police department who had ever dated her. He thought she had gone out with one of the assistant DAs five years before, but mostly she kept to herself and never talked about her personal life—except about her daughter.

Alexa had noticed that the cop with him looked young and intense. The earnest look on his face made her smile. Young cops always looked like that to her.

Jack and Alexa walked into Joe McCarthy's office at the same time, while Charlie waited outside. The DA looked happy to see them both. He was a good-looking man, of Irish origins, with a thick mane of white hair that was always a little too long. He said he'd had white hair since he was in college. It suited him. He was wearing jeans and cowboy boots and a worn-out old tweed jacket and a cowboy shirt. He was known for wearing western gear, even at meetings with the mayor.

"Did you two talk on the way in?" the DA asked, looking at Jack, who shook his head. He didn't want to steal the DA's thunder and knew better than that.

"Do we have a new case?" Alexa asked with interest.

"Yeah, I figured we'd keep it out of the paper for another day, until we get everything nailed down," he said as they sat down. "It'll probably leak by this afternoon, and then all hell will break loose."

"What kind of case?" Alexa's face lit up as she asked him. "Not another shoplifter, I hope. I hate the holidays," she said, looking disgusted. "I don't know why they don't just give them the stuff and forget it. It costs the taxpayers a hell of a lot more than it's worth to prosecute."

"I think we'll be putting the taxpayers' money to good use on this one. Rape

and murder one. Times four." Joe Mc-
Carthy smiled at Jack as he said it.

"Times four?" Alexa looked intrigued.

"Serial killer. Young women. We had a
tip. It didn't seem like a good lead at
first, and then bodies started showing
up, and the info we had started making
sense. There's been a small task force
following him from state to state for the
last six months, but they could never
catch him at it. All we had were victims
and no way to link them to him. The
snitch tipped us, from prison, but there
was no evidence to support the tip
for over a year. I guess our guy pissed
someone off before he left the joint, so
they gave us a call. The guy is very cool.
We had nothing solid on him till last
week, and now we've got him on two
murders almost for sure, and probably
two more. We're going to try and make
all four stick. That's your job," he said to
both Jack and Alexa, as they listened
with interest. And then he mentioned
that Charlie McAvoy, the kid outside,
was on the task force that had been following him around. He said the suspect
crossed state lines, so the FBI got into

it, but Jack and Charlie had made the collar last night. "All four victims are in New York, so the case is ours," he explained.

"What's his name?" Alexa asked him. "Have we seen him before?" She never forgot a face or a name, not so far.

"Luke Quentin. He got out of Attica prison two years ago. He pulled some robberies upstate. We've never had him in our court or on anything like this before. Apparently he told someone in Attica that he likes snuff films and watching women die during sex and wanted to give it a try when he got out. He's a pretty scary guy." He smiled at Alexa then. "He's your boy." Alexa's eyes opened wide, and she smiled. She thrived on hard cases, and putting away the people who deserved to be segregated from society forever. But she'd never had one as bad as this. Four charges of rape and murder one was a major case.

"Thank you, Joe." She knew that it was a tribute to her that he had given her the case.

"You deserve it. You're good at what

you do. You've never let me down. We're going to get a lot of press on this one. We have to mind our p's and q's. We don't want the guy getting a mistrial because we fucked up. The task force is working to collect data from the other states he's been in. If he's who we think he is, he's been on a killing spree for the past two years. His MO is always pretty much the same. First his victims vanish into thin air. Then we find the bodies but have no way to link them to him. We found two of them last week, and we got lucky. McAvoy got into his hotel room and got some dirt off his boots from the carpet. There was dried blood in it, and we're waiting for a final DNA match. It's a start. We had two other victims murdered in exactly the same way. Raped and strangled during sex. We found both of them in the East River, and two hairs off his carpet that match. That gives us four victims. Anyway, you two are going to have your hands full. I'm putting Jack in charge of the investigation, and you've got the case," he said, looking at Alexa. "Arraignment is at four o'clock."

"We'd better get busy," Alexa said, looking anxious. She was itching to bolt out of the office and start reading about the case. She wanted to be sure just how much they could charge him with that day, although they could always add more charges later on, as they got more information, more matches from forensic, and if more bodies turned up when they started checking unsolved crimes. All she wanted now was to put Luke Quentin away. This was what the taxpayers paid her to do. And she loved her job.

They left the DA's office after a few minutes, and he wished them luck. Charlie followed them out of the office, and Jack sent him back to work to check with the forensic lab for progress, and said he'd come back to him later on. Charlie nodded and disappeared.

"He's a quiet one," Alexa commented.

"He's good at what he does," Jack reassured her, and then decided to share some private information with her. "This is a tough case for him."

"How so?"

"If this is the guy, he killed Charlie's

sister in Iowa a year ago. It was pretty ugly, and Charlie got himself on the task force after that. He had to do a lot of talking to get them to allow it, even though it's a personal vendetta for him. But he's a great cop, so they let him do it."

"Sometimes that's not a good thing," Alexa said, looking worried, as they walked back to her office. "If he's going to help us, he needs to be clear-headed. I don't want him misinterpreting information or being overzealous because he wants to nail him. It could blow our case." She didn't like what she had just heard at all. She wanted everything about this case to be picture perfect, so the guilty verdict she got couldn't be overturned. And she knew she would get one. She was relentless in her prosecution and meticulous in her work. She had learned it from her mother, who was a lawyer too, and a good one. Alexa hadn't gone to law school until after the divorce. She had been married right out of college to the first and only man she had ever loved. And she had been madly in love with him. Tom Beaumont was a handsome southerner who had gone to

UVA and was working, more or less, at his father's bank in Charleston, where the spirit of the Confederacy had been kept alive, in part by the United Daughters of the Confederacy, of which Tom's mother was the head of the local branch, and a very grande dame. Tom was divorced and had two adorable little boys who were seven and eight at the time. She had fallen in love with them immediately, and Tom, and everything about the South. He was the most charming man she had ever known. Tom was six years older than she was, and much to their delight she had gotten pregnant on their wedding night, or maybe the day before. Everything had been idyllic for them for seven years, she had been the happiest woman alive and the perfect wife, and then Luisa, his ex-wife, came back, when the man she had left him for died in a car crash in Dallas. And the Civil War was fought again, and this time the North lost, and Luisa won. Tom's mother turned out to be Luisa's strongest ally, and Alexa never had a chance. To clinch the deal, Luisa got pregnant, while Tom sneaked off to see her, dazzled by her once again, as he had been when they met in college. Tom's mother showed him where his duty lay, not just to the Confederacy, but to the woman who was carrying his child, the mother of his "boys." Tom was torn between the two women and drank far too much while he tried to sort it out. In the end, Luisa was the mother of three of his children, Alexa only one. His mother kept reminding him of that and convinced him that Alexa had never really fit into their way of life.

It all happened like a very bad movie— a real-life nightmare. Everyone in town was talking about it, and his affair with his first wife. Tom explained to Alexa that he had to divorce her and marry Luisa. He couldn't let this child be illegitimate, after all, could he? He promised to work it out as soon as Luisa had the baby, but by then she was running his life again, and it seemed as though everyone had forgotten, including Tom, that there had ever been another wife—and child. Alexa had done everything she could to reason with him and talk him out of the insanity he was committing, but she couldn't stem the tides. Tom was too determined, and insisted that marrying Luisa for the baby's sake was the only option. It was the only one he saw.

Alexa felt as though her heart was being torn out of her body when she left Charleston. Luisa was actually moving her things in while Alexa packed. She took Savannah and her broken heart, went back to New York, and stayed with her mother for a year. The divorce had come and gone by then, and Tom didn't know how to explain it to her, but he said it just seemed better to leave things as they were. Better for him, Luisa, and his mother, and the little girl Luisa gave birth to. Alexa and Savannah had been banished, and went back to the North from whence they came, Yankees.

Luisa forbade Tom to bring Savannah back to Charleston, even for visits. She was back in full control. Tom came to New York to see his daughter a few times a year, usually when he came on business. Alexa wrote to her stepsons for a while, who were fourteen and fifteen when she left, and she worried about them both. But they weren't her children, and she could sense in their letters how torn they were between their two mothers. Their letters dwindled off within six months, and she let it happen. She started law school then, and tried to shut them all out of her heart. Everyone except her daughter. It was hard not sharing her anger with Savannah, and she tried not to, but even the six-year-old could sense how wounded her mother was. Her father was like a handsome prince whenever he came to see her, and sent her beautiful presents. But eventually even Savannah figured out that she wasn't welcome in her father's life. She didn't resent him for it, but sometimes it made her sad. She loved the time she spent with him. He was so much fun to be with. The fatal weakness that had led him back into Luisa's trap didn't show when he visited his daughter in New York. All that showed was how good-looking and fun and polite and charming he was. He was the epitome of a southern gentleman with the looks of a movie star. Alexa had fallen for it too, and so did Savannah.

"And the backbone of a worm," Alexa would say to her mother when Savannah wasn't around. "A man without a spine. Wasn't that a movie?" Her mother felt sorry for her, but reminded her not to be bitter, it did no one any good and would hurt her child. "She has no father!" Alexa would lament for her.

"Neither did you," her mother reminded her practically. Alexa's father had died of a heart attack on the tennis court when she was five, a congenital anomaly no one had known about or suspected. Her mother had been very brave about it, and went to law school, just as Alexa had. But it was no substitute for a good marriage, the one Alexa thought she had and didn't. "And you turned out fine," her mother reminded her often. Muriel Hamilton was proud of her daughter. She had made the best of a bad situation, but it had taken a toll on her, and her mother could see it. Alexa had a hard outer shell that no one could get through except her daughter, and her mother. She had only dated a few men since the divorce. Another assistant DA at one point, one of her investigators, and the brother of a college friend, and all of them briefly. Most of the time she didn't want to date and focused her attention on Savannah. The rest didn't matter to her, except her work, which she was passionate about.

Alexa had made a vow when she left Charleston. No one was going to break her heart again. No one could find it. She had locked it away in a storage vault, except for her daughter. No man was ever going to get near her again and hurt her. There was a wall around Alexa a mile high, and the only one who had the key to the door was Savannah. Her daughter was the light of her life. That was no secret. Her office was full of photographs of her, and she spent every weekend and spare moment she had with her. She was home with her every night. The hard part was going to come when Savannah left for college in the fall. Alexa had cautiously suggested NYU or Barnard, but Savannah wanted to go away to school. So they had nine months left of living together and enjoying each other. Alexa tried not to think about what would happen after that. Her life would be empty. Savannah was all she had and all she wanted.

Alexa carefully pored over the files that Jack had on Luke Quentin, his rap sheet, and the list of victims they were trying to match him up with sent by other states. They had been watching him for months, and a cop in Ohio had tied him to one of the killings, not conclusively or enough to book him, but enough to cause concern. There was no evidence to prove it, but he had been in the right place at the right time, as he had on several occasions since. The murder in Ohio was the first one that had made them think Quentin was their man. But they didn't have enough for an arrest. They had brought him in for questioning, and again on another case in Pennsylvania, which had turned up nothing. And he had laughed in their faces. It was only in the past two weeks in New York that Charlie McAvoy had been sure it was him when they found the bodies of two young women and fished the other two out of the river after that. They were exactly Quentin's type, and had all died in the same way, raped and strangled. There were no other signs of abuse. He didn't stab them or beat them up. He raped them and killed them while he did it. The only wounds on his victims other than the bruises on their necks from strangulation were the cuts and scratches they had gotten after their deaths, when their assailant dragged them away. Those cuts and scratches had provided the blood the forensic lab needed for DNA.

Alexa looked over the files that had come in from other states since the arrest the night before. They were trying to cross-check Quentin with a dozen victims. The photographs of the girls who had been killed were heartbreaking, and looked uncannily like Charlie's sister. There was a photograph of her in the stack too. All of the victims were between eighteen and twenty-five, most of them were blond and had a similar appearance. They had the look of wholesome young girls next door. All had been raped before they died—the bruises on their necks showed that all had been strangled, asphyxiated while their assailant raped them, which was consistent with his supposed desire to reenact "snuff films" and kill women during sex. All the young women had parents and friends who had loved them, brothers and sisters and boyfriends and fiancés whose lives had been forever changed when they died. Some of the bodies still hadn't been found, but many had. Some had just disappeared, and no one knew for sure if they had died, but the computer had spat them out as possible victims, and they had the same look as the others. In all, including those who hadn't been found, there were nineteen of them. Twelve whose remains had been located. Seven more whose hadn't.

Luke Quentin had a clear affinity for a certain type, if it was him. And if he wasn't, the killer liked a certain kind of woman, young, blond, beautiful, usually tall and lanky. Several of them had been models or beauty queens, the pride of their community, young girls on their way to happy lives and success, until they met him. He wasn't picking up sleazy women in bars, or killing hookers. He was on a rampage, seeking out the All-American Girl Next Door, which had left a trail of heartbroken, shocked, outraged parents across several states. Jack and Charlie and the rest of the investigation team and task force were all convinced he was the killer they were looking for. Now they needed to prove it, and the dried blood and hair in the soles of his boots and in his carpet was a first step. It had been their first lucky break, but that was all it took. One misstep on the killer's part, one infinitesimal forgotten detail, and sometimes the whole house of cards came down and got them their man.

It was hard to believe that one man could kill so many women, but it happened. There were sick people in the world. It was Jack's job to find them, and Alexa's to put them away. And she knew as she looked at the photographs that she was going to put Luke Quentin away, if he was the killer. If so, Alexa was going to be relentless and stop at nothing to convict him.

It would be small consolation to the families who had lost their daughters. She knew that in many cases they were astonishingly forgiving, and even spoke with the killers and said they forgave them. Alexa never understood it, although she had seen it often. She knew that if anything had happened to Savannah, she would never forgive the person who did it. She couldn't. The very thought of it made her tremble.

Jack went to the arraignment early with her at three-thirty. She had read all the pertinent files by then, and knew Quentin's history. She watched as they brought him into the courtroom in shackles and an orange jumpsuit. He was wearing jail-issue light canvas shoes, since his own boots had been taken as evidence for forensic, to analyze what was on them.

Alexa watched him move across the courtroom. He was a big man, powerful, but graceful. He moved with an arrogance that struck her the moment she saw him. And she didn't know why she thought it, but there was something subtly sexual about him. She could see why girls were attracted to him, or would be lured away to a quiet place to talk. He didn't look ominous, he looked sexy, handsome and appealing, until you looked into his eyes and saw how cold they were. They were the eyes of a man who would stop at nothing. As a prosecutor, Alexa had seen eyes like that before. He chatted easily with the public defender who had been assigned to him, a woman. And Alexa saw him laughing. It didn't seem to bother him at all that he was there, accused of four counts each of rape and murder. Murder in the first degree, premeditated, with intent to kill. They were throwing the book at him, and at the sentencing, if he was convicted, she was going to ask the judge to give him consecutive sentences. He was going to be in prison for the next hundred years at least, if Alexa had anything to do with it, and she hoped she would. This was going to be a long and complicated case to try to a jury, if he didn't plead guilty, and guys like him usually didn't. They brazened it out, and had nothing to lose. They had nothing but time on their hands and taxpayers' money to spend. In some cases, it was a media circus they enjoyed. Luke Quentin didn't look bothered by it at all, and as they waited for the judge to come out of chambers, Quentin turned slowly in his chair and looked straight at Alexa. His hands were cuffed, and his

feet were shackled, and a deputy stood
near him, and his eyes looked right
through Alexa as though he had X-ray
vision, and Alexa felt a chill run down
her spine. When you looked into those
eyes, it was terrifying. She shifted her
gaze after a moment and said something to Jack, who nodded. It was suddenly easy to believe that Quentin had
killed nineteen women, or maybe more.
Charlie McAvoy was sitting in the courtroom, staring at him, and wanting to kill
him. He had seen his sister's body and
what the killer had done to her. All he
wanted now was justice. No punishment would be enough for Charlie.

The judge came out of chambers
then, and Alexa spoke for the people of
the State of New York and stated the
charges. The judge nodded as he listened, and the public defender spoke
for the defendant and said he pleaded
not guilty, to every charge, which was
standard procedure. It meant that he
was not going to admit guilt or plea-
bargain for the moment, but none had
been offered. It was too soon. No attempt was made to set bail, not on four

counts of rape and murder, and Alexa said they would be seeking an indictment from the grand jury. And a few minutes later, Quentin was led back to the door where the prisoners entered, and taken back to jail. Just before he left the room, he turned and looked at Alexa again. He smiled an eerie smile, and then walked through the door another deputy had opened. It was as though he was looking Alexa over. She was older than he was, and twice the age of his victims, but his look said he could have her if he wanted. Alexa felt as though no woman would be safe from this man. He defined "menace to society," and he was outrageously cocky. Nothing suggested remorse or fear or even worry. He looked like a big, handsome guy who had the world by the tail and could do whatever he wanted, or acted that way.

There had been no press in the courtroom, because no statement had been made yet, but Alexa knew that almost immediately the media would be following the case. She was feeling uneasy when she left the courtroom. It was though he had run his hands over her, and she wanted to hit him. She was still feeling that way when she put her coat on in her office an hour later and went upstairs to another courtroom. Court was still in session, and a woman judge was on the bench, admonishing a man for having been delinquent in his child support for the last six months. She threatened to put him in jail, and he promised to pay promptly. It was the family law court, and half a dozen dramas were unfolding, as they always were.

Alexa waited until court adjourned, and followed the judge into her chambers. She knocked and opened the door, as the judge was stepping out of her robes. She was wearing a black skirt and a red sweater, and she was an attractive woman in her early sixties. She smiled at Alexa immediately, and came to give her a hug.

"Hi, sweetheart. What are you doing here?" Alexa didn't know, but she had needed to come here after her unsettling afternoon watching Luke Quentin in court.

"I just got a big case, and I went to the arraignment. The guy is so frightening, it freaked me out."

"What kind of case?" the judge asked with interest.

"Serial killer, and rapist. He seems to prey on young women between the ages of eighteen and twenty-five. We have nineteen murders we're trying to link to him, and four almost for sure here in New York. I hope we'll be able to nail him on the rest, but we don't know yet." As she listened, the judge winced. The sign on her desk said Muriel Hamilton. She was Alexa's mother and the family court judge.

"God, I'm glad I don't get cases like that. It would make me sick. It's bad enough watching guys who won't support their children but go out and buy a new Porsche. I made one of them sell his to give back support to his ex-wife. Sometimes guys can be such jerks. But this sounds ugly." And Muriel didn't like it. Not at all.

"Just looking at him, knowing what I do about him, the guy scares me to death," Alexa admitted. She wouldn't have said it to anyone but her mother. She didn't usually have that kind of re- action, but Quentin's arrogant, invasive glances at her had really gotten under her skin.

"Be careful," her mother warned her.

"I'm not going to be alone with him, Mom." Alexa smiled at her. She loved the fact that they could talk about work, among other things. Her mother had saved her life when she got back from Charleston. It had been her idea for Alexa to go to law school, and as usual she'd been right. "They bring him to court in cuffs and shackles," she reas- sured her, but her mother still looked worried.

"Sometimes guys like that have friends. As a prosecutor, you're going to be the focus of all his anger, if you indict him and bring him to trial. If you do, as far as he's concerned, you're the reason he's in jail. And the press will eat you alive on a case like this too." They both knew she was right about that.

"He doesn't seem to mind being in jail. And the guy who lost the Porsche was probably pretty pissed at you too."

Once or twice her mother had had to have a deputy sheriff at the house for protection during a tough case. Her mother laughed at what Alexa had said. And then Alexa had an idea. "Do you want to come to dinner tomorrow night?"

Her mother looked mildly embarrassed. "I can't. I have a date."

"You and Savannah. I can't keep up with either of you."

"No, and you don't try. When was the last time you had a date?"

"In the stone age. I think people were carrying clubs and wearing fur." Alexa looked ruefully at her mother. Muriel always brought it up.

"That's not funny. You need to get out more, and at least have dinner with friends." Alexa worked, went home to her daughter, and that was it. Her mother worried about her.

"I'm not going to have time to go out for a while now. I have to prepare this case."

"You always have some excuse," Muriel chided her. "I hate your having cases like this. Why don't you get a decent job?" her mother teased. "Like tax law or estate planning, or animal rights or something. I don't love the idea of you prosecuting serial killers."

"I'll be fine," Alexa said. She didn't need to ask who her mother's date was. She knew. She and Judge Schwartzman had been dating for years, since Alexa was in college. Her mother hadn't gone out much before that. She was too busy with her own work, and raising her daughter. Now she and Stanley Schwartzman went to dinner and movies, and sneaked away for the occasional weekend. Alexa knew that he usually spent the night on Saturdays. Neither of them wanted to get married, and the arrangement had worked for years. He was a lovely man, five years older than her mother and approaching retirement, but he was lively and in good shape. He had two daughters and a son older than Alexa, and sometimes they all got together over the holidays.

Her mother put her coat on, and they walked out of the courthouse together. It was just starting to snow, and they shared a cab uptown. Alexa dropped her mother off and went farther uptown to her apartment. She was looking forward to seeing Savannah at the end of a long day and was disappointed when she wasn't home. For a minute, a chill ran up her spine, thinking of men like Luke Quentin loose in the world, and Savannah was still so innocent at her age. It was a horrifying thought. But she turned the lights on and chased it from her mind. She looked around the room then and realized that in the fall, that was how it was going to be, a dark, empty house when she got home. She wasn't looking forward to it, to say the least. And then, as Alexa stood there thinking about it glumly, Savannah called and said she'd be home soon. She didn't want her mother to worry, and she said she was bringing friends. It reminded Alexa that things were still okay. Luke Quentin was in jail where he belonged. And Savannah was still part of her life every day. Alexa heaved a small sigh of relief, sat down on the couch, and turned on the TV. And there it was, the story of Luke Quentin on the evening news. And a still shot of Alexa leaving the courtroom after the arraignment. She hadn't even seen the photographer who took it. The report said she was a senior assistant DA with a history of convictions in major cases. All Alexa could think of as she looked at the shot on TV was that her hair looked a mess. It was no wonder she hadn't had a date in over a year, she thought, and laughed out loud as she switched channels and saw the same photograph again. The media circus had begun.

Chapter 3

As Alexa sat alone in a small dark room watching through a wall that was a two-way mirror, Luke Quentin was led into a larger room on the other side. Jack Jones and Charlie McAvoy were waiting for him, sitting at a long table. The other arresting officer, Bill Neeley, was there too, and two other cops Alexa had seen but didn't know by name. The full investigation team was present, as well as some people from the task force who would work with them later, but for now these were the primary cops involved. It was Monday morning, and everyone looked fresh after the weekend.

As he had been at the arraignment,

Quentin was led in, in shackles and handcuffs, and he looked calm and in control. The deputy sheriff with him took off the cuffs as soon as he sat down, and Luke looked at the men on the other side of the table.

"Anyone got a smoke?" he asked with a lazy smile. It was no longer allowed in the investigation rooms, but Jack figured it might be a helpful tool to put Quentin at ease. He nodded and slid him a pack of cigarettes and a book of matches. Quentin flicked a match with his thumbnail and lit up. Alexa could hear clearly everything that was said, and she sat in the darkness, watchful and tense. She wanted the interrogation to go well. Quentin took a long drag of the cigarette, exhaled a billow of lazy smoke, and then turned to precisely the spot where Alexa sat, as though he sensed her, and could feel her, and knew without question she was there. Through the darkened one-way glass, his ice-colored eyes met hers, and he smiled a small wicked smile, meant just for her. He knew almost certainly that she was there. The word that came to mind for Alexa was "insolent." She wasn't sure if he meant the look to be a caress or a slap, but it felt like both to her. She straightened in her seat, and without thinking, she reached for her own cigarettes. There was no one there to see it. She smoked occasionally and watched Quentin intently as she did.

"Tell us where you've been for the last two years," Jack asked him without expression. "What cities, what states." They knew exactly where he had been for the last six months, and Jack wanted to see if the suspect would tell them the truth. He did. He rattled off a list of towns and cities, in all the states they knew. "What have you been doing there?"

"Working. Visiting guys I knew in the joint. I'm not on parole. I can do what I want," he said cockily. Jack nodded assent. They knew he had taken jobs as a laborer, unloading freight, and in one of the farm states, he had picked crops for a few weeks. His size was in his favor and always got him a job. It wasn't in the favor of his victims and had cost them their lives. They knew that as well.

Quentin looked arrogant, but there was no threat of violence in his demeanor, and he had had no history of it in prison or before that they knew of. Luke was said to be a peace-loving man, but would meet the challenge if attacked. He had been stabbed once, when trying to break up a fight between two rival gangs, but he had had no known gang associations and kept to himself.

Quentin was known to be a jogger in prison. He ran track, and jogged daily in the yard. And he had continued running once he got out. They had watched him in parks several times, and it was often where the victims were found, but they still couldn't tie him to them. There were no witnesses to the crimes. The fact that he had run in the same park didn't mean that they had died at his hands. There hadn't been a single drop of sperm in any of the women, which meant that he had used a condom or had a disability of some kind, which maybe led him to rape. He was brilliant at what he did, if it was him.

Quentin was arrogant, but not a braggart. He waited for their questions and offered nothing else. He met their eyes, and from time to time glanced at the window where Alexa watched with a serious expression. Without realizing it, she had smoked half a dozen cigarettes by then.

"You know I didn't do it," Quentin said after a while, looking straight at Jack and laughing at him. His eyes had drifted past Charlie, dismissing him with a glance. "You guys just need someone to pin it on, to make you look good. You're playing to the press."

Jack decided to dispense with the amenities, as he met Quentin's eyes. There was nothing there, neither guilt nor fear, nor even concern. The only thing he saw there was contempt. Luke was laughing at them, and thought they were fools. He hadn't even broken a sweat, which suspects often did. The lights were hot. All the cops in the room were perspiring profusely, while Quentin looked cool. But they were wearing street clothes and bulletproof vests, he was in a thin jumpsuit, and totally at ease.

"There was blood in the dirt on your shoes," Jack told him calmly.

"So what?" Quentin looked completely indifferent. "I run every day. I don't look at the ground when I run. I run through dirt, dog shit, human excrement every day. I could have run through blood. It wasn't on my hands." And it wasn't on his clothes. They had already gone through everything he owned. It was only in the dirt on his shoes. And he could have been telling the truth, although it was unlikely. "You can't hold me forever. And if that's all you've got, your charges won't stick. You know that as well as I do. You'll have to do better than that. You're full of shit and you know it. The arrest is no good."

"We'll see. I wouldn't count on that," Jack said with a confidence he didn't fully feel. They needed some hard evidence to use in the case. They'd had enough to arrest him, although not enough to convict him yet. Hopefully it would come, with a few more lucky breaks. They had good men on their team. Maybe another snitch would turn up, although Quentin didn't look like a guy who talked. He was much, much smarter than that. And the forensic evidence they were waiting for would nail him.

The questioning went on for several hours, about where he'd been, what he'd done, who he knew, who he met, the women he'd gone out with, the hotels where he'd stayed. It checked out that he'd been in the cities where the women were killed, but so far there was nothing conclusive to tie him to the other girls. They were hanging by a slim thread, but it was good enough for now, and they were counting on the forensic lab to give them more with DNA.

"You've got to prove a hell of a lot more than that I ran in the same park." But the blood and hair would do for now. Even Luke Quentin knew that.

They had never mentioned his passion for snuff films during the entire interrogation. They didn't want to tip their hands yet. They had offered to have his public defender with him that morning, but Quentin said he didn't care. He was not afraid of cops, and he thought public defenders were jokes, they were always young and innocent, and most of the guys they defended were convicted anyway. The fact that they were guilty was irrelevant to him. And the PD he'd been given was no better. She'd been in the public defender's office for a year. He didn't care. He figured it would never get to trial, and for lack of evidence, they'd have to let him go. They couldn't prove a goddamn thing, and blood on his shoes wouldn't be enough.

The blood from all four victims came from scratches they'd gotten on the ground when they'd been raped, or dragged away, one from a cut on a victim's arm. The site of the bleeding hadn't been the cause of death. They had been naked when he raped and killed them, and when they were found. He always took their clothes off and didn't bother to dress them again once they were dead. The first two girls had been found in a shallow grave in the park, dug up by a dog. The other two had been dumped in the river, which was harder to pull off, but the killer had found a way, without being observed. The other bodies in the other states had been found disposed of in similarly casual ways, and some still hadn't been found, but were almost surely dead. They had disappeared and never returned, often while jogging in the very early morning, or at night, in parks.

The killer seemed to like a pastoral setting for his trysts. One girl in the Midwest had disappeared off a farm, she was just eighteen, and her parents said she had a bad habit of hitchhiking into town, but they knew everyone for miles around. This time, clearly, a stranger had picked her up. They waited for months, hoping for news of her, and that she had run off with some handsome young guy, she was a bit of a wild thing, but a beautiful girl. They never heard from her again, and her body was found in a field when a bulldozer was moving dirt months later. And she had died just like the others, raped and strangled.

They interrogated him for three hours, and then sent him back to his cell. Quentin sauntered out of the room, without even a look back. He didn't look in Alexa's direction on the way out, and she was as tired as the police officers and detectives when they met in her office to discuss what they'd heard. He hadn't given them anything, except confirmation of where he'd been, which they knew anyway, and a lot of names that would amount to nothing, just people he'd met along the way, had dinner with, worked for, or gone to bars with. He knew how to stay out of trouble, on the surface anyway. He had never been arrested since being released from prison. He had no history of drugs, except marijuana in prison. He liked tequila and cheap wine, but so did every kid in college, and they didn't rape and strangle women. Drinking cheap booze wasn't a crime, and those who knew him said he could hold his liquor, he wasn't a sloppy drunk who got into bar fights. He was cold and calculating, kept his own counsel, and watched every move he made. He had during the interrogation too.

"We didn't get much," one of the younger cops said, looking discouraged.

"I didn't expect to," Jack said calmly. "He's smarter than that. He's not going to give us some slip or the lead we've been waiting for. We're going to have to put this case together twig by twig and brick by brick and pebble by pebble, with grains of sand, like the three little pigs building their houses. He's not going to make it easy for us. We're going to have to do our jobs on this one, and work our asses off to nail him." Alexa liked the image, and smiled as the others left the office.

"So what do you think?" she asked Jack candidly, when they were alone again. They were both aware that Quentin had no history of convictions for violent crimes before this. But after his last stint in prison, he had changed his MO, and Alexa was convinced that he had done it, as was the task force that had trailed and studied him for months.

"Honestly? I think he did it. My gut says he killed them all, maybe even more than we know about. But I think we're going to have to work hard to get him. I think he's guilty. All we have to do now is prove it, and then you can do your job." Alexa nodded, she agreed with him. It was no slam dunk yet, but she wanted more than anything to get him, if he had done it, and she believed he had. Her instincts were the same as Jack's, but Quentin was as slick as a greased marble, and it would be hard to catch him. He had all the earmarks of a sociopath, a man who could commit heinous crimes, and remain indifferent and unruffled. He clearly wasn't frightened or remorseful. Maybe he would be later. "Want to share some lunch, guaranteed to give you indigestion?" Jack offered. "We can talk about the case, or not if you prefer. I still need to absorb what he told us this morning. Sometimes I pick something up later, when I think about it. It looks like nothing, but turns out to be a thread that's tied to something else." It was why he was good at what he did, he focused on every minute detail, and it always paid off in the end. It had on every case they'd worked on together. He was the best investigator they had, and she was the best assistant DA.

"Sure. I have to be back here at two for a meeting. I'm getting ready for the grand jury." It was in two days, and

Jack would go with her. She wanted to be well prepared. For lack of stronger, totally conclusive evidence, her arguments to bring Quentin to trial had to be tighter and better and more convincing. There was no smoking gun yet. But she was as good at what she did as he was.

They walked across the street together to the deli they all hated but frequented daily. Alexa tried to bring food from home but usually left in too much of a hurry to do so, so she either starved all day, ate junk out of the machines, or sacrificed her digestive system at the deli. The deli was awful but the closest to the building where they worked. They all agreed that you had to be either starving or suicidal to eat there. The food was heavy, greasy, and either fried into oblivion or dangerously under-cooked. Alexa usually tried to get by with a salad, which seemed minimally risky. Jack liked a man-sized meal, and took the daily special, which was lethal.

He ordered meat loaf and mashed potatoes, and she a Caesar salad, which arrived looking limp and wet.

"God, I hate the food here," she muttered as she started to eat it, and he grinned.

"Yeah, me too. That's why I try to eat here at least twice a day, sometimes three. I never have time to go anywhere else." Since his divorce years before, he spent most of his waking hours at work, even on weekends. He had nothing else to do and said it kept him out of trouble. Alexa had the same theory for herself.

"We both work too hard," she commented, making a face over the soggy lettuce that seemed weeks old and probably was, and had been the cheapest they could buy in the first place.

"So what else is new? How's your love life?" he asked casually. He liked her, he always had. She was smart, she worked hard, she was tough when she had to be, even relentless, but she was also fair, and kind, and a truly nice person, and pretty too. It was hard to find anything he didn't like about her, except that she was a little too skinny for his taste, and didn't do much with her hair. It was always tied back in a knot, although he suspected it would be long and luscious in bed. He tried not to think about it, and to remember that she was one of the "guys" in his life. It was how she acted, and the only relationship she seemed to want with him or anyone else. She'd been badly burned by her marriage, and her husband's betrayal. She had told him the story once, it was even worse than his.

"I assume you're kidding, right?" She smiled as she answered his question. "Who has time for a love life? I have a kid and a full-time job. That's good enough."

"Some people seem to manage more than that. They even go on dates, fall in love, and get married, or so I'm told."

"They must be on drugs," Alexa said as she pushed away the salad. She had had enough. "So what do you think of our case? Think we'll get him?"

"I hope so. I'm sure as hell going to try. He's as cold as they get. I think he would kill damn near anyone he chose to, if he could get away with it and had the chance."

"What makes you think so?" Alexa was intrigued by his comment and trusted his judgment, and always had before. He was rarely wrong. And he probably wasn't this time either. "He has no history of violent crimes, and he's never killed anyone before this spree, that we know of." She was playing devil's advocate for them both.

"That just means he's good at what he does. I don't know why I think so. But I've seen guys like him, and so have you. Ice cold and dead inside. They're like machines, they're not human beings. He's a classic sociopath, and they're usually smart, just like he is. The most dangerous guys around. They'd as soon kill you as shake your hand. He may not have killed anyone when he was younger, but I'm convinced he would now. Maybe something snapped the last time he was in prison. I think he's one sick, twisted sonofabitch, and he'll give us a run for our money. He's covered his tracks pretty well. I don't know why we got lucky with the blood on his shoes. Sociopaths don't usually make mistakes like that. Maybe he got too cocky, and he sure didn't know we were watching him." That had been clear in the interrogation, and they hadn't told him. They had just let him talk to see what he said.

"Shit, I hope we get him," Alexa said with fervor. She wanted nothing more. She wanted to put him away.

"So do I," he agreed.

"It makes me sick when I see those girls' faces. They're all so young and pretty. They look like my daughter." As she said it, a chill ran down her spine. She hadn't thought of it before, but they did. Savannah was just his type. But fortunately, he was safely in jail, and not wandering the world. For now.

"How is she, by the way?" Jack asked, changing the subject. He felt as though he knew her from the gallery of photos on Alexa's desk, and he'd met her once or twice at the office. She was a pretty girl just like her mother.

"She's applying to college. She wants to go to Princeton, at least that's in New Jersey. I'm scared to death she'll get into Stanford. I don't want her that far away. My life is going to be a wasteland when she goes."

He nodded and could see the real sadness in Alexa's face. She was too young to have given up her whole life for a child. "Maybe that's something for you to think about. You still have time to do something about it."

"Excuse me? This from a guy who works as hard as I do? My last date may have been in the stone age, but something tells me yours was several millennia before." He laughed out loud at her response.

"So take it from me, it's a mistake. It's too late for me now. By my age, I can either go out with younger women who want babies, and I don't, or women my age who are angry and bitter and hate guys."

"And there's nothing in between?" Alexa wondered if he had a point. She knew she was bitter herself, about Tom, and men in general. She had vowed never to trust any man again, and she hadn't, even those she had gone out with, rare as it was. Her walls were a mile high.

"Nope," Jack confirmed. "Hookers. But I'm too cheap to pay for sex." They both laughed at that, and he paid for their lunch as Alexa thanked him. "Don't say that I don't take you to the best places. If the theory about getting laid in exchange for a good dinner holds, you should probably kick me in the shins for lunch. How's your stomach holding up after that salad? Feeling sick yet?"

"Not yet. It usually takes about half an hour." The jokes about the deli were legion, but it was just as bad as they all said, and worse. All the cops swore the jail food was better, and it probably was.

They walked back into the building together, and Jack said he'd keep her posted on the latest developments about Quentin. The press was taking a major interest in him, and they were all being extremely careful about what they said. Reporters had already tried to interview Alexa and she declined. She was leaving that to the DA.

Alexa spent the rest of the afternoon in meetings, worked on her file for the grand jury, and left work earlier than usual, at six o'clock. Her mother and Judge Schwartzman were coming for dinner, and Savannah had just put a chicken in the oven when she got home. She looked pretty and fresh and had played volleyball that afternoon. She was elated that they'd won against a rival school. Alexa tried to get to her games whenever she could, but it wasn't as often as she liked. And she was struck again by the resemblance between her daughter and Luke Quentin's victims. It made the death of all those young women seem that much worse to her.

"How's your big serial killer case coming?" Savannah asked her as they stood in the kitchen. Alexa was making a salad, and they had just put baking potatoes in the microwave. Her mother and Stanley Schwartzman were due in half an hour. They could chat, as they always did, until dinner was cooked.

"It's coming along," Alexa answered. "I have a grand jury hearing on it in two days. How are the applications coming? Did you finish any more? I want to see them before they go out," she reminded her, but Savannah wrote excellent essays, and her grades and board scores were high. She was going to get in everywhere. Alexa had done her job well, and Savannah was a bright girl.

"I finished Princeton and Brown. I still have Stanford and Harvard to do. I don't think I'll get in anyway, they're both too hard. GW would be okay too. And Duke." Going to college still seemed unreal to her, like a dream, but she was excited about it. She was looking forward to talking about it with her dad when they went skiing.

Alexa and Savannah chatted in the kitchen, as they set the table and finished making dinner, and then the doorbell rang. It was Alexa's mother and Stanley. He was a handsome, distinguished-looking, vibrant man, despite his age, and exactly what a judge should look like. He was serious, conservative, but he had a great sense of humor and a twinkle in his eye.

The chicken was delicious, and everyone pretended not to notice that the baked potatoes were overcooked. The conversation was lively, and the three generations of women always had a good time together, and Stanley enjoyed being with them. Alexa reminded him of his own daughters, and Savannah of his favorite granddaughter who was the same age, and at Boulder, having a ball. They talked about Savannah's applications, and a funny case Stanley had heard recently, a suit brought by a man who had sued a co-worker for sneezing on him constantly and making him sick. The case had been dismissed for lack of malicious intent or tangible damages, and no damages had been awarded.

"Once in a while you have to ask yourself if people are all crazy," he said as he finished a dish of ice cream. "What are you working on these days, Alexa?"

"The big serial killer case that's been all over the press," Muriel answered for her, and he looked impressed.

"Those cases are always hard. They're very emotionally disturbing. Cases like that always haunt me for months." Alexa nodded. It was already starting to do that to her. She knew in every detail the faces of each dead girl, and their lives. The one she knew the least about so far was the defendant, how he had done it, when and where, and what made him tick, but she'd get there. She always did.

"I hate it when Alexa has cases like that," her mother complained as she carried their dishes to the sink and helped load the dishwasher. She loved coming to Alexa's for dinner, it was always easy and relaxed. And Stanley liked coming with her. They had a comfortable relationship and enjoyed many of the same things. Not enough to want to get married at this point in their lives, but enough to spend a lot of time together and talk on the phone every day. Sometimes they had lunch in his chambers or hers. "I always worry that the defendants are too dangerous and have equally dangerous friends on the outside."

"Any sign of that?" Stanley asked, looking mildly concerned, but Alexa shook her head.

"No. It's fine."

The evening ended shortly after that, and Alexa and Savannah went to their own bedrooms. Savannah spent the rest of the evening talking to friends on the phone, and Alexa pored over files, until she fell asleep on her bed, fully dressed. Savannah came in to say goodnight to her, and gently took her papers out of her hand, covered her with a blanket, and turned off the light. It was not an unusual occurrence. Alexa fell asleep that way on many, many nights, especially when she was in trial. Savannah kissed her, and Alexa didn't stir. She was purring softly, as Savannah smiled and closed the door.

Chapter 4

The next day, after Alexa's dinner with her mother, she got good news about the case. The latest, more extensive report on the DNA definitely determined that the dried blood caked into Luke Quentin's boots was a match with two of the women, and that the hairs were from the other two victims, and were a clear match too. Alexa considered the news a real gift, so they could now link him to all four women. How the blood and hair got there was up to them to prove. But it was solid evidence for their side, just in time for them to go to the grand jury the next day. Jack called and told her, and Alexa beamed when she heard the news. There were still more tests to do, which would be more conclusive, but the information they had now was reliable. Luke Quentin was in big trouble. As was proper, Alexa called and told his public defender, who was not thrilled to hear the news.

"Do you really think you can make this stick?" the other woman asked her. Alexa knew her and liked her, although she was still very green.

"Yes, I do," Alexa said firmly.

"You don't have a lot to go on." That much was true.

"I have four dead women, and a previously convicted felon, a repeat of-fender, with blood and hair of the vic-tims on his shoes. It didn't get there while he had lunch at McDonald's. He claims he may have jogged through it in the park. He didn't jog through four dif-ferent crime scenes. We're going with it. Let me know if he wants to plead."

"I don't think he will," the public defender said, sounding unhappy. She was not looking forward to this case. The killing of four young women would have public opinion heavily against him, and from what she had seen so far, her client was anything but remorseful, and extremely sure of himself. A jury was going to hate him the minute he walked in. All she could do was her best, but they both knew there was a good chance she was going to lose. And Quentin had no desire whatsoever to plead guilty to the charges. He had nothing but time on his hands, and a lot to lose. If he was convicted, he was going to spend the rest of his life in prison. He wasn't about to hand that to them. He was going to make them work to convict. "Thanks for keeping me up to date," she told Alexa, and they both hung up and went back to work.

As always, Alexa was impeccably prepared for the grand jury hearing the next day. It was held at the courthouse in Manhattan where her office was. Jack picked her up at home that morning, and drove her downtown in an unmarked police car. The hearing was closed to the public, and everything about it was kept in the utmost secrecy. Only she, representing the DA's office; Jack, as the head of the investigation;

the defendant and his attorney; and the grand jurors would be there. The hearing would determine if there was enough evidence for an indictment for the matter to be bound over for trial. Alexa knew that eighteen of the twenty-three members of the grand jury would be there—two more than they needed to indict. And at least twelve would have to vote for the indictment, and obviously she hoped they would. She and Jack didn't say much on the way downtown; it was early. Quentin would be brought to the courtroom with four guards, in case he tried to escape. The public defender would meet him there. She had had the right to file a motion to block the grand jury from convening, but she hadn't done it. There was too much evidence against her client to make a motion plausible.

Jack and Alexa hurried up the courthouse steps and into the grand jury room, just as Quentin was escorted in through a separate entrance. They had both been there many times before, with good results. It was rare, almost unheard of, for Alexa's indictments to be dismissed. And her paperwork and motions were all in order. She wanted no procedural mistakes on this case.

They took their places at the counsel table assigned to the DA's office, while the public defender sat down at the table across the aisle and Luke Quentin was brought into the room. Alexa was surprised to see that he was wearing a suit. She had no idea where the public defender had gotten it for him, but he looked good. She wondered if maybe it was his own. It seemed unlikely. He glanced across the aisle at Alexa then, and this time he didn't smile. His eyes bored into her and through her, like white-hot power drills that drove right through her head. There was pure hatred in his eyes, and then he turned away. She could all too easily imagine that same look in his eyes as he raped and killed some young girl. She had no doubts whatsoever about the case.

The grand jurors convened quickly and heard the evidence from Alexa's side. There were no witnesses to refute it. They were the only people in the room. Jack supplied enough evidence

to support the indictment, without giving any major secrets away. He said
there were investigations under way in
other states about fifteen more potential
victims, and they were still developing
the case, but they had four sure victims
so far. The jurors spoke to the defendant
briefly, and asked him a few questions
about his whereabouts and the forensic
evidence that had been found against
him, and then they thanked everyone for
coming, and said that they would hand
down their decision later that day, after
they voted on it. But Alexa knew from
their faces, as did everyone else in the
room, that they would vote to indict.
There was no other choice, with four
dead women and blood on Luke
Quentin's boots.

"So much for that," Jack said, as they
went back to their offices upstairs.
"Now we get to work." Alexa nodded,
and they parted in silence, each thinking
of all they had to do. The burden was on
the investigators now to give her the evidence she needed to win the case. She
trusted him completely.

Alexa got the call from the grand jury

late that afternoon. They had come back with an indictment in the Quentin case, four counts of rape, and murder in the first degree. They were off and running. She knew the coming months would be increasingly stressful until they tried the case. She called and asked the public defender if they would agree to a speedy trial, which she did. Joe McCarthy agreed with Alexa that the public's best interests would be served by trying and convicting him as quickly as possible and putting it to rest. The public defender admitted that she was not looking forward to trying this case. They set the date for May, which gave them four months. And by Friday night, after organizing all their files, clearing her desk, and setting the wheels of justice in motion, Alexa was wiped out.

She and Savannah ordered pizza for dinner, and after that Savannah went out with friends, and Alexa emptied her briefcase and went to work. She knew now that with the Quentin case scheduled for trial in May, she would have no social life whatsoever in the coming

months, but she didn't have one anyway.

Savannah had plans with friends all
weekend, which allowed Alexa to work
without feeling guilty, and finally on Sunday afternoon they looked over Savannah's college applications together. She
had finished the last ones.

"Looking good," Alexa said, smiling at
her proudly. As usual, Savannah had
met the deadline right on time. "Let's
stuff them in a bunch of envelopes and
get them out." Savannah agreed, and
they each filled several envelopes, put
stamps on them, and addressed them
to the admissions offices. Alexa said
she'd take them downstairs and stick
them in the mailbox, since she needed
some air anyway. She hadn't left the
apartment since Friday afternoon and
had worked straight through the weekend.

She was just about to leave the apartment when she saw an envelope that
had been shoved under the door. The
handwriting was stilted and awkward
and looked like that of a child as Alexa
picked it up.

"What's this?" she said more to her-self than anyone else. It was addressed to Savannah, and had been delivered by hand. She walked it into Savannah's room and handed it to her. "Looks like you're getting love notes from very young children," she teased her, and was about to leave the room as Savan-nah opened it and looked confused. The letter inside had been written on a com-puter and printed out. If it had been writ-ten by a child, it was one who owned a computer, but most children these days did.

Savannah looked faintly unnerved as she handed it to her mother without comment. It said, "I love you, and I want your body."

"Well, that certainly makes that clear. Any idea who it's from?" The note wasn't signed, and Savannah shook her head.

"That's weird, Mom. It's creepy. Kind of like a peeping Tom."

"Or a secret admirer. I wonder if it's someone in the building, since it didn't come through the mail. Just be aware when you go in and out, and don't get in the elevator alone with a guy you don't know." It was good advice.

"Why would someone write me something like that?"

"Because there are a lot of nuts in the world, and you're a very pretty girl. Just be careful and smart and you'll be fine." Alexa tried to treat it lightly and went downstairs to mail the college applications. She didn't want to admit to her daughter that she was somewhat unnerved herself. She was thinking about her mother's admonition to be particularly careful during the Quentin case, and her reminder that men like him had friends outside, even when they were safely put away in jail. So far Quentin didn't seem like a man who had a lot of friends, or any in New York. Some of his pals in prison had told investigators he was a lone wolf.

Alexa asked the doorman if anyone had hand-delivered a letter to them, and he said no one had, which led her to wonder how the sender of the note to Savannah had dropped it off. And more importantly, who would write the letter to her and why. She tried to look less upset about it than she was when she went back upstairs, but she admitted to being concerned. She had quietly put the letter in a plastic bag. Savannah brought it up again as they shared Chinese takeout that was delivered.

"I was thinking about that letter again, Mom. I think it's really scary, and I don't think it's the kind of thing that would be written by a kid," even though the envelope had looked that way. "Kids just don't write that kind of thing."

"Maybe a very repressed kid would. Some boy who admired you in secret from the distance, and disguised his handwriting on the envelope, so you couldn't guess who it was. I don't think it's a big deal. You should be careful anyway, but it isn't a threat." Alexa was trying to be cool.

"I guess so," Savannah said in response, finishing a spring roll. "It still creeps me out."

"Yeah. Me too. And actually, it's kind of insulting. I live here too, and nobody's in love with me or telling me they want my body." Savannah laughed, but in truth Alexa particularly didn't like that an anonymous stranger had written a note like that to Savannah. She was far more disturbed than she let on.

Without saying anything to Savannah, Alexa stuffed the letter in its plastic bag into her purse, and took it to the forensic lab the next day. Her favorite technician was on, a young Asian man who always got her fast results and gave her the most minute details.

"Who wrote that?" she asked bluntly, and he laughed when she handed him the plastic bag with the envelope in it.

"You mean hair color and shoe size? Or just what brand his jeans were?"

"I mean man, woman, or child?" She was afraid that it had not been written by a lovesick young boy, and maybe not even by a dirty old man. She had a feeling it had been written to unnerve her, and it had.

He narrowed his eyes as he carefully took the envelope out of the plastic bag, wearing rubber gloves, and looked at it, and then smiled at her. "Give me a few minutes. I have to finish something up, or the guys in narcotics are going to kill me. I'll call you in an hour. I assume you

want me to check it for fingerprints too."
She nodded.

"Thanks." She smiled back at him and went upstairs to her office. As promised, he called her within the hour.

"Okay, got it." Jason Yu got right to the point, he always did. "Adult male, steady hand so probably somewhere in his twenties or thirties. American. Possibly Catholic school education, so maybe it's a priest," he chuckled.

"Very funny."

"The handwriting was disguised, clumsily, to look like it was written by a child, but it wasn't. And there are no prints on the paper. He must have worn rubber gloves. Death threat?" he asked with interest. It wasn't unusual for cops and assistant DAs or even public defenders to get them. People who went to jail got pissed at lawyers and judges, and the cops who arrested them in the first place. It came with the job.

"No, nothing like that. Kind of a love letter of sorts, not to me, to my daughter."

"And you want to know who the boyfriend is?"

"She doesn't have one. It was an anonymous letter written by some guy who says he wants her body. Working on the Quentin case, I'm a little skittish about guys who go after young women. I'm probably just paranoid, and it's some kid in our building."

"It never hurts to check it out," he reassured her. "I'm working on your DNA studies right now. I'll let you know when I have something new for you."

"Thanks, Jason," she thanked him again, and they hung up.

He hadn't solved the mystery of Savannah's anonymous admirer, but at least they knew now that it was a man and not a child. As Savannah said, it creeped her out. There was no certainty in Alexa's mind that Luke Quentin was behind it, and there was no reason for him to know she had a child. But someone had written the letter. And if Quentin had somehow managed to look her up, or Google her online from the computer in the jail, and discover she had a daughter, then he had the information he needed, and could have had someone he knew write Savannah a letter to scare her, or follow her to discover she had a daughter. She didn't know how he could arrange it, but she did know that he had thought the grand jury wouldn't indict him, and they had. Inevitably, he would blame her for that, and the looks he had given her the few times she saw him had been to throw her off balance as well, to show her who was boss, and that to him she was just a hunk of female flesh like anyone else. There was a smoldering sexual quality to him along with the arrogance that hadn't gone unnoticed. And Alexa didn't like it. Not at all. And particularly not directed at her daughter. If he had sent the note, it was to frighten Alexa, and nothing else, to show her how far his reach was, and that he could get to her, even from jail.

"What's up?" Jack had walked into her office and looked startled at her expression.

"Why?"

"You've got murder in your eyes."

"No, I don't. That would be our defendant. I'm just worried."

"What about?" He sat down in the chair across from her desk.

"Savannah. We got a stupid anonymous letter this weekend, from some
guy who says he wants her body. I'm
probably being paranoid, but I wondered if Luke Quentin got someone to
drop it off. Do you want to look up his
visiting record and see if anyone has
come to see him, and let's check them
out."

"Sure," Jack reassured her. "But it's
probably not him. He's not that stupid. I
just spent another two hours with him,
and he's a smart guy. What's the point
of lusting after your daughter? Or sending anonymous letters to bug you? He's
in jail, and the last thing he wants to do
right now is beat a path to your front
door and piss you off. You're a pretty
formidable opponent, and you've got
the upper hand. I don't think he's your
guy. It's more likely just a random thing.
She's a pretty girl. Anyone could have
written that letter."

"I guess you're right. I'm just edgy.
And I don't like people stalking my
daughter." Alexa looked fierce as she
said it, a mother lioness protecting her
cub, and Jack smiled.

"Is she scared?"

"Not really. But we were both un-nerved."

"It's probably just some kid who likes her. Boys do dumb stuff at that age. Come to think of it, at every age."

"Jason Yu says it's a guy in his twen-ties or thirties."

"You asked him?" Jack looked sur-prised. Having the handwriting analyzed by forensics seemed like an extreme measure to him. "You *are* worried," he said when she nodded.

"I just wanted to be sure, so I know what we're dealing with. So it's a man and not a kid. But it's still probably nothing."

"I'll check Quentin's visiting record. And if it happens again, let me know." She nodded, and he filled her in on the interrogation that morning. Nothing new had turned up. But they were sending Quentin's early DNA results to the other states to see if there was any kind of match. And by late that afternoon, he was able to tell Alexa that Quentin had had no visitors at all, so it was unlikely that the letter to Savannah had been instigated by him. Alexa wasn't sure if she was relieved or not. If it wasn't Quentin, who was it?

It was two days later when Jack walked into her office again. Alexa was having a bad day. Everything had gone wrong, and she had just spilled her coffee over her desk, drowning her papers, and had ruined a new skirt.

"Shit," she was muttering to herself when he walked in, beaming.

"Bad time?"

"No, I just spilled my coffee." She was trying to salvage the papers on her desk. The skirt was a mess. "What's up?" He tossed a file onto the dry part of her desk.

"Bingo!"

"Bingo? What about?" It had been a busy morning, and her mind was going in a million directions at once.

"We have matches in Iowa and Illinois. Some of Quentin's hair under three victims' nails. So now we have seven. I think this is just the beginning." They had made the matches from the evidence in the rape kits put together by

the coroner in each case and meticu-
lously preserved.

"Holy shit!" She was both elated and
sorry at the same time. Sorry for the
families of the victims, but thrilled that
they had the perpetrator behind bars.
"Will they let us incorporate their cases
and add them to trial here, or do we
have to extradite him for trial there after
ours?" Their worst fear was that the FBI
would take the case away from them
since he had crossed state lines. Alexa
wanted to keep the case and so did
Jack and the DA.

"I haven't gotten that far." So far
they had him on a killing spree in three
states. It was going to get complicated
now. There were mechanics and legal
technicalities involved. And then Jack's
face clouded over. "One of the victims is
Charlie's sister, which was what got him
involved in the case in the first place.
But it's going to be hard on him knowing
that for sure."

"Did you tell him?"

"Not yet, but I will. I'm thinking of taking him off the case. This is a little too
close to home. He got the collar, that's

good enough." The "collar" in copspeak was the arrest.

"I think you should take him off. I don't want him losing it in court, and blowing our case. Or going nuts and shooting the guy. We'll have enough headaches without that."

"He's a good cop. He won't go crazy. I just don't want to upset him more than he already is." Alexa agreed, and she and Jack celebrated for a minute that they were about to avenge three more victims at the trial. It was all they could do for those girls and their families now.

But when Jack talked to Charlie about it later that afternoon, Charlie was adamant about not leaving the case, and he begged Jack not to take him off it. He had been involved in the investigation since the beginning and had been instrumental in bringing information to the task force. His feelings were hurt that Jack and the assistant district attorney thought he could lose it in court. He had been cleared to join the task force at the outset, and had made full disclosure about his sister. He had been closely observed, and made no slipups so far.

"What kind of cop do you think I am? A nutball? I'm not going to shoot the sonofabitch, although I'd like to. I've worked my ass off for the last year to bring this guy to justice and bring him in. I was one of the early ones who suspected it was him. And by sheer luck we nailed him on the crimes here first, which puts him in our jurisdiction. Jack, you can't take me off this case." There were tears of disappointment in his eyes. He wanted to do this for his sister. Jack hadn't realized they were twins until he read her birth date on the paperwork the Iowa police had sent him. Iowa was Charlie's home state, although he had moved to New York years before.

"All right, all right. But if it gets to be too much for you, I'll let you out. Or take you off it, if you get too stressed."

"I'm not too stressed," Charlie said calmly. "I've never hated someone so much in my life. That's different." Jack nodded, hoping he was doing the right thing, and remembering Charlie smashing Quentin's face into the pavement and breaking his nose the night they arrested him.

"I'm leaving you on the case, but I don't want you alone with him for interrogation, and I don't want you in his face, or him in yours. Is that clear?" Charlie nodded. "That's a little too much for your nerves and mine. Agreed?"

"Agreed." Charlie left his office then, having to digest the information he had suspected for months but never known for sure. Luke Quentin had raped and strangled his twin sister. He waited until he got home, to lie on his bed and burst into tears. It was early days yet, and they had a long way to go, but the case was taking a toll on all of them, in one way or another, and it was going to get a lot worse.

Chapter 5

The rest of January flew by, and Alexa was swamped at the office. They got a match on Quentin on five victims in Pennsylvania, and one they hadn't even known about in Kentucky. With the women in Iowa and Illinois, they had thirteen rape and murder victims now. The charges were incorporated into their case, by agreement with the other states, and it was in the press all over the country.

Alexa had made a brief statement to the media, but otherwise declined to comment. She didn't want to do or say anything wrong. The case was just too important. And there were at least a dozen more victims in question, in a variety of states where he had traveled. It had turned into a national story, and Alexa was constantly meeting with detectives from other states. Jack was gathering information, and Alexa was already busy preparing for the trial. Finally, in early February, Alexa had time for a quiet dinner with her mother after work.

"You look tired," her mother said, looking worried.

"It's going to get worse before it gets better. I only have three months till the trial." She was up till three in the morning every night, reading case law and making notes.

"Well, just don't wear yourself out totally. How's Savannah? Has she heard anything from the schools yet?"

"Not till March or April," Alexa answered with a sigh. "She's going skiing with her father next week. If he shows up. Most of the time, he flakes on her. He'll probably do it again," Alexa said with a look of irritation. She hated his disappointing Savannah, who always forgave him. It was enough that he had hurt her.

"Maybe he won't flake this time," Muriel said quietly. "I hope not."

"Why?" Alexa asked, looking exasperated. She hated her ex-husband, everything he stood for, and everything he'd done to them. He had banished them from his life, out of weakness. It had been easier for him to give in to his mother and ex-wife than to stand by them. She loathed the worm he had turned out to be. "Why do you hope he won't flake?" Alexa asked, suddenly angry at her mother.

"Because it's good for her to see her father, at least once in a while. She loves him. You may hate him, and I understand that, I don't like him either, for what he did to you. But he's still her father, Allie. Better the reality, with all its flaws and frailties, than a fantasy she makes of him." Alexa smiled at what her mother said. She hadn't called her "Allie" in years. But Alexa was still a child to her, just as Savannah always would be to Alexa and still was now.

"Maybe you're right," Alexa said,

backing down. "But I grew up without a father. It didn't kill me. And Tom is such a jerk."

"She'll figure that out for herself. Give her time."

"I think she already knows it but loves him anyway."

"Give her that. She needs it. For now at least."

"It always upsets her that I won't see him. I haven't seen him in ten years and hope I never do again."

"Is he coming to her graduation in June?"

"I asked her not to invite him," Alexa said guiltily. "She said she's giving me four years' notice, and she wants him at her college graduation." Alexa smiled ruefully at her mother. "I guess I have no choice. She's a good sport about it, and I try not to say too much, but she knows how I feel about him. It's no secret between us."

"You need to get over it," her mother said quietly, and Alexa looked at her in surprise.

"Why? What difference does it make if I hate him?"

"Because it poisons you. And you'll never have a decent relationship with another man if you don't put it behind you and stop hating him."

Alexa's jaw looked set in stone. "Check back with me in thirty or forty years. Maybe I'll have Alzheimer's by then." Her mother made no further comment, and Alexa went home to Savannah, who was lying on her bed and watching TV.

"How was Grandma?" she asked, looking sleepy. She had finished all her homework and had spent a quiet evening alone.

"Fine. She sends you her love."

Alexa went to hang her coat up in the hall closet, and saw the envelope sticking under the door. She hadn't seen it when she walked in. She picked it up cautiously by a corner. It was the same childlike handwriting as before. She didn't say anything to Savannah, and opened it after she put on a pair of rubber gloves she kept in a drawer. It said "I know where you are every minute of the day. Look around. You can't see me. You're a beautiful girl." There was no overt threat in it, but whoever had written it wanted her to know that she was being watched, and by a man who was lusting after her. Alexa was scared, terrified in fact, as she put the letter in a plastic bag, just as she had done before.

She didn't say a word about it, but walked into her bedroom and closed the door. She called Jack on his cell phone, he answered immediately, and she told him about the letter. Alexa was holding it carefully in the plastic bag.

"I don't even know if it's real. It may just be someone trying to be cute, or scaring her. But if some guy is following her, I don't like this at all." There was a long silence at Jack's end, and he finally admitted he didn't either.

"Why don't I give you a cop for her? He can go to school with her." Alexa hated to frighten Savannah, but she knew she had no choice. She had known when she took the Quentin case that there could be threats to her. She hadn't bargained on them being aimed at Savannah instead. These weren't direct threats, but there was a menace to them anyway. And if this was being orchestrated by Luke Quentin, it was even more frightening if he was having some previously convicted felon follow Savannah. She couldn't prove that, but even the remote possibility of it made her feel sick.

"I haven't told her about this letter yet, but I guess I have to. Thanks, Jack. I do want a cop for her," she confirmed. She was afraid for Savannah, not herself.

"No problem. Try not to worry about it. It probably has nothing to do with Quentin, but it's better to be safe than sorry. Who knows what kind of creeps he knows." Everyone he knew or hung out with had been in prison.

Alexa decided not to worry Savannah at bedtime and told her what the letter said over breakfast. Savannah made a face.

"That's so creepy, Mom. The guy is sick."

"Yes, he is. I called Jack Jones about it last night. He's going to give you a plainclothes cop to go to school with, just to be on the safe side, in case someone really is watching you. I'd rather be smart about this. It may just be a prank, but I don't want to take the chance." The case she was working on was a reminder of just how dangerous some men were.

Savannah looked instantly upset. "That's so embarrassing, Mom. How long do I have to have that?"

"Let's see if he writes to you again. It could be till after the trial." Until she knew if the notes were due to Quentin or not, she wanted Savannah protected and out of harm's way.

"That's three months away!" Savannah shrieked at her. "Maybe even four!" She knew enough about her mother's work to know that the trial could last a month, and this was going to be a big trial, with thirteen victims, and maybe more by then. "I'd rather stay home from school than look stupid with a cop with me every day."

"Well, you can't stay home from school. So suck it up," Alexa told her, relieved that Savannah was more upset about the cop than the potential danger. She was still ranting and raving when their doorbell rang five minutes later, and a handsome young boy with dark hair and big brown eyes wearing a baseball cap and jacket stood smiling at them both. He said he was Officer Lewicki, but to just call him Thad. He smiled at Savannah, and she stared at him as Alexa tried not to smile. It was easy to see that Savannah thought he was cute. Who wouldn't? He looked about sixteen years old, and was probably only a few years older than that, close to Savannah's age. She had imagined some old geezer in a uniform. Thad Lewicki was anything but that.

"All set for school?" Alexa asked sweetly, as Savannah put on her coat.

"Yeah, I guess so," she said, as Thad picked up her book bag.

"I thought maybe we could say that I'm your cousin from California, and I'm here for a few months. They're going to see me every day," he suggested with a boy-ish smile.

"Yeah . . . okay . . ." Savannah said as they opened the door to the apartment.

"I should probably warn you, I suck at history and math. I think it's some kind of learning disability or something. But I did okay in Spanish, if you need help."

"Thanks," Savannah said, smiling slowly. She glanced over at her mother cautiously, and Alexa nodded.

"Have a nice day," she said as the door closed. She called the school to explain the situation to them, and then called Jack. He had done exactly the right thing with Thad.

"Okay, so how come you never send guys like that for me? The last time I needed protection, you sent me some old warhorse who weighed four hundred pounds. This kid is mighty cute."

Jack laughed. "I thought you'd like him. What did Savannah think?"

"She didn't have time to tell me, but she had almost forgiven me when she left. He was offering to do her Spanish for her and carrying her bag. He's her cousin from California. He looks about fourteen years old."

"He's twenty-one, and a really nice kid. He's the oldest of nine children, and his father, grandfather, and brother are cops too. A nice Polish family from New Jersey. Hell, maybe they'll get married.

She could do worse." Alexa was laughing at the other end.

"You have it all figured out. Protection *and* a son-in-law all wrapped in one. Do you do windows and floors too?"

"Anytime, ma'am, if that's what it takes." He was teasing her, but there was always the faintest hint of flirtation in his voice when he talked to her about anything other than work. But he knew better than to try. She'd have run like hell, and he'd have lost a friend. "Anyway, problem solved." He was happy to take the worry out of Alexa's life. She had enough.

By the time she left for work that day, Alexa was relieved to know that Savannah was well protected. And by the end of the week, Thad was having breakfast with them before the two of them left for school. Savannah said he was a really nice guy. She said he had a girlfriend he'd gone out with since high school, they'd been together for seven years. He was a solid, reliable kid, and Jack said he was a good cop. Alexa had the sense that he and Savannah were becoming friends, although he kept respectful boundaries with her. And for the moment, there were no more letters. Everything was in control. Alexa hoped that the letters would stop, whoever had written them. She had enough on her plate without that. Jason Yu had checked the letter for fingerprints when she took it to him in the lab, and once again, whoever had addressed the envelope and handled the printed computer sheet had worn gloves. There were no fingerprints on it at all.

At the end of the following week, Alexa sat in on another interrogation of Luke Quentin, and this time she was in the room. She asked no questions, and only observed, but he never took his eyes off her. She had the feeling that he was undressing her with every move. Nothing showed on her face. She looked icy cold and entirely professional, but by the time she left the room, she was shaking and totally unnerved.

"You okay?" Jack asked her in the hallway. She looked pale.

"I'm fine. I hate that sick sonofabitch," she said, trying to calm down. They had linked two more murders to him. The house of cards had come down. His number of victims was at fifteen.

"Don't worry, he hates you too. Those looks he gives you are just an act to throw you off. Don't let him get to you, that's what he wants. He's not getting out of prison in this lifetime. He can't do anything to you."

"He acts like he can have any woman he wants."

"He's a good-looking guy. I guess it works for him." He had looked right into her eyes, and ever so subtly licked his lips. Just watching him made her feel sick.

"It didn't work so well for his victims," Alexa said tersely and went back to her office. She had work to do. And Savannah was leaving the next day for a week in Vermont with her father over ski week. He was picking her up after school, while Alexa was at work. So she wouldn't have to see him, which was fine with her.

Alexa and Savannah had a nice dinner that night, and said goodbye to each other the next morning, as Thad stood by, holding her books. Her bags for Vermont were all packed and waiting in the hallway. Alexa had helped her pack the night before.

"Have fun with Daddy," Alexa said kindly. They had told Thad he had the next week off, and he was going back on regular duty for a week. Alexa didn't need him. None of the letters had been to her, only Savannah.

"I'll call you from Vermont," Savannah promised as she hugged her mother and she and Thad walked out the door.

Alexa was sad to see her go, and she'd miss her, but she knew she'd have fun skiing with her father. He was a fabulous skier and had won races when he was younger. He had taught Savannah to ski when she was three, and it was still her favorite sport, probably because of the memories she'd shared with him.

Alexa worked late at the office, and came home after seven, braced to find an empty apartment, and was stunned to see Savannah still sitting there, looking glum. Alexa instantly tensed. Clearly, Tom had flaked on her again.

"What happened to your father?" Alexa asked gently, not wanting to upset

Savannah any more than she already was.

"He's late. His plane was delayed in Charleston. He won't be here till nine. He said we'd still drive up tonight." She sighed and smiled at her mother, who wondered if he'd really come. And as Alexa started to make something for them both to eat, she realized that she'd be there when he arrived. She told Savannah over dinner that she would stay in her room when he came. She didn't want to break a perfect record and see him for the first time in ten years. She wasn't ready for that. And wouldn't be for another hundred years, no matter what her mother said. Screw that. And him.

"Come on, Mom, be nice." Savannah didn't say it, but she wondered if they saw each other now, and it wasn't too awful, maybe her mother would let him come to graduation in June. She didn't want to seem like a traitor to her mother, after all she did for her, but secretly Savannah wanted him there. And he had already said he would come, if it was okay with her mom, but not otherwise.

He was respectful of his ex-wife's feelings about him, and knew all the reasons why she felt that way. He couldn't say she was wrong. He had been a total cad.

"I am nice," Alexa said tartly, putting their dishes in the machine. "That doesn't mean I have to see your father. Not tonight." Or anytime soon. Or maybe in this lifetime.

"All you have to say is hi and bye." Alexa didn't say it to her daughter, but she was still thinking more along the lines of "fuck you."

"I don't think so, sweetheart. I want you to have a nice time with him. We both love you. But we don't have to be friends."

"No, but you could at least be polite. You won't even talk to him on the phone. He says he would, but he understands why you won't."

"That's big of him. At least we know his memory is still intact," Alexa said, and walked out of the room. Savannah knew that her father had gone back to his first wife after leaving her mother, and they had had another child, whom

Savannah had never met. She had never met his wife either, or seen her half-brothers in ten years, although she still remembered things about them. She knew none of the details of the divorce or why it had happened, and her mother refused to discuss it with her. Alexa didn't think it right to explain it to her. Even if she hated Tom, he was Savannah's father after all. Savannah remembered her paternal grandmother vaguely, and being slightly scared of her. She had never heard from her in all these years either, not even a birthday card. There was a rift a mile wide between the two sides of her family, and her only contact with her father was when he appeared. He rarely called her and had told her years before that she could never call him at home, only in the office, but she never did. She had correctly sensed that it was okay for him to visit her, but not for her to go anywhere near his Charleston life. It was a silent pact between them, and the kind of thing a child knew, without ever having it spelled out.

Alexa and Savannah sat and watched

TV together, and the doorbell rang at nine-fifteen. Alexa leaped to her feet when she heard it and headed for the bedroom and was telling Savannah to come and say goodbye to her when she left, when Savannah pulled open the door, and there he was, and Alexa felt like a deer in the headlights as they stared at each other and said nothing. Ten years melted instantly like snow on their tongues. She had no idea what to say, and neither did he. He hadn't expected her to be there. She never was. And he looked exactly the same. He was wearing jeans, a black ski parka, and hiking boots, and he was as handsome as he'd ever been. His hair was just a touch too long, his eyes were just as blue, the gray in his hair didn't show among the blond, he had the same athletic body, and the same cleft in his chin. Tom Beaumont hadn't changed one bit.

"Hello, Alexa," he said quietly, as though afraid to approach her. She looked on the edge of panic and as though she were about to run from the room, and from him. And when he spoke, he had the same deep, husky voice, and the same southern drawl. What was different was that she wasn't his wife anymore, and hadn't been in years.

"Hello, Tom," she said politely, looking stiff. She was still wearing her work clothes, a quiet navy suit, and she had kicked off her shoes, and had on navy stockings and a lawyerly white blouse, and her hair in a bun. Unlike him, she looked like a different person than the carefree, happy woman she had been ten years before. Now she looked serious, professional, and extremely uncomfortable to be facing him. But Savannah was grateful that she was at least talking to him. It was a first. She was so glad his plane had been late. Alexa wasn't. "Well, I'll leave you two to get ready. Savannah can get you something to eat, if you haven't eaten."

"I can pick something up on the road," he said gently. What he had seen and startled him most was the look of sorrow in her eyes. It was all still there, everything he had done. It made his stomach hurt and made him want to cry. But it was way, way too late for that.

"We'll get going now," he told Alexa, as though to assure her that he would be out of her sight and her space soon. She nodded, somber faced, and left the room. She walked into her bedroom and closed the door. He looked at Savannah and said nothing. Savannah looked happy, as though something wonderful had happened. He wondered if she was used to the devastated look in her mother's eyes. That would be even worse. Alexa looked well, but the price of his betrayal was deep in her eyes.

They were ready to leave a few minutes later. Savannah was wearing black ski pants and a white parka, and she looked gorgeous when she came to kiss her mother goodbye in the bedroom. Alexa was going to miss her but had a ton of work to do. She could use the solitude, without having to feel guilty for the time she couldn't spend with Savannah. And she knew how much she had been looking forward to the trip with Tom.

"I love you," Alexa said as she hugged her. "Have a good time."

"I love you too, Mom. Don't work too

hard." And then she hesitated for a minute in the doorway. "Do you want to come and say goodbye?" She meant to her father. Her mother shook her head without a sound, and Savannah reassured her. "That's okay. Thank you for being nice when he came in." Alexa smiled, and Savannah closed the door.

Alexa heard them leave a moment later, and she lay down on her bed. She hadn't expected to see him, or to be so shaken when she did. What had shocked her was that he looked no different, not one jot. He looked exactly as he had when he was her husband, and for an instant she had to remind herself that he no longer was. It was as though her heart and body had hung on to all the memories she had tried to kill. Her soul remembered, her skin remembered, her heart remembered, and now she remembered how much she had loved him then, and how painful it all was. As she lay there, she wondered if there were some people you always felt the same way about, who awoke the same feelings and the same memories. No matter how much you had come to hate them, or how much things had changed, there was always some tiny part of you that remembered how sweet it had been. The worst part was that she knew that if she had met him for the first time that night, she would have been just as attracted to him, just as dazzled by him and how incredibly good-looking he was. He was hard to resist. And then slowly as she lay there, she remembered just how awful it had been, how badly he had hurt her, and how weak and despicable he was. But for just a fraction of a second, she had remembered the good times and felt the same things for him. She was sorry she had seen him, and then decided she wasn't. All it did in the end was remind her of how much she hated him, and why.

Chapter 6

Halfway into the week Alexa was relieved that Savannah was with her father. Her days had been insane. They had found another victim they could link to Luke Quentin. This time, a nineteen-year-old girl. He had sixteen victims that they knew of, and the forensic lab was working overtime on DNA. The task force was growing under the supervision of the FBI, since several states were involved now. Jack had a dozen investigators working on the case full time. The trial was three months away.

On Thursday Alexa met with Judy Dunning, the public defender, to discuss discovery with her. Alexa had to give her the evidence she had, all of which was incredibly damning. Alexa tried to convince Judy to get him to plead guilty, and Judy explained that she was beginning to think he had been framed, possibly by someone he had had bad dealings with in prison, who had sworn vengeance on him. She said that she was convinced herself that he hadn't done it. There were too many victims, and suddenly every dead girl in half a dozen states was being blamed on him. She told Alexa that he was a very sensitive man, and of course he didn't want to plead guilty, if he hadn't committed the crimes. Alexa stared at her as though she was out of her mind. It was clear to her what had happened. Luke Quentin had turned his smoldering sexual gaze on her, had done his sociopathic dance, and she was falling in love with him, in a frighteningly innocent way. It was what he did, and probably how he had seduced all his victims, made each one feel special and like the only woman in the world—for those few minutes, until he killed her. He wasn't going to kill Judy Dunning, but he had blinded her to the truth. Maybe it was what she needed to defend him, but Alexa came out of the meeting shaking her head.

"Where have you been?" Jack asked her when he ran into her in the hallway.

"On a UFO, eating Twinkies," she said, with a grin at him.

"Doing drugs again, counselor?"

"No, but the public defender is. She just spent a half hour trying to convince me of Luke Quentin's innocence. What's worse is that she believes it. He sure has cast his spell on her."

"Good. She can visit him in prison. That happens, you know. Women fall for them, no matter how heinous their crimes, and visit them in the slammer for years. We just got our seventeenth victim." The numbers grew almost every day.

"I feel like I'm following a presidential election," she said as they stopped at the coffee machine. She had already had too many cups that day. "How many states do we have now?"

"Nine," he said with a grim look. "The guy is amazing, and I don't think we're through yet."

"We're not overestimating him, are we?" She didn't want to get sloppy, and start pinning crimes on him that weren't his, and blow their case. She had "reasonable doubt" and a jury to think of.

"I think we may be *under*estimating him. So far it all matches up. We've got his DNA now with every victim." She nodded and went back to her office. She was there until nine o'clock that night, and had been all week. She was at her desk on Friday until ten-thirty, going over all the forensic reports from every state. It all looked solid. Nothing surprised her anymore, except that he wouldn't plead. He was still claiming he was innocent, and even more incredible, his attorney believed him. But no one else on the planet, and surely no jury, would. Alexa had a good case.

She was exhausted when she got home that night, dragging her heavy briefcase. It was nearly eleven. She had talked to Savannah at six o'clock. She'd had a great week in Vermont with Tom, and she was coming home the next day.

Alexa sifted through her mail and was about to toss it on the hall table unopened, and then a familiar envelope caught her eye. She tore it open and held the sheet of paper in a trembling hand. In the same boldfaced type, printed on a computer, were the words "I'm coming to get you now, and then you will be mine. Say goodbye to your mom." Alexa stood in the hallway with her coat on, shaking from head to foot as she read it again and again. What did he know about them? Why was he writing to her? Was it just a prank, or was Luke Quentin torturing them? There was no way to know, no way to trace the letters. She called the doorman, and he said that no one had dropped anything off for her. Whoever he was, he was getting into the building and slipping them under her door. It was frightening beyond belief. And what if sending Savannah to school with Thad Lewicki wasn't good enough protection? What if someone got her in the end?

She pulled her cell phone out of her bag, sat down on the couch, and called her mother. She hated to worry her, but Muriel had a level head. Alexa read the latest letter to her, and asked her what

she thought. Just how panicked should
she be? She was too frightened herself
right now to make sense.

"I think you need to take it very seriously," her mother said in a somber
tone. "If Quentin is behind it, he has
nothing to lose. And he wants to get
back at you. You can't take the risk."

"What am I going to do?" Alexa asked
her, as tears slid down her cheeks.
"Should I give up the case? I just want
Savannah safe." This wasn't just a case
now; it was a nightmare, if it was endan-
gering her child.

"It's too late for that. Turning the case
over to someone else won't change
anything. You've already brought the
roof crashing down on him. If they convict, he's gone for a hundred years. He's
after you and he wants revenge. And
even if he is masterminding this, whoever is dropping off the letters may
never do anything to her, other than
scare you, but you can't take the
chance."

"So what do I do?" Alexa felt overwhelmed, terrified, and confused. This
was more than she'd bargained for. She

was trying to seek justice for the families of all those girls, and in doing so had put her own at risk.

"Get her out of New York."

"Are you serious?" Alexa sounded shocked.

"I've never been more serious in my life. And get a deputy for you. At least till after the trial. It should calm down after that, eventually. It always does when the trial is over. He'll adjust. But right now, you're both in danger. You can stay here yourself if you want, and keep the case, but get Savannah out of town." Her mother sounded frightened too.

"Where?" All they had was each other. And she wasn't about to put Savannah in a witness protection program all alone, to stay God knew where, with people she didn't know. And she wanted to see the trial through herself, if she could, without putting Savannah further at risk. She wasn't as worried about herself. And no one was threatening her.

"Send her to Charleston with Tom," her mother said quietly, and all she could hear at the other end was her daughter's sharp intake of breath.

"I can't do that," Alexa said in a hoarse voice, brushing the tears off her cheek. This was serious business now, and she had to force herself to think. "Luisa would never let him," Alexa said quietly. "And he wouldn't have the balls to either. He cut us out of his life ten years ago. He doesn't want her back."

"You have no other choice," her mother said in an iron tone. "And neither does he. Your daughter's life could be at stake. Maybe this is only a prank to torture you, or scare you off the case. But neither of you can take that chance. You've got to send her away. This will be no life for her here, and it's too stressful. And for you too, worrying about her. Personally, I wish you would give up the case, but to be honest, I think it's too late. But Savannah doesn't belong in the middle of it. And you'll be worried sick if she's here." It was true. She already was. The words of the letter were burned into her mind. *Say goodbye to your Mom.* "Is she still in Vermont with Tom?"

"Yes. He's bringing her back tomorrow night."

"Tell him not to bring her back, just take her home with him. Or maybe he has relatives in the South that she could stay with. But she'd be better off with him, much as I hate to say it. The only thing I know for sure is that she can't come back here. Not now. Not till after the trial, and hopefully after that, things will calm down. Call Tom, Alexa. You have no other choice."

"Shit." It was the last thing on earth she wanted to do. She didn't want to send Savannah away, and surely not with him. But if her mother was right, and something happened to her, she would never forgive herself. "It's too late to call him tonight," Alexa said practically, "and I don't want to talk to him with Savannah sitting next to him."

"Then call him in the morning, but tell him not to bring her home." Alexa sighed deeply at her end. This was a high price to pay for sending a serial killer to prison. But her mother was right, she couldn't put Savannah at risk. She had made her own choices, with the career she'd chosen, and she took full responsibility for it. She wanted Luke Quentin in prison. But more than that, she wanted Savannah safe.

"I'll call him tomorrow," she said with sadness and resignation. She was going to miss her, but she didn't even know yet if Tom would take her. There was a good chance he'd say he couldn't. He had Luisa to answer to.

"Good. And call Jack Jones tonight. Tell him to put a cop at the door of your apartment."

"I'm okay, Mom. I have the chain on, and I'm not going anywhere." But after she hung up, she called Jack anyway, and told him what had happened. He listened, and agreed with her mother.

"If he is behind the letters, and I'm beginning to think he is, I don't think he'll have the balls to try anything at this point, and I'm not sure he has that kind of power, to make someone else grab her and hurt her. He's not connected to the mob. He's an ex-con and a sociopath. This is his deal, no one else's. He probably contacted someone he knows indirectly, and is doing this to rattle you, with nothing behind it. He hasn't had any visitors, but he can get word out of jail through someone else. It's probably just a sick game he's playing. But it's a lot to put your kid through. I think you should send her away, if you have somewhere to send her, and I'll assign a couple of cops to you. I'm sorry, Alexa, I know this is hard for you."

She nodded and tears rolled down her cheeks again. Savannah was her whole life and she didn't want anything to happen to her. She hoped that Jack was right and if it was Quentin, he was only trying to scare her, but she couldn't take the chance, and if it wasn't Quentin, it was scary anyway. Jack told her he'd have a plainclothesman at her door in half an hour. He agreed with her mother on that too, although Alexa wasn't nearly as worried about herself. It would take a lot of guts to kill the prosecutor, and it wasn't Quentin's MO. Savannah was, if he could have gotten to her himself. And Jack was probably right about that too. Whoever was dropping the letters off might never have the guts to grab her. But who knew? And worrying about it day and night would be hard on them both. She was better off somewhere else, although Alexa knew Savannah wouldn't be happy about it. She wouldn't want to leave her friends, mother, or school, especially for the last few months of senior year. It just wasn't fair.

Alexa was awake until the early hours of the morning. She slept fitfully for a few hours, and she woke up and called Tom at seven. He had the deep voice that he always had in the morning, and when she asked, he said Savannah was in the other room. They were having breakfast together in half an hour, and were hoping to get a few runs in before he drove back to the city at noon. He said he'd have her back at seven. His flight to Charleston was at nine.

"That's why I called," Alexa said, sounding exhausted. "You can't bring her home." She told him what had happened, and he was as concerned as she was. She tried to reassure him, but it wasn't a good situation, and it was impossible to predict.

"What about you, Lexie? Are you going to be okay?" He hadn't called her that since she left, not even by e-mail.

"I just want to convict the bastard. I owe it to all those families to send him to prison for the next hundred years. But I don't owe them risking my own kid."

"No, you don't," he said solemnly. "Are you sure you don't want to get off the case?"

"I'll be okay. It'll be over soon. The trial is set for May. She'd have to stay with you till then." She said it in a flat, unhappy voice.

"I understand. If it's safer for her to stay longer, that's fine too." It was the only conversation they'd had in ten years, but he was being more human about it than she'd expected, and he sounded concerned for both of them, and upset.

"Can you really do it?" She didn't want to ask him about Luisa, but they both knew what she meant.

"I'll work it out," he assured her. "What do you want me to do about Savannah? Do you want to tell her or should I? It may be easier for her to take it in person than on the phone." Alexa hated to admit it, but she thought he was right. "And then I think we should go home. I was on a nine o'clock flight, but it doesn't get in till nearly midnight. I'd rather drive back this morning and get an earlier flight." Showing up at one o'clock in the morning with his daughter would be even harder with Luisa. He'd rather get home earlier and settle Savannah in. The house they lived in was enormous, it was the same one he had shared with Alexa, and Luisa before that, the first time he had married her. There were several guest rooms where he could put Savannah. Alexa's stomach turned over when she thought about it. She didn't want Savannah there, but she didn't want her back in the apartment in New York now either. This was the best they could all do.

"Do you think you can get her into school?" Alexa asked him.

"I'll take care of it next week. I'll call you and let you know what time our flight is."

"I'll meet you at the airport, and bring her things. I can say goodbye to her there." It was going to be hard for both of them, and Alexa's eyes filled with tears as they hung up. They were tears of relief that Tom was willing to help her and keep their daughter safe, tears for Savannah for what she'd have to go through, and for herself for how lonely she would be without her.

Savannah called her half an hour later, and she was crying too. "I can't go, Mom. I can't. I want to finish senior year here . . . and I don't want to leave you." She was sobbing, and listening to her, Alexa felt sick.

"You have to, sweetheart. You don't want to live here like this, worrying about some lunatic sending you scary letters. I know it's hard, for both of us, but I'd rather know you're safe."

"I don't want to go to Charleston." She said it softly. She didn't want to hurt her father's feelings, he'd been really nice, and tried to make her feel better. But it was upsetting for them all.

"I'll come to visit you. I promise," Alexa said, trying to be grown up about it. But she felt like a sad, scared kid herself, and she was so sorry for Savannah. This was the most upsetting for her, to be uprooted like that, with no notice, to go to a place she didn't know, with a father she scarcely knew.

"You won't come to visit," Savannah said, sobbing. "You hate it there. You said you'd never go back there again."

"Of course I will, silly, if you're there. You won't be there for long, and it might be fun. You can go to school."

"I don't want to miss the rest of senior year at home." But she was rapidly figuring out that there was no arguing about it. Her parents, both of them, for the first time in ten years, had made up their minds and had made a unilateral decision. Savannah was leaving New York until after the trial, and that was it. Savannah just sat there and cried for five minutes while Alexa tried to soothe her, and then told her she'd come to the airport that afternoon to say goodbye.

"What should I pack?" Alexa asked, and Savannah started giving her instructions. She was still crying, but not quite as vehemently as she had before. "I'll give you both of my pink sweaters," Alexa said, smiling through her own tears.

"And the new black high heels?" Savannah was almost smiling. More than anything, she was in shock. They all were. Things were moving very fast.

"Okay, okay," Alexa conceded about the shoes, if it would help. "You can have them too. You drive a hard bargain."

"What if his wife hates me? I've never even met her. She probably won't like having me there," Savannah said, panicked. That sounded like a major understatement to her mother. Luisa was a bitch on wheels, and Savannah had heard her say it for years.

"Daddy will take care of it. You're not staying forever. It's only for three months. I'll try to come down next week."

"You'd better, or I'm running away and coming home."

"Don't you dare!" Alexa said sternly, but she knew Savannah wouldn't do that. She had been reasonable all her life. And she was being reasonable now too, even if it was a hard situation for her. "I'd better go pack now. I'll see you later, sweetheart."

Tom called her ten minutes later, and said he had gotten them on a six o'clock flight that would land in Charleston at eight-thirty, and they were leaving Vermont right then. He hoped to be at JFK by four or five.

"I'll be there at four with her bags. Call me on my cell phone when you get to the airport." She gave him the number, which he had never had before. All he had was her e-mail, but they had to work together now. "I'll be at the United terminal."

"I'll try to get there as soon as I can, so you have a little time together. She's pretty upset." He could hear that Alexa was too. But none of them were half as upset as Luisa when he called and told her the news.

"Are you crazy? You're bringing her *here*? You can't do that. Daisy doesn't know that she exists." Daisy was the ten-year-old daughter she had conceived to break up his marriage to Alexa and get him back. She hadn't given a damn about their boys during his marriage to Alexa—she had abandoned them for eight years. She had left him for an oil tycoon in Texas, and left the boys with their father, but as soon as her new husband died, she came running back. She had used a baby to get him, and he had stupidly fallen into her trap. He had bitterly regretted it in the years since. But it was too late to do anything about it now. All he could do was try to make it up to Alexa by taking care of Savannah. He owed her at least that— Savannah was his child too.

"Well, you'd better tell her," Tom told Luisa coldly, referring to Daisy's not knowing she had a sister and that her father had been married to someone else. "We'll be home tonight, and I'm not going to have Savannah pretend to be someone else. This is hard enough on her as it is."

"Hard on *her*? What about me and Daisy? Did you think about that? Or have you been screwing around with her mother? Is that what this is about?"

"I just saw Alexa for the first time in ten years. Our daughter's life is at risk here. I'm bringing her home, Luisa, like it or not."

"You sonofabitch. I always knew

you'd go back to Alexa someday." She knew Tom didn't love her. It didn't matter to Luisa. She had wanted her old life back, and him, when it was convenient for her. It was always and only about her.

"She wouldn't go near me with a ten-foot pole, and she's absolutely right," he said about Alexa. "I screwed her over ten years ago. The only reason she's talking to me now is because she needs someplace to send Savannah. Someone is threatening our daughter. Probably related to the case her mother is working on. I *have* to bring Savannah home. Her life may be on the line." It made him sick that he even needed to argue with her about it. Luisa didn't have a drop of human kindness in her, or compassion. She would never have done what Alexa had for her boys. It was ironic that now Luisa was in the position of having to take care of Alexa's child. Alexa had done it for Luisa for seven years.

"Well, don't expect me to do anything for her," Luisa said in a fury.

"I expect you to be civil to her, and make her as comfortable as we can."

"Is her mother coming to see her?" Luisa sounded suspicious.

"Probably. I haven't talked to her about it yet. I've only known about this for half an hour. She got another threatening letter about Savannah last night."

"Just keep her away from me, Tom. And I mean it. Keep her out of my sight." He loathed everything Luisa was and stood for. His punishment for what he had done to Alexa was living with Luisa now. It had been a long, hard ten years. But he didn't have the energy, or the guts, to get divorced again. So he had made his peace with it. At a very, very high price.

He and Savannah left the hotel in Vermont a few minutes later, and Savannah was silent and looked sadly out the window for most of the drive down. He tried to tell her how much she would like Charleston and how happy he was that she'd be there with him, but Savannah clearly wasn't in the mood to talk, and after a while he stopped talking and left her to her own thoughts. She was already homesick for New York, her mother, and her friends.

Alexa spent most of the day packing. She packed all the clothes Savannah liked best, everything she'd need for school and on the weekends. She gave her all the things Savannah coveted from her own wardrobe. She packed her schoolbooks, her favorite music, and two teddy bears she hadn't even looked at since she was a child, but Alexa thought they might comfort her now. And if she could have, Alexa would have packed herself in the suitcase. She hated to see her leave, but they had no other choice.

Alexa called her mother and told her what had happened, and that Tom had been decent about it. Whatever she thought of him, she had to give him credit for that.

She barely had time to dress and leave for the airport. She had three good-sized valises with her and got there at four o'clock. Half an hour later Tom called her on her cell phone. He was ten minutes away, and as soon as he drove up, Savannah jumped out of the car and flew into her mother's arms. She was sobbing, and it took her most of the time they had together to calm down. Alexa gently smoothed her hair that looked so much like her own, she held her and comforted her, and promised her she'd come to Charleston in no time, and before Savannah knew it she'd be home. Alexa barely had time to talk to Tom. He watched them unhappily, and walked away discreetly, so they could be alone. And then it was time to go. He had bought Savannah's ticket, and Alexa insisted on paying for the excess baggage, and they both cried when Alexa had to leave. Alexa couldn't walk them to the gate since she didn't have a ticket herself.

"I love you," she said over and over, and Savannah clung to her like a child. Tom finally put an arm around his daughter, and gently led her away from her mother as both women cried.

"Take care of yourself," he said over Savannah's head to Alexa. "I'll take good care of her, I promise. Just see that you stay safe." Alexa nodded and thanked him, and then they were gone, through security and heading for the gate, and Alexa couldn't see them anymore.

She was still crying when she hailed a cab to take her back to the city, and she was exhausted when she walked into the apartment and called her mother. The plainclothesman Jack had promised was posted outside her door.

"How did it go?" Muriel asked her. She sounded worried and had thought about them all afternoon.

"It was awful. But Tom was very nice. I'm going to try and go down there next week," Alexa said sadly. She couldn't even imagine her life without Savannah for the next few months. And in the fall she was leaving for college. Life as they had known it was about to end, or just had.

"I'll call her tonight," Muriel said somberly. She hated what was happening to them, and what the trial had done to their lives. "Do you want to come over for dinner?" her mother asked her kindly, but Alexa wasn't up to it. Seeing

Savannah cry at the airport had been too hard.

"No. I just want to crawl into my bed and cry."

"I feel terrible about this. Maybe I was wrong to tell you to send her to Charleston. But I think it's better to be safe. Come over and have dinner anytime you want." She knew how lonely Alexa was going to be without her daughter.

"Thanks, Mom," Alexa said miserably. And after they hung up, she did just what she had said she would. She climbed into her bed, pulled up the covers, and cried.

Chapter 7

The flight to Charleston took just over two hours. Savannah sat quietly in her seat, looking out the window, with tears rolling down her cheeks, and dozed off in the last few minutes. The shock of leaving home so suddenly had worn her out, and the emotions of leaving her mother had been overwhelming. Neither of them had expected this as a consequence of Alexa handling the trial. Tom watched her as she slept, and gently covered her with a blanket. He was well aware that his minimal presence in her life, and defection a decade before, had strengthened the bond with her mother to an unusual degree. Alexa was all Savannah had, and now suddenly she was being catapulted into a new world, without her. Worse yet, it was a world and life where she was not welcome, and was viewed as a threat. He was worried about Luisa, and with good reason. She wasn't known for her kindness, warmth, and compassion, and he knew that bringing Savannah home with him was going to start a raging battle. It already had. Luisa had declared war on him that morning, and she meant it. And knowing her, the worst was yet to come.

They landed in Charleston with a sharp bump on the runway, which woke Savannah up, and she looked at her father in surprise. For a moment, she had forgotten who she was with and where she was going. It came back to her in a rush when she saw his face.

"We're here, baby. I'm glad you slept for a little while. You needed it." She nodded, turned her phone back on, and saw a text message from her mother that said only, "I love you. See you soon." And Tom suddenly sounded even more southern than he had before.

He was home. And Savannah was far, far from hers, and felt like a lost soul.

She followed her father off the plane, and they got their luggage, her three big bags, and her father's small one and his skis. Her mother had taken her skis home. A porter followed them outside with their bags on a trolley, and her father hailed a cab. She settled in beside him, and looked around as they drove home. She had heard her father give his address in Mt. Pleasant, the part of Charleston where he lived.

"Do you remember anything about Charleston from when you lived here?" Tom asked her gently, and Savannah shook her head, her eyes wide. She looked beautiful as she sat there, still wearing ski pants and a heavy sweater, and carrying her parka. Her hair hung down her back like spun gold, and her eyes were the color of cornflowers, a rich, vibrant blue. She looked exactly like her mother when he had met her, and he knew Luisa would see it too. Savannah was only four years younger than Alexa had been when he fell in love with her, after Luisa had abandoned him and the boys for someone else. He had been devastated then, and had found happiness he'd never dared to dream of with Alexa. And seven years later, he had been a total fool when Luisa returned and spun her web. When he thought of it now, as he did often, he knew he had gotten everything he deserved after that. But when he'd seen Alexa again, he realized she was still paying the price too. He felt desperately guilty for that—he had hoped she was long over it by then. Instead, he could still see the pain in her eyes. He hoped that now he could help her in some way, by taking care of their child, and doing all he could for her. He wasn't going to let Luisa stop him this time, as she had so many times before, and he had let her. He was planning to do all he could for Savannah. She was his child too.

"I think I remember my school," Savannah said softly, "and maybe the house, or the garden . . . and Henry and Travis," her half-brothers. She had had no contact with them for ten years.

The air outside was mild. It felt more like spring in New York than winter, and she was warm in the heavy sweater on the short ride. In fifteen minutes, they had reached Charleston, and she could see church spires rising in the air. She looked with curiosity and interest at the beautiful old homes they were driving past, painted in ice cream colors, with wrought-iron gates and balconies. The architecture was intricate and ancient, and there were lovely old bridges reaching out to tiny islands. There was a spectacular harbor full of boats, mostly sailboats. Tom pointed out Fort Sumter in the harbor, where the Civil War officially began. It was a beautiful city, and had an aura of history and grace about it. Before she came to hate it, Alexa had always said it was the most breathtaking city in the South, maybe the world. There were tall trees with moss hanging from them, which were still green although it was February. As they approached Mt. Pleasant her father told her they were oak trees.

"I'll take you sightseeing tomorrow," he promised, and took her hand in his, as she smiled bravely and nodded.

Everything was so different and new, it felt like she was on another planet.

You could sense that everything here was different, a different culture, a different way of life, a respect for history, and a feeling of another world. She felt as though she was floating in space, although it was very pretty. The city seemed to be entirely about history and beauty. She knew that southerners were very proud of their history, and years before when she had asked her father about the Civil War, when she was studying it in school, he had corrected her and called it "the War Between the States," and said there was nothing civil about it. Her father was every inch a southerner, by ancestry and birth, and very proud of it. He was a southern gentleman to the core, although her mother had walked away without a word when Savannah had said that to her over the years. Clearly, he hadn't been "gentlemanly" to her, but he had extremely gracious manners. It didn't change what he'd done to her either, but it made him nice to be around.

And the old black man who drove the

cab had a heavy, warm accent. Savannah loved to hear it. Whenever she met someone from the South, it always reminded her of her father, and she said her father was from South Carolina. She was proud of it too, although in her style and habits and culture, she was a total New Yorker, like her mother. A Yankee.

The houses her father had pointed out to her in town predated the Civil War, and they bumped along over several cobblestone streets. He said there was a French Quarter he would show her too. There were two rivers, the Cooper and the Ashley. And her father told her that the beaches were terrific, at the Isle of Palms and Sullivan Island. He said she could go there when it got warmer. It was a small city, but there would be a lot for her to do. There were several colleges, coffeehouses where students hung out, and wonderful stores where she could go shopping. And he turned and asked her then if she knew how to drive a car. He was embarrassed not to know that about her but he didn't. There was so much about her that he didn't know—but he was about to learn now.

He wondered if, in some ways, this flight from New York would turn out to be a blessing for them both. Her coming to Charleston to be with him would never have happened otherwise. Luisa would never have let it, and hadn't for the last decade. Savannah had been banished. Thinking about it, he was deeply ashamed, and knew he should have been before this. It had made him uncomfortable, but never enough to do anything about it and challenge his wife.

"I have a license," Savannah said cautiously. "I got my learner's permit a year ago, and my license on my birthday, but I don't use it. Mom doesn't have a car—she rents one if we go away for the weekend. It's too much trouble in the city. And you have to be twenty-five to drive a rented car, so I haven't had much practice." She sounded apologetic.

"Charleston is an easy city to drive in, once you know your way around. You can get your practice here. I'll lend you one of ours. We have a couple of old ones." He didn't add "for the servants," but Savannah guessed it. It was nice of him to offer. "You can drive to school." Thinking about it scared her again, worrying about a school full of new faces, and being so different from all of them. She fell silent again as she thought about it. They drove over a beautiful bridge and entered Mt. Pleasant, the elegant neighborhood he lived in, east of the Cooper River. There were mile after mile of impressive mansions, each sitting on several acres of land, and always with the tall oak trees bordering the grounds and lining their driveways. He reminded her again that they were only ten minutes from the beach.

The architecture she was seeing was colonial, with tall white columns, stately entrances, ornate gates in some cases, and long driveways leading up to the houses. This was clearly the fanciest part of town, which didn't surprise her. Nothing looked familiar to her as she gazed out the window, until suddenly the cab slowed, and turned into a driveway. There was a huge expanse of grounds, and the driveway seemed endless. Savannah's eyes widened then as she turned to her father. She had recognized nothing so far, until this, but now she did.

"I remember this driveway." He smiled as she said it, and looked pleased. There had been a small brass plaque on one of the brick posts at either side of the entrance that said Thousand Oaks. He told her that in the early days, before the war, there were said to be a thousand oaks bordering the property. He had never counted and doubted there were as many now; the land had been reduced to ten acres that made a handsome expanse surrounding and reaching far behind the house. She remembered now that there was a tennis court, and a pool in the back, where she used to swim with her mother and brothers. Tom had put it in for them, amid much excitement, and Savannah had loved it too. She swam like a fish, and still did. She was on the swimming team in school, as well as volleyball. She was going to miss all of it now.

As they drove up the driveway, she could see the house better. It was huge, and absolutely spectacular. It looked like something in a movie. Savannah re-

membered it now, only it was *much* bigger than she had expected. And the gar-
dens surrounding it were exquisite, and
would be even more so in spring. Her
father smiled at the look of amazement
on her face, and was delighted. Maybe
she would like it here, and it would con-
sole her for the temporary loss of her
mother. He hoped so.

The house was white with tall
columns, and the front door was shiny
black with an enormous antique brass
knocker in the middle of it. The house
had been built in the eighteenth century,
and was part of the original plantation.
There was nothing left now except the
house and the ten acres it sat on. The
crumbling old slave quarters were at the
back of the property, and were used as
sheds to store tools and gardening sup-
plies. It was hard to believe that people
had lived in the tiny rooms, as many as
twelve or fifteen to a room. His mother
liked to say that the Beaumonts had
been extremely kind to their slaves, but
it wasn't something Tom was proud of.
Savannah had asked him about it years
before on their visits, and he had always

changed the subject. He didn't think slavery was a fitting topic of conversation.

The driver took their bags out of the car, and as though by magic two African-American men appeared, and greeted Tom warmly. One was a college student who worked for them part time, and the other was a dignified older man who looked kind and was well spoken. Jed had worked for Tom's family for years. He had been there in Alexa's day as well, and he had no trouble figuring out who the beautiful young blonde was, although he had had no warning of her arrival. She looked just like her mother, and he smiled widely when he saw her.

"Good evening, Miss Savannah. It's nice to see you again," Jed said, as though her visit had been much anticipated and warmly expected. She didn't remember him, but she was touched that he knew her name, and Tom looked gratefully at him. Jed's family had worked for the Beaumonts for generations, all the way back to the days of slavery. Even once freed, they had stayed. Jed felt a strong kinship with the Beaumonts, and their home, and had worked for Tom's mother when he was born. Now he was guardian, caretaker, and occasional waiter and driver, and he was almost like a father to Tom.

Tom introduced them so Savannah would know Jed's name, and he also introduced Forrest, the young student. Both men carried her bags inside, as Tom paid the cab, and Savannah stood close to her father, looking anxious. Tom had told them to put her bags in the blue guest room. It was the largest and most elegant of the four they had, and would make a nice home for her in the coming months, and for the duration of her visit. There was plenty of room for her to giggle with her friends there, once she'd met people at school.

Savannah followed Tom into the house. The ceiling in the hall was immensely high, with a gigantic crystal chandelier that the original owners had brought from France. And there was the kind of sweeping staircase you saw only in movies. Savannah remembered that now too, and running down it with her

mother when they were rushing somewhere. Her room had been close to her
parents' and down the hall from her
brothers'. It had been a pretty pink
room, full of sunshine, stuffed animals,
and toys, and flowered chintzes. It was
in sharp contrast to the room her mother
had decorated for her in New York,
which was simple, modern, and stark
white. She still had that same room now,
and had just left it. In its own way, it
had represented her mother's icy, barren state of mind when they moved into
the apartment in New York. Her life was
a blank page, and in some ways, Savannah thought their apartment still looked
it. Her mother was warm, but their
home wasn't. And Thousand Oaks was
filled with a sense of tradition, spectacular antiques, family heirlooms, and
grandeur. Alexa had had a wonderful life
there, for the seven years it had been
her home. And Savannah had been
happy too.

Her father led her into the living room,
which was equally opulent and full of
antiques. There was another beautiful
chandelier, and the furniture was uphol-

stered in delicate brocades. There were family portraits and statues, and vases full of flowers. The room had a delicate scent, and Savannah noticed that all the lampshades and the curtains were decorated with silk tassles. It reminded her of France. Everything was impeccable and in perfect order, but there was no one around. There was no sign of Luisa, or her and Tom's daughter, and the house was deadly silent.

They walked through the enormous dining room, where every wall boasted the portrait of a Confederate general, their ancestors. Tom escorted Savannah into the kitchen, which was large, bright, and modern, and he told her to help herself there whenever she wanted. Meals were prepared by a cook and two assistants, but there was no sign of them either. The house was deserted.

Tom led her up the stairs then, to her room, which took Savannah's breath away. It was a room for a princess or a queen, and her suitcases already sat on stands, ready for her to unpack them. But Luisa was nowhere in evidence.

Tom left Savannah then, and went to

his own room down the hall, and found Luisa there, stretched out under the canopy of their enormous four-poster bed with a damp cloth on her head and her eyes closed. She heard him come into the room and said nothing.

"We're here," he said simply, and didn't approach her. He slept in his study occasionally when she had "sick days," which meant they weren't speaking to each other. Her mother's migraines were how they explained their sleeping arrangements to Daisy, so he didn't "disturb" her. They tried to hide the fact that their marriage was rocky. She was too young to understand it, or so they thought. "Luisa?" he said more loudly, when she didn't answer. He knew she wasn't sleeping. Her jaw was tense, and she was fully dressed. She was wearing a pink Chanel suit, with a ruffled pink blouse, and her pink and black Chanel shoes looked hastily abandoned beside the bed. He suspected she had dived onto it, and grabbed the damp cloth when she heard them coming. She had no intention of welcoming Savannah. As far as

Luisa was concerned, she didn't belong here, and she was anything but welcome.

"I have a migraine," she said in a strong voice that suggested otherwise, and in a heavy South Carolinian accent, like his own. His family had been in Charleston for hundreds of years now, and hers had originally arrived in New Orleans, but had come to Charleston before the Civil War as well. Their histories and roots and traditions were deeply woven into the South. It wouldn't have occurred to either of them to live anywhere but here. Her seven-year sojourn in Dallas when she left him had been an agony for her. She thought Texans uncivilized and tacky, but liked the fact that most of them were rich, at least those she met with her husband. But all they had was money, she liked to say, not manners. Luisa was a snob about all things southern, and as far as she was concerned, Texas was not the South, and it was all new money. It had none of the history and dignity of Charleston.

"I'd like you to come and say hello to Savannah," he said firmly, offering no sympathy for her headache, which he did not believe for an instant. "She's in the Blue Room."

"Get her out of it immediately," Luisa said with her eyes closed. "That room is for important people who come to visit us, not a child. Put her in one of the rooms upstairs. That's where I want her." She said all of it with her eyes closed, and moving no part of her but her mouth. The room she was talking about was a maid's room in the attic, and Tom seethed inwardly at what she'd said, but wasn't surprised. Luisa had declared war on him and Savannah on the phone that morning.

"She'll stay in the Blue Room," he said firmly. "Where's Daisy?"

"Asleep." He glanced at his watch. It was nine-thirty.

"At this hour? What did you do? Drug her? She doesn't go to bed till ten."

"She was tired," Luisa said, and finally opened her eyes, and looked at him, but made no move to get up.

"What did you tell her?" he asked, his own jaw tensing now. And he knew that this was just the beginning. He was well aware of what Luisa was capable of. Her behavior was appalling, whenever she chose. He felt sorry for Savannah. He was used to Luisa's vendettas and venomous ways. Savannah surely wasn't, and had no idea what she was in for. He had brought her here anyway, he wanted her here, to keep her safe from the dangers she was facing in New York. He was going to do everything he could to protect her, as best he could. But Luisa was a loose cannon, and he knew it.

"About what?" Luisa stared at him blankly, in response to his question about what she had told Daisy.

"You know what I'm asking you. What did you tell Daisy about Savannah?" He studied his wife. She was as blond as Savannah and Alexa, but in her case it wasn't real and came out of a bottle. She wore her hair in the same flip to her shoulders she had worn since she was sixteen, and went to the hairdresser three times a week to maintain it, with a staggering amount of hairspray. She was impeccably groomed, fussy in her style of dress, wore too much makeup for his taste, and a lot of jewelry, some of which she had inherited from her mother, and the rest he and her last husband had paid for.

"I told her you had a youthful indiscretion, and Savannah was the result, and we've never wanted to tell her." He looked horrified at the suggestion that Savannah was an illegitimate daughter who had suddenly turned up, if that was what she had told Daisy.

"Did you say I was married to her mother?"

"I said that we didn't need to talk about it, and preferred not to, and Savannah will be staying for as short a time as possible, because her mother is in trouble."

"For God's sake, Luisa, you make it sound like her mother is in rehab, or jail." He was appalled, but not surprised.

"Daisy is too young to know that criminals are threatening Savannah's life. It would traumatize her forever." So would the lies her mother told her, Tom knew only too well. But it was hard to stop them, or the spin she put on every story, in her favor. Luisa was the worst of what people said about southern women, that they were hypocritical and dishonest and covered it with false sweetness and charm. There were lots of other southerners, men and women, who didn't use good manners as a cover-up for lies and were sincere. Luisa was not one of them, and always had an ulterior motive, a plot, or a plan. Her plan now was to make Savannah's life as miserable as possible, and Tom's.

"I want you to come and say hello to Savannah," he repeated with an unfamiliarly hard tone in his voice. Luisa didn't like it at all. She sat up on the bed, swung her legs down, and looked at him with narrowed eyes.

"Don't try to drag me into this. I don't want her here."

"That's clear. But she is here, for extremely important reasons. All I want is for you to be polite."

"I'll be civil to her when I see her. Don't expect more from me than that." He nodded and left the room. It was obvious that Luisa was not going to meet Savannah that night. He gave up the fight, and went back to her room by himself. He wanted to stop and see Daisy, but he went back to Savannah first.

"Luisa isn't feeling well, she's in bed," he said simply, and Savannah saw through it, but didn't comment. She was relieved herself not to meet her that night. "Do you want something to eat?"

"No, I'm fine, Daddy. Thank you. I'm not hungry, I'll just unpack." He nodded and went to his study, to look at his mail. He was so annoyed at Luisa that he decided not to visit Daisy after all. He was not in a good mood, and decided to sleep in his study that night. He had no desire whatsoever to spend the night fighting with his wife. There was time enough for that tomorrow, and for the next three months until after the trial. He closed his door softly, and in her own room, Savannah did the same.

She sat down in the large, comfortable chair and looked around the room. Everything was pale blue silk and satin. There were heavy curtains pulled back with blue tassels, a beautiful antique dressing table and mirror, and a little sitting area with a bookcase and two small couches. The room was warmly lit and elegantly decorated. It was much more elaborate than anything she was used to, and there was a large four-poster bed hung with heavy silk curtains as well. It was certainly a lovely room, even if it didn't feel like home. She had known that her father lived well, but hadn't realized that he lived in such grandeur. She had been taken aback by it when they walked in, and still felt daunted by it now. It didn't feel like a home where you could walk around in jeans and bare feet, or an old flannel nightie with holes in it. It was a house where you got dressed up and sat up straight on silk chairs and never relaxed or let your hair down. It was hard to imagine living here and feeling at ease. Even harder to imagine a child living here, and she had seen no sign of one yet. Like her mother, her ten-year-old half-sister was nowhere to be seen when they arrived, and the house was deadly quiet, as Savannah stared at her bags and tried to get up the courage to unpack. Instead she took out her cell phone and called her mother. It was ten o'clock, and there was no time difference in New York. She knew her mother would still be up, and was surprised to realize she'd been asleep. Alexa had fallen into a deep sleep after crying for hours but didn't tell Savannah that.

"How is it, sweetheart?" Alexa asked her quickly, and Savannah sighed.

"Strange. The house is amazing, and Daddy's been very nice. I'm in some big fancy guest room all done up in blue." Alexa knew it well, as it had been called the Blue Room in her day too, and she had always stayed there when she came to visit before they were married. And now Savannah was in it. Alexa could visualize it perfectly. "It just seems so fancy and uptight, like a museum." And it felt so far from home, even if she had lived there as a child.

"There's a lot of history in that house. Your father is very proud of it. Your grandmother lives in an even bigger house nearby, or she used to. It's an old plantation that her grandfather bought when he got married." It was too much for Savannah to absorb. She missed her mother and her familiar room, and her life in the city. It was all she cared about now, not the elegance and history of the South.

"I miss you, Mom," Savannah said sadly. "A lot." She was fighting not to cry, and so was Alexa.

"Me too, sweetheart. You won't be there long, I promise. And I'll come down as soon as I can." She wasn't looking forward to it, but she would have gone to hell and back to see her daughter. And as far as she was concerned, Charleston and all she'd lived through there at the end was hell. "How was Luisa?" Alexa held her breath as she asked. She knew what she was capable of, and hated having Savannah in the front lines exposed to it.

"I didn't see her. Daddy said she had a headache and had gone to bed." Alexa held her tongue and didn't comment. "I didn't see Daisy either. She had gone to bed too. Everything seems to roll up early here," contrary to New York, where the city was alive all night. "Daddy says he'll give me a car to drive."

"Be careful," her mother warned her. "You don't have a lot of experience yet." But the city was small and the traffic light. It was nice of Tom to give her a car. It would give her some freedom, particularly once she started school. "I can't wait to see you," she said sadly, wishing she were there with her.

"Me too. I guess I'd better unpack. We're going sightseeing tomorrow."

"It's another world there. You'll see. The Confederacy is still alive and well. For them the 'War Between the States' never ended. They still hate us and hang on to every shred of their history. They don't trust anyone but southerners. But there are a lot of wonderful things about it too, and Charleston is a beautiful place. I loved it when I lived there, and I would have stayed forever if . . . well, you know the rest. I think you'll like it. It has everything, beauty, history, gorgeous architecture, lovely beaches, nice weather, friendly people. It's hard to beat." It was easy to tell that she had once loved it no matter how she felt about it now.

"I just want to be home with you," Savannah said sadly. The scenic and historical aspects of Charleston didn't interest her at all, or even the school. She wanted to be with her old friends in New York to finish senior year, and now she couldn't because of a bunch of stupid letters written by some freak. It wasn't fair. "I guess I'd better organize my stuff. Did you pack my music?"

"Of course." Alexa was glad she had thought to do it.

There was no sign of a stereo in the room, but her mother said she had packed her Discman and iPod too. She was all set. And she wouldn't disturb anyone, which seemed like a good thing.

They ended the call, and Savannah slowly unzipped her bags and started hanging her clothes. It was all there, all her favorite clothes, and her mother's. Her eyes filled with tears when she saw the two pink sweaters, her mother's brand-new favorite black high heels, and a leopard sweater she hadn't asked for but loved, also new. She saw the two teddy bears and set them on the bed with a smile and was glad to see them for the first time in years. They looked like old friends, her only ones here for now. And she set her stack of CDs on the dresser with the Discman and iPod, and as she turned around to go back to the suitcase for more, she sensed someone in the room, and almost jumped a foot when she saw a little girl in a nightgown standing next to the bed and staring at her. She had long blond hair too and huge green eyes.

"Hi" was all she said. She had a serious expression, and the nightgown had bows and teddy bears all over it. She looked like a little doll. "I know who you are," she said solemnly.

"Hello," Savannah said softly, still startled by her, but not wanting to frighten her away. "We're sisters." It felt odd to say it.

"I didn't know about you till today. My mom told me. She said my dad was married to your mom a long time ago, for a few months, or something like that, when you were born."

"More like seven years," Savannah said, defending her history and her turf, and feeling more like ten than seventeen herself.

"My mom tells lies," Daisy said simply. It was a tough thing for a ten-year-old to say about her own mother, but it was true. "She does it a lot. She never told me about you. She said Daddy was embarrassed to tell me about you, so he never did. And you're here now because your mother is in trouble with the law." It was exactly what Luisa had said, and Savannah laughed out loud. It was an outrageous thing to say, and gave her a preview of who her stepmother was. "Is she in jail?"

"No." Savannah was still laughing as she walked over to the four-poster and sat down, and patted a space next to her for Daisy to hop up beside her, which she did. "My mom's a prosecutor, and she's trying to put someone in jail, a very bad person."

"Is prosecutor a bad word?" Daisy looked worried, and Savannah laughed again. She knew what Daisy thought it was, and it wouldn't have surprised Savannah now if Luisa said she was that too.

"No, it means lawyer. She's an assistant district attorney. She puts criminals in jail. She's going to be the lawyer in a trial, and put a very bad man in prison, who did a lot of nasty stuff." She knew enough not to frighten Daisy by telling her he had probably killed seventeen women and maybe more. "Probably one of his friends wrote me some creepy letters, so my mom wanted me to go away until after the trial so he wouldn't write to me anymore, so here I am."

"Does he know you're here?" Daisy looked worried, and Savannah shook her head.

"No, and he won't find out. That's why our dad brought me here, so no one knows where I am."

"Does your mom know you're here?" Daisy was interested in everything she said and took it all in. She believed her. She knew better than to believe her mother, as sad as that was. She had lied to her before, about people she didn't like, or to make herself look good. She had fired a nanny Daisy loved because she thought Daisy liked her too much and was too attached to her. So she told

Daisy that she had quit and run away and didn't care about her. But the cook told her the truth. Daisy had never heard from the nanny again.

"My mom and our dad agreed that I should come here."

"I don't think my mom is too happy about it," Daisy warned her with huge eyes, and Savannah nodded.

"I think you're right."

"I heard her yell at my dad. She does that a lot. They fight," she announced, as though it was a sport they played, like golf. She was giving her new sister a rundown on the situation in the first five minutes. But none of it surprised Savannah. She pretty much knew what to expect. And so far it was right on track, with no welcome from Luisa. "She can be pretty mean when she gets mad, so watch out. I like your bears," she said as she turned to look at them. "I have one too. I sleep with him." She smiled shyly at Savannah.

"Do you want to listen to my music while I unpack?" Savannah offered, and Daisy responded with a grin. Savannah went to get it and put her iPod on her, turned it on, and Daisy smiled broadly and started to sing, and then sang more softly so no one would hear them. She didn't want her mother to hear her in Savannah's room. She liked it here, and she liked her. She was still listening to the iPod when Savannah finished putting her things away. There was tons of room, more than she needed. There was a gigantic walk-in closet and built-in racks for her shoes.

Daisy was still sitting on the bed and took the iPod off so she could talk to Savannah again. "I like your music. It's cool." She had the same soft southern drawl their father did, and it sounded cute on her. It was eleven o'clock by then. "Do you like your mom being a lawyer? Mine doesn't do anything. She plays bridge and goes to lunch, and shops a lot."

"I like shopping too," Savannah admitted. "So does my mom, but she works hard. Her work is really interesting, except when something stupid happens, like the letters I got. That never happened before. My grandma was a lawyer too," she added. "Now she's a judge."

"I thought judges were men." Daisy looked puzzled.

"Nope," Savannah informed her. "They can be women too. She runs the family court, they do divorces and stuff, custody cases, a lot of stuff about kids."

"She must be smart." Daisy looked impressed.

"She is, and nice. I love her a lot."

"My grandma is the president general of the United Daughters of the Confederacy." It was a mouthful for a ten-year-old, but she whipped through it, never realizing that she was Savannah's grandmother too. "And I have two brothers, Henry and Travis." Savannah laughed at that.

"Me too."

"That's odd." Daisy looked surprised.

"Same brothers, because we have the same dad," Savannah explained.

"That is soooo weird," she said, smiling. "I always wanted a sister."

"Me too."

"Did you know about me?" Daisy asked, as she lay back against the pillows and looked at Savannah.

"Yes, I did," Savannah said gently.

"My mom told me a long time ago." And then she had an idea. "Do you want to sleep in here with me tonight?" There was room for ten of them in the huge bed, and Savannah thought it might form a bond between them that was already off to a good start. Daisy considered the offer, and then nodded. "Do you want to go get your bear?" Savannah asked, since Daisy had said she slept with him.

"I better not. Mama might hear me and not let me come back." She was smart, and right. "I can sleep with yours."

Savannah pulled the covers down for her, and Daisy slipped between the sheets with a grin. Savannah went to put her own nightgown on then, and was back in a few minutes while Daisy waited for her wide awake. And Savannah turned off the lights and got into bed too.

"Are you scared to be here?" Daisy asked her in a whisper after a few minutes. They were both lying on their backs in the dark, looking up at the blue silk canopy on the bed. The question made Savannah think of her mother and how much she missed her, and how strange it was to be here.

"A little," she answered in a whisper. "That's why I asked you to sleep with me tonight." In answer, Daisy slipped her small hand into Savannah's and held tight.

"You'll be okay," she reassured her. "Daddy won't let anything happen to you, and the bad man won't write to you anymore, and then your mama will put him in jail. And we have each other now," she said with the sweetness and innocence of childhood. What she said, and the little hand in hers, brought tears to Savannah's eyes.

"Thank you," she said softly, and leaned over to kiss Daisy on the cheek. It was soft and felt like a baby's skin to her. Daisy smiled and closed her eyes, and kept her hand in Savannah's. Her grip relaxed eventually, and they both fell asleep side by side.

It was after midnight when their father knocked gently on the door. When there was no answer, he opened it a crack to peek in. He saw that Savannah was in bed, and tiptoed into the room in the darkness, and then noticed two shapes side by side in the moonlight. He saw both his daughters there, sound asleep and holding hands. He stood looking at them for a minute with a tender smile, as tears ran down his cheeks. And then he left the room as silently as he had come in and closed the door.

Chapter 8

When Savannah woke up in the morning, sunlight was streaming into the room, and Daisy was gone. She was shocked to see that it was ten o'clock and she had slept like a rock. She hadn't heard Daisy steal out of the room in the morning, and there was no evidence that she'd been there. She had left the room at dawn so no one would find her in Savannah's bed, or there would have been hell to pay with her mother.

Savannah showered, brushed her hair and teeth and dressed, and made her way to the kitchen, where two women were sitting at the kitchen table. They smiled when she walked in.

"Good morning," Savannah said cautiously, wondering where her stepmother was.

"We've been waiting for you to get up. We didn't want to wake you," the older of the two said. "Mr. Beaumont said he'd be back at eleven to pick you up. He had to do some things at the office. And Mrs. Beaumont is at the hairdresser and has a luncheon in town after that." That meant her father would be back in half an hour for the sightseeing he'd promised. The two women introduced themselves as Tallulah and Jane. Tallulah was Jed's wife, and Jane was from Memphis, and had an accent but a different one. Savannah was fascinated by how they spoke.

They asked her what she'd like for breakfast, and she said cereal would be fine and she could help herself, but they insisted on serving her on flowered china, which they set on a delicately embroidered linen mat. Everything was fancy here. Nothing was simple or plain or practical, like at home. She felt totally out of her depth. She and her mother lived nicely, but nothing even remotely like this. This was another world. She realized now too what a shock it must have been for her mother to come back from all this after being banished. She must have felt like Cinderella after the ball, when the coach turned into a pumpkin, and the white horses into mice, and in her case Prince Charming into a rat. Savannah felt sorry for her.

She was just finishing her cereal when her father returned and strode into the kitchen looking handsome as ever in an immaculately tailored tweed jacket and gray slacks.

"Hi, Savannah," he said breezily. "How did you sleep?"

"Like a baby."

"Ready for the grand tour?" She nodded, thanked the two ladies in their white uniforms with starched lace aprons, and followed him into the front hall. She went to get a jacket and her bag, since it was cool but not cold and there was a breeze off the ocean, as there often was in Charleston, which translated to crushing humidity in summer. And five minutes later they were in his car, a Jaguar, and heading toward the heart of town.

They chatted easily about the city, and the first place he took her was Fort Sumter for a lesson in local history. It was where the first shot had been fired in the War Between the States. Savannah found it fascinating when they took the tour, particularly the totally southern slant they had on everything. It was all about the Confederacy, and never the North, which for them didn't seem to exist, except as the enemy they had loathed a hundred fifty years before, and in some cases still did.

From there he took her to the French Quarter to look around, and then to lunch at a quaint restaurant with a back garden. The food was spicy local fare, with crab soup and crab cakes, shrimp and rice, all in delicate sauces with aromatic spices. It was delicious, and they laughed together at lunch, and afterward he took her on a horse-drawn carriage ride down cobblestone streets, where they saw more historic sights, and he pointed out several popular coffeehouses to her, where young people hung out.

Afterward he drove her past several shops he said she might like to check out later, and past the spectacular beaches of Sullivan Island on the way home.

They got back to the house at four-thirty after a wonderful day together. And her father had told her over lunch that she was starting school the next day. It was all arranged. She would be a senior, of course, and she was welcome to attend their graduation and walk with the other students, although her official diploma would come from her school in New York. He had had her transcript faxed by her school, and the one in Charleston was impressed by her grades. He was going to drive her there in the morning himself, and pick her up on her first day, and after that he said she could drive herself. He had had the car detailed for her that day. He had left nothing out, and had taken care of everything, and she was touched.

They were both smiling and chatting easily as they walked into the house, and both of them were startled to find themselves face-to-face with Luisa, who had just come in too, from her lunch. And when she saw them, it was too late for her to avoid them or hide. The dreaded meeting between Savannah and her stepmother could no longer be put off.

"Hello," Savannah said shyly. She was the first to speak, as Luisa glared at her without a word. She was wearing a royal blue suit with satin lapels, and sapphires on her ears. Her hairdo looked like a helmet, and there was not a hair out of place. Her manicure was perfect, and her eyes looked into Savannah's like knives.

"This is Savannah," Tom said gently, to break the ice, as though Luisa didn't know. "And Savannah, this is Luisa, your stepmother." He knew instantly that it was a mistake, as his wife turned on him with a vicious look and ignored Savannah.

"I am *not* her stepmother," she said fiercely. "She may be your daughter, but she's not mine, in any way or form. And don't forget who your *real* daughter is in this house."

"They're *both* my real daughters," Tom said firmly, as Savannah wished she could melt into the floor and disappear. This wasn't fun. Daisy was right. Luisa was livid that she was there and made no attempt to conceal it. In fact, she wanted to be sure that Savannah knew just how unwelcome she was.

"I'm sorry you feel that way," Luisa said, as she walked past them to the kitchen to speak to the cook about dinner. Savannah wondered if she was going to be allowed to eat with them. It didn't seem likely, or appealing if she was.

Tom looked at her apologetically and shrugged. "She'll calm down. This is hard for her," he said lamely, unable to explain his wife's appalling conduct and embarrassed by it. Savannah was trying to reassure him as Daisy bounded down the stairs, and threw her arms around Savannah's waist. She was still hugging her when Luisa came back into the hall, and looked like she was going to have apoplexy when she saw Daisy wrapped around Savannah.

"Have you all lost your minds?" she said to her husband and daughter. "This girl is a stranger to us. She's a guest here, brought by your father. She is *not* part of our family, and surely not of mine. I'd like you both to remember that, and to keep in mind just who I am here. I'm your mother and your wife, and whatever mistakes your father made in his past are not my business or my problem, or yours," she said, looking straight at Daisy, who took her arms from around her sister's waist, so as not to upset her mother further. "We'll get through this, since we have to, but there is no need to act as though you've found some long-lost relative and brought her home. This is *our* home, not hers. And she is not my relative, or yours," she said to Daisy again, and with that she glared at her husband, ignored Savannah, and stomped up the stairs at full speed. And an instant later they heard the door of her room slam with a vengeance, as they stood looking at each other, embarrassed and confused. Tom glanced apologetically at his older daughter, who was shaken and near tears. Luisa had hit them with the force of a tornado, and had left them like rubble in her wake.

"Daddy, maybe I should go," she whispered to her father. "I'll be fine in New York. Mom was just being nervous. I don't want to cause any trouble here." Nor be treated like a pariah, or abused by a woman who clearly hated her.

"You're not going anywhere," her father said firmly and gave her a hug. "I'm sorry. Luisa has a terrible temper. She'll calm down." He glanced down at Daisy then, who looked crestfallen.

"Are you going?" Daisy asked Savannah.

"I don't know," she said honestly. "I think I should. I don't want to upset your mom."

"She's being mean," Daisy said, looking angry. "I like having you here. I want a sister. Don't go," she said pleadingly, and put her arms around Savannah's waist again. She was hard to resist.

Tom led them both up the stairs, with an arm around each of them. He liked having Savannah there too. He had always wanted her to visit, but Luisa would never allow it. Now the matter had been taken out of her hands by fate, and he was glad. He agreed with Daisy, and didn't want her to leave.

He told Daisy to go and do her homework, and left Savannah in her room and told her to relax. She thanked him for the nice day again, but her eyes were worried, and she called her mother as soon as he left the room, and told her what had happened.

"She is *such* a bitch," Alexa said in an exasperated tone.

"I don't know what to do, Mom. I think I should go. She's scarier than the guy writing me letters. She looked like she wanted to kill me a minute ago."

"She probably did want to kill you, but she won't. The 'guy writing you letters' might. I don't want you back here. I hate to do this to you, but you have to try and stick it out. Just stay away from her as much as you can. Did your father say anything to her to shut her up?"

"He tried. She ran right over him and told him off."

"She always did, and so does his mother. The two of them together are a force to be reckoned with, and he's no match for either of them. I don't mean to be ungrateful for what he's doing now, having you there, but he has no balls. Luisa cut them off ten years ago." Savannah didn't like hearing it, and Alexa was instantly sorry she'd said it. He was Savannah's father, but it was true. She was living proof. "I'm sorry. I shouldn't have said that," Alexa apologized quickly. "Just stay in your room, or go out, or wear your iPod. I don't want you back in New York until after the trial."

Savannah felt as though she had been sentenced to hard labor, or prison, no matter how pretty the furniture was or how big the house. She hated it here. And Luisa hated her. It was going to be a miserable three months. And her mother was right. Her father was no match for Luisa. Savannah had just seen it for herself.

"I'll try" was all Savannah would commit to, and promised herself to stick it out till her mother came to visit. And if it didn't get any better, she was going back to New York with her, or she'd run away. She wasn't going to live like this for three months, for anyone.

"I'm sorry, baby. I can't come down this weekend, but I'll be down the following one. I promise. Just keep your head down and ignore her."

"Yeah, right," Savannah said, and hung up. She was mad at her mother now too, for sending her here to live with this witch. She was worse than the evil stepmother in any fairy tale or bad movie. Cinderella's life was a snap compared to this. As she thought it, Daisy slipped into the room with a worried look.

"Are you okay?"

"Yeah, I guess so," Savannah said, looking discouraged, and then smiled at her. "I'm not used to this. I wish I were home," she said honestly, and Daisy nodded.

"I know. She can be pretty mean. She's like that to my dad a lot."

"That must be hard for you," Savannah said sympathetically, as Daisy shrugged.

"My dad is always nice to me, and my brothers." She smiled at Savannah and gave her a hug. "I hope you stay."

"We'll see how it goes," Savannah said noncommittally, but she couldn't imagine it for the next three months until after the trial, or even four, if the trial took a long time, which it probably would. It sounded like a complicated trial to her.

As the two girls sat talking in Savannah's room, Tom and Luisa were in a pitched battle in theirs.

"What the hell are you thinking?" he raged at her. "Saying those things, in front of Daisy, and Savannah. How can you be so threatened by a seventeen-year-old girl?"

"I don't want her here!" Luisa shouted back at him. "She's the result of a mistake you made, and I don't want her in my face, or my home." She looked righteous about it, and he stared at her in astonishment.

"Are you crazy? You can't rewrite history with me, Luisa. I was there. You walked out on me and our boys, you dumped me, divorced me, abandoned them, and married someone else who had more money than I did. I married Alexa while you were married to him, happily spending his money in Dallas, and you didn't give a flying fuck about us, me, or your boys. You didn't give a damn about me until he died, and you decided you wanted your old life back, God knows why. Lonely maybe, because you sure didn't need the money. And then you conned me into an affair with you, and I was stupid enough to fall for it, while you saw to it that you got pregnant and cried to my mother that I couldn't let you have an illegitimate baby, and I actually felt sorry for you, and left the woman I loved for you. Savannah is the result of a respectable marriage with a terrific woman who was wonderful to your boys, and whom I was dumb enough to give up for you, in order to be 'honorable.' What a crock of shit that was, and this marriage is. And I've allowed you to force me to keep Savannah away from here for ten years, to make you happy. I pushed out my own daughter. It's a wonder she even talks to me. And now when her life is at stake, and I bring her here for three months, you're rotten to her, and beat me up, and act as though she's a 'mistake' I made with some hooker while I cheated on you. You abandoned us, Luisa, flat and simple. And I'm not going to abandon my daughter again to make you happy. What I did to her mother was bad enough."

"If you're so sorry about it, go back to her," Luisa said coldly.

"That isn't the point. I may have been honorable to you, but I was anything but to her. We all know that, and so do you, so lay off, and be civil to Savannah, or you're going to have some very serious trouble with me." And without another word, and before Luisa could respond, he stormed out of the room and slammed the door. Both girls heard it from Savannah's room, but didn't comment. They could both guess what it was, and why. It was the first time in a long time, if ever, that Tom had stood up to Luisa like that, and she was in a rage, but she didn't pursue it, or him, any further and stayed in her room.

He went back to his study and called

their older son, and invited him and his fiancée, Scarlette, to dinner that night. He had told Travis that morning at the bank that Savannah was there. Travis was surprised, as his father explained it to him. And he could easily guess how unhappy his mother was about it. He hadn't been allowed to mention Alexa or Savannah in ten years, and had always felt guilty about not keeping up contact with them. He had tried to for a while, and then just let it slide, and he knew his brother had too. Travis was fifteen when Alexa left, and still young, although he had loved her and she had been good to him, which made him feel even worse. His mother had made it clear that any contact with her would be considered treason and a betrayal of his "real" mother, and he'd been young enough to buy into it. He was twenty-five now, worked at his father's bank in town, and was planning to be married in June, to a girl from a very social Charleston family, whose ancestors were even more steeped in the Confederacy than his. She had more generals in her family than they had oak trees on their property. She was a wonderful girl, and he was deeply in love with her. She was a nurse, and a very kind person. He liked the fact that she worked, and was unpretentious, no matter how illustrious or wealthy her family was. She wanted to keep nursing until they had babies, which his mother said was ridiculous. She didn't think it looked right for the wife of a Beaumont to be a nurse. Travis was entirely happy with it, and supported Scarlette's decision.

His father sounded tense and exasperated when he called and invited him and Scarlette to dinner. "Things are a little rocky around here," he said honestly. "Your mother is upset about Savannah. *Very* upset. You know how she is." Travis knew her raging temper tantrums only too well. She had them about everything, although he could imagine that the current one was a lulu. The only thing worse, in her mind, would have been to bring Alexa back instead of her daughter. But having Savannah there was bad enough, to her. Travis could easily imagine how unpleasant the atmosphere was at the house right now, and felt sorry for his father. "I thought if you and Scarlette came to dinner, it might distract her a bit, and ease things up."

"Sure, Dad. I'll see what Scarlette's doing. She just got off work an hour ago. I'll call you back." He did, and said they would be there at seven-thirty, in time to sit down to dinner, and Tom called the cook to tell her, after he thanked his son profusely. He announced it to Savannah and Daisy when he cruised past Savannah's room a little while later, and found both girls there, still talking. Daisy was excited to see Travis and her future sister-in-law.

"You'll like her," Daisy assured Savannah. "She's really nice. And Travis is great." Savannah barely remembered him after almost eleven years. She was six the last time she saw him.

The two girls trooped down to dinner together at precisely seven-thirty, just as Travis and Scarlette walked in. She was a pretty girl with features like a cameo, and long straight black hair, and he was the image of his father, but younger and even better looking. The young couple were both wearing jeans and nice sweaters, which apparently was allowed. Savannah had worn a skirt, sweater, and high heels, and looked very proper. Her long blond hair shone after she brushed it. And Daisy was wearing her school uniform with slippers. Tom had taken off his jacket and rolled up his sleeves, so apparently dinner at the Beaumonts' was not as formal as Savannah had feared.

Tom introduced Travis to Savannah, and the two stood smiling at each other, shyly. Travis said she had just been a little squirt the last time he saw her, and he didn't say it, but seeing her reminded him totally of her mother, just as it did everyone else. She was the image of Alexa. She and Scarlette chatted easily while they waited to be called in to dinner, and Scarlette talked about how busy her mother was with the wedding, which was going to be huge. She said they were inviting eight hundred people, which sounded like most of Charleston.

As they were talking, Luisa came down the stairs and walked into the living room, stunned to see her oldest son and his fiancée.

"What is this?" she asked coldly, fearing that Tom had organized some kind of dinner party to celebrate Savannah, and hadn't told her.

"Travis called and said he wanted to come to dinner," Tom said quickly, and Luisa wasn't sure she believed him. "I didn't think you'd object. It was half an hour ago, and you were resting." They both knew she hadn't been resting, but they hadn't been on speaking terms either, and still weren't, except in public. Privately, they were still furious with each other.

"Of course I'm happy to see Travis, and Scarlette," Luisa said, gushing as she rushed toward them. Her eyes were still smoldering, but she smiled broadly as she embraced them both, and made idle chitchat with them, while she totally ignored Savannah, which was a relief to her. She had no desire to talk to Luisa.

They went in to dinner, and Luisa sat between her husband and son. She put Scarlette next to Travis, and Daisy next to her father, lest he needed to be reminded who his "real" daughter was, and she seated Savannah between

Scarlette and Daisy, by simply pointing to the seat and saying nothing. Savannah was well aware that if Luisa could have seated her in the garage, or someone else's home, she would have. But Savannah had a nice time at dinner talking to Scarlette and Daisy. She liked Scarlette a lot, as Daisy had promised. She was warm, kind, well brought up, compassionate, and unpretentious. She was an oncology nurse and worked with people with cancer, and said she loved what she did. Travis was very proud of her and looked very happy. And they talked about the wedding a lot during the meal. Luisa was obviously very excited about it. They were giving a rehearsal dinner for three hundred at their club, and Daisy was going to be Scarlette's flower girl. Scarlette had already ordered a dress from Badgley Mischka, and the bridesmaids' gowns were being done by Vera Wang. Her own mother was planning to wear a very elegant brown satin coat and gown by Oscar de la Renta. And Luisa hadn't told anyone what she was planning to wear yet, but Daisy knew because she had seen it in her closet and overheard. Her mother was planning to wear red.

Everyone seemed to relax during dinner, and Tom's plan to have Travis there had been a good idea. Luisa seemed to have unbent a little by the end of dinner, and looked less angry. She said nothing to Tom after Travis and Scarlette left, but at least she made no vicious comments. She went back up to her room, and this time closed the door and didn't slam it. Tom said goodnight to his girls and went to his study, where he had moved his things. Daisy went to her room to finish her homework, but promised in a whisper to sleep in Savannah's room again that night so she wouldn't be scared. And Savannah went to her own quarters and collapsed on the bed with a groan. Being here was a lot of work. And she was starting school tomorrow.

She called her mother and told her she had met Travis and Scarlette, and they were really nice to her. Savannah and Alexa chatted for a while. Alexa was really busy. And as promised, Daisy showed up in her room at ten o'clock and sneaked into Savannah's bed. Her mother had already said goodnight to her, so the coast was clear.

The two girls held hands again after chatting for a few minutes, and this time, even faster than the night before, they fell asleep. For Savannah, it had been one hell of a first day.

Chapter 9

Savannah was nervous when her father drove her to Bishop England High School the next day. Daisy had already left on her school bus when Tom and Savannah drove away. Luisa was still in her room, and as she always did, Savannah had gobbled a quick bowl of cereal, and had been ready for her father promptly at eight a.m.

She said little on the drive north on Mark Clark Expressway. And she was obviously worried about it, as he tried to reassure her. Once they reached Daniel Island and the sprawling fifty-acre campus on Seven Farms Drive, he put his Jaguar in a space in the parking lot and walked her into the principal's office, where they congratulated her on her good grades in New York and welcomed her to the school. The assistant principal handed her a schedule, which looked reasonable to Savannah, and offered to take her to her classroom for her first class, and Savannah quickly kissed her father goodbye.

The school was much larger than the one she'd gone to in New York, and looked like the schools she'd seen in movies, with miles of lockers lining every hall. There were students congregating in little clusters, with books in their arms, laughing, and then hurrying to class. A few of the boys glanced at her with her lithe figure and long blond hair. She had worn jeans because they said it was allowed, Converse sneakers, and a plaid blouse that hung out of her jeans, with a sweatshirt from her volleyball team in New York. She knew it was too late to join the team here, but she was hoping to play intramural sports if she had the chance.

The first class on her schedule was French. She took AP French classes in

New York and had gotten good grades for her boards. The teacher was reading a paragraph from a book as Savannah slipped into her seat. She glanced up, looking slightly annoyed by the distraction, nodded, and went on. There were thirty students in the class, and most of them looked bored. The class lasted for fifty-two minutes, and when the bell rang, after the teacher had given them their assignment, everyone bolted for the door. The teacher smiled at her as she left, and Savannah wandered down the hall. She had been given a map, but everything was confusing and she had no idea where she was. She was turning the map around and around, with her books still in her arms, when a girl with bright red hair in a ponytail and freckles came over to her with a smile.

"Looks like you're lost. Can I help?" Like everyone else except Savannah, she had a heavy South Carolina drawl.

"I think I have history next. Thanks," she said as she handed the pretty redhead the map.

"You're on the wrong floor," the girl explained. "The class is straight up, right over our heads where we're standing, and Mr. Armstrong sucks. He gives too much homework and has bad breath. Where're you from?" She was still smiling and Savannah was grateful for the help. No one else had asked, although several boys were staring at her from their lockers across the hall, and Savannah thought they were cute. She hadn't had a boyfriend since the end of junior year. She just hung out with friends. And she knew that if she'd had to leave a boyfriend in New York to come here, it would have been worse.

"I was from here originally. I was born here. But I've been living in New York for ten years."

"Welcome back." The girl smiled broadly. "I have to go upstairs anyway. I'll walk you up. I have chemistry. I always flunk. I can't wait to get out of school. I'm taking a year off." Savannah nodded as they hurried up the stairs. The girl was wearing a sweatshirt and jeans, and so were most of the boys. It was no different than New York, although she felt out of place here somehow, as though there were a sign over her head, "I'm new." "Why'd you come back?" the girl asked her.

"I came to stay with my dad till the end of school. I live with my mom in New York." She didn't want to say that she was there because her life was at risk. That was too heavy to share with other kids, particularly one she didn't know.

"If you've been fighting with your mama, I know alllllll about that," the girl said with a grin. "My mama and I fight like cats and dogs, but I love her to pieces anyway, bless her heart. I can get around my daddy, but my mama is a bitch," the girl said, and Savannah couldn't help but laugh. "Yours too?"

"No, mine is pretty good. Great actually. We just thought it was a good idea if I visited my dad for a while." It sounded suspicious even to her, but she didn't know what else to say.

"What's your name, by the way?" She was curious about the girl from New York. She had style even in her sweatshirt and jeans, and a spark in her eye.

"Savannah Beaumont. What's yours?"

"Julianne Pettigrew. My great-grandfather was a general or something like that. Sounds pretty boring to me. I get so tired of all that crap. My grandmother's in the United Daughters of the Confederacy, and goes to tea parties all the time." She was tired of it but had mentioned it anyway. It made Savannah think of her father's mother.

Julianne had gotten Savannah to her classroom by then, and promised to catch up with her later. She said she'd be in the cafeteria for second seating at twelve-thirty and invited Savannah to join her. Savannah glanced at her schedule and saw that she was free then too and said she'd try to find it.

"Thanks for the help. See you later," Savannah said, and disappeared into her classroom. There were twice as many students in history as in French, and she got the last seat in the back row, behind a wall of boys who passed notes to each other and ignored the teacher completely, who did exactly what Julianne had said he would, and gave them too much homework.

She had two more classes after that, English Comp and a social studies class, and a break. And then it was lunchtime, and she found her way to the cafeteria, but didn't see her new friend. Two boys asked her to sit with them, but she felt awkward since she didn't know them. She was helping herself to a yogurt and fruit salad and a bottle of orange juice, when Julianne found her.

"You were right," Savannah said, happy to see her. Finding someone in the cafeteria was like looking for a lost sock at the airport. There were hundreds of kids milling around and sitting at large and small tables, and the noise level was tremendous. "Armstrong gives too much homework."

"I told you. I just got a D in chemistry again. My mama's gonna kill me. She's got this thing about good grades, but she never went to college herself. She just goes to lunch and plays bridge with her friends. You don't need to go to college for that." Savannah nodded. She didn't volunteer that her mother was a lawyer, it would have sounded too stuck up. "My daddy's a doctor. A pediatrician." Savannah nodded again.

They found a table and sat down, and

a flock of girls and boys joined them. Apparently, Julianne was popular and seemed to know everyone in the school. Halfway through lunch she admitted to Savannah that she had a boyfriend. He was the captain of the football team, which was a big deal.

Everyone at the table was making plans for the weekend, talking about the basketball game on Friday night, asking about friends, exchanging phone numbers and trading gossip. It was a lively group, and Savannah felt a little out of it, so she listened. She had been totally confident in New York, but she felt overwhelmed here, with so many new names and faces, and such a big school.

She was feeling somewhat dazed by the time her father picked her up at three o'clock. Julianne and two other girls had given her their phone numbers, which was a good beginning, but she felt too shy to call them.

"How was it?" her father asked as she got in. He thought she looked tired and ill at ease.

"Kind of overwhelming, but okay. I met

some nice people. There are just a lot of them, and it's hard having all new classes and new teachers. Most of the material is familiar, and not much different from what I've been doing in New York, except for the civics class, which talks only about the south and southern history. The Confederacy is definitely still alive and well in Charleston. I guess it wasn't bad for a first day," she said fairly, and he nodded, as they headed home.

"A lot of homework?" he asked with interest. He was being very attentive to her, far more than she had expected, and it touched her.

"About the same as at home. We're all kind of in the homestretch, waiting to hear from college. You've got to screw up pretty badly to blow it in the last term. It's pretty much coasting from here."

He laughed as she said it.

"I'm sure they'd be happy to hear that."

"They know it. We don't even have final exams at the end of senior year at home. You just have to get passing grades in your classes." She wasn't going to hear about her acceptances till the end of March, some of them even April, so she wasn't worried about it yet.

They were at the house five minutes later, and her father dropped her off and went back to the bank. He said he'd see her later. She went out to the kitchen for a snack, and there was no one there. The two ladies who usually sat in the kitchen had left a note that they'd gone grocery shopping. And there was no sign of Daisy or Luisa. Savannah went upstairs to her room with an apple in her hand and a can of Coke, just as Daisy bounded out of her room with a broad grin. She knew her mother was out, so it was safe to throw her arms around Savannah.

"How was school?" she asked, following Savannah into her room, where she put her books down and bit into the apple.

"Kind of scary," she admitted. It was easier saying it to her than her father. "Lots of new people."

"Mean teachers?" Daisy asked sympathetically, as she tossed herself onto Savannah's bed and watched her.

"No. Just different." And then she remembered something she had wanted to ask Daisy, who was now her official counselor on local customs. "What's this 'bless her heart' thing everyone says? They're always saying 'bless her heart.' " It had seemed a little weird to her, and Daisy laughed out loud when Savannah said it.

"That means they hate them. First, you say something really mean about someone, and then you say 'bless her heart' right after. My mama does it all the time. So does my grandma. We call that 'nasty-nice' here." Savannah laughed then too. Julianne had said it about her mother. "If you say 'bless your heart' to someone's face, that means you *really, really* hate them. My mama does that too." It was easy for Savannah to believe now that she would.

They heard the front door slam right after that, and Daisy ran back to her room, in case it was her mother. They didn't want to get caught together. Savannah heard Luisa's bedroom door close right after that, so she was glad that Daisy had left. Luisa would have had a total fit if she knew they were so friendly and sleeping in Savannah's room at night.

Alexa called Savannah shortly after that and asked her how school was, and Savannah told her all about it. She said she had made a friend, more or less. And just out of habit, her mother asked her what her name was, and Savannah told her. There was a silence at the other end as Alexa digested what her daughter had said.

"That's strange," she finally said, and sitting at her desk in New York, she had an odd look on her face. Savannah could hear it in her voice.

"What's strange?"

"There must be a thousand kids in that school, and you found the daughter of the woman who was my best friend for all the years I was in Charleston. She did the same thing, she sought me out as soon as I moved there, helped me with everything, showed me the ropes. She was like my sister." Alexa's voice drifted off as Savannah listened. She could tell there was more to the story. She knew her mother.

"And? So?"

"She claimed undying loyalty when your father told me he was divorcing me, and we'd be friends forever. I never heard from her again when I left. She stopped writing to me. She didn't return my calls. And last I heard, she and Luisa were best friends. Very southern. Watch out you don't get your heart broken there too. It's all a lot of phony bullshit."

"Don't be like that, Mom." Savannah scolded her. "There are people like that in New York too. People are friendly down here, some of them." She was thinking about Luisa then, who was anything but friendly and certainly hadn't shown any southern hospitality to Savannah. "There are real people and fake people everywhere. That's not southern or northern." She was right, but Alexa didn't want to hear it.

"Not one of those people stuck by me when I came back to New York. I never heard from them again, after seven years of thinking they were my best friends. I don't have anything to show for those years, except you." Alexa smiled sadly. "And I miss you so goddamn much. You've been gone for two days, and I can hardly stand it."

"Yeah, I know. Me too. It feels like it's going to be forever. When are you coming?"

"Not this weekend. The next one. It's the best I can do. This case is a killer." She was exhausted and Savannah could hear it. "How were your classes?"

"Boring. I'll get through it," she tried to reassure her. Her mother sounded stressed. And she knew that her mother was dreading coming to Charleston, but she would have gone to hell and back for her daughter. Savannah was thrilled she was coming.

Julianne called her on her cell phone before dinner, and had discovered the same thing Savannah had, that their mothers had been best friends when they were little. "My mama said to send yours her love, bless her heart," Julianne said, and Savannah had to fight to keep from laughing. She wanted to say she knew that meant Julianne's mother hated hers. But Alexa would have said the same thing if it were one of her idioms. Being from New York, she was more direct and had called Julianne's mother a traitor.

The two girls talked for a few minutes and promised to meet up at school the next day. Savannah started her homework, and had just finished history when it was time for dinner.

Without Travis and Scarlette for distraction, conversation was slim that night. Luisa spoke to her daughter, but ignored both Savannah and her husband. Tom spoke to all of them, Daisy only to her parents, and Savannah didn't dare speak at all—she thought it was safer not to.

Her father came to see her in her room afterward. She had her books spread out and was working on her computer, and sending e-mails to her friends in New York, telling them about Charleston. She hadn't explained to anyone why she went away. Her mother had told her not to. She just said she'd be back soon and missed them, and was visiting her father in Charleston. She didn't tell them she'd changed schools. And she was relieved she'd be back with them for graduation. At least she could say goodbye to them all then, before they left for college. For her, her New York school days were already over, but her friends didn't know it.

"How's the homework coming?" Tom asked her as he wandered into the room.

"I'm almost finished." She'd had an idea that afternoon and wanted to ask him about it, but hadn't wanted to bring it up at dinner. She didn't want to say anything in front of Luisa, bless her heart. She smiled as she thought it to herself. "I was wondering if sometime I should go and visit my grandmother."

"Do you want to?" He looked surprised.

"I thought it might be nice." He nodded. Savannah had arrived in Charleston so suddenly that it hadn't occurred to him so far, but it was a gracious thought. She was a good girl, and he was touched.

"I'll talk to her about it." His mother and Luisa were extremely tight, and he was concerned that taking Savannah to visit her might set off another explosion, maybe even a worse one. "She's pretty frail."

"Is she sick?" Savannah looked sympathetic.

"No, just old. She's eighty-nine now." She had been forty-four when he was born, and he had been a big surprise. His parents had never been able to have children in twenty-two years of marriage, and then he arrived. His mother still talked about what a miracle it had been. She had called him her little miracle as a child, and he had hated it. She still did.

"If she wants to see me, I'd like to," Savannah said. She hardly remembered her at all. She was extremely close to her New York grandmother, but her Charleston grandmother had totally removed herself from Savannah's life, out of loyalty to Luisa. And because Alexa wasn't southern, and an outsider, when they left, she closed the door on them and never opened it again. Savannah knew her mother was bitter about that too, and she wasn't sure how her mother would feel about her visiting Grandmother Beaumont, but it was something she wanted to do, as long as she was here. She was tasting every aspect of Charleston life. This was her family too, not just her father's. It was half of her, although saying that to her mother would make her sound like a traitor, and she felt a little guilty about it.

Tom stopped in to see his mother the next day. He had some free time, and drove back to Mt. Pleasant to pay her a visit. Eugenie de Beauregard Beaumont lived about ten minutes away from his house, on thirty somewhat run-down acres, in a colonial mansion surrounded by oak trees with extensive slave quarters still standing at the back of the property, though empty. She had two ancient servants living in the house with her, both of them women, and a man who came in the afternoons to do heavy work. They were nearly as old as she was, and they had neither the strength nor enough manpower to keep her enormous house clean. It was the house where Tom had grown up, and his father before him.

Tom had tried several times to get her to sell it, but she wouldn't. It had been her pride and joy for nearly seventy years.

She was sitting on the back porch, reading, wearing a heavy wool shawl, when he arrived. A cup of mint tea was sitting next to her, and her gnarled hands were holding a book. She was frail, and walked with a cane, but she was in good health, and she wore her white hair, as she always had, in a bun. She was the president general of the United Daughters of the Confederacy. She bore the title of general because her grandfather had been one, and an illustrious one. And several of her other ancestors had been as well. She liked to say that her family had been the pride of the South. She had been appalled when Tom had married a Yankee. Alexa had been extremely kind to her when they were married, but she was still a northern girl, and second best, or worse, to his mother. She had been thrilled when Luisa came back, and had done everything in her power to convince her son to marry her again. The decision had been made when Luisa very cleverly got pregnant, which Tom knew now had been no accident, but a careful plan, at his mother's suggestion, and it had worked.

"Mother?" he said gently, as he walked onto the back porch. Her hearing was perfect, and her vision was fairly good as well. Only her knees bothered her at times, but her mind was as sharp as ever, and her tongue. He didn't want to startle her, but she looked up and smiled as she set her book down.

"My, what a nice surprise. What are you doing here in the middle of the day? Why aren't you working?"

"I had some spare time and thought I'd come to visit. I haven't been out here since last week." He tried to visit her two or three times a week, and Luisa came at least once. She was very dutiful about it, which Tom was grateful for. And she brought Daisy with her every few weeks, but the child always got bored. There was nothing for her to do there. "What have you been up to? Has anyone come to visit?" he asked as he sat down. The woman who cooked for her offered him a cup of tea, but he declined.

"I went to the hairdresser yesterday," she said, rocking in her chair. "And Reverend Forbush came to see me on Sunday. I missed church and he was worried. My knee was acting up, so I stayed home."

"How is it now?" he asked with a look of concern. He was always afraid of her falling, that she might break a hip, and at her age it would be a disaster. She was pretty shaky on the stairs but insisted on getting up them under her own steam.

"Better. It's just the weather. It was damp on Sunday before the rain." She smiled at her only son. He was a good boy and she was proud of him. His father had been too, and had died three years before at ninety-four. His mother had been lonely since. Alexa had been very kind to him too. He was a feisty old man with a keen sense of humor, and he had never liked Luisa, but unlike his wife, he stayed out of Tom's business. Tom's mother had always had a million opinions about what he did, and she was a powerful influence on him. He revered her, even more than he had his father. His father had been more distant and more aloof. "Luisa said you went north."

"I did," he confirmed. "I went skiing in Vermont."

"She didn't tell me. I thought maybe you had business in New York."

"Not this time," he said.

He decided to brave it then and see what happened. She knew that he saw Savannah a few times a year. She never asked about her, and Tom didn't comment. As far as his mother was concerned, that chapter of their history was closed, though not as much as she thought.

"I took Savannah skiing." Eugenie said nothing.

"How's Daisy?" It was her way of saying not to go there.

"She's fine. Having fun at school." And then he decided, in a rare show of bravery, not to beat around the bush. "Mother, Savannah is here." For a moment, his mother said nothing, and then she looked him dead in the eye, and he returned her gaze.

"What do you mean, 'here'? In

Charleston?" He nodded, and she looked instantly disapproving. "What a terrible thing to do to Luisa! How could you do that?"

"I had no choice. Her mother is the prosecutor in a murder trial in New York, and the defendant was threatening Savannah. Her mother was afraid her life was in danger, and wanted her out of New York. We had nowhere else to send her." There was a long silence as his mother thought it over.

"Why is she handling cases like that? That's no job for a woman." She knew that Alexa's mother was a lawyer too, but she had been a divorce lawyer, which was different, and then a judge. She wasn't prosecuting murderers and putting her family in danger.

"She went to law school after the divorce, and she works in the district attorney's office. It's a very respectable job."

"Not for a woman," his mother said tartly, and clamped her mouth shut. She looked like a nutcracker when she did. She had been a pretty woman in her youth, but that was long gone. She was too thin now, and had a face like a hawk with hooded eyelids and a sharp nose. Her lips were set in a thin line, which meant she wasn't happy. It was a while before she spoke again, while Tom waited, and wondered if he should leave. If she didn't want to see Savannah, he wasn't going to insist. His mother only did what she wanted. That had always been the case. "How long is she staying?" she finally fired at him through narrowed eyes.

"Until May or June, after the trial." Her eyes flew open when he answered.

"Luisa must be very upset." She hadn't said a word about it, but they hadn't talked in several days.

"That's an understatement. She's ready to kill me. But Savannah is a very sweet girl." His mother said nothing. "She's my daughter," he added. "I can't just treat her as though I owe her nothing. It's not right. I never should have let Luisa talk me into keeping her away from Charleston and only seeing her in New York. She's part of my life too, or she should be, and she hasn't been for more than ten years."

"It's too upsetting for Luisa to have her here." Eugenie hadn't wanted him keeping any ties to Alexa, any more than Luisa did. She knew how much Tom had loved her, and she didn't want him going back to her. Luisa was his wife. And after her "little mistake," as his mother called it, Luisa had come back. His mother wanted it to stay that way. Luisa was a good southern girl from Charleston. Alexa was a stranger, from a totally different world. She didn't belong here. And neither did her daughter. But Savannah was Tom's too. She didn't want to admit that.

"Luisa will have to put up with it till after the trial," Tom said firmly. "She owes Alexa that. Alexa took care of the boys for seven years, while Luisa was in Texas. Three months now won't kill her." But she might kill him. It looked likely.

"What's she like?" his mother asked him. "How old is she now?" It seemed like a hundred years since they had left.

"She's seventeen, beautiful, sweet, polite, kind, gentle, smart. She looks like her mother." His mother's mouth shrank into a thin line again, and he decided to give up. "You don't have to see her, Mother. I wasn't going to ask. I knew how you'd feel about it. But Savannah suggested it last night, so I thought I'd mention it to you. I'll just tell her you don't see visitors anymore." His mother said nothing, and he got up to leave and gently stroked her hair. He was a loving son, and had always been devoted and respectful, and obeyed her commands. He bent to kiss her cheek then, and she looked at him with steely eyes.

"Bring her to tea on Sunday" was all she said, picked up her book, and began reading again. And without another word, he walked quietly off the porch and drove away. Savannah had gotten her wish. And Luisa would have another fit. He was used to it. She didn't scare him anymore. Savannah's visit had given him something back he lost a long time ago. Courage.

Chapter 10

When Alexa got to her office the next morning, she had a message from Joe McCarthy, the district attorney, to come and see him immediately. It sounded important. She went straight to his office, and his secretary waved her in. Joe was sitting at his desk, and Jack was with him. It looked like something had happened. Both men looked concerned. It didn't look good to her.

"Something wrong?" she asked as she took the seat Joe waved her into. He cut to the chase.

"The FBI wants our case." He looked unhappy about it.

"What case? Luke Quentin?" Alexa's

eyes widened, but she wasn't totally surprised. They had been moving in that direction ever since his victims started turning up in other states. Once state lines were crossed, the FBI always got involved. They all knew that.

"They want the credit for the investigation and the conviction." Joe McCarthy told her what he had just told Jack.

"They can't have it. They can help us with the investigation if they want, and they have been. But there are other local law enforcement agencies involved. And a task force, which, I have to admit, they've been running lately. But we found the first four bodies in New York, and we arraigned him here. The case is ours." She didn't want the glory of it, or the press, but they had worked hard on it, Jack especially, and so had she, and she didn't want to give it up now. And she was determined to put Quentin behind bars. "If they take it, it'll be a mess, with states crawling all over each other, dragging him around to try him. We need to associate their cases to ours and we have been. It's all nicely tied up.

We've arraigned him on each charge here. I don't see why the FBI can't sit in on it with us. We're not hiding anything from them, and we can use all the help we can get on the investigation, but he's going to cost the taxpayers a fortune if we start shipping him around to eight other states, and the FBI doesn't want to do that either. He's ours." She said it without hesitation, and Joe smiled at her.

"I like a woman who knows what she wants," he said, looking less worried. "You're not afraid of trying this case, Alexa? You've already got a cop at your apartment, and I hear you had to send your daughter away. You wouldn't rather just give it up?"

"No, I wouldn't," she said calmly. "I want to finish what I started. Luke Quentin is a sociopath, and a cold-hearted killer, and I want to try him. I'm not afraid of him. And my daughter is fine where she is. I miss her, but I've got too much work to spend time with her anyway. Let's do this, guys. We can't let the FBI rip us off. They're in it for the glory. We're not. We're working our asses off here. Let them help us with the investigation. We'll do the trial. Legally we have the right since we found the first four bodies." Technically, she was right, but the FBI had a lot of clout, and it could have gone either way.

"I'll see what I can do. How's the investigation going?" He hadn't asked in a few days—he'd been too busy battling the FBI director about the case.

"We've got DNA matches on almost every victim. We're missing two, and we're waiting for the results from Illinois," Jack filled him in.

"And he still won't plead?" Joe looked surprised.

"No," Alexa answered.

"What does the PD say?"

"That he's innocent and someone framed him," she said with a contemptuous smile.

"With DNA matches and seventeen victims? What's she smoking?"

"Her shoes. He's very seductive, and I think he cast a spell on her. She's young, and he knows just how to do it. He's a perfect sociopath."

"Do we have a psych evaluation on him yet?"

"We have two. Sociopath right down the line."

"Does she know that?"

"We're in discovery now. She has everything we have. No surprises."

"This is going to be ugly. A jury's going to hang him, and the judge will sentence him to about a thousand years."

"I agree," Alexa said with a sigh. She was tired, but doing a good job on the case, and both men knew it. She always did. She was unbelievably thorough, and the DA liked everything he was hearing. He didn't want to take the case away from her if he could help it. He was going to fight harder to keep it. She had convinced him. She was the right prosecutor for the case. No federal prosecutor could have done better. "Quentin wants his day in court. I think he likes the media coverage," Alexa said wisely.

"I hate that," the DA said angrily, but there was no way to stop it. Luke Quentin was national news now. And so was Alexa. She had been extremely discreet about it. She didn't want to blow the case with anything she said in the press. She knew better, and the DA liked that too.

He reassured both of them then that he would fight to keep the case, and pull all the strings available to him. And after that they left his office. Both Jack and Alexa were still concerned.

"Shit, I hope we don't lose the case," Alexa said as they stopped at the coffee machine for two cups, black. She was living on it, and candy bars, at her desk till midnight every night.

"Hopefully, he'll use his influence to keep it," Jack said as he followed her back to her office. He hardly saw her anymore, he was too busy working. He had just come back from Pittsburgh the day before, where he had gone to help with the investigation there, and trade information. "I must say, this sonofabitch is keeping us busy."

"That's our job," Alexa said as she smiled at him and sat down at her desk. She felt as though she lived there.

"Do you ever get tired of it?" he asked with a worn-out look, and sipped his coffee.

"Sometimes. Not this one. It's the shoplifters and the piddly stuff that gets me. At least with a case like this, I feel useful. I'm protecting society and young women. With the shoplifters, I'm torturing them for stealing panty hose in Macy's basement. Who cares?" Some of the cases were bigger than that, she knew, but most weren't.

"How's Savannah, by the way?" Alexa sighed when he asked her.

"She's okay. She's with her father, in Charleston. She's not loving it, but she's a good sport about it. I miss her." It was lonely without her, and Jack knew it.

"If the FBI gets the case, you could bring her back," he said, but Alexa shook her head.

"I don't want her back here till this case is over, no matter who tries it. The guy is a maniac. He could still torture her for what I've done so far, and I think he would. I think he'll give it up when he's convicted and goes back to prison. Then it's all over, and he knows it. Now he's King of the Hill." Jack didn't disagree with her. Quentin was thriving on the attention. Jack had seen him several times recently, and Quentin got bolder every time. He was drunk with excitement. And his defense lawyer's blind innocence and admiration just added to it. He thought he had the whole world fooled, but he didn't. He just thought so. He was suffering from grandiosity in the extreme. Nothing could touch him, or so he thought. Until he was convicted.

"I think you're smart to keep her there," Jack said honestly.

"I hope so," Alexa sighed again. "To be honest, I worry about her falling in love with it, the way I did. The South is very seductive, particularly a city as pretty as Charleston. People are friendly and charming. Everything is beautiful. It's a different world, a different life. It's true when they say the South is gracious. I loved it when I lived there. And then it turned on me, and all that warmth and kindness turned out to be bullshit. They stick with their own. They'd rather have a bad Confederate than a good Yankee in their midst. I got screwed over by everyone I knew there." And she was still bitter about it. Maybe she always would be.

"They can't all be like that," Jack suggested.

"Maybe not. But that's how it shook out for me. Savannah is still in the honeymoon phase. She's discovering all the beauty of it. The bad stuff comes later."

"Sounds like marriage to me." Jack chuckled as he looked at her. "I'm not so sure things are any different here."

"The South is a special place. It's from another century. It was a great place to live when I was there. I don't want Savannah to stay there, or want to. I'm hoping I get her back here before she gets hooked. Hopefully her evil stepmother will take care of that for me. Her father is married to a real bitch."

"Sounds like he deserved it." Alexa nodded in agreement, and with that, she picked up her voluminous files on the Quentin case and they got back to work. They sat there till three, and ate sandwiches at her desk. And then Jack went back to his own office. Alexa was in hers until midnight yet again.

*   *   *

Savannah didn't tell her mother she was going to see her paternal grandmother that weekend. She didn't want to upset her. She knew Alexa had enough on her mind with the case. And Tom didn't tell Luisa. It was none of her business.

He drove Savannah there on Sunday afternoon. And he was surprised to see his mother sitting in her drawing room, instead of on the porch. There was a tea tray on the table. Savannah walked in behind him, and was startled by how shabby the room looked. She only vaguely remembered it. The house had been beautiful at one time, but there was an air of decrepitude about it. Like her grandmother, it had seen better days, and was fading.

Tom's mother was sitting in a large chair, waiting. Her hair was perfectly smoothed into the bun she wore, and her sharp eyes observed them both. She could see instantly that her son was protective of Savannah, and attached to her, and his mother didn't like it. As far as she was concerned, Savannah didn't deserve it. She had tried to erase Savannah and Alexa from their lives. And she felt that his feelings for Savannah were a betrayal of Luisa. But she hadn't told Luisa about the meeting either. They were all in collusion and felt guilty. And his mother resented that too.

"Hello, Grandmother," Savannah said politely, extending a hand to her, and the old woman didn't take it.

"I have arthritis," she said, which was true, but not to that extent. She always shook hands with her minister when he came to visit. And she would have preferred it if Savannah had called her Mrs. Beaumont now, but she didn't say it. "I understand you're here until June," she said directly to Savannah, as her ancient maid came in to pour them tea.

"I might be," Savannah said quietly, sitting down carefully on a narrow chair near her grandmother. Everything in the room seemed fragile and dusty. Savannah hoped she wouldn't sneeze. "It might be May, if my mother's case goes more quickly. But it's a big case, it could take a while to try."

"Your mother wasn't a lawyer when I knew her," her grandmother said with an air of disapproval, and Savannah nodded. It was hard not to be daunted by this ancient, sharp-featured woman. She was old, but tough as nails.

"She went to law school after the"— she started to say "divorce" and then stopped herself instinctively—"after we went back to New York. My other grand-mother is a lawyer too."

"I know." Eugenie Beaumont nodded. "I met her. She was a very nice woman." She was willing to concede that, but nothing about Alexa, out of loyalty to Luisa.

"Thank you," Savannah said politely, still holding the cup of tea. She had worn a gray skirt and a white sweater, and she looked neat, clean, and de-mure. Tom was proud of her, for wanting to come here, and being brave enough to do it. His mother wasn't easy.

"Do you want to be a lawyer too?" Her grandmother scowled at her. She was looking to find fault with her, Tom could see, but had found none so far. She was clearly a northern girl, and lacked the softness of the South, but she was polite and well bred, and Euge-nie liked that.

"No. I think I'd like to be a journalist, but I'm not sure yet. I just applied to college, and I don't have to declare my major for two years." Her grandmother asked what colleges she had applied to, and was impressed by the list. They were all first-rate schools, including Duke.

"You must be a good student," Eugenie conceded, "to apply to schools like that. In my day, young women didn't go to college. They got married and had babies. It's different now, though. One of my grandsons went to the University of Virginia, like his father. The other one went to Duke." She said it as though Savannah didn't know them.

"UVA is a very good school," Savannah said easily, but she hadn't applied there. Her mother had discouraged her and said she'd be an outcast if she wasn't southern. Savannah knew it was her mother's prejudice about the South but had decided not to apply anyway. She smiled kindly at her grandmother, and took her empty teacup from her and set it down, and then offered her the plate of cookies. The maid had gone back to the kitchen. Eugenie took one of the cookies and nibbled it as she looked at her grandchild. "You look just like your mother." It was hard to tell if it was a compliment or an insult the way she said it. A complaint maybe. She didn't want to be reminded of Alexa, or how much she had liked her in the beginning. Until Luisa came home for good, and her allegiance had shifted back to her first daughter-in-law, not the second. Savannah thought it wisest not to answer. "Do you know what the United Daughters of the Confederacy is?" she asked her, and Savannah nodded. She remembered hearing about it, although it sounded a little silly to her, but she didn't say that. "I'm the president general. They gave me that title because my grandfather was a general in the Confederate Army." She said it with such pride that Savannah smiled at her. For all her toughness, there was a fragility and vulnerability that touched her. She was just a very old woman, and life had passed her by. She was alone in a dusty old house now, proud of an army that had lost a war nearly a hundred and fifty years before, like the Japanese soldiers who had hidden in caves and didn't know the war was over for years.

Eugenie looked at her son then and nodded. He understood the signal. She was tired. It was time for them to leave. He stood up and told Savannah they should be going.

"Thank you for letting me come to visit you, Grandmother," she said politely as she stood up too.

"Are you in school here?" Eugenie was curious about her. She was a bright girl, and on closer inspection, she looked like her father too, not just Alexa. She had southern genes in her, after all.

"Yes, I am. I started this week."

"Do you like it?"

"So far. Everyone's been very nice. And Charleston is beautiful. Dad showed me around on Monday before I started school."

"I hope you enjoy your stay here," Eugenie said politely, letting her know that she would not be seeing her again. It was hello and goodbye in one meeting.

"Thank you." Savannah smiled at her warmly, and then they left.

Savannah was quiet on the drive

home, thinking about her. She was so
small and old and not the dragon she
had expected at all. It hadn't been hard,
it was easy.

Luisa was waiting for them when they
got home. As usual, she ignored Savannah, and looked straight at her husband.

"I understand you just went to see
your mother, and just took her with
you." She always referred to Savannah
as "her" and "she" and never by name.

"That's right. I did. I thought Savannah should see her. She's her grandmother, after all. Did she call you?" It
surprised him, but maybe his mother
had felt a need to confess to Luisa.

"Someone saw you turning into the
driveway." Luisa had spies everywhere,
and knew everything he did. "Why didn't
you tell me?"

"I didn't want to upset you," he said
honestly, as Savannah left them quietly
and went to her room.

"It's a slap in my face to take her
there, and you know it," she accused
him.

"Savannah had a right to see her."

"She has no rights here," Luisa reminded him. "This is my home, and these are our children. She's not one of us, and she never will be. It's bad enough that you brought her here. You don't have to humiliate me further by showing her off, or taking her to your mother for tea."

"I'm sorry you feel that way. She's not the enemy, Luisa. She's a child. My child. Her being here is not going to hurt you or weaken your position." She didn't answer him, but gave him a quelling look and left the room.

Nothing further was said about it, until he visited his mother again two days later. He decided not to mention Savannah again, unless she did, and at the end of his visit, his mother brought it up. She amazed him by saying Luisa had called her, and was very upset about Savannah's visit. That didn't surprise him.

"She said she'd prefer it if I don't see her again," his mother said calmly. "I've thought about it, and I've decided I'd like to anyway. She seems like a very nice young lady. And it was kind of her to come to see me." He was floored by his mother's decision, and assessment of Savannah. She liked her. "I told your wife not to meddle in my business." It was the first time in years she had taken someone else's position, and not Luisa's. "There's no reason I can't see her again if I want to. No one is going to tell me what to do." Tom smiled at her as she said it.

"No one ever has, Mother. I have complete faith in you to stand up to anyone who would try. And I'm glad you liked Savannah."

"She's intelligent and polite, and a lot like you." He didn't challenge it, but the truth was that she was a great deal more like her mother, and they both knew it. She was far more courageous than he was. He had sold his soul to the devil years before, and had allowed his mother and Luisa to influence him into betraying someone he loved, and even abandoning his own child. He had nothing to be proud of, and he wasn't. "You did what you had to do, and you did the right thing," she said, reading his mind, as she so often did. She did it better than anyone, and sometimes she used it against him, but not this time.

"No, I didn't," he said quietly.

"It seemed like the right thing to do at the time." He wondered if she regretted it too, but he didn't ask her.

"They both suffered for my stupidity and weakness," he said honestly. "There's nothing right about it." And Luisa was the winner and didn't deserve to be. Everyone else involved had been losers, including him. And he had allowed it to happen.

"Maybe it will do you good to have her here now." And then she added with a wicked grin, "If Luisa doesn't make life too miserable for you. She's not happy to have the girl here." Tom laughed at what she said.

"No, she isn't. And she's making life miserable for Savannah too."

"She looks as though she can handle it. How is she with Daisy?" She was curious about her. Seeing her had whetted her appetite for more information.

"Very sweet. Daisy loves her." His mother nodded.

"Bring her to see me again. She ought

to learn more about her own history. There's more to her life than those two women lawyers in New York. She should know about our family too." It was a huge sign of acceptance that she wanted to share that with Savannah, and Tom was stunned as he thought about it when he drove away. He told Savannah that night that her grandmother wanted to see her again. Savannah looked pleased.

"I liked her too. Maybe she can tell me all about the United Daughters of the Confederacy next time, and the generals in her family."

"That's just what she wants to do," he said, as he gave Savannah a hug and left the room.

He moved back into his bedroom that night, with Luisa. She was still furious with him, but it was his bedroom too, and his house. He had no intention of sleeping on the couch in his study forever, because his daughter had come to visit. He took Daisy and Savannah to a movie that night, and invited Luisa. She didn't want to come, but he had asked her. He had a great time with both his daughters.

When he got into bed when they returned, Luisa turned her back on him, but she hadn't moved into one of the guest bedrooms, which he had thought she might do. She wasn't speaking to him, but he had reclaimed his territory, and his life. He felt like a man again, for the first time in ten years. Luisa no longer had him on the run, and she no longer owned him. He wanted to let out a shout of victory, but instead he just turned over and went to sleep.

Chapter 11

The week after Savannah's visit to her grandmother was another crazy one for Alexa. The FBI had backed down about taking the case, after a lot of pressure from Joe McCarthy, but they were still waiting to pounce and grab it if anything went wrong. So far nothing had. But Alexa felt she had to be constantly on her toes. And they had just gotten word of a link between Quentin and another murder, this one in a state where they didn't think he'd been. As it turned out, he hadn't, and the forensic evidence didn't match. She wanted to be particularly careful they weren't just throwing things at him to see what would stick.

She had to be absolutely sure that the murders he was accused of were in fact crimes he had committed, and all the evidence matched up, beyond a reasonable doubt. She didn't want to lose this case, or try to convict him for crimes he didn't commit. She wanted to be absolutely, totally, completely sure that she was on the right track in each case, and she believed she was. Without solid conclusive evidence from other law enforcement agencies in other states, she would not add their cases to her own. It was her cautious thoroughness so far that had convinced the FBI director to let her keep the case. He didn't think anyone could have done a better job, and Joe assured him that was true. All of which put additional pressure on Alexa to not make one minute slip or mistake. She looked and felt worn out. The trial was ten weeks away. And Quentin was continuing to hold court with a hungry press. Alexa refused to make further comment, which the FBI liked too, and at every opportunity she thanked them for their help, gave them credit where it was due, and was grateful for their enormous investigative machine that she was benefiting from to build her case.

Pennsylvania had found another victim, and the body had been exhumed, although her family had been reluctant to do it and had to be convinced. Jack flew out to see them, and begged them to cooperate, which they finally did, in tears. And it was a match with Quentin. That brought his number of victims to eighteen, and Alexa had a gut instinct that they had found them all. She wasn't sure why, but they had combed every state he had been in since leaving prison and checked him against every murder, rape, and missing person. There were no loose ends anymore. The twenty-two-year-old medical student in Pennsylvania was the last one. Eighteen beautiful young women, all dead because of him. It was unthinkable, especially to the girls' parents, but it happened every day. Alexa was grateful daily that she had sent Savannah away. There had been no letters since she left. She had decided to take Savannah to Europe in the summer, with the vacation time she had, and after that Savannah was leaving for college, and would be even harder to find. Quentin had robbed her of her last months with her daughter, but she was safe, and he had done worse to others, and robbed them of their lives. Talking to the parents of the victims had nearly broken Alexa's heart.

And throughout, his public defender was insisting they were wrong, in the face of evidence, victims, DNA matches, and three psych reports now that confirmed he was a sociopath. Alexa almost felt sorry for her, she was completely under his spell, and could have been yet another victim if they met when he was outside. He was a text-book sociopath, and every time he saw Alexa, which wasn't often, and too frequently for her, he undressed her with his eyes, just to let her know he could, and to let her know that she had no power and he did. He was a terrifying man, and smooth as silk. This was a case Alexa wanted to win, more than any case she'd had before.

They were interrogating him again that afternoon, about the latest Pennsylvania victim, and as always he strutted into the room. He had been working out, for lack of anything better to do, and his heavily developed muscles rippled in his jail-issue jumpsuit, and he observed everyone in the room with his now-familiar glacial eyes. This time Alexa decided not to hide behind the two-way mirror in the observation room. She sat among the cops across the table from him in the small stuffy room. The smell of male sweat hung heavy in the air. It wasn't pleasant, but Alexa didn't care, and Judy Dunning was there too, and gave him a sympathetic smile. With a half smile, Luke looked at the others as though to show them what he could do. He had completely turned her around, on her head, and upside down. There were also two special FBI agents in the room, Sam Lawrence and a new one she hadn't met, and Jack's original investigation team, Charlie McAvoy and Bill Neeley. The room was jammed, and the questioning began.

They asked him about the victim, about whom he claimed to know nothing, and showed him a photograph of her. She had apparently been approached on a dark street near her apartment, coming home late from the library of the medical school. Like the others, she had been raped and "snuffed" out, strangled during sex. Her body had been found in a shallow grave in a park. She hadn't been found for four months, and the body had deteriorated badly by then. And Luke had been in town when it happened. Luke shrugged when he looked at the picture of the girl when she was alive, and tossed it back on the desk. His eyes hooked Alexa's, and he paused for a long moment when he looked at her. She could have been wrong, but she had the feeling this time that he was silently saying "Watch out, that could be you . . . or your kid." Her eyes didn't waver, nor did his. This was becoming a personal vendetta between them now. She was not going to be bested by him, or fooled.

"Where do you guys keep coming up with these women? My dick would have fallen off by now if I'd screwed them all." The senior detective conducting the interrogation didn't comment, and Alexa noticed Charlie McAvoy shift in his seat.

He was still on the case and doing good work. He had handled his sister's case and several others and was working hours of overtime. He looked as tired as everyone else. Only the defendant looked rested, in top form, good spirits, and great shape. He was the center of attention and a star. He cast several glances at his attorney, who smiled at him encouragingly as the interrogation wore on.

Alexa had recently demanded that he have a further medical exam to see if his body ejaculated sperm, or if it remained trapped elsewhere, as happened sometimes with men who had severe kidney problems and had been on medication for years. There was no evidence that he was, and he had refused the exams, which he had the right to do, and had offered to come in their eyes.

Everyone was tired of it, and him, as the interrogation wore down. He was so completely without remorse or concern, claiming he'd had nothing to do with any victim, and had neither raped nor killed them, that if anything, he looked bored. And in passing he made a comment that all the women he'd met in Iowa had been dogs, sluts, or cheap whores. Alexa saw Charlie tense as he made the comment, and sat there willing him not to react. For some reason then, maybe knowing that one of the victims was Charlie's sister and wanting to goad him, he said that he wouldn't have stuck his dick into any girl in Iowa, or most of the states where he'd been.

Charlie was tired and had been up all night, after meeting with the parents of several victims, and trying to get more information from them. His sister had been dead for a year that week, and his own parents were still devastated and so was he. But Quentin wouldn't give it up. He kept talking about "dogs" and "sluts" and "cheap whores" and what he would and wouldn't do to them if he had the chance. And before any of them could grab him, Charlie was out of his seat like lightning, had literally flown across the table and had Quentin by the throat, and he was in even better shape than Luke. Charlie had a choke hold on him, and Quentin responded in kind. The two men were literally strangling each other, as every cop in the room and even Alexa dove toward them to break it up.

Someone hit an alarm, and there was chaos in the room as people shouted, grabbed, scuffled, it was nearly impossible to drag Charlie off him, but two of the men finally did. Jack was standing there sweating profusely, his own shirt torn from his attempts to break up the two men. He said not a word to Luke but shouted in his detective's face, who was choking and spitting on the floor. Luke was back in cuffs and being dragged away, spluttering too.

"What the *fuck* were you thinking? Are you out of your mind? You're off the case. *Now!*"

"I'm bringing charges!" Luke shouted through the door as it closed, with no time to cast smoldering looks at his attorney, or menacing looks at Alexa or anyone else. It had been an incredibly dumb thing for Charlie to do, and would probably win him a year's suspension for attacking a suspect, but he clearly needed the time off, and Jack was furious with himself for not taking him off the case before. He was quietly talking to Sam Lawrence and the other special FBI agent, who had actually been the ones to pull Charlie away from Luke. Jack explained again about his sister, and they nodded, and finally one of them laughed.

"Look, relax. I would have liked to do it myself. I just didn't have the balls. I have three sisters, and this guy is a piece of shit." But they also had a responsibility to protect him, and not kill him themselves. "I'm not going to file a report," Sam said. "He had it coming. You guys can do what you want." Jack knew he had to file one anyway. He told Charlie in his office half an hour later that he was suspending him for a year and sent him home. He had done a great job until then, but the stress had been too much for him. Quentin had killed his twin. Charlie had apologized profusely to Jack before he left, and said he would fly back to Iowa that night, but he and his family were planning to attend the trial.

Jack looked even more exhausted

when he showed up in Alexa's office after Charlie left.

"Shit. That's all we needed. Thank God the FBI guys were nice about it. McCarthy is going to kill me when he hears it. I should have taken Charlie off the case as soon as we knew his sister was one of the victims. I don't know what I was thinking. I must have shit for brains."

"You're human, like anyone else," she reassured him, but it had been a tense moment, and a very stupid mistake on Charlie's part. He had totally lost control. "This case is getting to all of us." It had impacted everyone's life, including hers.

They sat and ate Power Bars together for an hour, and to distract her, he asked about Savannah, and once again she admitted her concerns, and shared them with him.

"She went to see her grandmother there. She's settling in, and it worries me a lot. I don't want her falling in love with Charleston and deciding that's where she wants to live." It was a major concern for her, but the alternative, of bringing her back to New York, was worse, and out of the question until after the trial.

"I don't have any, but it seems to me, kids do what they want, and usually just the opposite of what their parents want for them. I don't think you'll have much control over what she decides. But even if Charleston is pretty, it's not New York. She's used to a bigger world, and she's going to college." He had a point and what he said reassured her, and they went back to talking about the case. She was going down to Charleston herself that weekend. She could hardly wait to see Savannah, but was dreading all the bitter memories it would revive for her, some of them even bittersweet.

In the end, there was no major fallout from Charlie's outburst in the interrogation room. Both the DA and the FBI were satisfied with Jack's suggestion of a year's suspension, and with the fact that Charlie was already gone and had left that day. There were extenuating circumstances, since his twin sister was one of the victims. And with him off the case, it wouldn't happen again, but it had been a close call. No one knew what could have happened if the other men hadn't been able to stop Charlie. It would certainly have solved the problem, but created others far worse for him. No one would have been sorry to see Luke Quentin dead, except Judy Dunning, whom Alexa now referred to as "the fool."

By five o'clock on Friday afternoon, when she had to leave for the airport, Alexa was flying around her office stuffing files into a bag. She wanted to do some reading on the flights down and back. The rest of the time would be dedicated to Savannah and whatever she had planned. She barely made it to the airport on time, and talked to her mother from the cab. She looked and felt a mess, and totally unprepared to face her old world. She had told her mother about Charlie McAvoy earlier in the week. Emotions were running high on the Quentin case, and Muriel commented that it would do her good to get away. Alexa wasn't as sure, except for seeing Savannah. She was terrified of the rest.

"What are you afraid of?" Muriel asked her from her chambers. She had just finished work for the day. It had been a good day for her. Her life wasn't fraught with the drama of her daughter's. She couldn't have lived that way, or worked as hard, although she had in her youth. Those days were over now. She was busy, but her life was not going at breakneck speed. Alexa's was. Muriel hated this case for her, and all the stress she had.

"I don't know, Mom," Alexa said honestly. "I guess I'm afraid she'll stay, that Tom will be so nice suddenly, and Charleston will be so seductive, all that beauty and southern charm. I fell for it hook, line, and sinker. Why wouldn't she? What if she never wants to come home, or live in New York again?"

"She may love what she sees there, and want to go back for a visit, but I'll be very surprised if she wants to live that far from you, for now anyway. And her sights are set on college, not on moving to the South, or discovering her roots. She should know about it, and I think it's good for her to see. I always thought that, it'll take care of any curiosity or magical beliefs she might have had about it. But Savannah is heading for college, that's all she cares about now. You were out of college and in love with a man older than you. That's a life Savannah can't even imagine and doesn't want. Not for a long, long time. If you ask, I think she'll tell you the same thing. She was curious about it, but no more than that. And being there for three months will put all those questions to rest."

"I wish I felt as sure." Alexa was only slightly comforted by her mother's words, although she made sense.

"Are you sure you're worrying about Savannah and not yourself?" Bingo! Alexa knew instantly her mother had hit a nerve, by how uncomfortable she felt. As she always did, she had gone right to the epicenter of the pain.

"Yeah, maybe I am," Alexa said honestly, trying to figure out what part of it she feared most. It was hard to say. "I was so happy there, I loved Tom so much, and his boys. I trusted him completely, and I thought we'd be together forever. And now all of that is gone, and someone else is married to him and living in that same house. It's a little hard to take." And she had hated him for it for years. He had stolen all her dreams, and destroyed all her trust. She had never been able to rebuild it since, with anyone. He had burned her to the ground. "I would have preferred never to go there again."

"Sometimes we have to face the things that hurt us most. Maybe you won't heal till you do. You haven't yet." They both knew that was true. "You can't move ahead until you bury the past, and all that agony and hurt is still alive for you. Maybe this will do you good." Alexa thought of it as the cab pulled up in front of the terminal, and she told her mother she had to go. But she knew that she was right. Her pain was still alive. None of it, nor the disappointment and feeling of betrayal, had dulled in the past ten years. If anything, it had gotten worse. She had no man in her life and didn't want one, because she couldn't forgive or forget the one who had hurt her most. Nor had she forgiven Tom's mother, or his wife, who had urged him to betray her in every possible way. It had been a cabal against her, because she wasn't one of them, hard as it was to believe now. It sounded crazy, but was true. Luisa had won by geography and tradition, and like Ashley in *Gone with the Wind,* Tom had been weak. She couldn't forgive him for it even now. And ten years of not forgiving him had poisoned her, like a radioactive substance she had ingested years ago, still coursing through her veins. It burned her insides with a searing pain. She hadn't wanted Savannah anywhere near those people, but she had had no other choice.

Alexa ran through security, and barely made her plane. She didn't want to miss it and disappoint Savannah. It left at six-thirty, and landed after eight. Her heart caught as she saw the airport. She had told Savannah she'd call when she arrived and meet her at the hotel. She didn't want her to wait alone. She got her bag and hailed a cab, and gave him the name of her hotel.

The drive to the city was familiar and

brief. Her heart ached when she saw the bridges, and the church spires she had loved. One of those churches was where they had christened Savannah. The city was full of memories for her, like a too ripe plum ready to explode. She had to force them from her mind. Before she got to the hotel she called Savannah, who was waiting for the call in her room. It was almost nine o'clock by then. She had been planning to drive over, but her father had said he would drop her off, since Alexa had arranged for a rented car through the hotel. He knew her mother probably wouldn't want her driving downtown alone. Savannah let him know when she got the call, and she ran downstairs with her small bag. She had kissed Daisy goodbye that afternoon, since she was spending the night at a friend's. Luisa was out playing bridge that night. Tom had opted to stay home. He and Luisa were on extremely tense terms, but sleeping in the same room. Barely, but they were.

"You must be excited to see your mom," Tom chatted easily on their way

to the Wentworth Mansion. Alexa had
remembered that it was the best hotel in
town, and had originally been built as
a home. It was still one of the city's
loveliest Victorian mansions, with every
possible amenity and comfort, and gracious, beautifully appointed rooms, Tiffany glass ceilings, fine antiques, and a
spa Alexa knew Savannah would enjoy
and where they could both relax. It was
in the heart of the city, with shops and
restaurants all around it, and spectacular views of historic Charleston right
from the hotel. Alexa was hoping it
would be a treat for them both, and Savannah wouldn't have cared if they
stayed in a motel. She just wanted to
see her mom. She could hardly wait.

"Yes, I am excited to see her," Savannah answered with a broad smile and
dancing eyes. "She's my best friend,"
she volunteered. "I miss her a lot."

"I know you do," Tom said, wishing he
could fill the void somehow, but even if
she enjoyed spending time with her father, it was too late for that. Thanks to
him, he knew, they were acquaintances,
not friends. He hoped to deepen their

relationship while she was there, but contrary to her mother's fears, three months wasn't long. And surely not long enough to make up for ten years.

Tom followed Savannah into the Wentworth Mansion, carrying her bag. She hadn't brought much with her, and said she could wear her mother's clothes. Savannah bounded into the lobby like a young puppy, and as soon as she did, she saw her mother standing at the desk checking in, and nearly jumped into her arms. The two women hugged so tight and clung to each other so fiercely that they looked like one body with two heads, while Tom stood quietly by, unnoticed by both of them. Alexa ran her hands over Savannah's hair and face and arms, as though she had been starving for her. Tom could see they both were, as Savannah clung to her mother like a child. It was a full five minutes before either of them remembered he was there. And he felt a secret sadness, watching them and knowing that he had created the fierce bond they shared, by abandoning both of them. He felt left out, and knew he had no right to more. He had it all once, and betrayed them, and now he lived in the ashes that were left. Both Alexa and Savannah were like rays of sunlight filtering into the darkness of his life through prison bars. It was a prison he had built himself, out of weakness and fear.

"Well, you two look mighty happy to see each other," he said, smiling at them both. None of his sadness showed. He appeared happy for them, and in fact was jealous of what they shared. Everything about them was pure gold. Alexa immediately stiffened when she saw him. She had forgotten he was there, and so had Savannah. Alexa tried to be polite. She was grateful for the haven he was providing their daughter, but he was still Tom, the person on the planet she hated and who had hurt her most. She watched him as he hugged Savannah, kissed her, and wished them both a good weekend. It looked sincere, but who knew with him, Alexa thought to herself, and blamed it on the South, as she always did, still convinced that every southerner was a hypocrite and a liar, waiting to betray a loved one or a friend. It was too late to convince her otherwise. For her, they were like a separate nationality she abhorred.

"She's been really looking forward to this," Tom said gently to Alexa, not knowing what else to say. Everything about her was slammed tightly closed except when she looked at her daughter and her entire being relaxed and softened. Like night and day.

"So have I," Alexa said coolly. "Thank you for keeping her here with you. I'm sure it can't be easy for you." She knew all about his fights with Luisa from Savannah, but didn't let on.

"She's our daughter," he said simply, "and I'm happy to make things a little easier for you, if I can. How's the case coming?" She really didn't want to talk about it with him, but with his good manners and easy southern charm, it was hard to avoid answering him. Even knowing what she did, he was still a handsome, seductive man.

"It's a lot of work," she said politely. "But we've got him. I'll be stunned if they don't convict."

"I'm sure you'll win it," he said, and then handed Savannah's bag to a bell-man. "Have a great weekend," he said to Savannah. "I'll pick you up on Sunday. Call me when you're ready, or if you need anything before that." He smiled at both of them and then strode out of the lobby on his long, lanky legs. There was no question about it, and even Alexa couldn't deny it, he was a handsome man, and his genes hadn't done Savannah any harm.

Alexa had reserved the best suite in the hotel, and Savannah looked around excitedly and exclaimed as she went from the living room to the bedroom and back again. It had a big four-poster bed like the one at Thousand Oaks, and this room was decorated in a deep yellow, with dark furniture, and lots of Tiffany glass. It was a classic antebellum mansion, and Savannah could hardly wait to see the spa. They had an appointment for massages, manicures, and pedicures the following afternoon before dinner. Alexa wanted to treat them both to a totally luxurious weekend.

They ordered something to eat in

the room, since Savannah had already eaten and Alexa only wanted a light meal. Afterward she unpacked the few things that Alexa had forgotten in New York, and two new blouses and a sweater she had bought her, which Savannah loved and said she could wear to school. They talked about school, the people she had met there, and her meeting with her southern grandmother, and they talked about Alexa's mother. They covered every possible topic and subject, hugged constantly, kissed each other often, teased each other, and Savannah told her about the "bless her heart" thing that southerners seemed to say before or after making a particularly bitchy comment, and Alexa roared with laughter and said it was true. They reveled in each other's love, and finally got into the four-poster bed together at two in the morning. And then with their arms around each other, they fell asleep like two puppies, happy for the first time in weeks.

And the minute they woke up in the morning, they started talking about everything they wanted to do. Alexa wanted to take her to a few cute shops that she remembered, if they were still there, and her favorite restaurant for lunch, and Savannah had a list of places too. They had enough to keep them busy for a week, and by ten-thirty they were walking down the streets of Charleston on a gloriously sunny day. Alexa felt a tug at her heart as she saw familiar places, but she tried not to let it upset her. This weekend was all about Savannah and not the disappointment she'd had here.

They went to a shop full of nothing but cashmere sweaters, mostly in pastel colors. Alexa bought her a pink one, and they were laughing as they left the store, and Savannah's eyes widened as she saw her friend from school. Julianne was with her mother, whose face lit up the moment she saw Alexa, as though she had seen her best friend too. She once had been, but had betrayed her as Tom had. It was the first time Alexa had seen or heard from her in ten years.

"Oh my God, Alexa! Dawlin', how *are* you? You can't even know how many times I've thought about you . . . I just miss you to pieces and Savannah is so gorgeous. Bless her heart, she looks just like you." Savannah and Alexa exchanged a quick look at her last words and tried not to burst out laughing. But Alexa was irked by her hypocrisy and pretense of a still-existing friendship and concern that she tried to pretend had lain dormant, when in fact it had died years before, at her hands. "How long are you here for?"

"Just till tomorrow. I came down for the weekend."

"My Gawwddd, we have to get together the next time you come. Call me before you do. We could have lunch with our girls." Not on your life, Alexa was thinking as she smiled back at her. "We're just so happy that Savannah is visiting her daddy. The girls are such good friends." Alexa nodded and said nothing, with a fake smile on her face. Savannah knew that look, and it was reserved for people her mother disliked intensely or had utter contempt for. And she knew that Julianne's mother was one. Her name was Michelle, and people called her Shelly. "What are you doing in New York now? Are you remarried?" Alexa had a strong urge to slap her when she asked. It was none of her business. Whatever the pretense, they were no longer friends, and never would be again.

"I'm a prosecutor in the district attorney's office," Alexa said quietly. She didn't answer the question about marriage. She suspected Shelly knew anyway, from the girls. She had always been nosy, loved gossip, and pumped everyone for all the information she could get.

"Bless your heart, that's such a big job, especially for a woman. You're quite the celebrity around here." Alexa thanked her and said they had to get going. The girls promised to call each other the following night, and Alexa and Savannah hurried away to the next shop on her list. And once they were out of earshot, Alexa turned to her daughter with a wry look.

"I counted a total of two 'bless your hearts' for you, and four for me. Watch out, she hates us!" Alexa warned her as they both burst into laughter.

"I noticed. I lost count after the first two. Julianne doesn't get along with her mother either. She says she's a total bitch."

"Yeah, I'd say she's right. She was about as sincere as poisoned ice cream, magnolia flavored!"

"Now, Mom, stop with your thing about the South. You just had rotten luck here." Savannah never failed to call her on it, and part of Alexa knew she was right. The other part hated the South too much to care.

"Yeah, yeah, whatever" was all she answered, as they stopped in a shop to buy lotions and makeup. They were having a totally girly weekend, just like they did in New York when they both had time, which was never often enough for Alexa. Savannah had a much busier social life than she did, and her mother was sure she would in Charleston soon too.

Their massages at the spa at the Wentworth Mansion were sheer heaven. They had their nails done, and padded back to their suite in rubber flip-flops with cotton between their toes. Alexa had made a reservation at Circa 1886 for dinner. It was in the former carriage house of their hotel and Alexa had never been there. But for most of the day, they had stopped at her old favorite places. And just as she had thought, it was bittersweet being there. She had lived there as a young wife and new mother, and since then her life had changed completely. They saw no familiar faces other than Julianne and Shelly, but Alexa was startled and touched when Travis called her. He apologized for being out of touch for so long. He said he'd love to see her the next time, but was in a tennis tournament at the club that weekend. He made a point of saying that Savannah was a fantastic girl, and he was happy to talk to Alexa. He was every bit as polite as his father, she just hoped he was more sincere. He mentioned that he was getting married in June and wanted Savannah to be there.

Savannah had told her that she really liked Scarlette, and Travis had been really nice to her. She hadn't met Henry yet, but he was supposedly coming home for a weekend soon. He was living in New Orleans, and working for an art dealer there, but that was all she knew.

Their dinner that night was even better than they'd been promised. And they both wore dresses they'd bought that afternoon. By the time they got back to their hotel room, they were happy and exhausted. The only bad part of the evening was knowing that Alexa was leaving the next day. Neither of them wanted to think about it yet.

They decided to go to church the next morning before going to brunch at Baker's Café.

They went to St. Stephen's Episcopal Church, where Alexa told Savannah she'd been christened, and slipped into a pew. It was a serious, traditional service, with beautiful organ music, and on the way out, Alexa and Savannah were holding hands and feeling good. They had just shaken hands with the minister outside the church, when suddenly someone ran up to Savannah, threw their arms around her waist, and nearly knocked her over. She tried to regain her balance and composure, and turned to see who it was and found herself looking down into Daisy's face, who looked immensely pleased.

"What are you doing here?" Savannah asked, still startled, and then introduced Daisy to her mother, who looked equally surprised but smiled at Daisy warmly. She was a very cute kid, and obviously crazy about Savannah. Alexa didn't have time to absorb what this child had meant in her own life and how she had been used. She was just a little girl in pigtails with a huge grin.

"My mom and I come here every Sunday, almost," Daisy explained to Savannah and then turned to her mother with interest. "Savannah says you're going to put a very, very bad man in prison."

"I'm trying," Alexa said, smiling at her, and then added, "That's why Savannah's here, so he can't hurt her."

"I know," Daisy said, looking important. "She told me all about it, and about you." She smiled broadly at Alexa again.

"She told me about you too," Alexa said warmly, completely ignoring who she was and who she belonged to. Daisy had a sweetness of her own that obscured all else. She was impossible to resist. Her face lit up at what Alexa had just said to her. She looked immensely pleased.

"She did?" Daisy asked happily. "I really, really love her," she said, putting her arm around her sister's waist again, as a voice behind them flew between them like a spear.

"Daisy! Take your hands off Savannah immediately!" the voice said sharply. Savannah knew who it was before she turned around to look, and Alexa could guess. "That's no way to behave at church." It was Luisa, glaring at the three of them with a venomous look, which was no way to behave at church either, Alexa thought to herself.

"Church is over, Mama. This is the part where everyone is friendly," Daisy insisted, with good reason. Apparently, Luisa had not come to church for that part, and surely not with these two women. She looked right through Savannah and Alexa, as though they didn't exist, as she scolded her child. Savannah decided to try and take the heat off Daisy.

"Luisa, I'd like to introduce you to my mother, Alexa Hamilton," Savannah said politely, nearly drawling herself, but not quite. Luisa looked at her in outrage, as though Savannah had just taken her clothes off in front of church, or grabbed her stepmother by her elaborately coiffed hair.

"We met, many years ago," she said through clenched teeth as her own daughter watched her with a look of resignation, wondering why her mother was always so mean. She was not a happy person, and angry most of the time. As Luisa said the words, she looked sourly at Alexa.

"It's nice to see you again, Luisa," Alexa said, lying through her teeth. She would have liked to add "bless your heart" but didn't dare. Neither she nor Savannah could have kept a straight face, or maybe even Daisy. "Thank you for having Savannah stay with you. I really appreciate it, and I know she does too."

"Not at all," Luisa said, and grabbed Daisy by the back of the neck in a firm grip, and propelled her toward their car without another word. Daisy looked back with a pained grin and waved, and both women felt sorry for her. In many ways, she was the victim in all this, as Savannah had been years before, and neither of them deserved it.

"What a *bitch*," Alexa muttered, watching Luisa snap at Daisy as she slammed the door to the car, and then drove her away. "Bless her heart," she added, and Savannah laughed out loud.

"Yeah, she is," Savannah confirmed. "But I'm glad you met Daisy. She's such a sweet kid."

"Your father sure got what he deserved with that one," Alexa commented about Luisa as they walked away from the church.

"He looks pretty miserable most of the time," Savannah confirmed, "or maybe that's just because she's so mad that I'm there. They've hardly said two words to each other since I got here, except when they're fighting."

"Sounds like a fun life." Alexa had been startled by the meeting, and rendered almost speechless by the look of venom in Luisa's eyes. She was a piece of work, and even worse than Alexa had imagined. Much, much worse.

They had a lovely brunch at Baker's Café, which was one of Alexa's old favorites. She said that they had gone there a lot when she was pregnant with Savannah. It was one of the old traditional restaurants of Charleston, with a pretty garden, and it was a lovely sunny day. Then they drove out to the beach, across several picturesque bridges, and eventually wound up back at the hotel in the late afternoon. They both hated to admit it, but their magical weekend was drawing to a close, and it made both of them very sad.

"How soon do you think you can come back, Mom?" Savannah asked, looking worried.

"I don't know, another week . . . or two . . . but I had a great time with you, sweetheart. I could even fall in love with Charleston again, here with you. Just don't you do it," she warned her. "I want you home soon!"

"Don't worry, Mom. I won't stay here. It's fun to visit, but I'm coming back to New York as soon as I can. I'd come home now if you let me," but they both knew that would have been a bad idea.

"Don't let Cruella De Vil get to you," Alexa said as Savannah laughed at the description. "Bless her heart, of course."

Alexa packed her bag, minus all the items she had brought for Savannah or that her daughter had taken a shine to. She had to leave for the airport at six-thirty for an eight o'clock flight. Savannah offered to come to the airport with her, but her mother didn't want her to. It was better for Savannah if they said goodbye at the hotel and she went home with Tom, instead of standing at the airport alone when her mother left.

Savannah called her father just before they left the room and went downstairs to pay the bill. She was relieved that her mother would be coming back soon. She knew that once the trial started in May that wouldn't be possible, but at least for March and April, Alexa was going to try and come down every couple of weeks, or more often if she could. She had promised, and she always kept her word.

By the time Alexa finished paying the bill, Tom walked into the lobby. He had come from the club and was wearing tennis shorts, and Alexa averted her eyes. She didn't want to see how handsome he was, or how good his legs were. It was no longer her problem, but she already knew that something about him would always stir feelings inside her. But it was nothing more than that.

"I'll bet you two had a great weekend," he said, smiling broadly at them, and then his face clouded just a little. "I hear you ran into Luisa and Daisy at church." His wife had nearly taken off his head about that, as though he had planned it. Luisa had told him that he should have warned Savannah not to go anywhere near their church. He had commented acidly on her warm Christian spirit, and could only imagine how unpleasant she must have been to Alexa. Instead of being remorseful, or feeling sorry for her, Luisa seemed to have a need to punish her further and grind her into dust. He looked at Alexa now as though to apologize for his wife.

"It was fine," Alexa said brusquely,

and then turned her attention to Savannah to say goodbye. They were both fighting back tears when Alexa got into the cab for the ride to the airport. Savannah stood on the sidewalk and waved until her mother disappeared, and then she got in her father's car and they drove to Mt. Pleasant. It felt weird to her sometimes—she had a father suddenly, and she wasn't used to it at all. She told him about the weekend and all the things they'd done.

She unpacked her bag when they got home, and the new things her mother had bought her. Daisy bounced into the room and chatted with her. Julianne and two other girls called her, and Travis and Scarlette came to dinner. Scarlette brought Savannah some magazines, and Travis a funny old photograph he had of her when she was three. By the time Alexa got off the plane in New York, Savannah had settled back into her new routine, and in an odd way, it almost felt like home.

Daisy had commented to Savannah that night that her mom was really pretty and seemed nice, and apologized to her that her own mother was so mean.

"I think my mom is jealous of your mom," Daisy said with the wisdom of young children.

"Maybe," Savannah conceded, and then they both burst out laughing as they both said at the same time, "Bless her heart."

Chapter 12

On her first day back after her weekend in Charleston, Alexa was busy with endless cops and investigators. Everything was coming together in the case, and she had dumped enough discovery on Judy Dunning to drown her. There was so much forensic evidence, and so many reports to go through, that the public defender was totally overwhelmed. Alexa took a break at noon, which was rare for her these days, and went to the family court to see her mother and have lunch with her in chambers. Alexa seemed like she was in a good mood.

"So how was it?" her mother asked

her. They were each eating a salad from the deli across the street.

"It was better than I feared," Alexa said to her. "Savannah was in great shape. And we ran into Luisa coming out of church, and she was a total bitch. But other than that, it was great. Charleston is as pretty as ever, and Savannah and I had a wonderful time together. I ran into an old friend of mine there, who defected when Tom divorced me, and that was creepy. But on the whole it was pretty good."

"I told you. This is interesting for her, and it's good for her to discover the other side of her family. She's a smart girl. She'll pick and choose. No one's going to pull the wool over her eyes. It sounds like Tom bought himself a one-way ticket to hell with Luisa. Why does he stay with her?"

"Probably for the same reason he went back to her," Alexa said curtly. "No guts. When he left me, he did what his mother and Luisa told him to do, and now she has him by the throat." Or worse.

"How does he look?" Muriel asked

with interest, and her daughter laughed. She was in good spirits. It had done her a world of good to see Savannah.

"Handsome and weak. I guess I never noticed. He's still the best-looking man on the planet, but I know what he's about now, and who he is. I guess I'll always think he's gorgeous, but thank God I'm not in love with him anymore. That's something at least." She sounded freer and less angry than Muriel had heard her sound in years. She wasn't as tense, despite the pressures of the Quentin case. She'd been working closely with the FBI, and now that they weren't threatening to take her case away every five minutes, she was enjoying working with them. There were no female agents on the case, and she didn't mind being the only woman in a world of men. She liked it. And the FBI agents were interesting to work with.

While her mother was back at work, Savannah was busy at school in Charleston. She had added a Chinese class to her AP French, and was having fun try-

ing to learn the language. She didn't
need it for credit, so there was no pressure on her. And she was starting to
make a lot of friends in school. She and
Julianne met for lunch almost every day.

She went to all the volleyball and soccer games, and rooted for their teams.
They let her join the swimming team because someone had dropped out with a
serious problem with her ears.

And the weekend after her mother
had been there, the captain of the soccer team asked Savannah out on a date.
Julianne nearly fainted when she heard.
He had just broken up with the prettiest
girl in school.

"Are you going to go out with him?"
Julianne asked breathlessly when Savannah confided in her.

"I might. I have nothing else to do."
She sounded very cool.

He took her to a movie on Friday
night, and they stopped at a coffee shop
afterward. His name was Turner Ashby,
a descendant of the general of the same
name, he informed her over burgers and
shakes.

"It seems like everyone in town is

related to a general," Savannah commented. She was wearing her mother's pink sweater and jeans, with high heels. She looked different from the girls in Charleston when she got dressed up. She had the sophistication of New York and was wearing just enough makeup but not too much. He looked crazy about her.

"That's a big deal around here," he explained.

"I know. My grandmother is the president general of the United Daughters of the Confederacy. She's the president general because she's related to a general too." Savannah grinned. She wasn't making fun of them, but she did think it was funny. He was a handsome boy with dark hair and green eyes, the oldest of four boys. "Where do you think you'll go to college?" she asked with genuine interest. She noticed that most of the people she talked to about it had applied to southern schools.

"Georgia Tech, or maybe SMU in Texas. I applied to Duke and UVA, but I don't think my scores are good enough to get in. What about you?"

"I'd really like to go to Princeton. It's close to home, which would be nice, and I liked the school. I liked Brown too. I think Harvard would be too serious, and I probably won't get in either. I liked Stanford, but my mom doesn't want me that far away." She went down her list.

"That's some list of fancy Ivy League schools you applied to," he said, looking impressed. She was smart but not stuck up, and the prettiest girl he'd ever seen.

He had her back at her house very respectfully at ten-thirty, and she had enjoyed him and the movie, and said she'd see him around school.

Julianne called her just after dawn the next morning to ask how it had gone.

"It was fun," Savannah said, and giggled, sounding younger than her age, and more like Daisy.

"That's it? You went out with the hottest guy in school and 'it was fun'? Did he kiss you?" Julianne wanted all the details. She had learned that from her mother. Gossip was their stock-in-trade.

"Of course not. We don't even know

each other. Besides, it would be dumb to get involved with anyone now. We're all leaving for college, and I'm only here for a few months." She was practical about it. She wasn't looking for romance, just friends, which made her even more appealing. She didn't have the desperation of some of the girls in school who were always looking for boyfriends.

"There's nothing dumb about going out with Turner Ashby. Did you know his father has oil rigs all over Biloxi? My mama says he's one of the richest men in the state. *And*," she said for emphasis, "he's cute. And the captain of the soccer team. What else do you need?" Savannah was well aware that playing soccer wouldn't get him far in life, it took more than that. And she didn't care about his father's oil wells. "Did he ask you out again?"

"No. Don't be silly. I just went out with him last night." She was totally relaxed about it.

"He will. Guys always like girls like you who don't give a damn about them."

"I didn't say that. I liked him. I'm just not going nuts about it, like you," she teased.

"I bet he asks you out next weekend," Julianne said, sounding moonstruck and hopeful.

"I hope not. I think my mom's coming. She said she'd try, but she may not make it till the following weekend."

Julianne made a disgusted sound. "Who would you rather go out with? Turner Ashby or your mother?"

Savannah answered without an instant's hesitation. "My mother."

"You're sick." Julianne promised to check in with her again later that day to see if Turner had called her yet.

Daisy was the next member of the interrogation team.

"Who was that boy who picked you up last night?" she asked casually over pancakes in the kitchen.

"Just a boy from school."

"That's all?" Daisy asked, looking disappointed. "Is he in love with you?"

"No," Savannah said, smiling. "He hardly knows me."

"Are you in love with him?"

"No. I don't know him either," she said, her feet firmly on the ground.

"Then why'd you go out with him if you're not in love with him?" Daisy asked, looking disgusted.

"Because we wanted to eat dinner and see a movie, and I figured I might as well do it with him, since he asked." Daisy nodded at the logic of what she said, but found it pathetically unromantic. Their father walked in, in his tennis clothes, while they were talking.

"Was that one of the Ashby boys I saw you leaving the house with last night?" he asked with equal interest. Clearly, her dating life was the hot topic in town.

"Yes."

"Nice kid?"

"I think so. He seemed like it," Savannah conceded.

"I play tennis with his father. They've had some hard times. His wife died last year. A drunk driver hit her on Highway 526, five miles from home. It must be hard on the kids."

"He didn't say anything about it. We just talked about school." Tom nodded, and told her that Henry was coming in from New Orleans that afternoon.

"He's anxious to see you. He'll be home for dinner tonight. Travis and Scarlette are coming over too. The whole family will be together," he said, looking happy, as Luisa walked into the kitchen and ignored him. She said she was going to the country club for a spa day that was just for women. Tom said he was picking Henry up at the airport, and Luisa said she'd be home in the late afternoon. She left the house five minutes later, and when they were alone again, Savannah offered to take Daisy to the aquarium, which sounded like fun to both of them. It was called the South Carolina Aquarium, and was said to be very good.

She and Daisy left the house at eleven o'clock, walked all over the aquarium, and had lunch there, and came back at three in the afternoon. Tallulah said their father had just left to pick up Henry, so they played Go Fish and War and Hearts and Gin Rummy, and shortly after five o'clock Tom and Henry walked in. Daisy flew down the stairs to greet her brother.

He was a year younger than Travis and was a handsome young man with a powerful athletic build. He had played football in college and instead of UVA had gone to Duke. Savannah knew that he had been an art history major and eventually wanted to teach. He wasn't interested in business like his older brother or his father, and he was working in an important art gallery in New Orleans, and as an intern at a museum. He was interested in curating too.

After Henry had lavishly hugged his younger sister, he looked up the stairs and saw Savannah smiling at him. She looked no different than she had as a little girl, as Travis had already told her, just bigger.

"I am sooooo happy to see you," Henry said softly, as he came up the stairs to where she stood and folded her into a bear hug. "I am so glad you're here. Travis and Daisy already told me all about you. I came home this weekend just to see you." And the way he said it, she believed him. They walked back down the stairs and into the living room. Fortunately, Luisa hadn't come home yet, or she would have objected to his making a fuss over Savannah. But Henry didn't care. He had never danced to his mother's tune.

They sat down and talked for a while, and he asked pertinent questions, what she liked, what she did, what her favorite music was, her favorite books and movies, the names of her friends. He wanted to know all about her. And his eyes grew sad when he asked about her mother.

"I didn't like to write when I was a kid, so I didn't. But I always thought about her, and about you. Your mom did something very special for me when she was married to our daddy," he said solemnly, as though he was about to share an important secret. "I'm dyslexic, and your mama tutored me for all those years. I hated the tutor I had, so she did it. I think she took classes to learn how to do it. Anyway, thanks to her, I got through school. I never forgot it. She was the kindest, most patient woman I have ever known, the spirit of compassion and love." Tom had been standing in the doorway and heard Henry say it, and walked away with a pained expression. Neither Henry nor Savannah had seen him there, and then he disappeared.

"She never told me," Savannah said honestly. "That's pretty good if you got into Duke."

"It's a good school," he confirmed.

They went on talking, and eventually Luisa came home from her spa day. She came to kiss her son, and then rapidly went upstairs to change. She wasn't happy to see him talking to Savannah, but she didn't comment, and she found her husband looking unhappy in their room. He had forgotten about Alexa tutoring Henry for all those years, and how loving she had been about it. Remembering it made him feel sick.

"What's wrong with you?" Luisa asked him, noticing how unhappy he looked.

"Nothing. Just thinking. How was your spa day?"

"Very nice, thank you," she said coolly. She had no intention of warming up to him again until Savannah went back to New York. She was planning to punish him for the entire time, to teach him a lesson. She wanted him to get the message loud and clear so he didn't bring her back again. She was not going to tolerate having Alexa's daughter in her house. But so far she was overruled.

The atmosphere at dinner that night was lively and jolly, thanks to Henry. He told funny jokes, did hysterical imitations, and teased everyone, including his mother. Travis was far more reserved, although a nice person too. Scarlette loved her soon-to-be brother-in-law, and he teased her mercilessly too, about the size of the wedding. Scarlette said her younger brothers did the same. Henry was twenty-four and he looked young, but there was also something more sophisticated about him. Savannah wondered if living in another city had shown him more of the world. Travis still lived in the family cocoon in Charleston. And even their father had done so all his life. Only Henry had really left home, although he had chosen another southern city. But New Orleans was bigger and more sophisticated than Charleston, and he seemed to spend a lot of time in London and New York. He knew all of Savannah's favorite haunts in New York.

With Henry in charge of most of the conversation, everyone was in a good mood, even his mother. She asked him at the end of dinner how that lovely girl was that he went out with the previous summer, and he gave her a strange look.

"She's fine, Mama. She just got engaged."

"Oh, I'm so sorry," she said, gushing sympathy for him, and he laughed.

"I'm not." Henry talked a lot about someone called Jeff who was his roommate. Apparently he was from North Carolina, and they had taken several trips recently. Luisa didn't ask about him.

By the time they finished dinner, everyone's sides hurt from laughing, and after they went back into the living room, Henry played cards with the girls. They were still playing when his parents said goodnight and went upstairs. Travis and Scarlette had left by then, since there was a breakfast shower for Scarlette the next day. She said she would have asked Savannah, but she'd be bored to tears. And Travis had told her she'd better not invite Savannah or his mother would be livid, so she hadn't, but felt terrible about it. But she did what Travis said.

Luisa would have liked to keep Henry away from Savannah too, but there had been no obvious way to exclude her from the evening, and she knew Henry would have objected and accused her of being rude. He never hesitated to challenge his mother, and tell her when he didn't like her behavior. He wasn't afraid of her. And Daisy had already told him on the phone that their mother had been awful to her, so he had gone out of his way to be nice to Savannah at dinner. And when he said he had come home just to see her, it was true.

Daisy fell asleep during their card game, and Henry gently carried her upstairs to her bed, while Savannah went to her room. Henry knocked on her door to see if she was decent. She was in her nightgown, brushing her teeth, when he came in. He strolled right into her bath-room to chat with her, like a real brother.

"I like having another sister, one I can really talk to," he said, smiling at her in the bathroom mirror. "You've been gone for way too long."

They sat down in her room and talked some more then. He said he wanted to move to New York or London in a few years, once he figured out if he wanted to work in a gallery, a museum, or a school. But working in the art field was his dream.

"You don't want to come back here?" She looked surprised. People in the South seemed to stay close to home and cling to their roots, judging from what she had seen so far.

"Too small for me," he said simply. "This is a very small provincial city. And being gay is too complicated for me here." She looked at him in surprise.

"You are?" She hadn't figured that out, and his mother had asked about a girl he had gone out with the year be-fore.

"I am. Jeff is my partner. I told my par-ents I was gay when I was eighteen.

Dad wasn't thrilled, but he's okay about it. My mother acts like she forgot and doesn't know, no matter how often I remind her. Like the girl she asked me about going out with. She knows I don't go out with women. I figured out I was gay about a year after your mom left, when I was fifteen. By sixteen I knew for sure. It shouldn't be a big deal, but for some people it is—my mother, for one. She's going to ask me about the women I go out with till I'm a hundred years old. She's probably hoping I'll get 'cured.' My being gay just wasn't in her plan. I think she's relieved I don't live in Charleston. It would be too embarrassing for her, and too hard for me. She still lies to her friends."

"How weird," Savannah said, looking puzzled. "What difference does it make to her?"

"It's not 'normal,' as she puts it, or 'right.' But it is for me."

"That's just who you are," Savannah said, smiling at him. "It shouldn't be a big deal. Does Daisy know?" she asked, curious about it.

"They'd kill me if I told her, but she'll

figure it out sometime. I don't think Travis is too thrilled about it either. He's a lot more like them than I am. He's a small-town boy who wants to do everything he can to make them happy and fit in their mold. I'd commit suicide if I married Scarlette, but she's just right for him, a nice southern girl."

"You're sounding like a Yankee," Savannah teased him.

"Maybe I am at heart. There are a lot of hypocrisies I don't like here, or maybe it's just a small-town thing. I hate seeing people covering up what they really think and feel, just to be polite or fit in. There's a lot of that here. It's all okay, if you have a couple of Confederate generals in the family, but not a gay son, at least not in this family. They tolerate it, but don't like it. Shit, for all we know, maybe all those generals were gay." They both laughed, and then he looked serious again. "It wouldn't have mattered to your mother. She was the most loving woman I've ever known. I didn't know I was gay when she was here, but afterward I wondered if she knew before I did. She's very sharp."

Savannah nodded, proud of her mother.

"Is your mom okay?" he asked her, and Savannah nodded. "She really got a shit deal from my mom and dad. I take it she never remarried, from what Travis said the other day. I asked him."

"No," Savannah said, "she didn't. She's only thirty-nine, though. But she's still pretty mad about your dad," she said honestly. "Or hurt, I guess."

"She has a right to be," he said, equally honest. "My mother really screwed her over, and Dad let her. I think their relationship has been lousy ever since, but Dad stays in it, and my mother walks all over him. She walked out on all of us when she left my dad. And everyone conveniently forgets she did. That's just the way it works." He looked disapproving as he said it.

"I've seen it," Savannah admitted. "She's furious about me."

"Too bad. He should have brought you back here years ago. I feel terrible that I never reached out to you or your mom. I let it happen too. I was fourteen then, and I hated what they were doing.

And then, I don't know, high school, college, life, I never did anything about it," he said. "But I'm glad you're here. I hope I see your mom too one of these days. I have a lot to tell her."

"She's going to try and visit me every couple of weeks. We had a great time last weekend. She didn't want to come back here, but she did."

"It must be tough for her," he acknowledged, as Savannah nodded. They were both thinking about Alexa, and then Henry finally got up, gave her a hug, and went to his own room. Daisy had slept in her own bed that night. And Savannah lay under the covers thinking about what Henry had told her. She didn't see what difference it made that he was gay. But she was from New York, not from Charleston. Things were different here.

Chapter 13

As Julianne had predicted, Turner Ashby asked Savannah out again. They went to RB's Seafood Restaurant and Raw Bar for dinner, and they talked about more personal things. He told her about losing his mother the year before. He said they were doing okay, but it was hard on his father and younger brothers. There were tears in his eyes as he said it, so it was obvious that it was hard on him as well, but he didn't say it. He didn't want to look weak to her. Turner said he was glad he was leaving for college, it was too sad at home without her. And Savannah talked about growing up essentially without a dad. They both agreed that it was nice she was getting to know him now, although it was difficult dealing with her evil stepmom. Savannah told him about it and he was shocked, although he had never liked her either, and always thought she was a snob. Now he knew she was cruel as well, and rude.

Turner was a very kind, thoughtful, respectful person, and he treated her with all the grace and good manners for which the South was known. He said he really enjoyed her company, and wanted to see her more often, but she said her mother was coming to visit the following weekend. He asked if she minded if he'd drop by the house sometime, and she said that was fine. It was more like an old-fashioned courtship than two high school seniors dating, but at the end of the second date, he kissed her, which Savannah liked a lot. They were having a very nice time together, and she promised to introduce him to her mother when she came back to town.

She told Alexa all about it, who started getting nervous again. What if Savannah fell in love? What if they got married and she stayed in Charleston? She rattled her worries off to her mother, who laughed at her this time.

"She's seventeen years old. She's not going anywhere. They're just having fun." Alexa realized it was true and calmed down.

Her nerves were on edge these days. The trial was seven weeks away, and she had a thousand details on her mind. No new victims had turned up, and she was preparing her case with infinite precision and care.

The day after Savannah had gone out with Turner Ashby, she drove over to see her grandmother on her own. She had a free afternoon, and she thought it might be a nice thing to do, although she wondered if she should have called first. She found her sitting on the porch, dozing in her rocking chair with a book in her hand. Eugenie's eyes flew open as soon as she heard footsteps on the porch and she was surprised to see Savannah looking down at her, in a yellow sweatshirt and jeans.

"What are you doing here?" her

grandmother asked sharply, startled to see Savannah there.

"I thought you might like a visit, so I came by," Savannah said cautiously, as her grandmother frowned.

"You should have called first. We don't like northern ways here," she scolded her. "Southerners are polite."

"I'm sorry." Savannah looked instantly apologetic and somewhat mortified. "I'll come back another time and call first." She started to leave and her grand-mother pointed sternly to a chair.

"No, you're here now. Sit down. Why did you come here?" She was curious about her, and Savannah looked scared. Her grandmother was a daunting figure, even as an old lady.

"I just thought it would be nice to visit. I like hearing all the stories about the war, the generals, the battles. We don't learn much about that in New York." It was true, but she had come mostly to be kind to an old woman, but couldn't say that to her.

"What would you like to know?" Her grandmother smiled and was intrigued by the request. There was southern blood in her after all.

"Tell me about your family. It's part of my history too."

"Yes, it is," Eugenie acknowledged, and she liked the idea of sharing it with this young girl. It was the best way for ancestors to be remembered and history to be passed on, telling stories from one generation to another.

She began with her great-grandfather, when he had come from France, and made her way down through several generations, marriages, and generals, when they came to Charleston, how much land they owned, and how many slaves. She made no apology for it, she said it was essential for cultivating the land, and how many slaves you owned was considered part of their wealth in those days. Savannah winced at that. It was a new idea to her, and not one she liked any more than any other culture that had owned slaves.

They eventually made it to the Civil War, and Eugenie's eyes lit up. She knew every date and detail about every major battle in the South, all the ones that had been fought in and around Charleston, who had won them, who had lost. She added personal stories about who people were married to, if they'd been widowed, and if they'd re-married. She was a walking encyclope-dia of Civil War and Charleston history, and Savannah was fascinated as she listened. Her grandmother had a fine memory for dates and details and talked for hours. No one had ever listened to her in such rapt attention for as long. It was dinnertime when she stopped. She had been revitalized by remembering every detail and sharing it with Savan-nah. And she had promised to share some books with her as well. Savannah actually loved it, and it intrigued her to think that she was related to some of those people. It was a whole other side of her life and history that she had never known anything about and wouldn't have otherwise, were it not for her grandmother's recollections.

Savannah thanked her profusely be-fore she left, helped her into the small parlor where she liked to sit at night, and left her with one of her two ancient maids and kissed her cheek.

"That's South Carolina blood in your veins," she reminded Savannah, "and don't you forget it! That's not just Yankee blood in you!"

"Yes, Grandmother," Savannah said, smiling at her. She had had a wonderful afternoon, and was still thinking about it as she drove back to Thousand Oaks.

Daisy complained about where she'd been so late, and Savannah said quietly that she'd been to see their grandmother.

"All by yourself?" Daisy looked surprised as Savannah nodded. "It's so boring there!" Daisy hated going to see her, there was nothing for her to do, and her grandmother was so old. She hated all that "general" stuff her grandmother talked about.

"No, it's not boring," Savannah defended her. "She knows everything about everything and everyone in the South. I learned a lot." Daisy made a face in response. She couldn't think of a worse way to spend an afternoon. When her grandmother tried to tell her about her roots, she didn't want to know. She'd rather stay home and watch TV. Seven years older, Savannah had soaked it up like a sponge.

Daisy's parents were out at a dinner party that night, together for once, so Savannah never got a chance to tell her father about the visit. But his mother told him the next day when he stopped by to see her after lunch.

"She's a very good girl," Eugenie said, looking at him. He had no idea who she meant, and he thought it was the maid, whom she often referred to that way. She also called male employees "boys," which seemed rude. But it was of her times.

"Who?" Tom said, looking blank.

"Your daughter," she said with a spark in her eye he hadn't seen in a while.

"Daisy?"

"Savannah! She came here for a history lesson, about the South. She listens carefully, remembers everything. That's southern blood in those pretty young veins. She wanted to know everything about our family, and more. She's a very special girl."

"I know she is," he said, looking amazed. "She came here alone?"

"Of course," his mother snapped at him. "You don't suppose your wife brought her here? Luisa is going to drive me insane if she doesn't stop complaining about that child." His mother looked sour about it and shook her head, which surprised him too.

"Does she call you about it?" Tom looked upset. He knew Luisa had called her once, but not more than that, about Savannah.

"Almost every night. She wanted me to use my influence on you to send her back. That's not right if her life is in danger, which you say it is, and that's probably true. Why would you lie about that?"

"I haven't. There have been some very upsetting letters sent to Savannah, presumably from a man who killed eighteen women. He's in custody, but he's got friends on the outside who have been dropping the letters off at their apartment. If it's him. If it's not, it's someone else just as bad. I think Alexa is right to want her out of New York."

"So do I. There's no reason to risk that child. Or even frighten her. Eighteen women, my word, how awful . . . what is Alexa thinking, taking cases like that?" She looked critical as she said it.

"She's an assistant district attorney," Tom said quietly. "She has no choice. She has to take what they assign her. That's her job."

"Noble of her, but much too dangerous, for a woman," his mother said, a little more gently. It almost amused Tom that now his mother was protecting her and Savannah, after telling him to banish them in the first place. How soon people forget their own perfidies and crimes. "In any case, Luisa wants Savannah run out of town, and she expected me to do it, and tell you to send her back. She got what she wanted ten years ago. She got you. She has Daisy. She got her boys back, she doesn't need to hurt Savannah now to prove the point further, or her mother. We all did quite enough ten years ago. I told Luisa to stop hounding me about it. She wasn't pleased." Tom imagined that she wasn't. Her mother-in-law had been her chief ally and partner in crime all those years before and ever since.

"Do you regret it, Mother?" he asked her honestly. He had never dared to ask her before. She hesitated before she answered, sitting in her rocking chair with a shawl over her lap, and looking very old and fragile. He knew she was less frail than she appeared, and strong as iron in her will and opinions.

"Sometimes. It depends how Alexa's life has turned out. If she's happy, I suppose it was all right. I don't know," she said, looking distressed. "I didn't want Daisy to be illegitimate, and Luisa was putting a lot of pressure on me then too, but I was younger then." He had fallen right into Luisa and his mother's trap for him. She had seduced him and gotten pregnant all in the same night, although he had been courting her secretly for several weeks and would have gotten there on his own. He had never gotten over Luisa leaving him for someone else, it had gnawed at him for all those years. He loved Alexa, but Luisa had been more powerful and more glamorous, and more southern. Alexa had

been kind and open and naïve and loving, and trusted him completely. He still
felt sick when he thought about it. "Is
she happy?" his mother asked him then,
and he sighed.

"I don't think so. I've never seen such
sad eyes. She's alone with Savannah,
and there's no one in her life. She's a
wonderful mother."

"Well, you can't go back to her now
and leave Luisa because Alexa is
alone." She looked panicked at the
thought.

"I don't think she'd have me, and
she's right," he said sadly. The idea had
crossed his mind.

"She probably is," his mother agreed,
which shocked him. "If you loved her,
you never should have left her for Luisa,
no matter what I said. You went right
back to her like a little lamb, and sent
Alexa to New York." He nodded. It was
true. He had wanted Luisa back, to
prove a point, but he loved Alexa. What
he didn't want was the life he had now,
with a woman he hated, who hated him
more. He had gotten what he deserved
in spades, and knew it. "I just want

Luisa to stop calling me about Savan-
nah. She needs to be decent to her.
She owes Alexa that. She took care of
Luisa's boys."

"I've told her that. She doesn't want
to hear it."

"She told me Savannah is a brat.
She's no brat, she's a lovely girl. She
came here all on her own, to see me.
She said she'd come to visit again. I
hope she does."

"I'm sure she will," he said kindly. Savannah was that kind of girl, to visit old
ladies and keep them company. She
had a warm heart. And both her father
and grandmother knew it. So did Daisy,
and her brothers. Only Luisa didn't care.
She had no heart at all. She had manip-
ulated him to recoup him, and had tor-
tured him ever since.

"I'm glad someone in this family
wants to know our history. Luisa isn't interested. She has her own. She has as
many generals in her family as we do,"
Eugenie said, looking miffed, and Tom
fought not to laugh. His mother took
those things very seriously, and always
had. Even he had a little trouble with it

sometimes. There were too many generals to count. And hearing about the battles and Confederate bravery and victories had bored him all his life. He was no history buff. His mother was.

Tom left his mother after that, and thanked Savannah that night for visiting her, and said that her grandmother had loved it and hoped she'd come back soon. Luisa overheard and snapped at them that Savannah shouldn't disturb her, she was too delicate and old. Tom turned on her instantly and told her he wanted Savannah to visit his mother. Luisa sniffed and said not another word. When she had spoken to her that afternoon, her mother-in-law had said the same. The tides had turned, and Luisa didn't like it one bit.

Savannah had told her mother about the visit, and the history lesson, and about Henry and his partner Jeff. She kept her abreast of the local news in their daily calls.

Her mother said she wasn't surprised about Henry. He was never interested in girls once he hit puberty, although he was young then, only fourteen. She had had a question in her mind once or twice, but never dared broach it with Tom. He was so closed on the subject, and Savannah said he still was, they all were. She said that Luisa, his own mother, pretended Henry wasn't gay. Alexa said she hoped he was happy, and would love to see him one of these days. She was coming back that weekend, and they were planning to stay at the Wentworth Mansion again. She'd made a reservation for the big suite.

"So am I going to meet that boy?" she asked about Turner, and Savannah grinned.

"Maybe. We'll see. If he's not busy. He has a game this weekend."

"Maybe we can go. If you're not ashamed of me."

"You know I'm not. I'm really, really proud of you, Mom, and you know it."

"I'm proud of you too, sweetheart," her mother reassured her. And after they hung up, she went back to work with Sam and Jack Jones, and Savannah went to meet Turner for a walk before dinner, and a lot of kisses.

Daisy saw her come in afterward. She slipped in discreetly before dinner, and Daisy was on her way back from the kitchen with a snack.

"So?"

"So what?" Savannah asked innocently.

"Don't give me that. I saw you leave with him. Is he cute? Did he kiss you?" Savannah decided to be honest with her little sister. She loved that idea, having a sister. And so did Daisy.

"He's cute. *And* he kissed me."

"Oh, yuk!!" Daisy said, running up the stairs. "How disgusting." And then she leaned over the banister with another question. "Is he your boyfriend?"

"Nope." Savannah shook her head, smiling. "Just a boy I like."

"Too bad," Daisy said, and scampered to her room, laughing all the way.

Chapter 14

This time when Alexa came to Charleston to see Savannah for the weekend, everything felt more familiar and comfortable for her. She didn't have to go through the shock of reentry into a world she had once known and loved and lost. The second time the Wentworth Mansion felt like home to both of them, and Alexa even managed to be pleasant to Tom when she saw him when he dropped Savannah off. Alexa had relaxed, and he could see it. It made him brave enough to ask her if she would have lunch with him. She didn't want to, and she didn't want to miss a minute with Savannah, but she didn't want to be rude to him either. He had helped her out in a major way with Savannah, and even risked Luisa's fury. Alexa hesitated before she answered, but when she saw Savannah's eyes pleading with her, she finally nodded and agreed to lunch with him.

"Not long, though," she cautioned. "I want time with Savannah. I'm here for her."

"Of course."

Alexa had the feeling that he wanted to bury the hatchet, somewhere other than in her back this time, or her heart. She wasn't ready for it yet, but she could almost conceive of being friends with him someday, not close friends, but civil ones, like at Savannah's wedding, or college graduation. She assumed he had the same goal in mind. The cold war between them had gone on long enough. She was slowly getting over it at last.

He suggested meeting her at Magnolias the next day, and Savannah said she could go to Turner's soccer game while they had lunch. Everyone was happy, although Alexa would have been happier having lunch with her daughter, but she had agreed, and Savannah thanked her when they went upstairs to their suite. It was just as pretty this time, and the flowers in it were even bigger. And they each had a glass of champagne to celebrate their weekend. There were chocolate-covered strawberries that were delicious with the champagne. And they each had only one glass. Alexa didn't like Savannah drinking, but once in a while, on a festive occasion, it was okay, and she didn't drink much either. She was nervous about her lunch with Tom the next day. They weren't friends, after all, at least not yet.

"Okay, so tell me about this boy you're so crazy about. When am I going to meet him? How about after the soccer game? We could have coffee or something."

Savannah hesitated and then nodded, looking embarrassed. "He's nice, Mom. It's not serious or anything. He's captain of the soccer team and he's hoping to go to Georgia Tech or SMU."

"A nice southern boy," her mother commented with a grin, but she wasn't sarcastic about it, just amused. They hardly ever went north for school. She'd noticed it when she lived there too.

"He has three younger brothers, and he lost his mom last year."

"I'm sorry," Alexa said softly. "He's nice to you? That's all I care about. My only requirement is that he treats you well. How often do you see him?" She had lost track in the chaos of her life right now, getting ready for the trial.

"He's nice to me," Savannah reassured her. "I see him every day at school. Sometimes we have lunch in the cafeteria, and we go out a couple of times a week, for dinner and a movie."

"Are you sleeping with him?" her mother asked her bluntly, and Savannah shook her head. It was too soon. "You're still on the Pill?" Alexa confirmed, and Savannah smiled at her. She had lost her virginity at sixteen and her mother had made her peace with it. Alexa was realistic, and Savannah had only slept with one boy so far, but her mother wanted to be sure she was prepared if something happened here with Turner. "And condoms, please!" she reminded her. Savannah groaned and rolled her eyes.

"I know, I know. I'm not stupid. It's too soon anyway. I hardly know him." Still, she liked him a great deal. A *great* deal. And they were kissing more and more. Things were getting serious and heated.

"Well, just in case, be prepared. People get carried away sometimes. Not that I'd remember," Alexa chuckled ruefully. She wouldn't have time anyway. She hardly got time to go to the bathroom or sleep, she was working so hard on the upcoming trial.

They had dinner at a cozy little bistro that night and ate fresh crab. It was a late dinner and they walked back to the hotel arm in arm, feeling closer than ever. They ordered a movie through the hotel, one of their favorites, and after it was over, they went to sleep in the huge comfortable bed, and woke up feeling relaxed and rested in the morning.

After breakfast, they did a little shopping as they had the week before, and then Savannah went to the soccer game and Alexa went to Magnolias, to meet Tom for lunch. He was waiting when she got there, and looked nervous. So was she.

They had a quiet table in the back, and were looking at the menus, when Alexa put hers down and looked at him.

"I'm sorry to say this, but this is weird. I just had to say it out loud. Maybe you feel that way too."

"Yes, I do." He had to laugh, she had always had a way with the truth. She put it right out there and refused to hide it or dress it up. It was anything but southern in style, but he had always loved that about her. No subterfuge. No games. She hadn't changed a bit. And if anything, he thought she was more beautiful now, eleven years later. She had grown into her looks.

"Why do we feel so weird?" Tom asked, as he looked at her. Luisa had no idea he was with her.

"Are you kidding?" Alexa looked at him. "You left me. I've spent the last ten years hating you. What am I doing having lunch with you? And our daughter is living with you. That's all pretty crazy."

"Maybe not. You had every right to hate me. And you're very gracious to have lunch with me, but you always were compassionate and forgiving."

"Don't count on that yet," she said honestly, and he laughed again. "So why do you feel weird? Did you hate me too?"

"I had nothing to hate you for," he said sadly. "I just had regrets, about what happened."

"It didn't 'happen.' You did it. With Luisa's help, and your mother's. They made the decision for you, to get rid of me and go back to her, and you did what they wanted. I guess you wanted it too." She looked wistful as she said it, and so did he.

He shook his head then. "It wasn't that simple. I didn't know what I wanted. I wanted to get my pride back because Luisa had left me, but I was in love with you."

"Then you did a really stupid thing, Tom." It helped her to say it, and she felt better after she did.

"Yes, I did. I agree with you. Totally. And if it's any consolation, I've regretted it ever since." She didn't want him to go there. She didn't want to know. They ordered lunch then, and both ordered crab cakes and lobster bisque. It had always been their favorite meal. Some things hadn't changed. Alexa told herself that the only thing they still had in common was the food.

They talked about other things then. Savannah. Her trial. His bank. Travis and Henry. Alexa mentioned in passing that Savannah had said Henry was gay and liked him a lot. She didn't think his lifestyle shocking and expected Tom to be reasonable about it, but she saw instantly that he looked pained.

"I'm sorry. Are you upset about it?" It was hard to believe in this day and age, but she also knew how conservative Tom was, and old-fashioned.

"Sometimes. I guess it's just the way he is. But it's not a life that I wanted for one of my sons. But in the end, I just want him to be happy. His mother denies it, which makes it harder for Henry."

"That's stupid of her," Alexa said bluntly, and then winced. "Sorry. I just feel sorry for Henry if he can't be himself with both of you. Is Travis okay with it? He's as conservative as you are." She knew them all well, even if she hadn't seen them for ten years, and left the boys in their teens. It was totally odd to her to be sitting at a lunch table with Tom, talking as though they were old friends, instead of her being the woman who had loved him, and been his wife, and whom he had spurned for another. Life really was strange.

"I think Travis tries to be understanding about it, but you're right, he's pretty straitlaced. The boys aren't as close anymore, now that they're grown up. They're very different."

"They always were," Alexa said quietly. "That's too bad if they're not close," she said sadly. "They were then." Tom was embarrassed not to have been more supportive of his son. It was one more thing for him to feel guilty about, like so many others. He had a lot on his list to repent for, and Alexa was at the top of that list.

"I meant what I said before," he said over coffee and warm peach cobbler for dessert. He took his with vanilla ice cream, she without. Same old habits again. For an instant, she could distinctly remember being his wife, what it had felt like, and how much she had loved it, particularly when Savannah was little. They had been so in love then, and Alexa had stayed in love with him right till the end.

"About what?" Alexa asked as she ate the dessert that melted in her mouth. She'd forgotten what he'd said earlier. They had touched on a lot of subjects, including their daughter, who he acknowledged was wonderful and gave her full credit for, which she deserved.

"I meant it when I said that I've regretted leaving you every day since." He looked sorrowful and depressed as he said it, and her eyes hardened at the words.

"I'm sorry to hear that, Tom. That's a hard way to live."

"Yes, it is." He was feeling sorry for himself. Alexa's eyes went cold.

"So is getting thrown out by your husband whom you love and trust, for another woman, who abandoned him before, and came back because it was convenient. It would have been nice if you'd seen through that." He nodded, he could see again how hurt Alexa was, and how unforgiving. Her walls had gone up the minute he brought up the subject.

"I'm not suggesting you take me back," he explained to her.

"Good, because I wouldn't. Not in a hundred years." She wanted that entirely clear, particularly if they were going to attempt to be friends. She wanted clear boundaries with him, and no confusion, for him, or herself. He was still a very attractive man, and she had loved him. She didn't want this to be dangerous for her. And he would be if she fell for him again. He had already proven to her once in no uncertain terms that he wasn't a man of his word. She could never trust him again, no matter how much she had loved him, or how handsome and charming he still was.

"I just wanted you to know how sorry I am."

"So am I. I've never trusted another man again, and probably never will." She blamed it entirely on him.

"That's awful," he said sadly, feeling guilty again and looking woebegone.

"Maybe. But it's real. For me anyway. I could never trust another man not to do the same thing. I thought we were married forever."

"So did I. And then Luisa came back, and I fucked it all up, for both of us." Alexa nodded. She didn't want to rehash their marriage with him over lunch. "Just know that I regret it, and I've never had a happy day since. She's a miserable person."

"Then why don't you divorce her? Not for me. For yourself."

"I just don't want to go through that again. Our divorce nearly killed me."

"Funny, me too," Alexa said bitterly, and then laughed at herself. "Sorry, I guess I'm still pretty pissed. My mother says I have to get over it, but it's hard to do. I saw a shrink about it for five years, and finally stopped going. I was just as pissed after five years, and just as hurt, and just as bitter. I guess it takes longer than that. For me, anyway. I'm a slow healer. I broke my arm once, and it took six months to heal instead of six weeks."

"I know," he said, near tears, "I was with you."

"Oh." She looked down at her plate for a minute and then back at him. "Look, let's be honest. I'm sure somewhere I still love you. If I didn't, I wouldn't hate you so much, or wouldn't have. I don't think I hate you right now. I'm not even pissed. We had a nice lunch and I enjoyed it. We have a beautiful daughter, and I loved you with all my heart. Maybe I always will in some secret place in my heart. Maybe 'until death do us part' is for real. I hope not, but it could be. I hate that you left me for Luisa and abandoned us. But you did.

"You're doing a nice thing for Savannah and I appreciate it, seriously. I don't have to worry about her right now because she's with you, and that means a lot. It's a huge weight off my shoulders. And you're still the most handsome man I know, and the most charming. I loved living here with you, and the South, until I hated that too because you were southern. And maybe we can be friends now. But I don't want to fool either of us that we can do it again. I won't do to Luisa what she did to me, or what you did. I won't sneak around with you. I don't want to fall in love with you again. I think it would be lethal for me, particularly if you hurt me again. I don't ever want to give that another chance, whether you're sorry or not. I can't. I don't have it in me. It's taken me over ten years to get this far, to get over you. And I want to keep going. Maybe now we can be friends, but that's all we can ever be, and all I want from you, if that. And if Luisa makes you miserable, then divorce her. But even if you do, all I want is to be your friend. We're Savannah's parents, so it'll be nice if we can be civilized. But I don't want to hold out any hope to you that it's more than that." She had been totally clear and totally fair with him. She always had been, which was one of the million things he loved about her and had forgotten, or tried to.

"I get it, Alexa. I'm sorry that I even brought it up. I just wanted you to know that I still love you and I'm sorry." Hearing it made her mad again. It wasn't fair of him to tell her that he was in love with her. Not now, ten years later, after all she'd been through since, all the pain, all the agony, all the tears over him. She looked at him with fury in her eyes.

"Don't ever tell me that again. It's self-serving. You're sorry now, but where were you for the last ten years? With Luisa. If you never say that again, maybe we can be friends. Deal?"

He nodded somberly, and knew he was lucky she was even willing to do that. "Deal. I'm sorry."

"Good. Go home to your wife now, or whatever you want to do. I'm going to meet Savannah at the soccer game." He nodded, a little shaken, or even a lot, by what she had said. Somehow, foolishly, he had hoped he could still get her back. He had thought of it when he saw her in New York, but didn't know how to do it. And he hoped that she might feel that way too. She didn't. He had hurt her way too much for her to ever come back to him. She might forgive him, but she would never take him back. There was no doubt in his mind now. Or hers.

They walked outside after he paid the check, and she smiled at him. "Thank you. I feel better." She had waited ten years to say those things to him, and had finally had the chance. She knew that that had been a gift. He didn't feel better, and she could see it. But that was no longer her problem.

She left him outside the restaurant and drove to the soccer game, and found Savannah just leaving the bleachers. There was a tall handsome boy waiting for her on the field, and other kids leaving the game too. Savannah was smiling at him, with a whole world in her eyes, and it made Alexa's heart ache to see it. She told herself that if this boy hurt her, she would have to kill him. Not really, but she would want to. She was still shaken by what Tom had said to her at lunch. If she had let him, he would have dumped Luisa and come back to her. Maybe. Or had an affair with her and broken her heart again. If his mother had even let him do that, or if he had the balls, which she knew he didn't. Luisa and his mother had them. It hadn't been fair of him to say he still loved her, but at least he had said he was sorry and seemed to mean it. Maybe that was enough. She felt lighter than she had in years.

Savannah introduced her to Turner when her mother walked across the field and reached them.

"Turner, this is my mom."

"Hi," Alexa said, smiling broadly. He looked like a sweet boy, and so young. And as she looked at him, she remembered that he had lost his mother and felt sorry for him.

"It's very nice to meet you, ma'am. I've heard a lot of great things about you from Savannah." He was very southern and very polite, but looked sincere.

"I've heard some pretty nice things about you too. How was the game?"

"We won," he said, grinning and pleased, as Savannah smiled at him and then her mother.

"Turner scored the winning points. Two of them," she said proudly, as her mother looked at them both and felt a thousand years old, but happy for them.

She took them to their favorite hang-out for a burger and shake. They chatted easily for an hour, and then Savannah and her mother went back to the hotel to get their nails done. It was a luxury they both enjoyed. Alexa told her daughter that she liked Turner very much, and Savannah looked delighted.

When they went back to the room after their manicures, Alexa told Savannah what had happened at lunch. She never kept secrets from her. They were best friends as well as mother and daughter, although Alexa was always clear what her role was, as the mother.

"Daddy asked me in a roundabout way today if I'd come back to him—he said that he still loves me and regrets what he did."

"What did you say to him?" Savannah asked with interest, watching her mother's eyes. She looked happy, happier than she had in a long time.

"I told him never to say that to me again. It's enough if we can be friends. That in itself is a miracle after what happened. I could never trust him again. I would never, ever trust him. And I don't want to go there again."

"What did he say?"

"I think he was shocked," Alexa said honestly.

"Was he pissed?"

"I don't think so. Sad maybe. It wasn't even fair for him to ask me, or imply it. It's been too long, and he hurt me too much." Savannah nodded. She agreed. She knew how hurt her mother had been, or could guess.

"I understand, Mom. I think you did the right thing." Even Savannah remembered her mother crying for hours every day, for years. It had been a terrible time. He couldn't just walk back in now, because he was bored and didn't like the choice he made. What about Alexa and what it had done to her? "I don't think he'll ever leave Luisa anyway," Savannah said wisely. "She runs the show. And he lets her do it."

"He always did," Alexa said quietly, "even when he was married to me, at the end. They deserve each other." Savannah nodded, although she felt sorry for her father too. Luisa was a terrible person. But he had made that choice, twice.

They had a wonderful evening and

talked late into the night. Turner called Savannah, and Alexa invited him to brunch with them the next day. And Travis called them in the morning. He wanted to see Alexa, and he and Scarlette dropped by after church for a few minutes. Savannah and Alexa were too lazy to go this time, and they didn't want to run into Luisa again. They were glad they hadn't gone when Travis said they had just gone to church with his mother.

He sat down with Alexa in their living room and talked about old times, and his life now. He apologized for not writing to her, and she said she understood. He had been young and his mother had forbidden it. Alexa knew that, although out of loyalty to his mother he didn't say it. He was as polite and sweet as he had been as a child, and he was very proud when he introduced her to Scarlette. She seemed like a nice girl, and Alexa hoped they would make each other happy. They talked about the wedding for a few minutes and how stressful it was organizing everything, and then they left. They were going to have lunch with Scarlette's parents to work on the guest list for the wedding.

The rest of the day sped by, and then it was time for Alexa to leave again. Tom met them in the lobby, as he had before, to pick up Savannah. Alexa thanked him again for lunch the day before. He had taken to heart all that she had said, and he met her eyes sadly.

"Thank you for being willing to have lunch with me." He realized now what a concession it had been for her, and how brave she had to be to do it. He understood now more than ever how much he had hurt her. He had focused on his own pain and loss for almost eleven years, but had never fully understood the depth of hers, and now he did. He had lost her forever. Just when he wanted her back. For her, it was way too little way too late, and no matter how much she had loved him, he was a man she could never trust again. For Tom, it felt awful. Hope died in him the day before. For Alexa, it had died ten years before.

Savannah kissed her mother goodbye again, and went home with her father. Her mother had promised to come back in two weeks. The time was going by, and Savannah was used to it here now. In some ways it felt like home, and in other ways she felt like a stranger. It was what Alexa said she had felt when she lived there, because no matter how much you love it, if you're not born in the South, you will never really be one of them. And now Savannah was beginning to understand that too. They still talked about southerners and Yankees, and the flag of the Confederacy was embedded in their hearts forever, and flew from many homes.

She noticed that her father looked unhappy as they drove home, and she glanced at him with concern.

"You okay, Dad?" He nodded and smiled at her, but his eyes were sad. She suspected that what her mother had said the day before had affected him deeply. But Savannah didn't blame her a bit.

When they got back to the house, Luisa was waiting for him. She was wearing a black Chanel suit and a lot of jewelry and makeup. She scolded him for being late. They were going to dinner with friends. This was his life now. For better or worse. It was the life and the woman he had chosen. The one he had truly loved, and who had loved him, was gone.

Chapter 15

It was the beginning of April, with only a month until the trial. It was still cold in New York, and it snowed the whole week after Alexa came back from her weekend with Savannah. In Charleston it was spring, and flowers were blooming everywhere. There were azaleas and wisteria vines, cherry blossoms. The garden at Thousand Oaks was resplendent and a fleet of gardeners worked on it every day.

Everything about the two cities and their lives there was in sharp contrast. In New York it was freezing cold, snowing, barren, gray, and Alexa was preparing the trial of a man who had murdered eighteen young women. The weather was as cold and dark as what she was doing.

In Charleston everything was blossoming, the weather was warm, and Turner and Savannah were falling in love. Daisy teased her about it constantly, and all the girls at school were jealous. He invited her to the senior prom. And her father allowed her to invite him to dinner at the house. Luisa wasn't welcoming, but at least she wasn't overtly rude to him since the Beaumonts and his father were friends.

The best part about Savannah being in Charleston, other than meeting Daisy, dating Turner Ashby, and developing a relationship with her grandmother, was that she had a chance to do things with her father that she never would have otherwise.

He went on long walks with her, showed her the places where he played as a boy, took her to the famous plantations outside the city, Drayton Hall, Magnolia, Middleton Place, and Boone Hall. They explored them together, and went for walks on the beaches near Mt.

Pleasant. They spent hours talking and getting to know each other. She had a real father now, not just a cardboard figure who showed up twice a year in New York, and wouldn't let her into his real life. And he knew for certain now, as did she, that he would never shut her out again. He wanted Savannah in his life.

He took both girls to the aquarium. He played tennis with them. He took Savannah to the country club and introduced her to everyone. And the more he did, the more Luisa felt he had betrayed her, but Tom no longer cared. Savannah's stay in Charleston, and Luisa's reaction to it, had driven a wedge between them that widened the gap that had been there before Savannah arrived. Tom and Luisa hardly spoke to each other anymore, and Luisa was either out, in a rage with him, or in bed with a damp cloth on her head. She just couldn't get past it and didn't try. She hadn't had a single kind word, or made a single hospitable gesture toward Savannah, since she arrived. Her father apologized to her for it, but he just couldn't make his wife behave. It was open civil war.

Her grandmother got a touch of the flu, and Savannah went over several times to keep her company and nurse her. She had read all the books her grandmother had given her, and was learning a great deal about the Civil War.

Savannah was sitting with her one afternoon on the porch, when Luisa came by unannounced. She looked furious the moment she saw Savannah there and told her to go home. Savannah started to get up. She didn't want to cause a problem.

"Sit down," her grandmother told her harshly, and looked at her daughter-in-law. "She's not going anywhere, Luisa. Why don't you try to relax? She's not going to hurt you. She's just a child. She doesn't want anything from you. And her mother doesn't want him either." Her son had reported to her what Alexa had said to him over lunch. His mother wasn't surprised, and respected her for it. She told Tom that Alexa was right, and at least had pride and self-respect. She was sure she probably did love him, but she didn't want a man who could hurt her that badly, and wait ten years to come back, when it was convenient for him. Tom had been shocked by what his mother said.

"I have no idea what you're talking about," Luisa said grandly, as Eugenie looked at her with narrowed eyes.

"Yes, you do. You're afraid that Tom will do the same thing to you that you and he did to Alexa. He won't. She won't let him. You've got him. And Savannah has nothing to do with it. She's stuck here. So there's no reason to punish her."

"I haven't punished her!" Luisa looked outraged. "Did *she* tell you that?" She looked daggers at Savannah, and her mother-in-law shook her head.

"No. Tom did. He says you've been mean-spirited and rude to her since she arrived." Eugenie pulled no punches, southern or not. And she ran the show. Savannah was mortified to be listening to their conversation. She didn't want to defend her stepmother, but she didn't want to confront or condemn her either. She was too formidable an opponent to

take on, and already bad enough without that. "I think you should just sit back
and enjoy yourself for a change, and
have some fun. You got him. He's not
going anywhere."

"How do you know that?"

"He's not that kind of man." She knew
her son, and also that he didn't have
the guts. "You dragged him out of that
marriage, and I pushed him. Without our
help, he's not moving. And a seventeen-
year-old girl is no threat to you. All she's
doing here is waiting for her mother to
finish her trial so she can go home."

"Why is she spending so much time
with you?" Luisa sounded suspicious
and suspected a plot between them. It
was the kind of thing she would have
done, but not Savannah. It was the far-
thest thing from Savannah's mind.

"Because she's a nice girl," her
grandmother said kindly. She had grown
fond of her in a short time, and she was
grateful for the time they had shared.
"And she's probably lonely here, without
her mother. You haven't done anything
to make her feel at home."

"I . . . I . . ." She started to splutter, but she had no response.

"Why don't you come back and visit some other time, when I'm alone?" She was sending Luisa away, and Savannah stood up, embarrassed to be witness to a conversation where they talked about her as though she weren't there. Luisa acted like she didn't exist.

"I have homework to do anyway," Savannah said, bending to kiss her grandmother. She promised to come back soon, and a few minutes later she drove away, and Luisa was left with the mother-in-law who knew too much, and had been part of it, but now held it against her.

"I thought you'd be good to him," she said as Luisa sat down across from her, angry that Eugenie had championed Savannah's cause, but not hers. Savannah was a lot easier for the old woman to love than Luisa. "You haven't been good to him. You've been mean to my son. You won him, like a dog at a fair. He's yours now, he has been for ten years. There's no need to kick him. He might be nicer to you, if you treat him well."

She was defending her son, with good reason. Luisa had treated him badly for years.

"I really don't know what you're talking about, Mother Beaumont." Luisa would have liked to say that they were the rantings of an old woman, but they both knew that she was totally clear-headed and what she was saying was true. Luisa pretended to look hurt but in fact was livid.

"I think you ought to go home and think about it," Eugenie said to her. It was late in the afternoon, and she was tired. Savannah had stayed for a long time, and her grandmother had enjoyed it. But now she was worn out. Too much so to deal with Luisa. "You'll lose him in the end, if you treat him badly. Alexa won't have him back. But someone else will. He's a fine-looking man."

"I've already lost him," Luisa said hoarsely, looking crestfallen, and for once was sincere. "He never loved me, not since I got him back. He never stopped loving her." They both knew it was the truth, and Eugenie had regretted it ever since. Her son had been miserable for ten years, and in great part it was her fault. She felt guilty for it now, and was repaying the debt to Savannah, and felt guilty about her too. Luisa was only thinking about herself, and the fact that her husband didn't love her, and never stopped loving Alexa.

Her mother-in-law knew she was right. "We were wrong, Luisa. Both of us. We had no right to do what we did. We hurt both of them, and their child. If I were you, I'd do everything I could to make it up to him, and to Savannah while she's here. That would mean a lot to him." Luisa was bereft of speech for once, nodded at her mother-in-law, and went back to her car. She was no different to Savannah that night, or to Tom, but she was very, very quiet. Tom could see she had something on her mind. He stayed away from her, because it was easier for him. Luisa went upstairs instead of having dinner with them. She said she had one of her sick headaches, and went to bed.

* * *

Spring was in full bloom when Alexa came back to Charleston again. She was bringing two important things with her, Savannah knew, her college acceptance letters, and her grandmother from New York. Savannah was excited about both, and threw herself into Muriel's arms the moment she saw her.

"You look wonderful, Savannah," her grandmother said, looking pleased. She'd been afraid that being away for so long had been hard for her granddaughter. Instead, she looked happy, and was thriving, and seemed even more grown up and poised. She could see why Alexa was worried. Savannah seemed so comfortable in Charleston that it was hard to believe she would ever want to leave. But Muriel was still certain that ultimately she would want to come home. And New York with her mother was home.

"Okay, so shall we open the letters?" Alexa asked excitedly after Savannah greeted her grandmother in the suite. Savannah hadn't allowed her mother to open them and read them to her. She didn't want to hear the news on the phone. They had all finally come in that week, some several weeks late, others right on time. Some were thicker envelopes than others, which usually meant acceptance. She had heard back from every college where she'd applied, and she looked nervous as she held the envelopes. Her future was about to be decided, and where she would spend the next four years. And more than likely, she would have several choices. She hoped they were the ones she wanted, and not just her backups.

There were six envelopes. Some of her friends had applied to a dozen schools, but Savannah had narrowed it down to six. Alexa and Muriel sat on the couch and waited with bated breath. Savannah began.

She opened Stanford first, and they had turned her down. She looked crestfallen for a moment, and her mother quickly said that she wouldn't have let her go there anyway, so it was a moot point, which softened the blow. Savannah knew that was true since her mother had said it all along, unless it was her only option.

Harvard declined her as well. Savannah hadn't been in love with it either. The school seemed too big and scary to her.

Brown had wait-listed her, and congratulated her on her good work. She was a little disappointed by that. Brown was her second choice.

That left Princeton, George Washington, and Duke. She opened Duke next and got in. The three women in the living room of the suite let out a cheer. They hugged each other, Savannah was grinning, and they sat down again. She had a school. A good one.

"Why do I feel like I'm at the Academy Awards? And for best picture . . . ," Muriel said as Savannah giggled, even more nervous than she had been before. She opened GW next. Another yes. She had two schools now. And the last one was the one she wanted most. Princeton. The envelope seemed slim. They had probably turned her down. She sat holding it in her hands. "Will you open it, for God's sake?" Muriel prodded her. "I can't stand the suspense."

"Neither can I," Alexa admitted. But

this was Savannah's show. She had worked hard for this and waited a long time to know. Her applications had been sent in three months before. She ever so slowly tore open the last envelope, agonizingly, and carefully unfolded the letter. She closed her eyes for an instant, and then read it, jumped to her feet, and let out a scream.

"I got in! I got in! Oh my God! *I got in!*" she shouted as she danced around the room, and both her mother and grandmother cried. They were on their feet in a minute hugging her. "I'm going to Princeton," she chortled, and then remembered instantly that Turner would be disappointed when she didn't accept Duke. He had gotten in and was going there. But they could visit each other. Princeton was her dream. She wasn't giving that up for a boy, not even one as nice as Turner.

The excitement in the room was overwhelming. Alexa opened the champagne, while Savannah went to call her father. He had known Alexa was bringing the letters, and he was anxious to know too.

He picked up his cell phone at the house. "Stanford, Harvard no, Brown wait-list, yes GW, Duke, and . . . *Princeton*!" she screamed into the phone, and he grinned broadly. "I'm going to Princeton, Daddy!" Like Turner, he would have preferred Duke, but he was partial to southern schools. And Princeton was very impressive. All her choices were. She had aimed high and done well. He was very proud of her.

"Congratulations! Let's celebrate tomorrow night. I'll take everyone to dinner. Congratulations, sweetheart. I'm so proud of you!" She thanked him and went back to her mother and grandmother then. They sat talking about it for ages, and then went out to dinner at Savannah's favorite restaurant. It was noisy and friendly and full of college students. Most of her friends had heard about their colleges that week, and true to her word, Julianne hadn't applied and was taking a break year, but was a little sorry now. She felt left out, so Savannah didn't call her and rub it in. But she called Turner before they left the hotel, and he was thrilled for her, although disappointed she didn't want to go to Duke with him. But he knew how much Princeton meant to her, and he promised to come and visit her as often as he could, and she vowed to do the same.

It was a wonderful night, and Savannah still looked ecstatic as they walked back to the hotel. Her grandmother was enjoying the city. She had always liked it when she visited Alexa there when she and Tom were married. She thought it had a huge amount of charm. They sat and talked for an hour before they all went to bed, still excited by Savannah's great news. And the next morning Travis called to congratulate her, and so did Daisy. She wanted to know if she could visit Savannah at Princeton, and her older sister said of course she could. Henry called her after that and was thrilled, although he said he was hurt she wasn't going to his alma mater, and asked to speak to her mother after that. He and Alexa chatted for a few minutes, and Alexa was smiling when she handed Savannah the phone. Everyone had called. And her grandmother Beaumont was next. She told her she should have gone to a southern school, but if she was going to a Yankee school, Princeton would do very well.

"Isn't that all men?" Eugenie asked, somewhat confused.

"It used to be," Savannah answered. "Not anymore."

"What's the world coming to," Eugenie said, smiling on her end of the line, and then said that she would like to come to tea to see Savannah's mother and grandmother at the hotel that afternoon. Savannah was stunned. She said she was sure they'd be delighted, and thanked her grandmother for making the effort. "I'll have your father bring me." She suggested four o'clock. Savannah hung up, and hoped her mother wouldn't object to the visit.

"I think that's very sweet of her," Alexa said nicely, with a somewhat reserved tone. This was the woman who had orchestrated her downfall ten years before, and destroyed her life, but she was Savannah's grandmother, and she was willing to be gracious about it. Alexa was determined to make the effort for her daughter, and her own mother was proud of her. Alexa said she had seen Tom, she supposed she could see his mother, although she didn't have warm feelings about her.

"Thanks, Mom," Savannah said gratefully. She knew what a huge gesture it was for her grandmother Beaumont to come out. She very seldom left her house anymore. She was old enough to be her other grandmother's mother.

They continued to celebrate all day, and went to the spa together. Muriel loved it, and got her hair and nails done after a massage. They were all back in the suite at three-thirty to dress to meet Mrs. Beaumont for tea at four.

She arrived promptly with Tom. Savannah was excited to see her, Muriel greeted her cordially, and Alexa looked tense. Grandmother Beaumont walked straight to Alexa first.

"I owe you an apology, Alexa." She stood resting on her cane and looked straight into Alexa's eyes with a serious expression. "I ruined your life, and my son's. No apology will ever cover that. But I want you to know that I'm aware of it and I'll answer to my Maker for it one day. But you have a wonderful daughter, and I love her very much." Alexa thanked her quietly and embraced her graciously. It was true, an apology would never make up for her marriage. But at least she had the grace and the courage to acknowledge what she'd done. Tom stood behind her looking embarrassed, and didn't meet Alexa's eyes.

And after that, it was pure celebration. Alexa showed Grandmother Beaumont the brochure of Princeton. It was a beautiful school and campus, and Savannah could hardly wait to get there. She had called several of her New York friends that morning, and e-mailed others. And two of her friends were going to Princeton. She was planning to room with one. They had it all worked out.

Tom's mother stayed for an hour, and then he took her home. It had been a big outing for her, especially after her recent flu, which had left her feeling weak. She embraced Alexa as she left, and congratulated her again on Savannah.

Tom reminded them all on the way out

that he would meet them at the restaurant at eight, and Daisy, Travis, and Scarlette would be with him, and Turner was coming too. Eight of them to celebrate Savannah's acceptance to Princeton. He dropped his mother off then, and went home. And when he got there, he went to look for Luisa, and invited her again to come with them. Her face was set in hard lines. It was a familiar look to him.

"Don't be ridiculous, Tom. I'm not having dinner with *her*." She meant Alexa, which he knew. "And I don't care where Savannah got into school. She's not my child. What's more, I'm sure Alexa doesn't want to see me either. I wouldn't in her shoes."

"You may be right," he conceded. "But you could at least participate somehow. You've done everything you could to avoid Savannah since she got here, and make her feel unwelcome. She's my daughter."

"But not mine," Luisa said again. She looked somber, and sad. "I don't want her here. You knew that and brought her here anyway."

"I had no choice. You don't have to make it as difficult as possible for everyone, Luisa. She's not going to hurt you, and neither is her mother. They don't want anything from you, or even from me."

"They already have it," she said sadly. "Alexa has had you for the last eleven years. You never left her, Tom." He was stunned by what she said.

"What are you talking about? I left her eleven years ago, for you, and Daisy. I left her so we could get remarried. I never saw her again, or even spoke to her until February of this year." Luisa nodded. She believed that, and checked up on him often. In her mind trust did not exclude supervision.

"And you never stopped loving her either. I knew it every time I looked at you, and the way you looked at me. I thought I could steal you from her, and you'd forget about her. You never did. You never loved me, Tom. You wanted me back to get even with Thornton, because I left you for him. Your ego was hurt, not your heart. Alexa has always had your heart." Tom didn't say a word when she said it.

He couldn't deny it. It was true. And they both knew it, and so did Alexa, even though she didn't want him. "You never stopped loving her, and now you love her child, who looks just like her."

"Savannah is her own person," he defended.

"You had lunch with Alexa the last time she was here."

"Yes, I did." She always knew everything he did. "We share a daughter."

"And what else?"

"Nothing. She doesn't want me," he said grimly. This was not a conversation he wanted to have with his wife.

"Did you ask her?"

"No. But I'm not happy, and you know it. You've been hard on me for years. You got me, and then for some reason I don't understand, you've been punishing me ever since."

"Because I knew you still loved her. You never loved me."

"But I stayed with you. That must count for something. Loyalty at least." But they both knew he wasn't loyal. He had proved it to Alexa. He was weak.

That was different, and Luisa knew it, and so did he.

"I don't know why you stay," Luisa said to him, honest for the first time in years, maybe ever. "For Daisy maybe. Out of laziness. Because your mother told you to. Even your mother has turned on me." She knew about the visit to Alexa and her mother that afternoon. Tom had told her. "You turned on me when you brought Savannah here. You have no respect for me at all."

"It's hard to respect a woman who is so angry, and so often mean, Luisa. Think about it. You're not even nice to Daisy, your own daughter. You walked out on our boys. And on me. It's hard to forget those things. So now what do we do? Hate each other for the next forty years, or give it up, or just limp along? It would be nice if we could at least be friends. You don't have to come tonight. And you're right, you probably shouldn't. It would be awkward for both of you, and Savannah. She's very protective of her mother."

"So are you."

"No. I feel guilty. That's different. I

didn't protect her when I should have. From you. I cheated on her, and slept with you, and I got you pregnant. For all I know you did it on purpose." She didn't answer one way or the other, which told him what he knew anyway. "I let you and my mother manipulate me. But I didn't protect her for a second, and she was my wife then, not you. But I did it. And you're my wife now. It would be nice if you'd act like one, once in a while, and not as though you hate me. We created this mess together. It was what you wanted. You got it. Why don't we make the best of it, or at least try to? It's going to be a very sad, lonely life for both of us if we don't." Everything he had said was true.

"I'll feel better when Savannah leaves," she said quietly. "We can start then."

"Whatever you want," he said with obvious disappointment, and a few minutes later, he left, without seeing her again. She stayed upstairs in her room. They had both been shaken by the conversation. Luisa never reached out to him, or even tried to be kind. It was just who she was. And their marriage was a disaster as a result, for both of them. And probably always would be, he realized now. And Luisa would do nothing different when Savannah left. His punishment fit the crime.

The dinner at FIG for Savannah was lively and fun. Travis had a little too much to drink and was very funny, telling stories from his college days at UVA, which was something of a party school. Scarlette was adorable to Savannah, and they talked about the wedding. Daisy was all excited and loved Savannah's mother and grandmother, who were younger and much more fun than her own. And Turner looked adoringly at Savannah throughout dinner and sat next to her holding her hand under the table. And at one moment Tom and Alexa's eyes met across the table and the years faded away. Whatever had happened between them, they were both proud of their daughter, and this was a very special day. It was a lovely evening for all of them. They were the last to leave the restaurant, and it had been a perfect celebration for Savannah. Her dreams had come true, she was surrounded by people who loved her, and this was just the beginning. And for the entire evening, no one had even thought about Luisa, not even Tom. She was at home, alone, hating them all.

Chapter 16

Alexa sat next to her mother on the flight home. The whole weekend had been festive and fun, and Muriel was glad she had gone with her, particularly for the opening of the envelopes when Savannah found out she'd gotten into Princeton. It was an unforgettable moment for them all.

But Muriel also noticed something different now about Alexa. She wasn't as angry, or bitter, and seemed more at peace. Her mother suspected that having to go back to Charleston had done her good. She had faced all the demons of her past. Tom, his mother, Luisa. They seemed to have shrunk over time. She knew that Alexa's marriage was still a huge loss to her. But when you saw who Tom really was, how weak and self-serving, maybe she hadn't lost so much after all. She hoped Alexa knew that, and had seen it better now. He was a very selfish man, and the only reason he wanted Alexa back was because it hadn't worked out with Luisa. If it had, he'd have had no regrets at all. Muriel thought he had gotten what he deserved, a woman who respected him as little as he respected himself. As Alexa had been recently, she was reminded of Ashley in *Gone with the Wind.* What her daughter needed now was Rhett Butler. She just hoped she'd find him one day. She had a right to some happiness after all these hard, lonely years. And she had done a great job with her daughter. That job was over now too. Savannah was all grown up and running. Her life had begun.

And best of all was Savannah, glowing with all that lay ahead. Muriel thought her boyfriend in Charleston was a very nice boy. She wondered if the romance would last when Savannah went to Princeton and he went to Duke. Those things were always hard to predict. Some early romances lasted. Some didn't. Time would tell.

Muriel looked over at her daughter as they flew toward New York, and Alexa was sound asleep. It had been an emotional weekend for them all.

Savannah still had two big events ahead in the months to come. She would be attending graduation with her class in Charleston, and would then come back for the one at her school in New York. She was going to catch up with her friends again, just in time to say goodbye. And Turner had promised to come up. That was going to be fun for Savannah too. Her father still wasn't coming, since he would be at her Charleston graduation, and he felt New York was her mother's turf and he didn't want to intrude. Savannah was fine with that. But first, her mother had to get through the trial. And then Savannah could come home. She was ready. Charleston had been great. She had gotten a father, sister, two brothers, and fallen in love. But New York and her mom were still home to her.

Alexa didn't think she would be able to go back to Charleston again until after the trial. There was too much going on now, but Savannah understood. The final crunch was on.

The morning after their Charleston weekend, Alexa was in her office at seven. She had gotten up at five to read some material she needed to prepare for the trial, and motions that the public defender had submitted to the judge.

The public defender had filed a motion to dismiss the case, which was so ridiculous it was laughable. No judge was going to grant it, but she filed it anyway, pro forma. She owed it to her client to try. And she had filed a Sandoval motion as well, to prevent Alexa from cross-examining Quentin on his prior convictions. She had a shot at winning that, but Alexa didn't really care. The evidence against him in this case was so damning, and the crimes so heinous, that the earlier fraud and robbery charges he'd been convicted for were almost irrelevant, and certainly not pertinent to this case, although the fact that he had prior convictions would certainly tell a jury what kind of man he was.

Both motions were being decided on that morning in chambers. Alexa objected to them, and the judge dismissed them both. The public defender walked back into court looking glum.

"So much for that," Jack muttered under his breath as he and Sam followed Alexa out of court with a member of the FBI elite Serial Crime Unit, which had helped them investigate and prepare the case. The motions had been routine, and the judge looked impatient that the public defender had filed them. There was no sympathy for Luke Quentin in court, and there would be even less from a jury. Alexa had all their evidence and expert witnesses lined up. The prosecution was airtight.

Alexa went to see Judy Dunning that afternoon.

"Sorry about the motions," Alexa said

pleasantly, trying to sound sympathetic, although she wasn't.

"I think the judge was being unreasonable about the Sandoval," Judy complained. "The jury doesn't need to know he was convicted of fraud and robbery to try this case." Alexa didn't comment but just nodded. She had come to see her to try to convince her again to get her client to plead guilty and avoid a trial.

"I can't offer him a deal in a case like this," Alexa said honestly, "but he may get better treatment in prison if he's reasonable now. A trial is just going to be a circus, and a jury will convict. You have to know that. There's so much evidence against him, I must have twenty boxes of it in my office. Judy, talk to him. No one needs the grief." The public defender had even tried to challenge the warrant the DA had gotten to allow Jack and Charlie to search his hotel room initially, but that had held up too, so the incriminating evidence they had gotten was admissible in court.

"He has a right to a trial," the public defender said through pursed lips. It

was like talking to a wall, and Alexa
went back to her office more than anything annoyed. The trial was going to be
a media circus, and he was going down
for a hundred years. So be it. She had
work to do. She had meetings with the
FBI all week, forensic witnesses to line
up from nine states, testimony to organize, her opening statement to finish.
She had a thousand ducks to get in order, and only a few weeks left to do it.
There were so many investigators on the
case now that she didn't know all of
them by name, and the FBI was sitting
in on every meeting, to make sure that
all proper procedure was maintained.
No one wanted a mistrial and to do it all
again. A change of venue had been dis-
cussed but rejected since Quentin was
known now in every state. The case had
made national news. And the judge they
had been given was notorious for being
tough on the press, so that was good.
For the next several weeks before it
started, and as long as it took after,
Alexa was going to be eating, sleeping,
and dreaming the trial.

She called Savannah from the office

every day, but never had time to talk long, and by the time she got home at night, it was too late to call her. Savannah understood and was busy with her life in Charleston, with school, friends, and her boyfriend.

It was two weeks before the trial, as Tom was watching the news in his den one night, when he saw a news conference come on and realized it was Alexa. He shouted to Savannah to come in and watch it, and Daisy came in too. They stood in front of the television and watched Alexa speak eloquently about the upcoming murder trial involving eighteen victims. There were swarms of police and FBI around her, but the microphones were all pointing to Alexa as she gave careful, coherent, intelligent answers to the questions they asked her. She looked calm, cool, and competent. Not knowing what the fuss was about, Luisa came in too, and stood there, watching her for a moment, and then walked away with pursed lips set in a hard line.

When the press conference was over,

Tom looked at his oldest daughter and complimented her mother.

"She was very good. That's going to be one mess of a trial for her to handle, and the media's already going crazy. I thought she was very impressive, didn't you?" Savannah agreed with him and was very proud of her, and Daisy was excited too. She'd never seen anyone she knew on TV before, and she smiled up at her sister.

"She looked like a movie star," she said as Savannah smiled, and Luisa came back in and told them it was time to go down to dinner. She made no comment about the broadcast, and it had obviously irritated her. She seemed to be absolutely incapable of being gracious about Alexa. She didn't want to hear about her, see anything of her, or have anything to do with her daughter, and she was constantly aware that Tom had forced her to have Savannah there. All she wanted was for her to go away.

The coup de grâce for Luisa came three days before the trial when the invitations to Travis and Scarlette's wedding arrived in the mail and Savannah got one. She was opening it as Luisa came home from the hairdresser. She recognized it immediately and snapped at Savannah.

"Where did you get that?" She acted as though she had stolen it or was opening someone else's mail.

"It's mine," Savannah said, instantly sounding defensive. "It came in the mail. It had my name on it," she said to the evil stepmother who tried to turn every day into a living hell for her and sometimes succeeded. Without her father to defend her constantly, Savannah's life would have been miserable. He buffered everything for her, but now and then Luisa got the best of her anyway.

"They sent you an invitation to the wedding?" She looked horrified and snatched it from Savannah's hand. She marched into Tom's study with it five minutes later and waved it at him in fury. "I will *not* have her at our son's wedding!" she said, trembling with rage as she faced him. "She doesn't belong there. She's not his full sister. And I won't be humiliated at my own son's wedding." He understood quickly what had happened when he saw the invitation she was holding and shook his head.

"If she's here when they get married, you can't *not* have her at the wedding. She's not going to sit home like Cinderella while the rest of us are there."

"And if she's not still here at the time of the wedding?" She didn't want her coming back for it. She wanted her gone. Forever. And surely not coming back for a family event as important as this. Everyone who was anyone in South Carolina would be there, and from neighboring states.

"Then it's up to Scarlette and Travis if they want to invite her. May I remind you that we're not giving the wedding? Scarlette's parents are. It's entirely up to them." He tried to sidestep it, but Luisa wouldn't let him.

"Who put her on the list?"

"I have no idea," he answered.

Luisa called Scarlette about it five minutes later and told her daughter-in-law in no uncertain terms that she didn't want Savannah at their wedding.

"Mother Beaumont," Scarlette said gently, "I don't think that's right. She's Travis's sister, and I like Savannah very much. There are going to be eight hundred guests at the reception, although only three hundred at the church. I don't think it will hurt anyone to have her at our wedding." Scarlette persisted, making it clear that she was not going to be rude to Savannah.

"It will hurt *me*!" Her future mother-in-law shouted into the phone. "And you wouldn't want that, would you?" It was a clear warning shot across her bow.

"Of course not. I'll seat her at the opposite end of the tent from you," Scarlette reassured her, and Luisa hung up on her brusquely and was in a rage for the next two hours.

"Maybe I'll be gone," Savannah said quietly to her father a little later. "The trial should be over by then."

"It would be fun for you to come to the wedding. Half of Charleston will be there. With eight hundred guests, you won't be able to find anyone you know, if you want to. Luisa will calm down about it." He reassured her, and tried not to look as upset as he was himself. Luisa was like a dog with a bone and just wouldn't let go of it. She wanted Savannah out of their lives. It was a difficult position for a seventeen-year-old girl to be in, and even harder for him, constantly torn between his wife and his daughter. It was hurtful for Savannah and exhausting for him. Daisy tried to stay under the radar as much as possible.

Savannah spoke to her mother that night and mentioned the invitation to her, and Alexa startled her daughter when she said she had gotten an invitation to the wedding too.

"Would you go, Mom?" Savannah couldn't imagine her going, not if Luisa would be there.

"No, sweetheart, I wouldn't. But it was nice of them to ask me. You can go if you want to. I don't think I should. Luisa would have a coronary, or she might poison my soup." Savannah laughed at what she said.

"There will be eight hundred guests there. Dad says she'll never even see us if we're there."

"I don't want to make her uncomfortable, Savannah."

"I know, Mom. But I'd like to go, and I'd rather go with you."

"We'll see. Let's talk about it after the trial. I can't think about it right now. Weddings are the last thing on my mind." Alexa was going in a thousand directions at once.

She'd had another press conference that day, and the public defender had given one too. The PD insisted that this was all an unfortunate misunderstanding, of an innocent man who had been framed, and it would be cleared up at the trial. She said she had every confidence that Luke Quentin would walk free, as the innocent man he was.

She looked and sounded even crazier when Savannah saw it on TV later that day. Daisy was watching with her and looked confused. Savannah had the news on in her room now constantly. Her mother was on TV every day.

"Did he do it or didn't he?" Daisy asked her.

"That's up to the jury to decide. But

he did it. Believe me. They're going to convict him and send him to prison."

"Then why did the other lady say he didn't?"

"That's her job. She has to defend him. And it's my mom's job to prove he did it." Daisy nodded. She was getting daily lessons on the criminal justice system from Savannah. The judge had banned cameras in the courtroom, but once the trial started, it would be a madhouse in the hallways and on the courthouse steps.

The day the trial started, Savannah watched the news before she went to school. She watched it again in the cafeteria during her lunch break, and knowing that Savannah's mother was the prosecutor, a crowd of students gathered around. Alexa had been surrounded by reporters before she went into the courthouse, but she didn't stop. They would be doing jury selection for the next several days.

Arthur Lieberman, the judge in the case, was a stern-looking man in his fifties. He had short white hair, and eyes that took in everything in his courtroom. He was an ex-Marine and tolerated no nonsense. He hated the press, and he didn't like attorneys, neither for the prosecution nor for the defense, who wasted his time with useless motions and frivolous objections. He called Alexa and Judy Dunning into his chambers at the beginning of the case, and gave them a sobering lecture and stern warnings about what he expected of them.

"I want no nonsense in my courtroom, counselors, no funny tricks, no playing with the jury in any way, no improper procedures. I've never had a trial overturned, there has never been a mistrial in my courtroom, and I don't intend this one to be the first. Is that clear?" Both women nodded and said, "Yes, Your Honor," like dutiful children. "You have a client to defend," he said, looking at Judy, "and you have eighteen victims to prove the defendant is responsible for killing. There is no more serious matter than this one. I don't want any irresponsible shenanigans in my courtroom, or histrionics or unnecessary drama. And watch what you say to the press!" he admonished and dismissed them summarily.

Jury selection began half an hour later and seemed endless. Alexa sat at the prosecutor's table flanked by Jack Jones on one side and Sam Lawrence on the other.

Alexa had come to respect Sam as they prepared the trial. He was a nit-picker, about everything. But she discovered rapidly that he was right, and he had made her even more careful than she normally was. They had shared lunch at her desk many times in the past months. He was in his fifties, she knew he had been a widower for years and had devoted his entire life to the FBI. She knew that when they won the case, it would be in part due to his help. He hated Quentin, and the case, and was as determined to put him away as Jack and Alexa and the DA. That was his only goal, she realized early on, not trying to screw her over or take the case away from her, even if the regional FBI director would have liked to. Senior Special

Agent Sam Lawrence wanted the best person to do the job, and to prosecute the case, and Alexa had his full support. He smiled as she sat down next to him, and jury selection began.

It was a long, exhausting process. A hundred potential jurors had been selected, after all those were dismissed who were pregnant, sick, couldn't get away from their jobs, spoke no English, were taking care of dying relatives, and had been able to come up with convincing reasons to be excused. And Alexa knew that there would be many more with similar excuses amid the hundred who sat crowded into the courtroom, praying they'd be sent away. The judge explained to all of them that it would be a long case, that it involved multiple homicides, and that testimony and arguments would go on for many weeks or even more than a month. Those to whom that presented an undue hardship, or had medical conditions that prevented them from serving, were to identify themselves to the clerk of the court. He pointed him out, and within minutes, there was a line of about twenty people standing in front of the clerk. The other eighty sat waiting expectantly to be questioned by both attorneys to see if they would qualify or be dismissed. Among them were people of all races, ages, both sexes, all of whom looked like ordinary people and were, everything from doctors to housewives, teachers to mailmen to students, all sat staring expectantly at Judy and Alexa.

Luke Quentin had been quietly brought in as the process began, wearing a suit, and he was neither shackled nor cuffed. Since he had shown no signs of violence during the months in jail, awaiting trial, he was allowed to appear like a civilized person, and not in handcuffs and chains, so as not to unduly influence the jury or make him look more menacing, although they knew what he was there for. Alexa noticed when she glanced cursorily at him that he was wearing a brand-new white shirt. She did not meet his eyes, but saw that Judy smiled a reassuring smile at him when he came in, and patted his arm when he sat down. He looked calm and collected and anything but scared, as his eyes roved over the jury, as though he were planning to pick them himself. Technically, he had the right to question them too, but Alexa doubted he would.

The first juror was Asian and misunderstood Alexa's questions four times, and two of Judy's, and was thanked and dismissed. The second was recently arrived from Puerto Rico, a young woman who looked terrified and said she had four children and two jobs and couldn't stay, and she left too. Alexa knew the kind of juror she wanted, solid citizens, preferably of an age to be the parents of people the same age as their victims, and of course the parents of girls. The public defender was going to do everything in her power to keep them off the jury. It was a game where each attorney attempted to set the chess pieces up to her best advantage. The prosecution and defense each had twenty peremptory challenges, simply based on the fact that they didn't like the answers to their questions. Relatives of law enforcement officers, or anyone too closely related to the legal or the criminal justice system, were rarely kept on juries. Cops themselves were dismissed, so were certain professions, notoriously lawyers, anyone who might be prejudiced, or who had a relative who had been murdered or the victim of a violent crime. They tried to weed out all forms of bias or excessive sympathy for either side. The process was laborious, and slow, and took the entire week, which Alexa had expected. She thought it might take even longer.

And during the entire process, Quentin sat quietly meeting each juror's eyes, and either smiled at them or drove his eyes right through them. He seemed to alternate between an aura of intimidation and one of innocence and gentleness, or indifference. Most of the time, he ignored his defense counsel, although she leaned over to whisper explanations to him frequently, or ask him questions in notes. He would nod or shake his head. And at the prosecution table, Alexa consulted frequently with Sam and Jack, but most of the time she made her own decisions about the jurors she rejected or kept.

Two of the jurors were dismissed

when they said they knew the judge, and he agreed, many claimed health problems, others wanted to serve but were not the jurors Alexa wanted, or Judy let them go because she felt, as Alexa did, that they would be likely to convict. It was a guessing game for both of them, and they could use only the material at hand, they couldn't pull their ideal jurors out of a hat. They had to carefully assess how these people would react to the evidence, the crimes, and the defendant. It was an educated guessing process and at the same time a crapshoot, where you tried to divine human nature and predict how they would respond to what they heard, and if they would fully understand the rules that applied to them, which the judge would explain once the trial started. They had to convict beyond a reasonable doubt, or acquit. Their final decision had to be unanimous. All twelve had to agree, and anything less than that meant a hung jury. And the last thing both Judy and Alexa wanted was either a hung jury or a mistrial, and to have to try the case in front of a different jury all over again, although Quentin might have liked a mistrial, to stall the process of convicting him and sending him to prison forever.

The judge decided on the sentence, not the jury, and would do it a month after the verdict. The one thing they didn't have to worry about was the death penalty. New York's State Court of Appeals had overturned the death penalty in 2004, and had been battling motions to reinstate it in the years since. For the time being, there was no capital punishment in New York State. If convicted, Luke would serve life in prison without parole, but would not be sentenced to death. So the jury didn't have the burden of knowing that their decision could cost his life, which made things a little easier for them. All of his other cases had been associated to the one in New York, and he was being tried for the rape and death of all eighteen women in this trial. He had been charged with eighteen counts of rape, and eighteen counts of first-degree murder, with malicious intent.

It was late Friday afternoon when

twelve jurors had been selected, and four alternate jurors had been chosen, in case one of the regular jurors could not serve and had to be replaced. Of the twelve regular jurors, eight were men and four were women. Alexa didn't mind that. She thought that men might be more protective of young women, more outraged by the crimes and more sympathetic, and angrier at Luke Quentin. She was counting on it. Four of them were old enough to have daughters that age, two were slightly younger than she wanted and would be hard to predict, but she had used up her challenges by the time they were selected. All were employed and seemed respectable and intelligent. Of the four women, all were older. Judy had objected to young women on the jury. But the four alternate jurors were mostly young women in their thirties. All races were represented, white, Hispanic, Asian, and African-American. Looking at them, Alexa was convinced they were a good jury and had worked hard to pick them, and get around some of Judy's objections. Judy wanted men on the jury, because she thought they would be more sympathetic to Luke. Alexa didn't agree, but in the end, they both liked the makeup of the jury. There were always loose cannons, and unpredictable surprises, but from what she could tell, with the knowledge they had of them, Alexa thought this jury was a good one. They would know after the trial.

Once the jurors were dismissed for the day, Quentin was handcuffed and then shackled, and led out of the courtroom by four deputies. He looked confident and relaxed, and stopped to glance at Alexa on the way out. Her face was expressionless, and his was slightly mocking, and then he moved on.

They had done good work that week, and Sam and Jack were pleased too. They took a minute to talk before they left the courtroom. Sam was always impressed by her precision and good judgment and had said as much to his superiors. The proof would be in the trial, of course, but he was extremely pleased by how she handled every detail. And so was Joe McCarthy, who had slipped into the courtroom several times that week to watch the jury selection process. He had added his approval to her choices, and thought she had wisely avoided some bad ones.

"Well, we've got our jury of twelve peers for Mr. Quentin," Alexa said to Jack and Sam, as she put her papers and legal pads back in her briefcase. It was so heavy now that she had to pull it on wheels.

"Ready for your close-up, Ms. Hamilton?" Sam teased her as they left the courtroom. It was no surprise they were met by a wall of press who wanted to know what she thought about the jury. What felt like a million lights went off in her face.

"We're satisfied with the jury" was all she would say as she pushed through them without further comment or expression. Jack tried to lead the way, and Sam stayed close to her with several policemen, but the heat was on her and she took it well. There was a van waiting for them outside so they could make their getaway. Alexa had a cop with her all the time now, and she had to go back to her office before wrapping up for the weekend. Jack said he'd go with her, and they dropped Sam off at the FBI office, and wished each other a good weekend. And he said he'd be available on his cell phone all weekend, they all would. Alexa had thought briefly about flying down to Charleston to see Savannah, but she knew she couldn't. She had too much material to go over and her opening statement to polish some more.

She was just walking into her office when her cell phone rang. It was Savannah.

"I just saw you on TV," she said proudly, "leaving the courthouse. You were great." Alexa laughed.

"That's rank prejudice. All I said was 'We're satisfied with the jury,' and no further comment. I don't see how you could think I was great, but thank you." It touched her that Savannah was following it so closely.

"Daisy and Dad thought so too," she confirmed. It had been a consensus. Luisa was out playing bridge. "You looked calm and collected, and you didn't let them push you around.

You just said what you wanted to and kept going and you didn't let them make you nervous. At least you didn't look it. And your hair looked good." She had worn it in a ponytail with a satin ribbon, instead of a bun, all week. It seemed less uptight.

"Thank you, sweetheart. Well, we'll see what happens next week. I think they're a pretty good jury. I hope I'm right. I was thinking I might come down this weekend, but I just can't," she said, sounding disappointed, but Savannah wasn't surprised.

"I didn't expect you to, Mom. Things must be crazy for you right now."

"Pretty much," she admitted. "What do you have planned for the weekend?"

"I'm going to one of Turner's games tomorrow, and he's coming over tonight to hang out." There was an old playroom in the basement that her brothers had used when they were young. There was a Ping Pong table and a pool table, and her father had suggested they could visit there. Luisa never went down to the basement, and it seemed more respectable than having Turner in her room.

"Say hi to him for me," Alexa said, and then got back to work at her desk. Sam Lawrence called her a little while later.

"Am I disturbing you?" he asked respectfully. It was Friday night by then.

"Not at all. I'm still at work," she said in a pleasant tone. He was a nice man, and working with him had gone well so far. They had a great deal of mutual respect, and he and Jack had become friends in the past months.

"Sounds like we keep the same kind of hours. I'm going to move into my office pretty soon," he laughed. But they were all going to work night and day during the trial. Judy Dunning was too, and even more so, since she had less support, and she didn't have the FBI helping her. "I just wanted to tell you that I'm really happy with the jury, and I thought you handled the selection process very well. You're a real pro," he complimented her, which was high praise coming from him. FBI agents rarely approved of anyone except FBI.

"I hope so, with a case like this." She smiled.

"Let me know if I can do anything to help over the weekend."

"Thanks, I'll be fine," she assured him. And with Savannah away, she had no distractions and no obligations other than her work.

She spent the rest of the weekend working at home, going through boxes of forensic reports and evidence, working on her opening statement, and organizing the prosecution down to the last detail. By Monday morning, she felt fully prepared.

On Monday morning, they met in Sam's office and went to the courthouse together. The press were waiting, and it was a pushing, shoving, shouting match to get through them, and Alexa made her way through the crowd, looking calm, with five cops and Jack and Sam to help. She didn't have a hair out of place when she got into the courtroom and sat down at the prosecution table, looking unruffled. She seemed businesslike, competent, and totally in control.

Judy Dunning was already at the defense table. Luke Quentin came in with four deputies, and sat down next to her. And five minutes later the judge walked to the bench and sat down. Court was convened. Without pause, he instructed the jury as to what was expected of them. He spoke in simple, clear terms about the process, and thanked them for giving up their time to be there. He said they had a very important job, perhaps the most important job in the courtroom, more than his as judge, or the attorneys. And they nodded and looked at him seriously as they listened.

And then Alexa rose to give her opening statement. She had been preparing it for a month. She was wearing a serious black suit and heels. She introduced herself to the jury and explained what her role was, as prosecutor. She explained that the man sitting next to her at counsel's table, Jack Jones, was the chief investigating detective on the case, and she spoke about him for a minute. She then mentioned Sam Lawrence and explained that he was the chief senior representative of the FBI on the case. That was their team.

"And why do we have the FBI here?" she asked quietly, walking in front of them, and looking each one in the eye. "Because these crimes were committed in many states. Nine states. Eighteen young women were killed in nine states." She didn't overemphasize it but said it perfectly, as though to engrave the numbers in their minds. "And when state lines are crossed, when a defendant goes from one state to another to commit crimes, then the FBI gets involved, to coordinate information, so there is no mistake or confusion between local law enforcement agencies. All that information is pooled so that what we submit to you, ladies and gentlemen, is correct. Having the FBI here means it's an important case. And it *is* an important case. Not because the FBI is here, but because eighteen young women died. They were violently attacked and killed. Brutally raped, strangled during sex, and killed. Eighteen of them. The youngest one was eighteen, and the oldest twenty-five, a medical student. The eighteen-year-old was a theology major." She wanted to stress their respectability to the jury and did so effectively. All eyes in the courtroom were riveted to her, as she spoke calmly and with enormous dignity and strength. She had talent at what she did, as Jack and Sam and everyone in the courtroom observed her.

"Their murderer didn't happen on them, he didn't just run into them and rape them and kill them by accident, which would have been terrible too. He planned it. He sought them out. We believe he looked for them and observed them, and chose them, and did exactly what he *planned* to do, with malicious intent. He planned to rape them and kill them, because that's what turned him on. He killed them because that was his ultimate pleasure. The defendant in this case likes 'snuff' films, where women are killed during sex. He wanted to live out that fantasy and went out of his way to do it, killing eighteen young women for thrills. Murder in the first degree is when you plan to kill someone, you intend to kill them, and you do. It's not an accident, it's planned, 'with malice aforethought.' You know what that means. These young women were violently raped and murdered. It was a *plan.* And the plan was carried out. And now they're dead.

"I know some of you have children. I asked you that question when we selected you as jurors. But even if you don't have children, I know you must be shocked by these crimes. We all are.

"I have a daughter, she's seventeen. I think she's beautiful, and she means everything to me. *Everything.* She's a senior in high school, and she's going to college in the fall." She didn't say Princeton so as not to appear elitist. "She plays volleyball and is on the swim team, and I think she's the sweetest kid in the world. I'm a single mom, and she's an only child, so she's all I have." She paused, and looked at each one closely. She had just become human to them. She was a single mom with a child, and they could trust her. She wanted them to know that. Some nodded understandingly as she spoke. She had them now.

"Six of these eighteen girls were only children. Seven of them had single moms. Nine of them were students and had jobs to support their education and help their families. Two were oldest children whose moms had died, and they took care of their siblings. Four were outstanding students. Eight had scholarships or had had them. Eleven of them were religious and active in their churches. Five of them were engaged. They played sports, they had siblings and moms and dads, and dogs, and teachers who knew and loved them, and boyfriends and friends. *All* of them were respected and loved in their communities, and are greatly missed. And *all* of them were killed by the defendant sitting in front of you. *All* of them. Eighteen girls. We believe that's the truth. The State believes it, eight other states believe it, the FBI believes it, and I think that when you hear the evidence in this case, you will believe it too.

"It takes a special kind of person to commit crimes like this, to be so without conscience, so unfeeling as to kill eighteen young women, while raping them, because that's what turns you on, and you planned it. That's a terrible way to die, and a terrible reason.

"The State believes beyond any doubt, and will prove to you, that Luke Quentin, the man at the defense table in this courtroom, raped and killed these eighteen young women, with malicious intent.

"We can't allow people who behave this way to walk among us, to hurt our children, to kill people we love. People who commit crimes like this need to be put in prison and punished for those crimes. If not, none of our children or loved ones are safe, and we aren't either.

"We feel sure that Luke Quentin killed these eighteen women. We can prove it, and we will prove it to you during this trial, beyond a reasonable doubt. And if you agree with the evidence, and the State, we will ask you to find him guilty of killing and raping eighteen women. It's all we can do now for the eighteen girls who died." She looked at them for a long moment, and then spoke softly. "Thank you." She went back to sit at the prosecutor's table. The jury looked shaken, and several were squirming in their seats. Sam Lawrence nodded his approval when she sat down. It had been a powerful opening statement and proved to him again she was the right person for the job.

As she sat down, Luke was whispering to his attorney, and she nodded. The defense was not obliged to make an opening statement, but Judy Dunning had decided to anyway. She knew that what Alexa would have to say would be too powerful to let it just hang in the air, without at least trying to mitigate it before the trial began. The public defender had told the judge earlier that she would be making an opening statement too.

She got up and walked to where the jury was sitting, and she looked sad, and serious as she gazed at them. She told them who she was, and that she would be defending Luke Quentin.

"I wanted you to know, ladies and gentlemen, that I'm sad about those eighteen girls too. We all are. So is Luke Quentin. Who wouldn't be? Eighteen young lives and beautiful girls gone forever. What a terrible, terrible thing.

"And you will hear a great deal of evidence in this case, some of it very technical, of what happened, how it happened, when it happened, and who may have done it. The State believes that Luke Quentin did it. Ms. Hamilton just told you that. But we don't believe it. Not for a minute. Luke Quentin did not kill those women, and we are going to do everything we can to prove that to you.

"Sometimes terrible circumstances come together, being in the wrong place at the wrong time, people making it look as though you did something you didn't. It looks like you've done something awful, but you haven't. All the stars and circumstances and bad luck conspire against you, and you're blamed for something you didn't do."

She looked at each of them intently, from one face to another. "Luke Quentin did *not* commit those murders. He did *not* rape or kill those women. And we will prove that to you, beyond a reasonable doubt. If you believe us, or have any doubt whatsoever that Luke Quentin committed these crimes, then we are asking for an acquittal. Don't punish an *innocent* man, no matter how terrible these crimes." And with that, she went back to her seat. The judge called a twenty-minute recess immediately after.

Both Jack and Sam congratulated Alexa on her opening statement and its impact on the jury.

"Judy's wasn't bad either," she said fairly. She didn't have much to work with, and would have even less as the days wore on, but at least she had raised a question in their minds. Alexa knew it was the best she could do.

They went to get coffee out of the machine, drank it quickly, and were back at the prosecution table when Judge Lieberman rapped his gavel and brought the court to order again. He told Alexa to call her first witness.

She called Jason Yu from the forensics lab because he was personable and would make the DNA tests easier for the jury to understand. Afterward she would call experts, whose information would be harder to digest. With Alexa questioning him, he explained the DNA tests that had first linked Quentin to the bodies in New York. She had him on the stand for close to an hour, and then the judge called a recess for lunch. Jason Yu had done well, and she thanked him. Judy was going to cross-examine him after lunch.

Sam, Jack, and Alexa went out to lunch, but Alexa was too nervous to eat. She was running on adrenaline and spent most of the lunch hour making notes and jotting down additional questions. The two men chatted about sports while she worked, and then they went back to the courtroom.

The public defender's cross-examination of Jason Yu was weak. She tried to confuse him, unsuccessfully, and make his information and tests sound unreliable and inconclusive, but each time he explained his material more precisely and more clearly. She was starting to look foolish and dismissed him, and said she had no further questions. Neither did Alexa.

Alexa called one of her expert witnesses after that, and his testimony was long, drawn out, and potentially confusing. But there was nothing she could do. The evidence he presented was important to their case. She knew there would be many witnesses like that from several states. And she was afraid it would bore the jury, but they each had something important to contribute.

On the whole, the first day went well, and so did the first week. Despite the heinousness of the crimes, there was little emotional testimony in the case. It was all very technical. There were no eyewitnesses, the parents had no testimony to give.

The most emotional factor in the courtroom was the enormous section of seats cordoned off for the relatives of the victims. There were a hundred and nine people in those seats, watching the proceedings intently and many of them crying. Instinctively, the jury knew who they were and looked at them often. Alexa had referred to them once, so they'd know, and Judy had objected. But by then the jury knew, and it was too late. Charlie sat among them with his family, who had come to see justice done.

Mostly the case involved the presentation of technical forensic data that systematically linked Luke Quentin to each victim and her death. Cross-examination involved refuting that evidence, and the public defender didn't have the skills or evidence to do it. It was a hard case to beat. Alexa and Sam met with Judy on Friday afternoon after court was recessed for the weekend.

"I just wanted to suggest to you again," Alexa said calmly, "that you get your client to plead. We're all wasting our time here."

"I don't think we are," Judy Dunning said stubbornly. "People make mistakes in DNA tests. Sometimes all they do is exclude one group of people without accurately pinpointing others. I think the cops in every state pinned every unsolved murder they had on Luke. If there was one mistake made, just one, if one of those cases was wrong, or poorly handled, it will raise a reasonable doubt that could overturn all the others." It was a long shot, but the only one she had. And investigation teams in nine states and the FBI had seen to it that there were no mistakes. Alexa thought she was being foolish and committing legal suicide for her client in open court. "He has nothing to lose and he has a right to a trial," Judy said darkly, as though she were watching an innocent man be crucified, instead of a merciless killer being brought to justice. She still believed in her client's innocence, that much was clear. She wasn't just doing a job, she was leading a crusade, for a lost cause. Judy seemed painfully naïve to Alexa.

"He has a lot to lose," Alexa pointed out to her. "The judge is going to be much tougher on him if he wastes everyone's time. No one is going to be sympathetic to him, or give him a break. He'd be a lot better off if he strikes a deal now, before we go through weeks of trial. The judge is going to get pissed," Alexa warned her, and Jack agreed with her completely, and felt that a good attorney would have forced Luke to plead. Judy was too weak to do it, and too enthralled by Luke. "If I were his attorney," Alexa said quietly, "I would make him plead." The judge might give him concurrent sentences instead of consecutive, which could extend far beyond Luke's lifetime. Concurrent sentencing was the best he could hope for.

"Then he's lucky you aren't his attorney," Judy said firmly and stood up, looking huffy. "I'm his lawyer, counselor, and he's not pleading." Alexa nodded, thanked her, and she and Jack left the room without comment.

"See you Monday," she said as she left him in the hall.

Four policemen helped her down the courthouse steps into a waiting police car, and two stood outside her apartment all weekend. They were back in court on Monday.

The technical testimony went on for three weeks, and was impressively conclusive, beyond a reasonable doubt, Alexa thought. Again it was less emotional than she would have liked. And the photographs of the victims were absolutely awful, because most of them had been found later and the bodies had been badly decomposed. The jury had been warned that they would have to view them. They looked sick when they did, but the photographs were evidence in the trial, and part of the State's case.

After three weeks of testimony, the prosecution rested and turned the case over to the defense. Alexa had produced volumes of expert testimony and DNA testing that couldn't be refuted. All Judy could do was try to confuse it, which she attempted, without much success. And the most damning element in her case was that Luke wasn't going to take the stand in his own defense, because of his previous convictions and criminal record. He could have, but it would have been foolish in the extreme. Even Judy wouldn't risk it, so he said nothing in his own defense, which spoke volumes. Instead he sat in the courtroom for three weeks looking arrogant and without remorse, as the victims' families cried.

The case for the defense took less than a week, and then the public defender rested her case. Alexa called only two defense witnesses for rebuttal and made hash of them. They were incompetent, and it showed. And then Judy made an emotional closing statement, begging the jury not to convict an innocent man, and hoping that she had convinced them he was. The jury looked stone-faced as they watched her.

Alexa's closing argument summed up the evidence for them, reminded them of each case and instance when Luke Quentin had been linked conclusively to one of the women, as their murderer. She went down the list of proofs, both simple and complicated, that should convince them that the defendant was guilty of all of these crimes. She then made a brief emotional speech reminding them of their responsibility as jurors to bring criminals like Luke Quentin to justice and convict, not an innocent man, but a man who had been *proven* to have raped and killed eighteen women. She thanked them for their attention during the long trial.

The judge then instructed the jury for their deliberations. The foreman had already requested charts and evidence that had been presented during the trial. Throughout the trial the judge had warned the jury that they were not to read anything in the press about the proceedings, but he had not sequestered them.

They would be taken to a hotel that night, however, if they had not reached a verdict, and for as many nights as it took. The jury left the courtroom, and Alexa let out a long sigh. Her job was done. Sam and Jack looked at her with admiration.

"You did a hell of a job," Sam said, somewhat in awe of her strength and precision. Watching Alexa in court was like watching ballet. She had an amazing way of making complicated information sound simple and reasonable to the jury, as she questioned witnesses and asked them to explain in simple terms what they'd said before. It was a very clever way of not confusing a jury with overly technical details.

As she stood up, Luke Quentin was led away in handcuffs by the four deputies who had been with him throughout the trial. He looked at her in open hatred this time. He knew too that it hadn't gone well. He said nothing to

Alexa and moved on, but if he could have murdered her with a look, she would have been dead on the spot. She was more than ever grateful that she had sent Savannah away. Until he was behind bars in a maximum security prison for life, she didn't feel safe.

Sam, Jack, and Alexa had to stay near the courtroom but not in it while they waited for the jury to deliberate. They were all available on their cell phones, and decided to go back to Alexa's office. It was hard to believe it was almost over. Alexa hoped they'd convict, and it was difficult to imagine they wouldn't. But juries were unpredictable and quixotic. If they had a "reasonable doubt," even if they had been too confused to assimilate the information, he'd go free. They had all seen it happen.

Sam sprawled out on the couch in Alexa's office, while Jack relaxed in a chair, and Alexa sat down with her feet on the desk. She was excited, but exhausted, and had been running on adrenaline and fumes for almost five weeks, since jury selection. It was the

first of June. Savannah was graduating
in Charleston in ten days. Life would
be normal again by then. The DA had
promised her a week's vacation as soon
as the verdict came in. He stuck his
head into her office as she sat there and
said he had seen her closing argument
and it had been excellent. He had been
in the courtroom frequently during the
trial, as had several senior members of
the FBI.

There was no call from the court that
afternoon, and little conversation in her
office. They were too tired and anxious
to speak.

Finally, the judge's clerk called, and
told them to go home. The jury was going to a hotel for the night, and would
reconvene to deliberate in the morning.
Alexa reported it to Jack and Sam, and
they both groaned. They were hoping
the verdict had come in, although it was
early for that. They invited her to dinner,
but she said she was too tired. She went
home and sat on the couch and stared
at the TV mindlessly. It had been an incredibly grueling five weeks. Alexa fell
asleep on the couch, in her clothes,

without dinner and with the TV on, and didn't wake up until seven a.m. the next day. She looked at her watch as she woke with a start. She had to shower and dress. The jury was reconvening in two hours.

Chapter 17

Sam, Jack, Alexa, the judge, the public defender, and the families of the victims waited through another long day, while the jury deliberated, with no results. They were all about to leave so the jury could be sent to a hotel for another night, when the foreman sounded the buzzer in the judge's chambers that announced they had reached a verdict.

Court was immediately reconvened, and the defendant was brought in.

The elderly man who was the foreman of the jury stood up and looked at the judge.

"Have you reached a verdict, Mr.

Foreman?" the judge said formally, as the man nodded.

"Yes, we have, Your Honor. The jury has reached a unanimous verdict." Alexa heaved a small sigh of relief. No hung jury. No retrial. Whatever it was, it was over. They had all done their jobs, the jury as well.

The judge instructed the defendant to stand at the defense table and then turned to the foreman again.

"And how do you find the defendant on eighteen charges of rape, Mr. Foreman?"

"Guilty, Your Honor," he said clearly, as Alexa glanced at Sam. They hadn't won yet, but they were halfway there. There was an intake of breath in the courtroom.

"And how do you find the defendant on eighteen charges of murder in the first degree?"

"Guilty, Your Honor," the foreman said, looking at the judge, but not at Luke. Guilty on all counts.

There were shouts and screams and crying in the courtroom from where the family members sat, and a moderate amount of pandemonium, as the judge rapped his gavel and called everyone to order. Alexa noticed Charlie and his mother hugging and crying as the judge thanked the jury for their hard work and civic responsibility, and many weeks of their time, and they were led from the room immediately, as was Luke, this time in both handcuffs and leg irons, which they had ready for him. She couldn't help herself, Alexa watched him go. He turned toward her as they led him away and in the most venomous tone he could muster, looking like the killer he was, he spat "Fuck you!" at her, and was gone. Judy had tried to comfort him before he left, and he had pushed her away, and she was sitting in her seat, stunned. Alexa went across the aisle to her to shake her hand.

"You couldn't win this one, Judy. You never had a chance. The case was just too tight. He should have pleaded." She looked up at Alexa with sad eyes.

"I don't think he did it. That's the awful part," she said as Alexa looked at her in silent disbelief. The awful part was that she believed a man who was a stone-cold killer and a sociopath. Alexa said as gently as she could, "I think he did." She hoped Judy would never see him again after the sentencing. She was sorry she had to see him again then herself.

The judge rapped the gavel again then and said that sentencing in this matter would be held on July 10th, and both prosecution and defense were expected to be present, and the defendant. And then he thanked everyone, dismissed the court, and disappeared into his chambers. It was seven-thirty at night, and he wanted to go home. And so did Alexa. All she wanted was to see Savannah now. She hadn't seen her in a month.

It took ten cops to get her through the wall of photographers on the steps this time. They were pushing and grabbing and wanted comments from her and interviews, and she just smiled at them and hurried down the steps to the patrol car as they ran after her.

"What do you have to say? How does it feel?" They were calling her name, and she turned to them just before she got in the car and smiled. "Justice has been served. That's all that matters. The murderer of eighteen women was convicted. That's what we're here for. That's our job," she said, and the police drove her away.

Savannah called her on her cell phone before she got home. She had just heard the news, and what her mother said.

"I'm so proud of you, Mom."

"I'm proud of you, sweetheart. I'm sorry it took so long."

"Everyone thinks you're a hero, and you are to me."

"You're my hero," Alexa said, relaxing for the first time in months. She was going to enjoy every minute she could with Savannah over the summer, to make up for lost time. "I'll fly down tomorrow, sweetheart. Are you ready to come home?"

"Right after graduation, Mom. It's just another week."

"I know." Alexa had already agreed to it. "And then you graduate here. I have to be at the sentencing in July, but I thought we could go to Europe then for a few weeks. I need a vacation!" She laughed.

They chatted for a few minutes, and Alexa promised to be there the next day. She was a free woman. It was over. Luke Quentin would be in prison forever. She still had two detectives protecting her for the next month, but life could become normal again. And Savannah could come home at last. She was smiling broadly to herself when she let herself into her apartment. She had done her job. And it was a great feeling knowing she had done it well. She was flying.

Chapter 18

As promised, Alexa was on the plane to Charleston at noon the next day. Savannah had taken time off from school, and was going to meet her mother at the airport, and they could hardly wait to see each other.

Alexa had spoken to her mother the night before, while she was packing. Her mother had congratulated her profusely on the case. Stanley had called her too and done the same. He had slipped into the courtroom a couple of times to watch her, and said she had handled the prosecution brilliantly and with poise. She had never tried to turn it into a circus and had relied on facts and forensic evidence, which he thought was the way to go, and had won the case.

Sam had called that morning before she left for the airport and said he would miss her. He was based in Washington, D.C., normally and was going back, although he was in New York often and suggested they have lunch in the fall. Jack had called to congratulate her, as had Joe McCarthy the day before. There was an atmosphere of victory and celebration, and now she could bring her daughter home, which was even better. There had never been another letter. Quentin had hinted recently to one of the guards in jail that he had played a "little game" to scare Alexa, and Jack had told her about it. Quentin had been toying with her by having a friend drop off the letters to Savannah. Quentin thought it was funny, and it had made Alexa even more pleased with her decision to send Savannah away. The letters had stopped as soon as his friend reported Savannah gone, and Quentin lost interest in the "game." It hadn't been a game to Alexa. It had been pure terror, worrying about Savannah and the letters.

And Alexa was willing to concede that the time in Charleston may have done Savannah good. It had established a real bond with her father, which meant a lot to her, even if it had angered his wife. And Alexa's mother reminded her again that it was nice for Savannah to know something about her father's family too, and to meet a grandmother who was very old and wouldn't be around forever. The timing had been right, and it had been a blessing for them all. Even for Alexa, she had put old ghosts to rest, and was no longer as bitter as she had been for so long. When she looked at Tom now, she saw a weak man who had paid a high price for his betrayal of her. She didn't see a man she loved, or even hated. She felt freer than she had in years.

Savannah was waiting for her when she got off the plane, and they hugged each other and held tight. Savannah drove her to the hotel in the little car her father had loaned her, and she went back to school, and promised to come back later.

Tom called her while she was unpacking, and congratulated her too. He had seen her on television the night before when she left the courthouse, and as always, had been impressed by how humble she was when she said justice had been served and let it go at that. She wanted no glory, just the conviction, and she had done it.

"You must be exhausted," he said sympathetically, and she admitted she was.

"But it was worth it, for the conviction."

"Are you staying for Savannah's graduation next week?" he asked hopefully.

"No, I have to get back. I only have a week off, and I'll be at the one in New York." She was still grateful to him for keeping Savannah for four months. It had worked out perfectly for her too, and gave her the time she needed to prepare for the trial without worrying about Savannah.

"I'm going to be very sad when she leaves," he admitted to her. "And so will

Daisy. I hope you're planning to come down at the end of June for Travis's wedding." She didn't know if he was being honest or polite and just southern. It was hard to tell.

"It was sweet of them to ask me, but I think it would be awkward for your wife." He was disappointed when she said it. He had hoped she'd be there.

"With eight hundred guests, you could bring a bear in a hula skirt and no one would notice."

"But maybe not an ex-wife," she said honestly. "I'm sure Luisa doesn't want me." This was her turf, not Alexa's. She was respectful of that, although Luisa hadn't been of hers.

"It's not up to Luisa, it's up to Travis and Scarlette. And I know they'd like you to come. Savannah wants to come down too."

"She can do that if she wants to. I'll talk to her about it. She's a big girl, she could come alone."

"I hope you come, Alexa," he said softly, and she ignored it. The softness in his voice was too familiar and bittersweet, and much too late.

"We'll see," she said noncommittally, which they both knew meant no.

"I'll see you sometime this week, before you go."

"I'm just going to take it easy and spend time with Savannah, and get over the trial. I'm beat," she said honestly, and she sounded it, but happy too.

Savannah was back by six o'clock, and they wandered the cobblestone streets together. The weather was hot now, the flowers lush and fragrant. It was Charleston at its most beautiful and romantic. Alexa spent her days wandering around when Savannah was in school, and went to visit one of the old plantations and took a tour. She and Savannah went to the beach that weekend, and Turner joined them. And Alexa took Savannah and a dozen of her friends out to dinner for a pre-graduation celebration. They were all in high spirits, and Alexa was too.

The week in Charleston flew by, with no problems or unpleasant moments, or even encounters with Luisa. She was ignoring Savannah completely these days, which seemed to work well.

Savannah waited until the last night to ask her mother about Travis's wedding. She really wanted to go, and wanted Alexa to come with her. And it was a huge wedding, so Tom's point about it not being awkward with Luisa was well taken. The rehearsal dinner that he and Luisa were giving at the country club would have been awkward, but not the wedding reception. Alexa had had lunch with him again, and he had pointed that out. He didn't mention again how much he missed her, or how sorry he was, or how unhappy with Luisa. He respected the boundaries she had established, and she was grateful for that. She wouldn't have seen him again otherwise. She was past it. It was over for her, all behind her now.

"Will you, Mom?" Savannah pleaded, looking more like five than seventeen, and her mother laughed.

"What difference does it make if I'm there? You'll be having fun with your friends." Everyone she knew was invited, even Turner and Julianne, as their parents were going too. It was a very small social circle in Charleston, and eight hundred guests represented everyone who mattered in town. Savannah said that even the governor was coming to the rehearsal dinner, and several senators to the wedding, at least two. Luisa loved showing off her social and political connections, and so did Scarlette's parents. The two families were well matched, as were the bride and groom.

"It'll just be more fun if you're there. We can come down together." She hadn't told her mother yet that she wanted to come back in August to see Turner before they both left for college. The romance had lasted and was going strong. They were in love.

"All right, all right," Alexa finally conceded, "but it's awkward for me. I knew all those people while I was married, and now I'm an outcast." She looked awkward and forlorn as she said it, but she felt that way.

"You're not an outcast, Mom. You're a national media star. You're a famous prosecutor from New York."

"Don't be silly," Alexa said humbly, denying it. But it was true.

"You don't have anything to be ashamed of, Mom," Savannah insisted.

"Only that your dad dumped me, which was a big deal here, and to me. Huge, in fact." No matter how important she was in her job, that still mattered to her too.

"You're bigger than that. Besides, I think you're over it," Savannah said cautiously, not wanting to upset her mother. "You don't want him anymore, and I'll bet you could have him, if you did. He's miserable with Luisa."

"I know," Alexa said quietly. He had told her as much himself. "And you're right, I don't want him now. But I did then."

"I know, Mom," Savannah said, putting her arms around her mother. "So you'll come?"

"Yes, yes." She rolled her eyes. "I'll send the reply card back tomorrow."

"I already told Scarlette I'd go," Savannah giggled.

They spent a lovely last night together, and Alexa left for the airport when Savannah went to school the next morning. She had thought it would be her last visit to Charleston, but it appeared there would be one more, for the wedding.

Alexa told her mother about it when she got home.

"I don't know how I let Savannah talk me into it," Alexa complained. "And now I have to buy a dress."

"It might do you good. Maybe you'll meet someone," Muriel said hopefully. It had always seemed ironic to both of them that Muriel had more of a love life than she did.

"That's all I need is to meet some other southern charmer," Alexa said ruefully. "One is enough in a lifetime. Been there, done that. I don't need another one."

"They're not all like Tom," her mother reminded her.

"That's true. Or like Luisa. But their society is certainly inbred at times, and if you're not one of them, you're screwed. I hope Savannah doesn't wind up there, and comes back to New York after college."

"God knows where she'll want to be, depending on her jobs, or who she falls in love with. I managed while you lived in Charleston."

"Yeah, but you had Stanley even then. I don't. I have Savannah."

"Maybe you need more than that in your life," her mother reminded her again. "You can't hang everything on her. It's not healthy for either of you."

"Well, I'm about to get dumped anyway, when she leaves for college." Alexa was worried about it, but their time apart for the last four months was a good practice run. Alexa was terrified of the empty nest thing. And even in the last four months, the apartment had been agonizingly quiet without Savannah. Alexa was glad she was only going to Princeton, and no farther. "Do you want to go shopping with me this weekend?" she asked her mother. "I need a dress for the wedding. It's black tie."

"I'd love it." Muriel sounded delighted, and they made a date to go to Barney's on Saturday, and have lunch.

"I haven't bought an evening gown in years," Alexa said, sounding excited . . . eleven years . . . since she was married to Tom . . . and now she was going back, not as his wife, but as her own person . . . the prosecutor from New York, as Savannah put it . . . how life had changed.

When Savannah graduated in Charleston, her mother was already back at work, handling a number of small cases that were a breeze after the Quentin case. She was still very much a local star for that. Several magazines had wanted to interview her, and she had declined. But she had admitted to Jack that she was a little bored with the minor cases she was handling now. It was hard to get back to routine cases after one as challenging as the one she had just done. And she was surprised to find she missed working with the FBI. Jack wondered if she was burned out, but didn't ask.

At Savannah's Charleston graduation, the girls wore white dresses under their gowns, and the boys wore suits. The girls carried flowers, and everyone cried when they sang the school song. It was emotional and tender and everything it should have been. And her father gave her a lunch afterward at the country club. Travis and Scarlette came, and Turner, Daisy, and her father of course, and Grandmother Beaumont came to the graduation and lunch. Luisa had been invited to both but made no pretense of caring and declined. At least, she was true to what she felt till the end. The only thing she wanted to celebrate was Savannah leaving in two days. And she was still furious that she was coming back for the wedding. She hoped that it would be the last they would see of her for a long time. She didn't want her in Charleston again, although Tom was already making noises about Thanksgiving. Luisa wouldn't hear of it. No one missed her at lunch.

It was lovely in the garden of the country club. Her grandmother gave her a small pearl necklace that had been her own mother's, and her father gave her a very handsome check and told her how proud of her he was. She said she was going to buy what she would need for college. And she was coming back to Charleston to see Turner in August, and all of them of course. Tom hoped that Luisa would be away then, visiting her family in Alabama, as she did every summer. She had relatives all over the South.

For the two days after graduation, Savannah spent as much time with Turner as she could. He had a job working in the oil fields in Mississippi for June and July, and he was going to miss her terribly when she left. She was the love and light of his life. He was coming to New York for her other graduation the following week but could only stay for two days, but they were grateful for that.

Savannah's last night at Thousand Oaks was bittersweet, as she lay in bed with Daisy, holding hands, just as they had the first night. It was a hot, moonlit night, and the girls whispered and cuddled until they fell asleep. Savannah wanted her to visit in New York or at Princeton, but both girls were afraid Luisa wouldn't let her, and they were going to try and arrange it with their father.

Daisy stood crying on the front steps when Savannah left. Jed had put all her things in the car, and Tallulah was dabbing her eyes. Julianne had come to say goodbye too, and was sobbing. And just before she left, Savannah went back inside to say goodbye to Luisa, who hadn't come out. She found her stiff-backed at the kitchen table, eating breakfast and reading the paper.

"Thank you for everything, Luisa," Savannah said politely, as her father watched from the doorway with an ache in his heart. Savannah was such a good girl and had tried so hard, and Luisa had no mercy at all. "I'm sorry if I was a nuisance while I was here. It was wonderful," Savannah said, with tears in her eyes. She was genuinely sad to leave, although happy to go back to her mother. She had gotten something here that she had never really had before, a father. And that wouldn't stop now.

"You weren't a nuisance," Luisa said coldly. "Have a safe trip." She made no move to come toward Savannah, and then picked up her newspaper again.

"Goodbye," Savannah said softly, and left the kitchen with her father. It was about as warm a goodbye as she'd ever get from Luisa.

Savannah gave Daisy a last hug and got into the car. Daisy and Julianne and the two old servants were waving as she and Tom drove away from Thousand Oaks. Savannah would never have believed it, but she hated to leave Charleston, and what felt now like her second home. Even Luisa hadn't been able to spoil it for her. Savannah thought that even though she had missed her mother, they were the happiest four months of her life. She had two real parents now and loved them both.

Chapter 19

Savannah's New York graduation was the antithesis of the one in Charleston. All her friends wore jeans with holes in them, and tank tops and sneakers or flip-flops under their gowns. No one carried flowers or wore pretty white dresses, and the boys wore T-shirts and jeans, and Nikes or flip-flops, but they let out the same wild war whoop of glee the moment they had graduated, and threw their caps in the air, and then tore off the rented gowns.

Everyone had been thrilled to see Savannah, and she had stayed in touch with most of them by e-mail and phone from Charleston. But it felt strange to be back here now. Everything seemed so different in New York. She wasn't sure where she was most at home now, she loved both. She didn't say it to her mother, but she really missed Charleston at times.

Turner had come up for her New York graduation, and she showed him all the sights. All her girlfriends thought he was gorgeous and really nice, and even the boys she knew liked him. And her grandmother took them both to lunch, and she showed him her court. Turner was impressed that her grandmother was a judge, and her mother an assistant DA. His own mom had never worked before she died.

"Neither did mine when she was married to my dad," Savannah explained. "She went to law school after they got divorced, and my grandma went when my grampa died. Sort of to keep busy and not be so sad." Turner had admitted to her that his father had a twenty-six-year-old girlfriend and was thinking of getting remarried, and he and his brothers were really upset about it. He was lonely without his late wife.

Savannah and Turner did everything they had hoped to in New York. She took him to the top of the Empire State Building, which he wanted to see, they rode on the Staten Island Ferry, and went to the Statue of Liberty and the museum at Ellis Island. And they went to the Bronx Zoo, saw the animals, and felt like little kids again. And they went to Long Island and walked on the beach. They were already figuring out how they were going to spend time in Duke and Princeton with each other in the fall. They had every intention of continuing their romance. And whenever they were apart, even for an hour, they called and texted each other constantly. They both felt like it was going to be an eternity before she came back to Charleston to visit in August, after Europe with her mother. But at least they had the wedding ahead of them. It was ten days away when Turner left New York.

And the day after he left, Savannah found a dress. Alexa had found hers with her mother the day they went shopping at Barney's. She had bought something totally out of character for her. It was a peach-colored strapless chiffon gown that was low cut and very sexy, and the skirt was long and graceful. She had bought high-heeled silver sandals to wear with it. She tried it on for Savannah and was worried that it was too low cut and too revealing for her.

"Mom," Savannah scolded her, "you're thirty-nine years old, not a hundred. You *should* look sexy."

"That's what Grandma said. I don't know what you two have in mind. Maybe you're planning to pimp me out. I have nowhere to wear this afterward." It seemed like a waste of money, but she had fallen in love with it and hadn't had a dress like it in years.

Savannah was pleased that her mother had bought such a pretty dress. "You're wearing it to Travis's wedding. That's enough. You look beautiful."

"Maybe I can have it shortened and wear it to the office," her mother teased. "It'll look great in court at my next trial."

"There is more to life than work," Savannah scolded her again, and Alexa shrugged.

Sam had called her a couple of times to see what she was up to, and they both admitted that there was a let-down after the trial. Everything else seemed so insignificant compared to what they'd been doing. But serial killers with eighteen victims in nine states didn't come around often in any-one's career. It was nice to feel they'd made a difference in the world and done their jobs well. The sentencing was scheduled for the day before she left for Europe with Savannah. They were going to Paris, London, and Florence, with maybe a weekend in the South of France. Alexa was planning to splurge, and they were staying for three weeks. And then Savannah would go back to Charleston to see Turner for two weeks. Alexa had agreed to that too. She didn't want to stand in the way of romance.

The dress Savannah had bought for her brother's wedding was a pale blue satin, strapless like her mother's, though not quite so low cut. It was long too, and she had bought sexy high heels to match. They were both going to be knockouts, Muriel assured them. She and Stanley were going on vacation that summer too. They were taking a long driving trip in Montana and Wyoming, which was what they liked to do, hiking, riding, and fishing. Savannah said it sounded awful. She was much more excited about her trip with her mother, especially Paris.

Savannah and Alexa arrived at the Wentworth Mansion in Charleston on Friday afternoon, even though they weren't going to the rehearsal dinner hosted by Tom and Luisa, nor the church service, which was only for immediate family and close friends. St. Stephen's was too small to hold all the guests they had invited to the reception. But they wanted plenty of time to relax and get ready for the next day. They had an appointment at the hotel spa that night.

Savannah called Daisy as soon as she arrived, and her father drove her over to see them briefly. She was all excited about being the flower girl and said she was wearing a really pretty dress. She checked out Savannah's dress in the closet and liked it, and afterward they went out for an ice cream cone, and then her father took her home. She had to go to the rehearsal dinner that night, and her mother would have a fit if she was late. So it was a short visit, but a nice one. Daisy had thrown herself into Savannah's arms like a cannonball, and the two girls had hugged and kissed and giggled. It touched Alexa to see it. Daisy was a wonderful addition to Savannah's life, and the little sister she had always wanted. Alexa had just never expected it to be this one. And Savannah had already promised Daisy a weekend in Princeton and a visit to New York, which Tom swore he would make happen.

Turner had dinner with them that night, after they were finished at the spa. He and Savannah went out for a drive, and he offered to escort them to the reception the next day, which sounded great to Savannah and even her mother. She didn't want to take a cab or rent a limo and show off.

The reception was at six o'clock, and Turner picked them up promptly at five-thirty, in an old Mercedes he had borrowed from his father, and he whistled when he saw them. Alexa looked like a princess in the peach chiffon gown with her hair in an elegant French twist, and Savannah looked spectacular in the blue dress that was the color of her eyes, with just enough but not too much cleavage. Her mother's dress wasn't inappropriate, but a little more daring. Turner said they looked absolutely gorgeous and he was proud to escort them. He was wearing a summer tux, with a white dinner jacket and traditional black trousers with a satin stripe, and the black patent leather pumps that were old-fashioned but proper, and a real black satin bow tie, not a clip-on.

"You are one *very* handsome young man," Alexa complimented him, happy for Savannah. They looked adorable together, so young and innocent and hopeful, the way people in love should be.

The wedding was at St. Stephen's Church where Alexa had gone with Savannah and they'd run into Luisa and Daisy. But Alexa and Savannah went straight to the reception afterward with Turner in his car, as they were not invited to the church. Luisa had seen to that. Alexa expected to be seated in the parking lot at the reception, or the kitchen, and suspected that Savannah wouldn't fare much better, but they didn't really care. They had come for Travis and Scarlette, and to have a good time. Neither Alexa nor Savannah cared where they sat. And as long as Turner was there with her, Savannah was happy.

As they reached the receiving line at the reception, Scarlette looked like a medieval queen, standing proudly beside Travis. Her gown was exquisite, and Scarlette looked prettier than anyone had ever seen her. And Travis looked like the happiest, proudest man in the world, with Henry beside him as the best man, and a dozen groomsmen and bridesmaids stood around them. Scarlette's older sister was maid of honor, and Daisy as the flower girl was wearing a billowing white organdy dress, carrying a satin basket of rose petals. There were banks of flowers everywhere, including orchids, gardenias, and lily of the valley. The flowers had been flown in from all over the world. It was a spectacular wedding.

"Wow!" Alexa whispered to her daughter, as she leaned toward her. "This is quite a wedding." Scarlette's parents were very important, and Luisa was extremely proud of the match, as though she had pulled off a major coup herself. And just as Daisy had said she would, she was wearing a screaming red satin dress, with a borrowed diamond tiara and ruby necklace. Tom looked faintly embarrassed when he saw it, but had said nothing. Luisa did what she wanted. He thought she had overplayed her hand a little, but no one seemed to notice.

Tom saw Savannah and Alexa, and he left the reception line for a minute to kiss them both.

"You look fantastic," he told Alexa with a tender expression. "I love the dress. Save me a dance." She was tempted to say "Whatever," as Savannah would have, but didn't. It was nice of him to say hello, and Henry came over soon after and crushed his sister in a bear hug.

"Oh my God, I'm going to eat you up, you look so good." He nuzzled her neck with kisses, and she laughed, and then he grinned at her mother too. "You look beautiful too, Alexa. Really, really great. Sexy dress."

"Not too much so, I hope," she said, looking nervous.

"You're a media star from New York. Screw them," Henry said, looking dashing in his tuxedo. His was more modern than what most of the men were wearing there, and he had bought it in LA. The groom was wearing white tie and tails.

As predicted, Luisa was too busy to notice Alexa and Savannah. The crowd filtering in to the reception was huge. Scarlette's parents' estate was vast. And as people drifted by them, Henry introduced Alexa as his step-mother, which touched her heart. People vaguely remembered the story when he said it, but had forgotten until then that his father had been married before.

They thought it was lovely that she and the boys were still close.

She and Henry milled around together for a while, Savannah came and went, Tom appeared for a moment again and reminded her about the dance. And then the family disappeared to take photos with the bride and groom, and Alexa wandered around alone, with a glass of champagne in her hand. She saw some vaguely familiar faces in the crowd, but no one she knew well, and she was relieved.

Henry surfaced again half an hour later, and walked her in to dinner. She had been given an escort card at the door, with her seat and table number.

"Ooops," Henry said, as he glanced at hers. "You're in Siberia. To be expected. My mother must have helped them with the seating." They were both laughing, because she had expected it too.

"Bless her heart," Alexa added, and they laughed even harder.

"Precisely. She's ignoring me tonight because I refused to bring a woman. I can always tell her I brought you." Alexa was happy to be with him. He was great company and very attentive when he took her to her seat, and then left her for his own at the other side of the tent. Savannah wasn't at Alexa's table either. Before he left her, he had warned her that many dignitaries would be there that night, probably the President, the Queen of England, and almost surely the Pope. He was as much fun as he had been as a child, and she had always loved him, although she loved Travis too. Travis had been a much quieter child, but Henry had always been funny and outrageous.

The people at Alexa's table seemed perfectly pleasant. There were four older couples, most of them her mother's age, and she was seated next to a Catholic priest, who was very interesting and nice to talk to as they chatted. But contrary to her mother's hope for her, she was not about to meet Prince Charming tonight. She hadn't expected to anyway, and didn't care.

Henry came to visit her several times throughout the evening. She caught glimpses of Savannah and Turner now and then in the distance, and when the music started after dinner, Henry led her onto the floor for a dance. The entire wedding reception was in an incredibly enormous tent.

"Do you suppose they got it at the county fair?" Henry asked her as they started dancing, and she giggled. The tent looked like ten thousand miles of white satin. They had had two dances when Tom spotted them and cut in. The music had just changed to a fox-trot and Tom glided her gracefully around the floor. It was a strange feeling for Alexa to be dancing with him, but she decided to be a good sport and ignore it. They had just made a turn when they crashed heavily into a man walking across the dance floor, probably to get to the bar. Tom ignored him at first and then realized he knew him. He kept Alexa's hand in his own, but pulled her a few feet with him so he could say hello to the man and not lose her. He looked vaguely familiar to Alexa, but she had no idea who he was. He was about fifty years old, tall and distinguished, with salt-and-pepper hair, and he smiled when he saw Tom, and then even more broadly when he saw Alexa.

"What are *you* doing here?" he said with a smile, and she assumed he had mistaken her for someone else. Hopefully not Luisa.

"I'm sorry?"

"I've been watching you on the news for the last month. That was quite a case you won, counselor. Congratulations!" She was amazed that he had recognized her here, and both embarrassed and pleased to be complimented on the case. She had been worried for a minute that his smile of acknowledgment and delight had been aimed at her cleavage, not her brain. This was better.

Tom introduced them then. And it was her turn to be surprised. "Senator Edward Baldwin," Tom said formally, and Alexa realized why he looked familiar. He had the same heavy Charleston drawl as everyone else there, and was senator from South Carolina. One of the dignitaries Henry had promised, if not the Pope.

Alexa smiled at him. "It's an honor to meet you, Senator." They shook hands, he nodded, and headed for the bar, and she and Tom continued dancing and commenting on what a beautiful wedding it was. They both knew it must have cost Scarlette's parents a million dollars, but they could cleary afford it. Alexa liked the fact that Scarlette was so unassuming and that all she wanted to do was be a nurse, and have babies in a few years. There was nothing showy or pretentious about Travis's bride. Alexa approved, and so did Tom. Luisa was thrilled with the wedding and the obvious expense. And the rehearsal dinner had gone off well. Luisa had pulled out all the stops, not to be outdone by the parents of the bride, but she was anyway.

Tom danced another dance with Alexa, a slow waltz in honor of the old folks, which reminded her of their wedding in New York. And then he took her back to her table. There was too much noise to really have a serious conversation, and she was grateful for that. He had a wistful look in his eye and was drinking a lot of champagne. She thanked him for the dances, and went back to chatting with the priest.

It was two hours later, as she was thinking of making a discreet escape back to the hotel on her own, when Senator Baldwin appeared out of nowhere and sat down in the seat the priest had vacated.

"Is anyone sitting here?" he asked, looking worried.

"Just the Pope," Alexa said casually, and he laughed out loud. "I was told by my stepson he was going to be here, but it was just a priest from the local church. He left."

"I was fascinated by your case," he launched back into the subject. "How did you keep it out of the hands of the feds with all those states involved?"

"I refused to give it up." She smiled at him. "And my DA put up a good fight. We got the first four cases, so it didn't seem fair to lose it to the feds after we did all the work. They kept a pretty close eye on us, but they let us keep it to the end."

"That was quite a victory for you," he said, looking impressed again.

"Not really. We had an airtight case, with DNA matches with every victim. Are you an attorney, Senator?"

"Used to be. I've been in politics for twenty-five years." She knew that about him too. "I was a prosecutor for about two years when I started. I didn't have the stomach for it, or the talent. I like politics better than the law."

"What you do is a lot harder," she said admiringly. She wasn't impressed by his position, but thought he was smart. He obviously thought the same of her.

"What brings you to Charleston?" he asked with interest, and she hesitated for only a fraction of a second, and then answered.

"I used to be married to the father of the groom, a long time ago." He smiled when he heard it and nodded.

"That's great that you stayed close. My ex-wife and I have been divorced for twenty years. We spend all our holidays together. I'm crazy about her husband. Great man. Much better husband for her than I was. I've been married to the Senate for twenty years. She married him and had three more kids. We have two.

It makes for wonderful holidays together." She didn't tell the senator that her relationship with Tom and Luisa was not that way at all, and Luisa was not her best friend. Luisa would have had a stroke if Alexa showed up for Christmas. Alexa just laughed and nodded, it was simpler. He asked her for a dance then, to be polite.

She asked if he was from Charleston. And he said from Beaufort, which she knew was nearby, and a pretty place. He was pure South Carolina through and through, was undoubtedly related to a dozen generals, and probably had a mother in the United Daughters of the Confederacy, like Tom's.

They danced for a few minutes. He was an elegant dancer who was easy to follow, and was surprisingly tall once she was in his arms. And then he totally startled her with a confession, and said that he didn't enjoy spending time in the South. He said he spent most of his time in Washington, D.C., and preferred it. "I don't have a lot of patience with all the local gossip, all the grande old dames waving the Confederate flag, and everyone being 'nasty nice' about everyone else while smiling and putting the knife in their back. It's a little complicated for me. Washington is a lot simpler." That wasn't always simple either, Alexa knew. But what he said was exactly how she felt and would never have dared to say, especially here, or to him, about the South.

"I have to admit," she confessed in return, "I've had thoughts in the same vein." And as she said it, Luisa danced past them in her bright red dress with her tiara askew. When she saw who Alexa was dancing with, she looked like she was going to have a tantrum, but there was nothing she could do about it as her partner led her away on the floor. "I loved it when I lived here, but then it all kind of blew up in my face. I went back to New York, very sour about the South. I just came back to Charleston for the first time in ten years a few months ago."

"It's nice of you to come back. We don't always treat northerners well." They certainly hadn't, but she didn't say it. And she was amazed that he had, and was so honest.

"Was your wife from the South?" Alexa asked politely, and he laughed.

"Certainly not. She's from Los Angeles and hates the South with a passion. That was one of the reasons why she left me. Once I got into politics, she knew I'd have to spend time here, so she bailed out. Now she and her husband live in New York. She's a writer and he's a producer." They sounded like interesting people, and so was he. She hadn't met a handsome prince that night, as her mother had hoped, for her to fall in love with. But instead she had met an interesting senator to talk to. He teased Alexa then. "If you tell anyone what I just said about the South, I'll lose my seat and blame it on you." She put a finger to her lips, and they both laughed, and then he took her back to her table.

Henry came and kept her company again after a while, and eventually she found Savannah and told her she was leaving. A wild rock band had just started playing, and she knew that she and Turner would want to stay for hours. Alexa was ready to go home. It had been fun, but she'd had enough. They cut the wedding cake finally a few minutes later, and then she left. She congratulated Travis and Scarlette again, kissed Henry, and caught a glimpse of Tom as she left. He was at the bar, alone, looking unhappy and very drunk. Luisa was dancing wildly to the rock band, with her tiara over one ear and a wild look on her face. Alexa hadn't seen Tom go near her all night.

Alexa didn't say goodbye to him when she left. She didn't want to deal with him if he was drunk, that was more than she wanted to take on. So she got in one of the cabs waiting outside the tent and went back to the hotel. It was after midnight, which was late enough for her. And at the hotel, she took off the peach dress and put on her comfortable nightgown.

"Goodbye, pretty dress," she said, putting it on the hanger. "See you again never." She knew she wouldn't be wearing a dress like that again in this lifetime. Or not for a hell of a long time, if ever. She never went to parties like this. It had been an amazing wedding and she'd had fun talking to Henry, the senator, and the priest, and even dancing, which she hadn't done in years.

She heard Savannah come in around three-thirty, and smiled as she slipped into bed beside her.

"Have fun?" Alexa muttered with her eyes closed.

"I loved it, it was terrific. Thank you for coming," Savannah said, and kissed her mother's shoulder. Alexa smiled and went back to sleep.

Chapter 20

"I feel like Cinderella after the ball," Alexa admitted to Jack the following week when he stopped by her office to give her some files.

"After the wedding in Charleston?" he asked as he sat down.

"No, after the Quentin case. I'm back to real life and human-sized cases. It's a little tough after all that excitement." He laughed.

"We'll try to find you another serial killer sometime soon." But he felt the same way. They dealt with a lot of routine cases, not just big ones. And most of the time it was tedious work.

He had just left her office when the

phone rang on her desk, and she picked it up herself. Her secretary was out to lunch. There was a deep voice on the other end that she didn't recognize.

"Counselor?"

"Yes, Alexa Hamilton here," she said officially.

"Senator Baldwin," he said, equally so, and then laughed.

"Are you showing off, Senator? You outrank me." It was a bold thing to say to him since she hardly knew him, but she knew he had a sense of humor.

"Absolutely, and yes, I do. I'm in New York for two days and wondered if you'd like to have lunch." He was as straight-forward as any northerner and didn't beat around the bush.

"That would be fun," she said, smiling.

"Are you very busy these days?" he asked her.

"Not busy enough. I'm buried in paperwork."

"How disappointing." He suggested a time and place for lunch the next day, sounded rushed and hung up. She was startled by the call, but he might be a good man to know, and he was certainly interesting to talk to. She had no idea why he had called her. He hadn't flirted with her at the party, and she liked him. He seemed like a bright, amusing person.

She had a minor court appearance the next day, and took a cab uptown to the restaurant he had suggested. It was a chic, busy Italian bistro with good food, that she'd been to before, but not in a long time. He was waiting at a table when she arrived, looking at some papers, and slipped them back into his briefcase. He had a town car and driver waiting outside.

They talked about everything from politics to law to his children, who were twenty-one and twenty-five. His twenty-one-year-old daughter was at UCLA and loving it, and his twenty-five-year-old son was in London, with the Royal Shakespeare Company. He had recently graduated from NYU, at the Tisch School of the Arts. He said his daughter wanted to be a doctor, everyone else in the family was literary or artistic, including their mother, who he said was somewhat eccentric but great fun. He spoke of her like a sister. Alexa hadn't reached that point yet with Tom, and probably never would. But at least they had finally reached a good place. Tom had come to say goodbye to her and Savannah the day after the wedding. He looked depressed and hungover, and she felt sorry for him. But not sorry enough to want him back.

Alexa said that she and her daughter were leaving for three weeks in Europe right after the sentencing in the Quentin case on July 10th. It was still two weeks away.

"I'm going over too," Edward Baldwin said easily. "I use my ex-wife's house in the South of France, in Ramatuelle. It's near Saint-Tropez, but not as crowded. I'm going to Umbria after that. I've rented a villa. Where will you be with your daughter?" He was interested in her and friendly, but she didn't have the feeling that he was pursuing her, and she liked that. Maybe they could be friends.

"Paris, London, Florence, and maybe something in the South, like Cannes or

Antibes. I haven't been in a long time, but this is a graduation present for my daughter and we had kind of a tough spring. I had to send her away for four months during the trial and before. She was getting threatening letters, from the defendant. He was doing it to unnerve me apparently, I learned later, and it did."

"How awful."

"Yeah. It was pretty scary. That's how she wound up in Charleston with her father. I had nowhere else to send her."

"Have you stayed close since the divorce?" He had assumed she had the same kind of relationship with her ex that he did. Alexa laughed and shook her head.

"We didn't speak for ten years. And he hardly saw his daughter, until February. But the last four months changed all that, so I guess it was a blessing for us all, except his wife." She decided to give it to him in a nutshell. "Simply put, he got dumped by his wife, who abandoned him and their two boys. He married me, everybody was happy, and his first wife came back seven years later, I got dumped, and he went back to her. And his mother helped. I'm not from the South, his first wife is. All very simple. So I came back to New York, became a lawyer, and lived happily ever after. I have one daughter from that marriage, and two stepsons I love and just saw again for the first time in ten years, one of whom was the groom at the wedding. And my ex has a very cute ten-year-old who was the vehicle wife number one used to get him back."

"Let me guess," Edward Baldwin said with a look of disapproval. He didn't like the story, although she told it lightly and with a touch of humor, but he could see the hurt in her eyes. "And now they hate each other, and he wants you back."

"Something like that." Alexa nodded. "I'm not interested. It's all over for me."

"It sounds like a bad southern novel," Edward Baldwin commented. His divorce had been simple and clean. His wife left him, but he didn't blame her, and they were still friends. She had done it nicely. "Do you hate him?" He looked curious as he asked. He wouldn't have blamed her if she did.

Hearing the story, he disliked him. He despised men like that.

Alexa didn't hesitate this time. "No. Not now. Something healed it for me when I went back there, and saw him, and how weak and pathetic he really is. He betrayed me, but ultimately he betrayed himself, and now he would betray her. I don't hate him now. I feel sorry for him. But I was pretty angry for a long time. Ten years. That's too long to carry a grudge. It's heavy lifting." She had discovered that the hard way, and realized it when she finally set it down.

"You never remarried?" She laughed at the question and shook her head.

"Nope. I was too hurt. And too busy with my work and my daughter. I'm happy like this. I don't need more than that."

"Everybody needs more than that. I do too. I just don't have time. I'm too busy taking political junkets to Taiwan and Vietnam, keeping my constituents happy, and playing the political game in Washington. It's fun. But it doesn't leave time for much else." They both knew that wasn't true either. There were lots of married senators—most of them, in fact. For whatever reason, he didn't want to be married again either. They had that in common. They were both afraid of something, getting hurt or commitment. And he didn't have the excuse of a nasty ex-wife who had screwed him over, since he said they were good friends and got along. He was obviously alone by choice. He had said in the course of lunch that he was fifty-two years old. And had been divorced for twenty. That was a man who either liked to play a lot or was afraid of getting tied down. Either way, Alexa thought he'd make a fine friend.

Eventually, he paid the check, and she thanked him for lunch. She hailed a cab to go back to work, and said good-bye to him in front of the restaurant. She had given him her card, and was surprised when he called her on her cell that afternoon.

"Hello, Alexa, it's Edward." His deep voice and southern accent were easy to recognize.

"Thanks again for lunch. It was fun."

"I enjoyed it too. I just had a thought. I'm having dinner with my ex-wife tomorrow night and her husband, and I wondered if you might like to meet them. She's a wonderful person."

"I'd like that very much," Alexa said. She gave him her address, and he said he'd pick her up at eight. She was startled when she hung up, and didn't even know what to say to Savannah, so she said nothing. She just got dressed for dinner the following night, and put on a black suit that she usually wore to court.

"What are you all dressed up for?" Savannah asked her as she came out of her bedroom. She was going to the movies with friends.

"I'm having dinner with a senator and his ex-wife." Even saying it sounded absurd.

"You're what? What senator?" Savannah didn't know of any that her mother knew.

"Senator Edward Baldwin, from South Carolina." Savannah vaguely remembered hearing that he was at the wedding but hadn't met him. Luisa had been bragging about him.

"Did you meet him at the wedding?"

"Your father introduced me. He's very

nice. Just as a friend. He followed the Quentin case on TV."

"So did the whole country." She looked at her mother more closely then. "Is this a date?" She was stunned. Her mother hadn't said a word.

"No. Just a friend," Alexa repeated. She looked blank.

"What's with the ex-wife?" Savannah looked suspicious, and her mother laughed.

"They're good friends." And with that, the doorman buzzed the intercom in the apartment and told her that there was a car waiting for her downstairs. She kissed Savannah, picked up her purse, and ran out the door, as Savannah stood staring after her and then rushed for her cell phone. She called her New York grandmother immediately, and Muriel answered on the first ring.

"Hi, cutie." She could see that it was Savannah. "What's up?"

"Red alert. Holy shit. I think Mom has a date."

"How do you know? With who?" Muriel was immediately interested.

"She got dressed up, and she was

having dinner with a senator she met at Travis's wedding, and his ex-wife."

"His ex-wife?" That sounded strange to her.

"They're friends," Savannah said in a conspiratorial tone.

"What senator?"

"Baldwin, from South Carolina."

"Well, I'll be damned," Muriel said, and they both burst into gales of excited laughter.

Chapter 21

The evening with Edward Baldwin's ex-wife was fun, unexpected, and totally crazy. She and her husband had a penthouse on Fifth Avenue, three unruly teenage sons, and he was a successful movie producer. As soon as Alexa met him, she recognized the name. And his wife was a best-selling author. She said she had only started writing after she left Edward, but Alexa knew she had had an extremely successful career ever since. She had met her husband when he had bought her book and produced the movie eighteen years before. They were attractive and funny and nuts. Sybil was wearing some kind of flowing robe she'd bought in Morocco. Her husband was in jeans and an African shirt. They had four dogs who were everywhere, King Charles Spaniels, and a parrot on a perch in the living room. Alexa had read several of her books. She was the daughter of a famous Hollywood producer, and now married to one. And it was obvious that she and her ex-husband genuinely liked each other, and he got on famously with her husband. Their children treated Edward like an uncle, which was a far cry from Luisa's performance with Savannah.

This was straight out of a movie, but it was also a lot of fun. They boiled lobsters for dinner and all helped while the dogs barked, the phones rang, the stereo blared, and the kids' friends came in and out as though there were a party going on somewhere. Their whole life was a party, and they enjoyed themselves. Sybil was very pretty and about ten years older than Alexa, somewhere around forty-nine or fifty.

It was the funniest and most entertaining evening Alexa had ever had. They all had a great sense of humor, even the kids, who had been friendly, and the parrot spoke only four-letter words.

"She wasn't quite that zany when I married her," Edward explained as he took Alexa home. "Brian has kind of brought it out in her, and it works for them. But she was a lot of fun then too. She was a terrible practical joker, and always had a whoopee cushion in her purse. She's basically just a really wonderful woman." He smiled lovingly as he said it.

"Do you miss her?" Alexa asked boldly.

"Sometimes," he said honestly. "But I was a lousy husband. In those days, I wanted politics more than my marriage. She deserved better than that. And she got it with Brian."

"And now? Do you still want politics more?" She liked him, and he had an interesting life. He was a collection of odd contrasts, the old and the new, the North and the South. His ex-wife said she hated the South. She thought it was hypocritical, antiquated, and uptight. Alexa liked it more than that, but she could see her point, in some circles. Luisa embodied all the worst of the South. But others were shining examples of everything good about it. And there was so much about Charleston Alexa had loved.

"I don't know," Edward said in answer to her question. "Politics are still the driving force in my life. But I don't want just that. At one point I did. I don't want to wind up alone, but I don't want to go through all the bullshit you have to go through to wind up with the right person, or maybe the wrong one. I want to wake up married to the right person. But I don't want to make any effort to get there, or take the risk of making a mistake. Which means, I'll probably wind up alone." He laughed. The prospect didn't seem to disturb him. "I guess I'm lazy."

"Or scared," she challenged, and he nodded slowly.

"Maybe," he admitted. "And you?"

"Teriffied for the last ten years," she said honestly.

"And now?"

"Maybe thawing out." She wasn't sure.

"You have good reason to be scared after what your husband did to you. That was rotten."

"Yes, it was. I never had any desire to try again with someone else. I thought the risks were too high. I think I feel more relaxed about it now. But I was gun-shy for a long time."

"Relationships are so damn complicated," he said gruffly, and she laughed.

"Ain't that the truth." And then they talked of other things, until he dropped her off. She thanked him, they shook hands, and his limousine drove off as she walked into her building. He was going back to Washington in the morning.

Predictably, his cell phone rang as the car took him to his hotel. It was Sybil, his ex-wife.

"She's perfect for you. Marry her immediately" was Sybil's opening line, and he groaned loudly.

"I knew that would happen if I introduced her to you. Mind your own business. I just met her."

"Fine. Then give it two weeks and

propose. She's terrific." Sybil had loved her, and so had Brian.

"You're nuts, but I love you," he said happily. He loved his friendship with Sybil, better than he had their married life. It had been more commitment than he wanted then. All he really cared about then was his political life. Sybil knew it, so she made a graceful exit, before Brian came along.

"I love you too," Sybil said sweetly. "Thanks for bringing her. I really like her. She's smart and honest and fun and beautiful. You won't do better than that." He had done all right with her, but that was a long time ago.

"I'll let you know how it works out," he said firmly, with no intention to tell her.

"Goodnight, Eddy," she said, as he reached the hotel.

"Goodnight, Sybil. Give my love to Brian, and thanks for dinner."

"Anytime." And she clicked off. She truly was nuts, but he loved her, in the nicest way.

*   *   *

Edward called Alexa again before she left for Europe, and got her schedule there. He wasn't sure, but he thought their paths might cross in London or Paris, and he said he'd call her if that was the case. He had to go to Hong Kong first. He seemed to travel constantly.

The day before they left for Europe, Alexa attended the sentencing in the Quentin case. Luke Quentin was no longer wearing a suit. He was wearing a jail-issue jumpsuit, as he had in the interrogations. He looked unkempt and angry, and was curt with his attorney and blamed her for his conviction. He was far angrier now at Judy than Alexa. His defense counsel took the brunt of his blame. He ignored Alexa completely, which was a relief.

Jack was there, but Sam wasn't. He was on another case.

The judge did what he said he would, and gave him the maximum sentence for each charge, and ran them all consecutively, a hundred and forty years in prison, life without parole, several lifetimes. He would never see the light of day again. He said something rude to the public defender as he was led from the courtroom, and didn't look at Alexa. The war was over. He no longer cared. He would be transferred to Sing Sing prison within the next few days.

Alexa left the courtroom with Jack. Some of the relatives of the victims had come to the sentencing, but most hadn't. Charlie and his family weren't there. They had all gone back to work, and were satisfied with the convictions. They could guess the rest and would be notified later. It was over for them too. And sadly, the eighteen young victims were gone forever.

The press was there, but not as forcefully as they had been at the trial. Alexa left the courtroom when it was over, and drove away with Jack. Luke Quentin was just another case, a dangerous criminal they had put away. There would be other cases, although less sensational than this one. The Quentin case had been the high point of her career.

*　　*　　*

The next day Alexa and Savannah flew to London and stayed at a little hotel that Alexa had remembered from her youth. They had tea at Claridge's and visited the Tower of London, walked New Bond Street, and gaped at all the jewelry and pretty clothes. They watched the changing of the guard at Buckingham Palace and visited the royal stables. They did all the fun tourist things and shopped in Knightsbridge, Carnaby Street, and the flea market in Covent Garden, where Savannah bought a T-shirt for Daisy. And they went to see several plays. They had a wonderful time, and flew to Paris after five days.

They checked into a small hotel on the Left Bank, and started their stay out with lunch at an open-air café, planning their attack on the city and what to do first. Alexa wanted to go to Notre Dame, and Savannah wanted to take a boat ride on the Bateau Mouche on the Seine, and walk along the quais. They decided to do all three and had time that afternoon. And they wanted to see the view from Sacré Coeur the next day, and visit the Louvre and Palais Tokiyo. They went back to the hotel to rest for a while before dinner, and Senator Baldwin called Alexa there. He had just arrived in Paris and was in the city for two days on his way to the South of France.

"What have you ladies been up to?" he asked her, and she reported on their assorted doings. He was impressed by all they'd done. "Could I talk you both into dinner tonight, or do you have other plans?" Alexa asked if she could check with Savannah and call him back.

"What do you think?" Alexa asked her, extending Baldwin's invitation to them both.

"I think it's great. Why don't you go alone?" She had just turned eighteen, and felt very grown up, and capable of wandering around Paris for an evening on her own.

"I don't want to go alone. I'm here with you. Do you want to do it, or is it too boring for you?" Savannah was her priority, and this was their trip. Savannah wanted to meet him and check him out, and it sounded fun to her. He was a senator, after all. How bad could it be?

Alexa called him back five minutes later, and said they accepted with delight. He was staying at the Ritz, and suggested they come there for dinner, and they could eat in the garden. The weather was beautiful and warm. He invited them for eight-thirty. And at the appointed hour, Alexa and Savannah met him at the restaurant, wearing skirts and sandals and pretty blouses, with their blond hair brushed straight down their backs. They looked more like sisters than mother and daughter, and he said they looked like twins.

The hotel was very beautiful, with an ornate mirrored lobby and huge vases of flowers everywhere. And the garden table where the headwaiter settled them was relaxed and balmy in a marble courtyard with a fountain, and there was music coming from the main restaurant. It was a perfect way to spend a warm Paris night, and he looked happy to see them.

"How was Hong Kong?" Alexa asked him after introducing him to Savannah, who was unusually quiet. She was watching him and how he looked at her mother. No question, he liked her, and not just as a friend. Savannah approved. He seemed nice, he was friendly, he wasn't pompous, and he had a good sense of humor. It was a good beginning.

"Short, hot, and busy," Edward Baldwin said about Hong Kong. "I'm looking forward to the South of France. I haven't had a vacation in months. I need one." He led a stressful life, and so did she. Particularly after the Quentin trial and four arduous months of preparation.

They ordered dinner, and he asked Savannah about her plans for school. He was impressed by Princeton, and said that his daughter was a senior at UCLA and wanted to go to medical school. She didn't want to come back to the East, and was hooked on California and hoping to get into Stanford.

"My mom wouldn't let me go there." Savannah smiled at him. "Too far away, but I didn't get into Stanford anyway. UCLA's a great school. I should have applied there, but I didn't."

"Princeton will be fine, thank you," Alexa interjected. "I don't want you three thousand miles away. Four months in Charleston was bad enough. I miss you too much," she said, and both the senator and her daughter smiled at her. She was honest about it. "You're the only kid I have."

They talked about art and theater then, and what Savannah wanted to study. It was like an easy evening with an old friend, and he was good with kids. She had seen that when she had had dinner at his ex-wife's house with her three teenage sons, who were in and out constantly and seemed totally at ease with Edward and he with them. He told Savannah she should come to Washington and visit the Senate. She looked interested, and he told her she was welcome anytime. He had an easy, comfortable way with people and a sharp mind. And by the end of the evening, Alexa and Savannah were totally at ease with him. He walked them out after dinner and put them in a cab back to their hotel. They stood in the Place Vendôme for a minute, admiring how beautiful it was. It was all lit up and spectacular looking with the obelisk in the center. And then they got in the cab and gave the driver the address of their hotel on the Left Bank. Edward waved and strode back into the Ritz.

"I like him," Savannah said, as they drove across the Alexandre III Bridge to the Left Bank.

"I do too," Alexa admitted. "Just as a friend."

"Why just as a friend?" Savannah challenged her. "Why not more than that? You can't stay alone forever. I'm leaving in September. Then what are you going to do?" Savannah was serious. She worried about her. And it was time for her mother to have a man in her life again. It had been too long, and she was still young. She wasn't even forty yet, although she would be soon. Edward Baldwin was fifty-two, which Savannah thought was a good age for her mother.

"Stop trying to get rid of me," Alexa complained. "I'm fine like this."

"No, you're not. You're going to wind up an old maid," Savannah threatened her, and Alexa laughed.

She called Edward Baldwin the next

day to thank him for dinner. He was leaving that night for Ramatuelle, and said he'd call her when he was in New York again, which sounded nice to her. She wasn't sure if he would or not. She wasn't worried about it, but she had enjoyed her two evenings with him, and lunch. She was flattered that he'd asked her out at all.

Alexa and Savannah spent the rest of the week in Paris, enjoying all the sights, and decided not to go to the South of France. They went straight to Florence instead and loved it, spending hours in museums and galleries and churches. Then they decided to go on to Venice and do more of the same. They spent five days there in a funny old hotel on the Grand Canal. It was magical. And they flew home from Milan after nearly three weeks in Europe. They were both thrilled with what a perfect trip it had been.

And it was hard getting back to New York and real life. Alexa hated to start work again, and two days after they returned, Savannah flew down to Charleston to see Turner. She stayed with Julianne for a few days, and then her father. She was planning to stay for two weeks. Luisa was away, and Daisy was at camp for the month.

And in New York, Alexa was shocked by how lonely she was in the apartment without Savannah. She didn't have the trial to keep her busy now, and she hated coming home to the empty apartment at night. Her mother and Stanley were away too, on the trip to Montana and Wyoming.

She had dinner with Jack and complained about it.

"You'd better figure something out quick," he warned her. "She's leaving for college in a couple of weeks, and then it's forever."

"Thanks," Alexa said glumly. They had just gotten a robbery case to work on together that day, and it didn't interest either of them a lot. She was in the doldrums at home and at work.

Things got better and livelier again when Savannah came back from Charleston. Her friends were in and out of the apartment constantly to say goodbye. Alexa and Savannah had things to buy and pack, all her favorite clothes to pack again, she needed sheets and towels for school. They dragged a trunk home to put everything in. They managed to get it all together by September 1st. And on her last night in New York, they had dinner with her grandmother and Stanley. They had just gotten back from Moose, Wyoming. They were both wearing new cowboy boots and jeans and cowboy shirts, and Savannah laughed and told them they looked cute.

They had dinner at Balthazar in the Village, which Savannah liked, and her grandmother promised to come and visit her at Princeton soon. It was only an hour and a half away. And Tom and Travis had said they'd come up too in October.

As Alexa lay in bed that night, it was hard to believe that it was all over. All those years of living together, and taking care of her, and being alone with her, and now she was going. Alexa felt devastated, and knew it would never be the same again. Savannah would come home for visits now, but never to live again, except in the summer. That seemed a long time away right now. The best was over, or so it seemed.

Alexa had rented a van to take her things to Princeton the next day. Savannah was taking a bicycle, her computer, a small stereo, pillows, blankets, a twin bedspread, framed photographs, all the things she needed in college. Savannah had spoken endlessly to the friend who was going to be her roommate. They were already making plans. Savannah was excited and called Turner four times on the ninety-minute drive. He had gotten to Duke the day before and had three roommates in a suite. Savannah having only one roommate in Princeton sounded very civilized to him. He was coming up the following weekend, and Savannah was thrilled.

Savannah had a map of the campus that she used to tell her mother where to go, once they got to Princeton. They had to leave the van in a parking lot. And Savannah used Nassau Hall, the oldest building on campus, and Cleveland Tower behind it, as their main landmarks to figure out the rest. Her room was in Butler Hall, and they found it after walking around for a few minutes and asking people where it was. Her room was on the second floor. And it took them two hours to get everything into her room and organized. They still had to hook up the stereo and the computer, but all else was in place, and the roommate's parents were doing the same thing. Her father helped Alexa with the computer. And the girls were going to share a microwave and tiny refrigerator they rented for the room. Each girl had a phone line, a bed, a desk, a chair, and a chest of drawers. The closet space was minimal, and as Alexa struggled with it all, the two girls walked into the hallway to meet other students. In another hour, Savannah had been absorbed into dorm life and told her mother she could go.

"Don't you want me to hang your clothes up?" Alexa asked, looking disappointed. She had just made the bed. They had brought some snacks too, and she thought they should buy more groceries. But Savannah was impatient to move on now, and meet the other students in the dorm and on campus. Her new life had just begun.

"No, Mom, I'll be fine," she said as the other girl did the same with her parents. "Honest. You can go." It was a polite way of telling her to leave. Alexa hugged her close for a minute, and forced back tears.

"Take care of yourself . . . call me . . ."

"I will, I promise," Savannah said as she kissed her, and Alexa smiled bravely as she left, but there were tears rolling down her cheeks when she reached the parking lot, and she wasn't the only mother crying. It was wrenching, leaving her there. It was like setting a bird free after loving it and nurturing it for eighteen years. Were her wings strong enough? Would she remember how to fly? How would she feed herself? Savannah was ready for it, but Alexa wasn't. She got into the van and started it, and cried all the way home. It was the final severing of the umbilical cord and felt like the worst day of her life.

Chapter 22

Alexa felt as though someone had died when she dressed for work the next day. Her cell phone rang just before she left the apartment, and she thought it was Savannah. She had forced herself not to call her the night before. The number that showed up on her cell phone was blocked, and when she answered it was Sam Lawrence, not Savannah. She hadn't talked to him since July and was pleased he was calling.

"That's a surprise," she said pleasantly. "How are you?"

"Pretty good." He sounded busy and in good spirits. "Will you have lunch with me today?" he asked her. She really wasn't in the mood.

"To be honest, I feel like shit. My kid left for college yesterday. I feel like my life is over. I suddenly became obsolete. I hate this. How about lunch next week? I'll be in a better mood." She didn't want to see anyone right now. She was mourning Savannah's childhood, a huge loss for her.

"Let's have lunch today anyway. I can cheer you up." She hoped this wasn't a date of some kind, because she was even less in the mood for that, and they were work buddies, and that was all she wanted with him. She tried to weasel out of lunch some more, but he wouldn't let her.

"Okay. I'll meet you at the deli across the street. Maybe the food will kill me and I won't have to worry about being depressed anymore."

"You'll feel better in a couple of weeks. You were fine when she was in Charleston during the trial," he reminded her.

"No, I wasn't. I missed her like crazy. But I was busy. I don't have a hell of a lot going on right now." He didn't comment, but they agreed to meet at twelve-thirty.

He was there when she arrived, and he could see that she was miserable. Her hair was pulled back in a barely combed ponytail, and she hadn't worn makeup, and had put on jeans for work. She looked like she was convalescing from an illness. She was pining for her child.

Sam made small talk with her for a few minutes, as they talked about how bad the food was, and then he smiled at her. "Maybe I have something to cheer you up," he said hopefully. He hoped he wasn't making a mistake meeting with her when she was in such low spirits. "I have a proposition for you," he said mysteriously, as she looked at him with both curiosity and suspicion.

"What kind of proposition?"

He took a breath and said it. "A job."

"What kind of job?" She frowned at him. "Like a case?" And then she laughed. "You guys have a case you want my help on? Now, that is a compliment!" She was very flattered that the

FBI wanted her help, but they had worked well on the Quentin case together.

"Not a case, Alexa." He smiled at her. "A job. We want to offer you a job with the OCG, the Office of the General Counsel of the FBI. It's a desk job, not a field job, so you're not going to be shooting bad guys. You know what the OCG does. They were all over our asses on the Quentin case. Only now you'd get to be the one bugging everyone else, watching everything, or taking the cases on yourself and kicking ass. They're going to make you an official offer, but I wanted to talk to you about it first. I've been wanting this to happen since we worked together on the Quentin case. I think you've done it in the DA's office. This could be a really exciting career move for you. The benefits are great, it's interesting, and hell, it's the FBI." She'd never even thought of that before. Not once. She assumed she'd be in the DA's office till she retired.

"Here? In New York?" she asked, still looking amazed. It was definitely a prestigious job, and a huge compliment to be asked.

"No," Sam said awkwardly, "in Washington, D.C. But your kid is gone, Alexa. As far as I know, you don't have a guy in your life. Why not Washington, D.C.?"

"My mother is here," she said, looking distracted and confused. It was a lot to absorb all at once. New job, new city, new life.

"New York is three hours away by train. It's not a big deal. It's not Venezuela, for chrissake."

"No, it isn't. What's the money like? Better than what I make now?"

"Yes." He smiled at her. "You can't lose on this one. And if you hate it, you can always come back here. But you won't want to. You've done this. It's over for you. You're burned out, and you know it." She had been feeling that way before the Quentin case, and that had spiced things up for a while. Now she was back to robberies and shoplifters, drug busts, and the occasional murder. She missed having something more important to do. "Will you think about it?"

"Yes." She nodded, smiling, and feeling a lot less depressed than she had an hour before. She was scared but excited. "I thought you were asking me out on a date." She laughed then.

"I can do that too." He grinned at her. "I didn't think you'd go out with me if I asked, or I would have."

"I wouldn't. I don't go out with guys I work with. I did that once. It was stupid and a mess, so I don't."

"I figured." He had guessed correctly from the vibes she put out that she was only interested in being buddies while they worked together. And he saw her treat Jack that way too. "Just take the job. They want you, and you'll love it. You need something new in your life. Maybe a guy too."

She shrugged. "You sound like my mother. And my daughter."

"Maybe you should listen to them." She laughed again, and they spent the rest of lunch talking about the OCG.

They made her an official offer two days later. The job sounded interesting, the benefits were great, and the money was terrific. It was hard to beat. But she felt guilty leaving the DA's office. She had been there since she'd graduated from law school seven years before, and they'd been good to her. And she liked Joe McCarthy. She hated to leave them, but they didn't really need her.

As she always did, when she had a difficult decision to make, she turned up in her mother's chambers at the end of the day, looking troubled.

"Everything okay?" her mother asked. "Savannah okay?"

"Disgustingly happy," Alexa answered. "It's my job."

"You got fired?" Her mother looked shocked. She had done such a great job on the Quentin case. How could they fire her? But Alexa shook her head.

"I've had an offer. From the FBI." Her mother's eyes opened wide.

"That's impressive. Are you going to take it?"

"I don't know. The money is good, and I like the job. The FBI would be more fun than the DA's office at this point." And then she sighed. "But it's in Washington. How do you feel about that?" she asked her mother honestly, and Muriel thought about it.

"That's an interesting question. Thank you for asking." She appreciated the relationship she had with her daughter and Alexa's thoughtfulness toward her. "I don't want you turning a job down for me." Her mother smiled at her. "I'm not that old. I'm still working and busy. It's like Savannah leaving for college. You have to let go and let your kids move on to where they're supposed to be. I had to face that when you married Tom and moved to Charleston. And Washington's not that far away. I would miss you," she added, "but I can visit, and so can you. How do you feel about Washington? That's more important. You don't have a lot going on here. These haven't been happy years for you. And I think you'll get bored with the job you have now eventually."

"I already am," Alexa admitted. "It's been dead since the Quentin case, and before that really."

"Maybe you need a change, and with Savannah leaving, this is a good time." And then she smiled at her. "Maybe you'll meet a guy in D.C."

"I'm not worried about that. I'm think-ing about you and Savannah."

"She's gone, and I'm fine. And she can just as easily visit you in D.C., from Princeton. And if she wants to come to New York, she can stay with me. I think you should do it." She was being self-less and honest because she would miss her.

"Me too. I think I should do it. Are you sure you'll be okay?"

"Yes." And then her mother sighed too. "Stanley's been bugging me about living together. We don't want to get married, but he thinks getting older, nei-ther of us should live alone, and he wants to live together, in his place or mine." It had taken seventeen years to ask her, and Muriel had been happy the way things were till now.

"What do you want, Mom? Never mind what he wants."

"I think I like the idea. I was afraid you wouldn't approve." She smiled at her daughter, looking a little embarrassed.

"I think he's right. And I approve. I worry about you too. So is that settled?" Alexa grinned at her mother.

"Maybe. I want to think about it some more. I don't want to rush into anything."

Alexa laughed out loud. "How long have you two been dating?"

"I think it's seventeen years. Stanley says it's eighteen."

"Either way, I don't think you're rushing."

"I'll probably do it. I'd rather he move in with me. I don't want to give up my apartment, and I don't like his. He says he's fine with it. Maybe after Christmas. I've got a lot to do before that. What about you. Think you'll do it?" Alexa nodded.

"Yeah, I think so. Thanks, Mom." She leaned over and kissed her, and they walked out of the courthouse together.

Alexa thought about it that night, and called Savannah. She was doing homework, and Alexa told her about the offer. She was surprised and impressed. She thought the move to Washington would be fun and good for her mother, and she agreed with her grandmother, she could stay with her in New York, if she wanted to see her friends there. It was a time of transition for all of them.

"Change is a good thing, Mom. Have you heard from the senator, by the way?" Savannah liked him. So did Alexa.

"I think he was staying in Europe till mid- or late August. He's probably busy." But in any case, Savannah had given her full approval for the move, and she thanked her mother for asking her too.

Alexa gave Joe McCarthy notice the next day. She felt terrible about it, but he said he understood. He said he figured it would happen sooner or later. He had always assumed she would go into private practice with a big law firm. He had never thought of anything like the FBI.

"They're smart to hire you." He gave her a hug. "So when are you leaving us?"

"Does a month's notice sound reasonable?"

"Very. That gives me time to reassign your cases."

She thought of something then that she wanted to thank him for again.

"Thank you for fighting to let me keep the Quentin case, and not just giving it to the feds."

"Maybe I should have," he teased her. "Then they wouldn't be offering you a job." And then he hugged her again. "I'm happy for you. I think this is a good career move for you. I hate like hell to lose you, but I approve."

"Thank you."

Word of her leaving spread like wildfire in the office. Jack was glaring at her from across her desk by four-thirty that afternoon.

"What the fuck is that about?" he said unhappily.

"I'm sorry, Jack," she said apologetically. "They made me an offer I couldn't refuse."

"It's going to suck around here without you," he said miserably, and walked out of her office again, too depressed to talk about it any further.

She was thinking about all she had to do, find an apartment, break her lease on this one, move, start a new job, get her cases reassigned here, when Edward Baldwin called her just before she left the office.

"Can I talk you into a last-minute hamburger? I'm in town for the night. Sorry I haven't called you since I got back. I've been dealing with about four hundred headaches, and I had to spend a week in Charleston. How's Savannah doing at Princeton, by the way?"

"She loves it." Alexa smiled. He sounded full of life and busy and like he was running in two hundred directions. And now, so was she. "And the hamburger sounds great. Where should I meet you?"

"I'm about two blocks from your office. Why don't I pick you up, and we'll figure it out together?"

"Sounds good."

She was downstairs five minutes later, and so was he in his town car. He opened the door and she got in, and they sped uptown to his hotel for a drink, and a hamburger later.

"How was the rest of your trip?" he asked her.

"Wonderful. How was yours?"

"Perfect." He smiled as he said it. "I thought about you a lot. I kept meaning to call you, but I didn't. I saw your husband in Charleston last week, by the way. I have to admit, he looks miserable. I can see why, his wife was with him, and she looks like she sucks lemons for breakfast and beats him up every night. I'd say the fates got even with him."

"Maybe so." She smiled at Edward. It wasn't her problem anymore.

She told him over their hamburgers that she was moving to Washington and going to work for the FBI, and he looked stunned.

"You are? Now, there's a huge change. How brave of you."

"I figured it was a good time to do it with Savannah leaving for college. I probably wouldn't have before." But she had made a lot of brave moves recently. She had let Savannah go to Charleston, had visited there herself, she had buried the hatchet with Tom, and now she was changing jobs and cities. It was a time of growth for her too. "I have to start looking for an apartment pretty soon."

"I'll help you," he volunteered with a

broad grin. "When do you start with the OCG?" He liked that a lot. He was in Washington most of the time. He had wanted to see her, even if she was living in New York, but this would make it a lot easier for him, and give them more time together to get to know each other.

"I start on November first. And I have a lot to do before then."

"Why don't you come down this weekend and start looking?" She thought about it. She had nothing else to do. She looked across the table and smiled at him.

"Okay."

"We can look for apartments all weekend," he suggested. It sounded like a plan to her.

Chapter 23

Alexa left the DA's office as planned on November 1st. It was a bittersweet day for her, and Joe McCarthy hosted a dinner for her before she left. They gave her a plaque and a lot of silly joke gifts.

She was leaving for Washington the next day, via Princeton. She had put off starting at the OCG by a week, to give herself time to move into her new house. Her furniture was due in Washington two days later. She had been staying at her mother's for the past week, which was kind of fun. And Edward was calling her several times a day with plans and invitations. He had invited her to dinner at the White House with him in two weeks.

And she wanted to visit Savannah in Princeton on the way down. When Alexa got there, Savannah looked busy and happy. She'd already made a lot of friends, and Turner was coming up from Duke again that weekend. Savannah's new life was well off the ground. Now Alexa had to get busy on her own.

She drove to Washington with the last of her things, and when she got to Washington, Edward met her at the tiny house she had rented in Georgetown, instead of an apartment. It looked like a dollhouse. He had helped her find it, and she knew Savannah was going to love it. The top floor was just for her. And it had all the room that Alexa needed. It was near Edward's apartment, which was spacious and modern and convenient for him. He helped her unload the car, and they walked around her empty house together. She loved it. This was a whole new lease on life. New city, new home, new job, and maybe new man. She wasn't sure yet. But the other changes took the sting out of Savannah leaving for college. They had both graduated to new lives, and Alexa was very excited about her own, as much as Savannah was about being in Princeton.

Edward took her to dinner at Citronella that night, and afterward he escorted her back to her hotel. She was staying there for only one night, and he kissed her before he left. It was the first time he had kissed her and it surprised them both. But she liked it a lot and so did he.

He came to see her at the house when the movers arrived the next day. He stayed till midnight, helping her unpack boxes. She found her linens and he helped her make the bed. He was telling her silly stories and bad jokes, and they were both laughing, as they fell onto the bed, exhausted, and looked at each other, still laughing. He was a nice man, he was good to her, and he made her happy. And he stunned her with what he said next.

"I think I'm falling in love with you, Alexa. Is that all right with you?" He knew how badly burned she had been before, and he didn't want to upset her, do what she didn't want, or move too fast.

"I think so," she said softly. "I think I'm falling in love with you too." It frightened her to say it, but it felt good too, and was true. She was crazy about him, in a way she hadn't been in twenty years. He felt just right to her. And she trusted him completely.

"That could be a very good thing for us both," he said, as he put his arms around her and pulled her close. Everything had fallen into place. Her new life in Washington gave them all the time they needed.

"Would you like to stay here tonight?" she asked him, surprising them both again. Her life was getting crazier by the minute. It felt scary but great at the same time. It was very exciting and so was he.

"I'd love that." He smiled at her and held her in his arms. A little while later, she took a shower and got into bed, between the clean sheets, and he did the same and came to bed a few minutes later. And a whole new world began for them that night. A world neither of them had thought they'd find again, or even wanted to. It felt like a miracle to both of them.

Alexa spent the rest of the week organizing the house, and Edward came over when he had time. He stayed there with her every night. They didn't tell anyone what was going on. They decided to keep it to themselves until they figured it out. Maybe it wouldn't last, but it was wonderful for now. Alexa didn't need or want more than that.

She started her new job and loved it. It was everything she had hoped it would be and more. She loved the excitement and prestige of working for the FBI. And the following week, Edward took her to the White House dinner he had invited her to. They were photographed by news cameras going in, and they made a very handsome couple. The dinner was in honor of the president of France. And the next day, the news ran a clip of the senator going into the White House dinner with a very pretty woman on his arm.

Tom and Luisa happened to be watching the news together when it came on, and because he was the senator from South Carolina, they ran the clip several times in Charleston. Luisa bolted out of her seat like a shot when she saw it, and stood in the study, looking irate.

"That *bitch*! Did you see that?" She glared at Tom.

Tom hadn't seen it. He had looked away for a minute and missed it. "Who are we talking about? The First Lady or the wife of the president of France?"

"Of course not! Alexa! Did you see Edward Baldwin going into that dinner at the White House? That was Alexa with him!"

"Alexa? Our Alexa?" Tom looked stunned.

"Your *ex*-Alexa, thank you! She was his *date*! She must have picked him up at the wedding." Luisa was incensed.

"She didn't pick him up. I introduced them." He looked as crestfallen as Luisa looked livid.

"Why would you do a thing like that?" Luisa berated him.

"Because we bumped into him while we were dancing, so I introduced them."

And now he regretted it bitterly. He had lost her, but he hadn't meant to introduce her to the next man in her life. He liked knowing that she was alone.

"She's a whore," Luisa said, and turned the TV off.

"No, actually," Tom said tersely, "she's not. You were, and I was. She wasn't. And she wouldn't do what we did. She wanted nothing to do with me now because I'm married, or even if I weren't. We're the whores, Luisa. She isn't. You slept with another woman's husband, and I cheated on my wife. Not too pretty, is it?"

"I don't know what you're talking about." She looked indignant.

"Yes, you do, and so do I. So maybe she deserves the good senator after all." Luisa said not a word and left the room. It enraged her even more to know that Edward Baldwin had taken Alexa to the White House. She didn't deserve anything of the sort.

And after Luisa left the room, Tom sat staring at the blank screen, knowing just how much Alexa deserved it. She deserved anything good that happened to her now, to make up for what he'd done to her. And as he thought about her with Edward Baldwin, two silent tears rolled down his cheeks.

"What are we doing about Thanksgiving?" Edward asked Alexa the weekend after they'd been to the White House. Thanksgiving was two weeks away, and she looked blank.

"I hadn't even thought about it, I was so busy getting organized here. We usually do it at my place, just Savannah and me, my mother, and her friend Stanley. But I don't know if they'd want to come down here. I'd better call her, and Savannah. Why? What did you have in mind?" She leaned over and kissed him. They were in bed with the Sunday paper all over the bed and the floor and a cup of coffee on the night table on either side of the bed. She loved their life together, and so did he. It was comfortable and easy, and cozy and happy. He was a warm, loving person, and as kind as she had hoped he would be. And he thought Alexa was every bit as perfect as his ex-wife said she was.

"I usually go to Sybil's. My kids fly in, and we all spend it together. I'd love to have you with us, and I want you to meet my kids."

"I'll call Savannah and my mom." She did that morning, but was startled by what they said. Savannah said that if her mother didn't mind too much, she wanted to go to Charleston to spend it with her father and Turner, and of course Daisy, Henry, Travis, and Scarlette . . . and Luisa. She was the only fly in the ointment. Savannah begged her mother to let her do it, so Alexa said yes.

And when she called her mother, Muriel said that Stanley had just bought tickets for a cruise in the Bahamas and she hadn't had the guts to tell Alexa yet.

"I won't go if you'll be alone." Alexa had just told her about Savannah going to Charleston. In a way, her time in Charleston earlier in the year had prepared Alexa to be without her. It would have been even harder now otherwise. It had broken her in.

"I'll be fine," she reassured her

mother. "Go on the cruise. You'll have a good time."

"What will you do?" Muriel sounded worried.

"Edward just invited me to spend it with his kids and ex-wife."

"Edward? As in Senator Edward Baldwin?" her mother asked.

"Yes," Alexa said softly, not ready to say more. She hadn't told her about dinner at the White House either, and her mother had somehow missed the press on it. Savannah hadn't and was pleased. She had texted her grandmother about it.

"That's interesting." She could tell Alexa didn't want to talk about it, and wondered if she was with him. "I'll tell Stan we can go on the cruise, then," she said with a grin. She could tell that something was going on.

"Looks like we're all set," Alexa reported to Edward after speaking to her mother. "My whole family has ditched me." She was grinning at him. "So I'm all yours for Thanksgiving."

"Excellent news," he said, and kissed her. He called Sybil and told her on

Monday morning, and she was pleased too. Everybody was happy. Particularly Edward and Alexa, and the fan club rooting for them in secret.

Thanksgiving with Sybil was as chaotic and loving and warm as everything else she did. Instead of turkey, she served a delicious leg of lamb, done French style, with garlic and green beans. They had caviar before dinner, and sautéed foie gras as a first course, and she served pumpkin pie because the children liked it, but she served Baked Alaska too. It was an exceptional even if unorthodox meal. And the wines Edward brought were superb.

All of Sybil's children were there, and hers with Edward too. Alexa loved his daughter, who reminded her of Savannah and was three years older. His son John was interesting and smart and funny and a little eccentric like his mother. He wanted to be a Shakespearean actor, and was getting decent reviews in London. His hair was almost as long as Alexa's, and his girlfriend looked ten feet tall and was an actress too.

"It's a wonder I ever get elected, re-lated to all you people," Edward teased them. They played charades after dinner, and the dogs barked constantly. The parrot told everyone to go fuck them-selves, and several friends dropped by, one of whom was an extremely famous artist.

Being at their home was like being on a movie set, and after things started to calm down a little, Sybil turned to both of them over excellent Château d'Yquem, which tasted like candy.

"So what's happening with you two?" she asked with a mischievous grin. "I'm dying to know. I think you're in love," she said to Edward. "I don't know Alexa well enough to ask her. She's not my sister-in-law yet. But will she be?"

"It's none of your business," Edward said to her good-naturedly. "When we have something to tell you, we will. Meanwhile, find something else to do, other than meddle in my life."

"Edward, how rude!" But she was only teasing him, and he was very pleased that his children had obviously taken to Alexa. That mattered to him a lot, and he liked Savannah as well, and he thought his children would too.

"I hope you'll come to us at Christmas," Sybil said to her as they left.

"I'll have to be at my mother's," Alexa explained. "But maybe you could all come for drinks," she added hopefully.

"We'd love it," Sybil assured her, and Alexa realized that she had to warn her mother of what was about to hit her, even for cocktails. A famous writer, a well-known movie producer, a senator, and five additional children. It was going to be a shock to her mother in her small apartment. But at least it was only drinks. Her mother could never have handled dinner. She could hardly cook for her and Stan. He did most of the cooking. When she was alone, she ate salads she bought on the way home from work. Muriel had never been much of a cook.

Edward and Alexa were staying at the Hotel Carlyle for the Thanksgiving weekend, and they were planning to see his son and daughter again the next day. Sybil and her three younger children and husband were going to their house in

Connecticut for the weekend. They were a busy group. But it turned out to be a wonderful weekend. They went to dinners and movies with his kids, went for walks in Central Park and to the Guggenheim and the Museum of Modern Art. By the time the weekend was over, they were all friends, and she told Savannah all about it. She missed her, but Savannah sounded happy. And Luisa hadn't ruined Thanksgiving for her, which was something. Daisy was thrilled to have her home. Henry had brought his "roommate" Jeff, and Savannah loved him too.

Muriel was in shock when she got back from her cruise and Alexa told her who was coming to drinks on Christmas, and how many of them.

"Are you kidding? They won't even fit in my apartment." Muriel sounded panicked. But she wanted to meet Edward and see him with Alexa. And she was curious about his ex-wife and children too. She read all of Sybil's books.

"Yes, they will, Mom," Alexa reassured her. "It's just for a drink, and they're very casual people. Actually, to tell you the truth, they're certifiably crazy, except for the kids, but they're a lot of fun. I think you'll like them."

"You sound happy," Muriel said in a tender tone.

"I am," Alexa said softly. "He's a wonderful man."

"Do I hear wedding bells?" her mother asked, getting excited. Being the wife of a senator sounded good to her. And a good man for her daughter sounded even better. It was time.

"No, just happy bells," Alexa said. "I don't need to get married. I did that." *And got burned too badly to do it again* was the rest of Alexa's sentence, but she didn't say it. And Edward wasn't Tom. There was nothing weak or dishonest about him. He was a totally straightforward, decent man.

"That's how I feel about marriage," Muriel said. "But I'm a lot older than you are, and I can't see the point. At your age, you should be more courageous."

"Why? I'm happy like this."

"If he's a good man, you might be

happy married to him too. Just don't rule it out. You never know how you'll feel about it later."

"Maybe," Alexa said, sounding unconvinced. Marriage scared her, and probably always would.

When the Senate recessed for Christmas, Alexa took a week off, and they flew to New York. Savannah was staying with her grandmother and Stan, and Alexa and Edward checked into the Carlyle again, as they had over Thanksgiving. She took a room there for Savannah too, who was going to stay at the hotel with them. And Turner was coming up the day after Christmas. They were going skiing in Vermont over New Year's with their friends, and Edward and Alexa were staying in the city. Alexa was loving her job too.

On Christmas Eve, Sybil arrived with her small army at Muriel's apartment. The only ones she didn't bring were the parrot and the dogs. She had all five children and John's girlfriend, who had come with him from London again. Brian had brought his niece unexpectedly, and two grown children from a first marriage Alexa hadn't known about, and they all crowded into Muriel and Stan's apartment and drank eggnog and champagne. Muriel told Sybil how much she liked her books, Brian and Stan talked about favorite old movies and fly-fishing, John and his girlfriend were talking to Savannah, and Ashley, Edward's daughter, was fighting with her boyfriend in California on her cell phone and crying. It was total chaos, and Alexa stood back, watching it with Edward, and laughed.

"My family has certainly grown. Last Christmas was just me, Savannah, and my mom. Stanley came by after dinner, he had to visit a sick friend."

"What do you like better?" Edward asked her honestly. "That or this?"

"This," she said without hesitation. "It's so alive and so happy and so loving." And the next thing she knew, her mother had suggested they order Chinese takeout and camp out in her kitchen and on the living room floor. She had put a small turkey in the oven, which they could eat the next day. Sybil and her troops loved the idea and voted to stay, and scrap their own dinner at home, which Sybil said was a mess anyway.

The young people sat on the floor in Muriel's living room. The grown-ups sat in the dining room, which only seated eight. And somehow it all worked. It was the best Christmas Alexa had ever had, even better than the good days in Charleston.

They left Savannah at her mother's for one more night, and Edward and Alexa walked to the Carlyle as it started snowing. They sang "White Christmas" together off-key and he stopped on the street and kissed her. It was the happiest Christmas of her life, and he felt the same way. He had loved being married to Sybil in the beginning. But this was better, it was more grown-up. And sometimes Sybil was a little too wild, even for him, although he loved her dearly.

"Maybe it'll keep snowing and we can have a snowball fight tomorrow," Alexa said, sounding hopeful, with a hand tucked into his arm.

"I don't think so," Edward said, looking down at her with a serious expression.

"No? Why not? Don't you like snowball fights?" It seemed so unlike him not to. He was a good sport about everything else.

"I do like snowball fights," he conceded, as he stopped walking again and looked at her. "I just don't know if it's a good idea for a senator's wife to be lobbing snowballs at people in the park. You might hit a stranger and wind up on the news." Her eyes opened wide as he said it. "What do you think about that?" he asked softly.

"The snowball fight?" she asked breathlessly.

"No . . . the other . . . the senator's wife thing. Does that sound too crazy?" He knew how terrified she was of marriage, but he was sure now himself. He had waited a long time to find her. Sybil was right. Alexa was the one. The perfect one for him.

"I . . . yes . . . no . . ." She stumbled on her words, and he kissed her again. "Yes. I mean no. No, it doesn't sound too crazy . . . and yes, I want to." She was crying and laughing when he kissed her again, and then with her hand tucked tightly into his arm, they walked into the Carlyle. Alexa was grinning broadly, and looked ecstatic, despite the butterflies doing somersaults in her stomach, and the senator from South Carolina looked extremely pleased.